Praise for
A RIVER OF GOLDEN BONES

"I inhaled this novel. *A River of Golden Bones* by A.K. Mulford is a gorgeously written queer fairy tale fantasy conjured with the bones of wicked worldbuilding and laced with decadent spice. Get ready to devour this wolfish tale"
Charissa Weaks, bestselling author of *The Witch Collector*

"A beautiful journey of self-discovery and queer identity, filled with heart-stopping romance and page-turning adventure. *A River of Golden Bones* is a must-read for fantasy and romance readers alike. I couldn't put it down!"
Cait Jacobs, author of *The Princess Knight*

"The relationship between Calla and these performers becomes the most compelling part of the book, giving rise to questions about gender and the difference between a protector and a tyrant. Defeating evil is important, sure—but the real thrill is finding people who make you want to be your fullest self. It's lovely, life-affirming stuff"
Washington Post

"I was taken by the expert dismantling of the gender binary amidst a quest that is sexy, romantic, and heroic all at once"
Book Riot

"A steamy romance between Calla and Grae unfolds amid battles against monsters and dark magic, intertwined with Calla's fight against patriarchy and oppression and her burgeoning acceptance of her own genderqueerness. This series is off to an exciting start"
Publishers Weekly

"It's one of those books that just sucks you in and makes you want to keep reading into the night"
Smexy Books

"I've been waiting for this one for a long time, and I'm happy to say that it was one of the most moving books I've read in quite a while. . . . Really, really beautifully done!"
The Book Review Crew

"If you've been looking for a queer adult fantasy to sink your teeth into, this is the one! . . . If you love shapeshifters, stories about overcoming odds and re-examining our beliefs, and politics, this is for you. It's a series I know I'll be keeping up with"
Utopia State of Mind

"An incredible book. From the depth of the characters to the beautifully described scenery. The sense of mild humor even when things are tough and the overarching sense of loyalty. This is a found family book and it shows in their interactions. I didn't want this book to end, and now that it has, I can't wait to read the next one"
Nonbinary Knight Reads and Reviews

"*A River of Golden Bones* by A.K. Mulford is a romantasy full of wolves, malicious power and the path to acceptance. I'm completely in love with this first book in The Golden Court series. . . . This is a book you need in your life"
Immersed in Books

"I just want to hug this book!!! I loved it so much for the comforting characters and the author's smooth storytelling. . . . Most meaningful to me is the author's incredibly kind and understanding way of expressing Calla's gender and the very real fears that go along with self-discovery. This not only made me feel seen but just so comforted by these characters"
Laughing Loving and Books

A HEART of CRIMSON FLAMES

ALSO BY A.K. MULFORD

The Five Crowns Of Okrith
The High Mountain Court
The Witches' Blade
The Rogue Crown
The Evergreen Heir
The Amethyst Kingdom

The Okrith Novellas
The Witch of Crimson Arrows
The Witch Apothecary
The Witchslayer
The Witching Trail
The Witch's Goodbye

The Golden Court
A River of Golden Bones
A Sky of Emerald Stars

A.K. MULFORD

A HEART *of* CRIMSON FLAMES

HARPER
Voyager

HarperVoyager
An imprint of HarperCollins*Publishers* Ltd
1 London Bridge Street
London SE1 9GF

www.harpercollins.co.uk

HarperCollins*Publishers*
Macken House,
39/40 Mayor Street Upper,
Dublin 1, D01 C9W8
Ireland

First published by HarperCollins*Publishers* Ltd 2025
1

Copyright © A.K. Mulford 2025

Designed by Angie Boutin
Map design by Nick Springer / Springer Cartographies LLC

A.K. Mulford asserts the moral right to
be identified as the author of this work.

A catalogue record for this book is available from the British Library.

ISBN: 978-0-00-860188-1 (HB)
ISBN: 978-0-00-860189-8 (TPB)

This novel is entirely a work of fiction.
The names, characters and incidents portrayed in it are
the work of the author's imagination. Any resemblance to
actual persons, living or dead, events or localities is
entirely coincidental.

Printed and bound in the UK using 100% Renewable Electricity
by CPI Group (UK) Ltd

All rights reserved. No part of this publication may be
reproduced, stored in a retrieval system, or transmitted,
in any form or by any means, electronic, mechanical,
photocopying, recording or otherwise, without the prior
written permission of the publishers.

Without limiting the exclusive rights of any author, contributor or the publisher of
this publication, any unauthorized use of this publication to train generative artificial
intelligence (AI) technologies is expressly prohibited. HarperCollins also exercise their
rights under Article 4(3) of the Digital Single Market Directive 2019/790 and
expressly reserve this publication from the text and data mining exception.

This book contains FSC™ certified paper and other controlled sources
to ensure responsible forest management.

For more information visit: www.harpercollins.co.uk/green

Dedicated to all the readers who exist between the ink and the pages. I hope you felt seen in this world. Thank you for coming on the journey with me.

CONTENT WARNING
Mention of domestic violence and sexual assault, including of a minor (not on page), attempted sexual assault, war, grief, violence, gore, abuse, fire, monsters, transphobia, BDSM, including mild restraint, spanking, blood, and magical CNC, as well as sexually explicit scenes

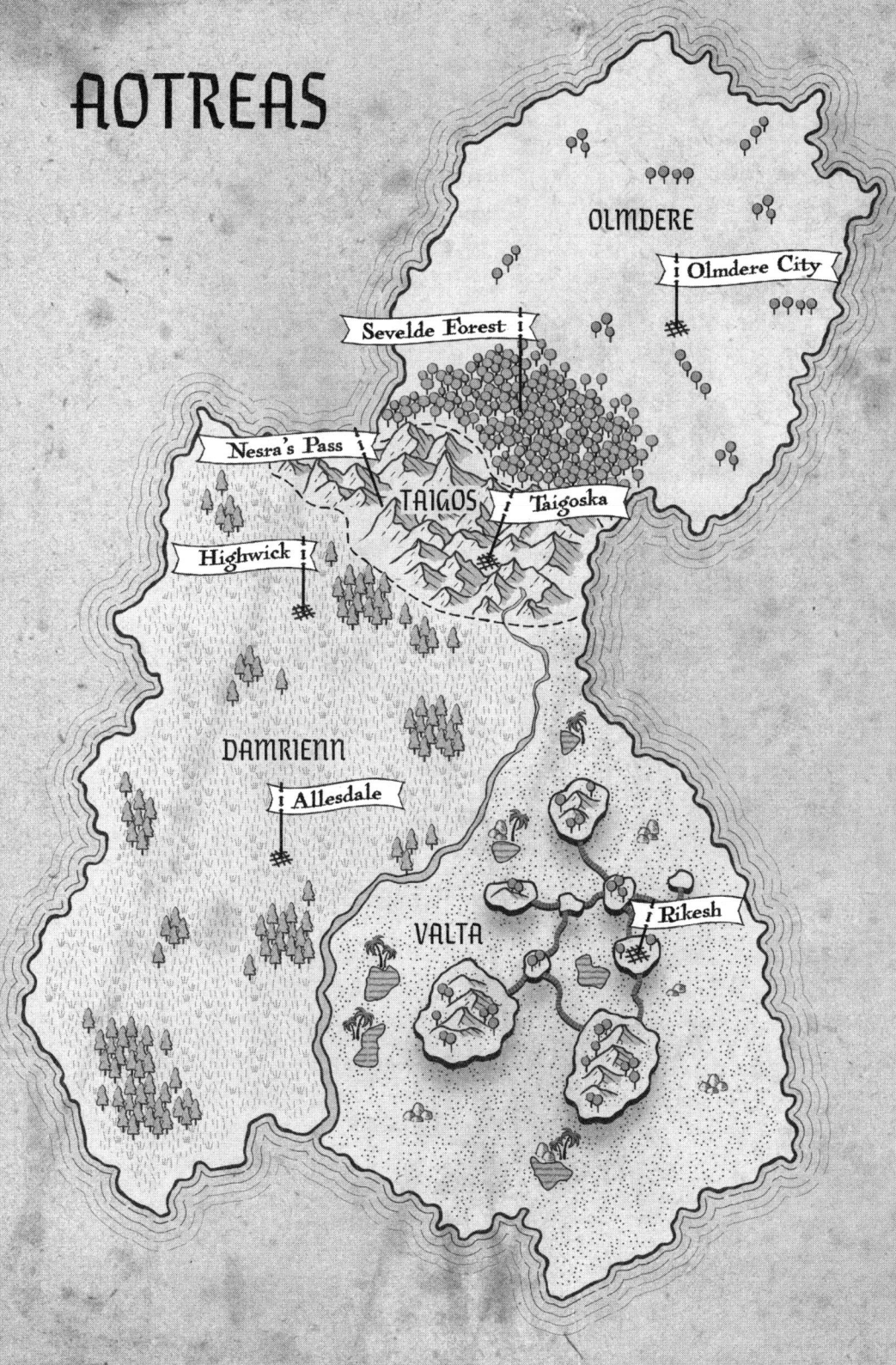

ONE

BRIAR

SHADOWS CLUNG TO MY MIND, HOWLING, MY VISION SPINNING. I didn't know if they knocked me unconscious via an elixir or a blow to the back of my head; I just knew I didn't remember the journey here. I also knew I was in a dungeon, a dress folded neatly beside me on the wet stone floor. I frowned down at the crushed velvet gown. It was a brilliant shade of crimson with a detailed silver filigree neckline. Atop it sat a crescent diamond necklace.

Every detail was designed to craft me into a Silver Wolf trophy.

They want me to play the part of the Crimson Princess once more?

The costume—for that's what it was, nothing more—told me clearer than a sign above my head: play the role. *Behave.*

That dress would imprison me more than the bars and the stone walls.

This is all they'll let me be. A Wolf in a frock, held in place by a leash of silver and velvet. An instrument for someone else's glory.

Instead of taking the dress, I stayed in my golden furs. For one thing, it was far warmer than the velvet dress. For another, it was safer if anyone entered the dungeons while I slept. With my keener senses I could hear the slightest shuffle of footsteps overhead, the tinkling drips of water on the moldy stones, the groan of a warped wooden door opening, and the sound of anyone approaching.

My Wolf form also staved off the hunger far better than my human stomach. Wolves gorged on a fresh kill and then went days, even weeks, without food before another hunt. As I imagined tearing into a bloody stag, invisible claws raked through my empty insides. I pushed that gnawing feeling to the back of my mind. I didn't know how many days we'd traveled to get here, didn't even know if it was day or night, but of one thing I was certain from the must and sweat and distant reprieve of pinewood: we were in Highwick.

I'd been unwillingly returned to Nero's castle, right back to where it all began.

This was what the Silver Wolves had always wanted from me—beauty and obedience. It had been thinly veiled before, when I was engaged to Grae, but now it was clear they would lock me up until I submitted. There was never truly a choice, not when the only options ever given were by the ones with all the power. The thought that I had gone along with it for so long without protestation was laughable now. Not a fierce Wolf royal, but a bird in a gilded cage. Because of my sex, in their eyes, the only thing I was good for was being on the arm of a Silver Wolf prince.

When the only hand I wanted was so, so far away.

My senses reached out in every direction, craving a familiar pair of arms and her hushed words of comfort, but could not feel her. Where was my mate? Did she know I was Nero's prisoner? Was Maez tearing the world apart to get to me right now? Would they kill her for it?

Dread pooled in my gut, its acid churning in my unfed stomach. I hoped the others would be able to stymie Maez's blind rage, plan a smarter tactic to come rescue me than simply slaughtering anyone in her path... *not* that I would particularly mind seeing her in all her battle glory, but one Wolf against the entire Silver army was a death sentence.

My family *would* come, I had no doubt, but whether they would survive their rescue attempt was another thing entirely. Anxiety and weariness clashed within me. Here I was, once again the damsel in distress, needing my pack to come rescue me from the clutches of a tyrant. I didn't think my smiles and pleasantries were going to get me out of this one alive.

Moments before the door to the dungeons screeched open, I had heard steps in the hall, and now I strained my eyes trying to see who was beyond the brazier's flickering firelight. Every sound was a threat. I didn't know if it was a guard come to bring me food or take me to the gallows. I just knew it wasn't a friend.

And when *he* appeared through the bars of my cell, it wasn't a guard at all. My maw curled into a snarl, baring my teeth.

Evres—Nero's chosen heir, Grae's replacement, and now Crown Prince of Damrienn and future pack leader. He had hard sharp features that some would've considered handsome if he didn't have such disdain in his piercing silver gaze. Those haunting eyes trailed me now from nose to tail.

"Hello, dearest," he crooned, drawing out every syllable. There was a glinting flash to his teeth as he spoke.

I forced myself to stay still, to not cower in front of him and stoke his need to dominate. But neither did I shift nor speak. I knew his type, had been trained since birth to deal with these arrogant royals. I knew any movement, any indication in my expression would only add more fuel to his fire.

Evres tipped his head to the dress beside me. "Don't like your outfit, love? I can have the maids send another."

More than his loathsome words, I hated the way he smiled. He was mocking me, goading me. His delightedly malevolent expression screamed: *go on, try me.*

I didn't move.

"Look at you, Briar. Dainty, meek, helpless," he said, licking his tongue across his canine tooth as if wishing he could take a bite out of me. "Curled up into such a tiny little ball. You'll need to be made of stronger stuff when you sit by my side. Now put on the dress like a good girl and I'll let you go to your chambers instead of rotting in this awful place."

I wanted to growl, wanted to shoot forward and see if I was fast enough to grab a hand wrapped around the bars before he had a chance to retreat. But I just stayed exactly as I was. Placid. Demure. Nonthreatening.

Domesticated.

"My betrothed wishes to stay down here, hungry and cold, another night?" He pursed his lips, his eyes seeming to light up, enjoying the challenge. "That is fine by me. Give yourself some time to get acquainted with this place. I have a feeling this won't be your last visit." His hands trailed along the bars with a *clunk, clunk, clunk* as he winked at me. "Once you put that dress on . . . then we can talk about better arrangements for you."

The dungeon door wailed shut again and I stared into the inky darkness, unmoving, for several more breaths.

I knew Vellia would've told me to always submit to the first request, that it makes them more trusting and malleable to know you give in so quickly. The faery taught me how to play the part of obedient wife to my own gains—make them think they'd brought me to heel, grant me a longer leash, so that I may then exploit it. It would be much easier for Maez and the others to rescue me from the throne room than from the dungeon. Maybe I could even manage to flee toward the Stormcrest Ranges when out on a pack hunt through the forest. Calla had managed to outrun them; maybe I could, too.

But I wasn't my twin.

That brought me up short. It felt like a knife to my side just thinking of them. I hoped Calla was okay—too far for me to sense them.

But that reminded me that I should've been able to still feel my mate. Yet even in my shifted form, I couldn't feel Maez anywhere, no connection to her or the rest of the pack. Like a puppet with its strings cut, I was free-falling, reaching out but unable to feel her anywhere. What did it mean? Where was she? If she was dead, I'd be dead, too. At least that gave me hope. If she was alive, we'd find a way back to each other.

Sweet Moon, I missed Maez. Missed her scent and her warm soothing words and the way she'd kiss my temple when I was concerned. I missed her jokes and her cavalier confidence and the feeling of being so safe in her arms . . .

I permitted myself one single whimper as I curled into a ball against the dungeon wall.

At least when Sawyn had cursed me, I'd been asleep. At least I was laid on a bed in a high tower and not in a cold cell. At least I was somehow nourished in that magical dream state. It was a paradise compared to this—at least for me.

I thought of Maez, of how she had endured this for weeks under Sawyn's imprisonment. But even then, in some small ways it was a blessing she'd been captured by someone other than a king or prince, even then it was safer. I knew Evres planned to take my body by force, a vessel for his future offspring. And I wondered, too, how much of my soul I'd have to give just to remain alive.

Bile rose up my throat, and I was somewhat thankful to have no food in my belly. It was foolish of me to think I could've ever escaped this fate, to not be a pawn in a world ruled by men.

To simply be happy with my mate.

I swallowed and lifted my chin skyward, howling at the Moon Goddess even though she, like everyone else I loved, felt so far from me here.

I just have to survive until Maez comes for me. Whatever it takes.

I would not die here, not in body or spirit. I wouldn't let them crush me like they had so many Wolf queens before. I was a Golden Wolf, I was the twin of the Golden Court Queen, I was the mate of the most gorgeous and fearsome warrior in all of Aotreas. I wouldn't be leashed by some stuck-up prince.

He will not win.

With my newfound resolve, I cried for the last time, buried my nose into my tail, and fell asleep.

TWO

BRIAR

MY GROWLING STOMACH WOKE ME. I KNEW THERE WAS NO POINT trying Evres for a second time. Let him think one hungry night would break me—maybe he would decide that's all it took.

When the dungeon door opened the following day, I was ready. I'd put on the heavy bloodred dress, the diamond necklace choking me like the collar it was around my neck. I finger-combed my ratted and tangled hair to the best of my abilities and braided it off my face with practiced hands. Prettying myself up for a monster, donning the appearance of someone braver than myself. I even pinched my cheeks, pinking them up as I waited.

Evres's expression was more than a little smug when he saw me sitting at the back of my cell, carefully avoiding the rivulets of suspicious liquid dripping from the ceiling. My very life depended on how good an actress I could be. Luckily, much of my young life had been exactly that: pretending to be something else. That had been to keep me safe, too. Except then, I'd had my sister. I'd had Vellia. Now it was just me, and so it took a greater force of will to pretend alone. But ultimately I conjured an image in my mind that I projected outward—pretending I was sitting eagerly at the edges of a ball, waiting for an invitation to dance, and not a prisoner in a cell.

"You're going to be good for me now, aren't you, Briar?"

Evres asked, though we both knew it was more command than question.

I fought the urge to shudder at his poisoned tone and softly said, "Yes, Your Highness."

Evres seemed to like the sound of his newly appointed title on my timid lips. He studied the way I moved to stand with a practiced poise as if rising from a moon prayer. I folded my hands and bowed my head, waiting for him to speak, the picture of subservience.

"I was there the night of your failed wedding, you know?" That was not what I was expecting him to say. "Look at me." His command was soft yet threatening as he casually leaned against the bars.

My eyes were the hardest part of me to control. Too wide, and I was surprised. Too narrow, and I was angry. I pulled my senses further inward, far from the surface. *Be the porcelain doll, expressionless, unruffled.*

"You looked so beautiful in that dress," Evres continued, "though I think we can do better for our own wedding. Something that will catch the moonlight and make those blue eyes sing." He pursed his lips, considering me. "I remember the way your eyes drifted over the crowd the last time. Did you even see me then? You looked right through me."

It was a testament to my training that I managed to hide my surprise. Was he . . . jealous? What an incredibly arrogant and petty thing to say to me while I was trapped behind bars. Evres really thought *he* should be a memorable part of my wedding ceremony to someone else? Yet we'd had no introductions. Not a single handshake or exchange the last time I was here. He wasn't even royalty until this year. This man really thought the Moon Goddess shined out of his ass, didn't he?

I thought back to my almost wedding day. I remembered the maid with the raven hair bringing my breakfast. I remembered the seamstress with her full lips and freckled cheeks fixing my hem. I remembered searching for Maez's dark eyes and mischievous smirk in every room I entered . . . but the only men I ever took notice of were the ones I was trying to protect myself against. And Evres wasn't important enough to be a threat to me back then.

Instead of voicing my disdain for his jealous sentiments, I said meekly, "I was frightened, Your Highness. I was trying to do as was expected of me."

I kept my gaze averted, but from my periphery, I could see Evres cock his head like a predator locking in on his prey. "Expectations." His chin dipped. "I will *expect* more from you, Briar Marriel, daughter of the last King of Olmdere. Perhaps now with better instruction, you will rise to the task," he mused. He tossed something at me, a small object that bounced off my dress and clattered onto the ground at my feet: a ring. "Put that on."

I stooped and picked up the golden band—two rubies sat on either side of a giant crescent-shaped diamond that matched the one around my neck. I slid the ring over my finger without hesitation, the weight of the heavy stone making it wobble on my slender finger. "It's beautiful; thank you, Your Highness," I said, masking that—to me—it was one of the most heinous sights I'd ever seen.

His ring on *my* finger. His *promise* of subjugation, and not honor and cherishment.

Maybe he felt what I'd been trying to hide, but either way, Evres didn't seem to care for that level of gratitude, ignoring me. *He expects me to be grateful. Me saying such things is redundant to him.*

I noted that for future consideration.

"Now that you are my betrothed," he said, eyeing the ring as if its presence was proposal enough, "you are mine to do with as I please. I will erase you and reshape you into everything I desire you to be and you will *smile* while you do it"—his eyes stabbed daggers into me and held, a fly caught in his web—"you will spread your legs for me whenever I command and I will breed you and break you until I have as many heirs as my heart desires and then I will keep going. I *own* the air in your lungs and the blood in your veins. Do you understand?"

It wasn't a question—or rather, it was a trivia question, with only one right answer. It took every single year of training for my mouth not to fall open, for my eyes not to widen in shock. I lowered my gaze out of self-preservation and feigned obeisance, feeling instant relief from breaking our eye contact. I gave another short bow. "Yes, Your Highness."

I heard the jangling of metal against metal as Evres produced the keys from his pocket and opened the dungeon door. As he yanked it ajar, I wanted to push past him and flee the cell, but instead I stood stock-still and waited for his command, imagining my bare feet tethered to the wet stone.

"Then you may go to your room," he said. "I trust you will be able to find it. It is the same one you resided in last time you were here."

"Yes, thank you, Your Highness." I offered another quick bow. There could never be too many with someone like him. In truth, I had no idea where I was going but I wasn't about to ask a venomous beast like him to guide me.

I took a tentative step forward, waiting for Evres to make way, but he didn't move from the doorway, forcing me to get within a hair's breadth from him to push past. I kept my eyes trained on the silver buttons of his tunic, the skirt of my dress brushing over the tops of his boots as I moved past. My heart punched against my sternum. I had just skirted past him when his hand snapped out, grabbing me roughly by the upper arm and slamming me back against the bars.

I tried not to yelp as my head smacked against the steel, but there was only so much I could contain. Evres shot toward me, his mouth hovering over my own. A cold hand lifted to cup my cheek and he swept his thumb across my bottom lip. His chest pressed into mine as he breathed me in and I fought with every ounce of restraint not to let my shoulders bunch up around my ears. I fought the tension building in my muscles, desperate to fight and flee.

He wants you to flinch. Stay calm. Stay calm. Stay calm . . .

I'd felt unsafe with men my whole life. I caught their lingering stares, their lust-filled looks tinged with violence; knew with acute surety that I never wanted to be trapped alone with one of them, let alone give one my heart. When Grae had told me our marriage would be in name alone, I'd felt such relief. For one thing, I knew him and trusted him. For another, it meant nothing would ever be forced on me. Bedding a man would've been just another way I was forced to pretend. And when I'd found my mate, I felt so blissfully confident that no man would ever touch me again. Tears welled in my eyes at the thought, but Evres was too close to see them.

I wondered what he'd think of them. They'd likely spur on his violence; worse, they'd probably turn him on.

His mouth dropped, his lips colliding with mine in a bruising kiss, one I was forced to return. *You have to move; react!* It was all I could do to listen, to not let the fear freeze me. So I worked my tongue over his, meeting each of his kisses with a disingenuous passion of my own. His mouth tasted as rotten as his soul. As I kissed him, I dreamed of biting out his tongue, blood dripping down my neck as I chewed it, masticating and swallowing as he choked on his own blood.

Surprisingly, this fantasy was enough to keep me engaged. I held on to the thought like a prayer, like a curse: *he will die at my hand.*

I could do it, I told myself. *I* will *do it*, I affirmed . . . once I knew I could survive to tell the tale.

Oh yes, I was made of stronger stuff. But Evres didn't need to know that . . . yet.

When he pulled away his eyelids were drooped, his lips parted as he stared at my seemingly eager mouth. I prayed to all the Gods that I could work my magic over him like I had Wolf men before. He shook the spell of that kiss from his eyes and released me, taking a step back, eyes just slightly hooded.

"Go to your room," he commanded once again. I took a step when he continued, "And get ready for a reception with the King. You will face the wrath of your pack ruler for your crimes."

He said it so nonchalantly—like an afterthought, I wasn't sure if what I'd heard was real. I had somehow forgotten about Nero. About the brute that had *created* this Wolf standing before me. The one staring pointedly at me, making it clear he could kiss me and threaten me in the same breath and not blink.

I would note that to myself, too.

My cheeks flamed, fear coiling in my heart, as I turned and walked toward the dungeon door.

Don't run, don't run, don't run.

It would only make him want to chase me.

I battled the tears threatening to spill as I reached the threshold and stared at the cloudless sky through the stained glass windows.

Please, Maez, I begged the sky and the Moon Goddess hidden by the daylight, the Goddess who had gifted me a mate, one who I'd found my way back to against all odds, against dark magic itself.

Please. Come save me.

THREE

CALLA

"BRIAR!"

The scream shredded my throat as I raced through the snow. I could hear Grae shouting my name from behind me, but I just ran and ran and ran. I didn't feel the ice burning my feet or the blood gushing from the wound on my thigh. I had to reach that sleigh. I had to save her. I couldn't lose her again, not when I just got her back.

What was happening to her in that sleigh? Naked and frightened. No. My heart couldn't take it.

I ran faster, not caring if I bled to death on the snow if it meant I could reach her.

But Grae was too fast. He caught up to me, grabbing me and yanking me back against his hard, bare chest. I wailed, thrashing in his grip. Let him tear me in two if it meant reaching my twin—

"Calla! Open your eyes!"

At his command, my eyes flew open. At first all I saw were shadows, my gasping breath filling my ears. Then the world started to become clear, stars blinking out from my vision. I wasn't on that mountain covered in snow. I was slicked by sweat, in my bed, in my castle, in my homeland.

In so much pain.

Grae held me tight to his chest, spooning behind me, so warm and powerful as we lay on our sides. "Breathe. Breathe." He spoke softly as he coached me through another nightmare. They had plagued my sleep since Briar was taken by the Silver Wolves.

"I'm okay," I rasped, wiping hair off my damp forehead. My throat was raw, so scratchy it felt like I had swallowed a bucketful of sand.

"You're not." Grae gently soothed his fingers down my bare side. "But you will be soon. I vow it."

"As if you could will it into existence from sheer determination," I replied, catching my breath.

"Do not doubt my powers," he said, almost but not quite eliciting a snort from me. Serious again, he added, "Soon, we'll have her back," and that assurance—that confidence—cut to the quick of me.

Maybe because, for the first time since I'd known him, I wasn't sure I could believe it.

A lump formed in my sore throat and I battled back tears as I shook my head. "I don't think anything will be right again."

I couldn't dare say it aloud to anyone else, not to my citizens who feared another war, not to people who looked to me to promise a better future. Not to the humans I'd sworn to protect. I couldn't voice my terror to them. But even queens needed reassurance, and in that, Grae had always been my guiding star.

Once again, I needed to believe him. Believe *in* him. Believe in his belief of me.

My breathing steadied as Grae circled lazy fingers over my rib cage and up my arm.

"I would say go back to sleep," he murmured into my hair. "But I know you too well for that."

I looked at the curtains, the pink of the predawn sky limning the edges.

"It's almost sunrise," I replied with a weary sigh. "Might as well start my day. There's so much to be done. Especially now."

I moved to sit up and Grae's hand splayed low across my belly and pulled me back against him. And despite my still racing heart, a smile curved my lips when I felt the outline of his erection against my bare ass.

"Perhaps I could be persuaded to stay in bed for just a little bit longer . . ."

Grae's hand lifted to knead the muscles of my tense shoulder. "You're wound tighter than a trapped bunny." His mouth dropped to the shell of my ear. "Maybe I can help with that."

"Maybe," I taunted.

The suggestion lingered in the air between us for a beat before Grae moved again. His hand circled lower across my skin until he cupped my sex. I leaned my head back against his shoulder, arching into his touch. I didn't know what I would've done without this—the distraction, the comfort, the release, the *connection*. Grae had been taking care of me in a way that only a mate could, saving me from my racing thoughts and ratcheting pulse if only momentarily.

And I thanked every star in the sky for these sacred, quiet moments. When the wool of lust covered my eyes to everything else. When nothing existed except Grae and me.

His finger slid down my center, circling my already swelling clit. He touched me with such deftness, as if my body was an extension of his own, as if he could *feel* the pleasure unfurling within me. Grae knew the exact pressure and tempo to make me come undone, and yet he also knew how to perfectly tease me. To take me to the edge . . . and sometimes keep me there, taunting me until I was panting for more. Not knowing what to expect—the anticipation—took my delight to new levels each time.

A little moan escaped my lips as he worked over me, his other hand coming up to cup my breast.

I reached behind me, finding his hard cock and stroking its silken length. "Is my mate hungry?" I asked in a goading tone as I stroked him up and down.

"For you? Insatiable," he said, biting my earlobe.

I guided him to my slick entrance as his finger kept working me in tauntingly slow circles. Grae pushed into me slow and sleepy as if he had all the time in the world, as if we could take all morning to melt into each other. Everything quieted in my mind as he began to move, and in that moment, time meant nothing to me. I wished we could stay in bed all day, wished there weren't any other responsibilities aside from making him repeat that low sound at the back of his throat.

Grae picked up his pace, pushing me higher, and I came before I had a chance to slow him down. A bright flash of an orgasm zapped through me, making my body light as air and heavy as the mountains. Tingles of ecstasy coated my skin as Grae chased after me, his release rushing through him just as quickly.

We stayed there, intertwined, our limbs entangled as we caught our breath. I stared at the brightening light around the curtains, time slipping away from us like the mist lifting from sunlight. Soon the castle staff would be awake. Soon there would be meetings, debriefings, and fight training. Soon I'd have to unflinchingly face the uncertainty of the future ahead with confidence and grace.

Soon.

But I stayed there, stealing just one more moment intertwined with my mate.

Grae kissed my shoulder, his stubble scratching across my skin. In that sated rasp, he spoke as if hearing my own worried thoughts. "Sadie and Navin will have a dragon at their beck and call. Maybe even a dozen more monsters if Ora decides to join them. And Mina—"

"Mina stays with us," I said too quickly. "I promised her she could remain with the Golden Court, and I'm not about to go back on my promises. Besides, having a Songkeeper by our side may prove useful."

Grae hummed thoughtfully. "She may be of more use with Galen den' Mora."

"It will have to be enough without her," I said, finally moving and climbing out of bed, my thighs sticky with Grae's release, wondering at how my life could contain such pillow talk. I wasn't frustrated with it, though. Rather, it actually made me happier knowing I could have *all* of Grae—both his fantastic body *and* his incredible mind. He was a confidant, lover, friend, and strategist all in one.

Still, controlling monsters had never been in my battle plans. It was far more likely that my allies would get eaten or seriously maimed by these monsters than have them marching off into battle for us. But I wouldn't stop them from trying, not if it meant getting my sister back and ending King Nero once and for all.

I thought of Sadie at the ends of the world in a wagon filled with musicians and a bloodred dragon trailing her, and knew then, as bad as I had it, it could always be worse.

"Gods, I hope they know what they're doing."

FOUR

SADIE

"I can't believe you conjured a fucking dragon," Kian said, holding a hand to the sky to block out the sun. His eyes trailed the flash of glittering carmine shooting through the sky.

We sat around a midday campfire, roasting a gamy lunch of squirrel and hare—a meal that I offered to catch seeing as I was the only Wolf of the bunch. I would've been happy to just eat it raw, but I was sure that would garner some unwelcome looks from the others. I was still on the back foot being surrounded by all these Songkeepers. We'd crossed the Stoneater River on Galen den' Mora—the wagon now packed with seven of us, including Navin's little brother *and* my sworn enemy, Kian.

I hadn't had a good chance to look at Kian when he was in his Rook uniform trying to *kill* me, but whenever I saw him now, it made me grab for my knives. At the very least, he deserved for someone to pluck out an eyeball, *but no*, Navin said that would hurt the group morale. And now that Navin was the involuntary leader of this group until Ora returned, I didn't want to cause any dissent . . .

Well, not publicly.

"Do you think there's a reason it was a dragon," another musician, Svenja, mused. She was a flautist with curly blond hair braided back off her temples, piercing ocean eyes, and a lithe body that she moved like dancing underwater. "Why a dragon and not another creature? Is it the way you sang the eternal song? Or is it like your own personal brand of monster?"

"*That* is one of the many things we need to figure out," Navin said as he licked the grease from his fingers. "There will be much to learn from the temple of knowledge." I heard the unspoken word: "hopefully."

Navin looked back up to the dragon circling the sky like a vulture. She was every shade from rust to burgundy to bright scarlet, her scales every color of gore as if created from the Onyx Wolf blood itself, her body a reminder of the slaughter. I swore she'd grown twice the size in only a week. Already larger than a crishenem or samsavat, maybe she was still just a baby. The thought was terrifying. Maybe she'd be big enough in a few more weeks that just the swipe of her tail would topple Nero's castle.

Maybe . . . a dragon would be all we needed to win this war.

But first we needed to learn how to wield her. Right now, Navin treated her as no more than a scaly red puppy trailing our crew. We had to find a way to make her a weapon.

"You should've never done it," Kian said, easily commanding the attention of the group, still ever the soldier. His eyes were a cold hazel, his skin the same warm brown as Navin's own. He was incredibly tall and lean, only slightly smaller than his brother—undeniably related. Both cunning and powerful in their own ways. Though where Navin was passionate and creative, Kian was nothing but cold stoicism.

"You're one to talk," I muttered, flicking my knife back and forth.

Kian frowned down at the blade in my hand. "Do you always do that when you're angry?"

"No," I snarked, "sometimes when I'm angry, I stab smug little boys."

Kian was about to reply when Navin held up a hand to his brother. "Don't," he commanded. "Or even I won't be able to spare you from her steel."

I smirked at Kian, satisfied that Navin was once again demonstrating he was firmly on my side. Navin made a point of letting me know it at every available opportunity. He wouldn't make the same mistake of defending his brother again, and it was clear there was no love lost between the two. Navin seemed to hate his brother even more than I did. Still, we needed every advantage in this coming war and that meant having Songkeepers to wield their magic.

"You should give her a name," Svenja said, squinting up at the dragon.

"I already have," Navin replied, dusting his hands down his legs. "Haestas. After the old Valtan song 'Nanesh ahm Haestas.'"

"That is a song about a phoenix rising from the burning sands of Lower Valta." Svenja gave Navin an incredulous look. "You named your mythical beast after a different mythical beast?"

"Haestas means firestorm," Timon said with a nod. "Good name."

The crew started breaking out into song around the campfire. And while "Nanesh ahm Haestas" wasn't part of their normal rotation, I couldn't stomach listening to one more evening ballad. Apparently, Navin couldn't, either.

"Save the songs for our travels. We should pack up and keep moving," Navin said, nodding to Timon to go fetch the oxen.

Timon gave a grunt and pushed up from the log where he perched. He was a short, stout man of few words, but Gods could he sing. At night he'd regale us with sea shanties sung so deep that it made my chest vibrate. It was amazing watching all of them together, performing music and improvising harmonies just for the fun of it. It certainly made traveling far less boring . . . although not entirely. For Navin and I also had to share the cramped wagon with all of them, which made finding any alone time nearly impossible. I prayed that the temple of knowledge had lots and lots of bedrooms . . . with excellent soundproofing.

Or not. I was starting to not care if they heard—and felt—us set the wagon rocking.

You just have to wait a little longer . . .

But not too much longer.

Navin gave a whistle and Haestas sailed across the sky, off to go hunt for some lunch of her own. I wondered if he could whistle for her to bring back a kill for us heartier than rabbit and squirrel. If she could be trained to bring us back a goat or deer, what would stop her from one day bringing us back the bodies of Silver Wolves . . .

"She knows not to go too far north, doesn't she?" Asha asked, nervously nibbling her bottom lip. She was the youngest of the musicians who'd come to Navin's call—a mousy brunette, timid and shy, but according to Navin an incredibly powerful Songkeeper, too.

I'll believe it when I see it.

"I can't *talk* to her," Navin said for what felt like the hundredth time. "But she knows. I don't know how she knows," he added quickly before someone could ask. "But she knows."

We were all still trying to pick apart this bond he and his dragon shared, figure out all the working mechanisms to his magic. Navin only had one quick peek at the vase engraved with the eternal songs in Valta before conjuring the beast, unable to study the intricacies. With a little more time, he might've been able to fully decode communication with her like Rasil had with his samsavat.

"Hopefully the library of knowledge will contain hidden songs," Svenja added, giving voice to my own thoughts. "It's time to see what else your dragon can do."

"Aye," Timon added.

Ignoring their comments, Navin tipped his head to the fire. "Put that out—let's go."

I liked the new aura of command in his voice since Navin had become our de facto leader of this splinter group of the

Songkeepers. We needed this leadership, as it now seemed the musicians of Galen den' Mora were on the other side of a war from their musical brethren—the ones who still backed Rasil.

Rasil—the Head Guardian of the Songkeepers, traitor, friend to the Onyx Wolves . . . *and* Navin's husband. That last part still grated me just as much as the rest, maybe more. I couldn't wait to help annul their nuptials by slicing Rasil's throat open and letting him bleed dry. It was the least he deserved for what he'd done to us. The world would be safer for it, too. Who knew if Rasil would use the eternal songs to conjure more monsters into the world. Gods, there might be no world left to save if the continent became overrun with beasts and dark magic again.

As if Nero wasn't enough of a monster to deal with.

Navin slung his long arm around my shoulders and guided me back to the wagon as I frowned up at the familiar trees. The heat of the desert had morphed to the cool lushness of the pine forests of Damrienn. I'd never been this far south in my homeland. No Wolf had. We'd always stayed close to the capital and our pack.

Guilt crept through me at how good it felt to be back in Damrienn. Something in me eased at the smell of the trees and wet earth. It was like an old friend welcoming me back home.

The humans were sparse down here, too, nothing but rolling forests as far as the eye could see . . . except—

I sniffed the air again. Just the faintest whiff on the wind.

Navin paused. "What is it?"

My eyes narrowed as I stared through the endless trees. "A scent in the distance." I focused on it, more certain now of the acrid decay that lingered in the air.

"What is it?"

My hand drifted toward my knives. Fire, ashes, blood, bile, rot.

"Death."

BILE ROSE IN MY THROAT AT THE OLFACTORY OVERLOAD IN MY nostrils, the repelling stench not only of death but also of rot, the kind that had been festering for weeks. Scavengers feasted across the rubble. Vultures, foxes, rats, and creatures I'd never even known all fed. Most of all the insects. Some corpses were so covered in ants, no flesh could be seen underneath the carpet of writhing black. Others were like nurseries for maggots and the wriggling horror they became. The decay choked my throat. I'd seen gore, I'd known death, but this was a kind of devastation that would haunt me for the rest of my days.

There were no survivors, and for that I thanked the Moon Goddess.

Rockford had been the town's name, the southernmost dot on our map of Damrienn. Below it had been only forests and a few hunting cabins, too small to be noted. How many dots would be left on the map if Nero had his way? *One*, I thought. Highwick and then nothing but forest and scorched rubble, pockmarked ashes of the humans that no longer existed in his kingdom. *Someone must avenge them.* As I surveyed the eyeless sockets of decaying corpses, I vowed that Rockford wouldn't be forgotten.

Navin and I took the lead, scouring the village reduced to ashes. The others I tried to encourage to stay in the wagon and let it travel through the outskirts of town. They were musicians for Moon's sake; they didn't need to see this kind of carnage. I'd known my fair share of death and even I found the site haunting.

But I had once again underestimated the Songkeepers. They were made of stronger stuff than they appeared. Their nostrils flared and they covered their mouths with cloths, but still they searched. Kian turned over beams and doorways, Svenja flipped over bodies that were clearly gone, and even Asha searched. Still, the farther we moved through the town, the more we abandoned any hope.

I couldn't hear a single heartbeat, couldn't sniff out the pumping blood of a single living soul. Some of the bodies were far from intact, injuries that weren't inflicted by those scavenging their flesh. A few had fought valiantly, it seemed. I scented Wolf blood, saw a few patches of silver fur torn out by panicked fingers, but humans were no match for trained Wolf soldiers.

Nero's Silver Wolves had torn them all to shreds, and it was soon apparent they'd been *unleashed* on this little town. In all my years as a soldier for the Silver Wolf King, never had I seen such untethered wrath. I shuddered to think of the murderous frenzy that played out across Rockford, for the mutilation of these corpses was far beyond what was required to kill. This was the epitome of hatred.

The state of the world around me was the clearest indicator that the Silver Wolf King had gone from ruthlessly calculating to utterly insane.

My fear of him grew with every step. If he inspired this kind of violence. If he commanded it to spread . . .

If he brought this wreckage to Olmdere . . .

When we'd turned over every corner left of the little village and found nothing but despair, the Songkeepers gathered to sing the souls into the afterlife. The harmonies of their voices were rousing and hauntingly beautiful, blanketing the silent landscape in song.

I cleared my throat and wandered to the far side of the wagon, permitting myself a few tears before squaring my shoulders and returning.

I stared up at the brilliant red dragon circling high above us and I once again thought of Nero. We needed to end him. I once called his pack my own, but I now knew he needed to be gone for good, and perhaps the entire depraved pack along with him. Too much was at stake. How many human villages were there even left? How many towns sat poised at the edge of his domain, living in fear of becoming the next Rockford? My homeland was in ruin, the humans the whipping boys of Nero's jealous anger.

Except sometimes whipping boys lived. There was no such hope here.

Their song finished, we solemnly loaded back into the wagon before pressing on toward the temple of knowledge, resolute in our mission. The only thing that mattered now was stopping Nero, whatever it took.

I thought of Navin's dragon and once more wondered if it would grow big enough to handle that task.

FIVE

BRIAR

THE ROOM WAS THE SAME AS THE DAY OF MY WEDDING—PLUSH carpets, sparkling chandeliers, gilded mirrors—but no longer did it fill me with nervous excitement but instead a deep-seated fear. I saw a vision of my former self in that mirror, wearing a wedding dress with seamstresses milling around her, Calla lounging on the bed behind, her reflection eating candied almonds, all of them more excited than fearful.

Despite my nerves, I'd once relished the thought of moving out of my cabin in the woods and to a castle with such opulent furnishings. But now the luxury felt like a bribe for obedience, not that one needed to be bribed when they would inevitably be forced. The memory of this place warped and distorted in my mind's eye.

That I never wanted to marry Grae had always been true. But more, I had never wanted to be a *queen*. Still, I had been enthusiastic to have a life outside the little town of Allesdale. I was excited to have a pack, and a purpose, and a world that I would add value to.

Now, however, standing here, I knew the only value they ever wanted me to add was my silent presence—a decorative display of their wealth, just like that gilded mirror.

No seamstresses today. No maids to attend me.

I restyled my hair, combing out the last of the tangles my fingers had missed and anointing myself with oils and perfumes. I hoped it would cover the stench of dread that wafted off me like its own sickly fragrance. I rouged my cheeks and painted my lips that crimson red that I knew they all wanted to see—the vixen, the princess, the beauty. I'd resigned myself that Wolf kings would only ever appraise me for my looks, my money, my title. Resigned myself that was *okay*.

But then I found Maez, someone who loved me so far beyond either, and now I knew I was worth more.

Normally, there was this strong connection between the two of us like a rope wrapped round my waist, a tugging right behind my navel. But that tether felt frayed now, the solidness with which I navigated through the world now all fuzzy, as if my limbs were filled with sparkling wine.

I heard the clamor of barked orders out the window and mindlessly drifted over to peek through the warped stained glass.

What I saw made my stomach drop.

A line of humans were tied to poles like dummies upon which the Silver Wolf soldiers practiced. Slicing and hacking at the air inches from the humans' flesh . . . except not always. Because I spotted several who had actually been struck, blood trailing down their tattered clothes. *What world is this?* This was cruelty I had never seen before. Why wasn't anyone stopping them? I searched down the line of steely-faced guards. Why wasn't anyone doing anything?

But I knew why. Because this *was* them doing something. This was what the Silver Wolves were.

As if sensing my surveillance, the one who had been issuing the commands looked up at me and saluted.

"Come on, lads," he shouted, squinting against the sun to stare up at me, sword now raised high. "Let's show our princess what happens to traitors of the crown."

I stared back at him without emotion, vowing inside that if I ever had the power to, I would cleave his head from his body myself. But for all my bravado, nothing could prepare me for what happened when he dropped his sword.

The sight made me want to scream and retch, the truest part of me wailing beneath the surface. But I only stood there woodenly and watched, stone-faced, as my soul withered a little further and tears pricked my eyes.

The bound humans didn't even cry out, their bloodshot eyes wide with shock as the Wolves sliced them open one by one, gutting them from navel to throat. Their last vision of this world was their insides spilling out, splattering on their bound feet, as they bled out onto the mossy earth. My eyes welled until my vision was glassy, but I still didn't look away, staring hatefully at that commander as he craned his head back up to me and winked.

Wolves killed to feed, to protect, to defend. This was none of that. This was a horror like I'd never known. Nero had truly gone mad, and his pack had followed him into that madness.

What scared me more than anything was that it had somehow gotten so much worse since the last time I was here. Before, the Wolves mistreated the humans, sure—an imbalance in power, land, wealth—but they weren't outright murderous. Not like this. Now the Wolves seemed like the humans were little more than sheep, but at least sheep provided food. The only thing the Silver Wolves were feeding off here was fear. And not just the fear of the humans. This was clearly staged for me, and the warning to me was abundant: fall in line, start acting like a Wolf, or be treated like a human.

When the palace guards came for me, I struggled to regain my composure, the vision of the humans' gruesome deaths burned into my retinas. I stuffed that sorrow as deep as it could go and tried to put on the persona of the woman I'd always been trained to be—poised, elegant, fearless. It would be the greatest act of my life if I could pull it off.

When we reached the grand hall, the doors were already open, the pack milling about as if in a casual gathering, no waiting with bated breath this time. There would be no grand sweeping ceremonies for me like there had been on my first arrival to Highwick. There would be no reverence, either. Still, the pack parted, creating a makeshift aisle for me to walk down.

My eyes swept over the leering group as my gut clenched. I gathered my courage as my gaze landed on Nero sprawled across his throne. He looked like he'd aged rapidly since the night of Sawyn's last curse, years compounded over the space of months. For the first time since I woke up in the dungeon, I had a spark of happiness: I liked the thought of stress plaguing him. I hoped he feared the retribution that my court would bring down on him for all that he'd done. Maybe he knew his time would soon be up.

My eyes then darted to Evres who sat on a smaller throne beside Nero, looking for all the world like he was born to sit there. I held his pewter gaze, making sure this time he knew I wasn't going to look through him. A wicked smile curled his lips at the way I held his stare as I walked to him and only him.

"Princess Briar," Nero said, his voice cutting through the murmuring crowd, which swiftly fell to silence. "You've returned home to us at last."

I forced my expression to look pleased.

Slow, slow, I urged myself. I was the smallest minnow in a sea of sharks, and I knew I needed to stay calm and play their games until help arrived.

Time to lie through my teeth.

"I am so pleased to be back in Damrienn, Your Majesty," I said, dropping into a deep, decorous bow. "I have missed my home and my pack."

The pack behind me broke into murmurs again.

"Yes," Nero mused, studying me with a frown. There was a crazed tinge to his gaze, one that hadn't been there the last time, or perhaps one he managed to hide better. "You've gone so long without a proper ruling hand, daughter of kings. Wolf bitches will go wild without a leader to guide them."

Nero gestured off to the shadowed corner, and it was only

then that I spotted it: a body swinging by the ankles, hoisted up for all to see.

My stomach curdled as the pack murmured their agreement. I knew that face. Even with his head discolored from the rush of blood and many bruises—even with the bright red bloodshot eyes, purpling in the corners—I knew him.

Hector. The one who had betrayed Calla to the Silver Wolf pack.

I stared, only to see if his bare and bloodied chest rose and fell.

Ostekke gut me, he's still alive.

I almost let loose a snarl at him. A warped pleasure coursed through me to see the traitor in such a sorry state. I hoped he regretted what he did to us with each painful breath. I hoped Nero tortured him until he begged to be ended.

But I kept my expression neutral as I turned back toward Nero, not lingering on Hector and all my ill will as the Damrienn King said, "Tell me, Marriel princess: if you were so eager to get back to us, why ally yourself to your traitor of a sister?"

The pack snarled, pushing in closer. I felt the hairs on the back of my neck stand on end, waiting for one of them to take a swipe at me.

I bowed my head. "I am not a fighter like the others," I admitted, making myself into a wayward pup and not the adult I was. "I was taught to follow, to obey. I fell under Sawyn's curse in this castle and I awoke in the castle of Olmdere. I made no choices. I didn't travel to my twin's aid." All of that was true, though I wasn't about to admit it had been a relief to wake from my sleeping curse in my true homeland with my twin claiming our family's crown. "I didn't know what else to do, Your Majesty."

Nero leaned forward, the small action capturing the rapt attention of the room. "I don't know if I believe you, Briar Marriel."

I felt the pack pressing in closer with each of his words, my heart punching through my rib cage. Nero stood and wandered down the dais toward me. The air stole from my lungs as he prowled toward me and reached out.

Don't flinch, don't flinch, don't flinch, I coached myself as his cold fingers tilted my chin up.

"I don't know what else—"

"Do you know what it means to be loyal to your pack?" His head tilted. "Do you know the lengths I would be willing to go to? The lengths *you* should be willing to go to as their princess?"

"I..."

He leaned in closer, stale breath on my face. "There is no advantage I will not take, no power I will not grab, no darkness I will not embrace to protect my crown and my pack. *That* is what loyalty is."

A chorus of howls echoed through the cavernous hall, making me jolt. Did his pack truly believe the venomous lies he purported? That he was doing this all for them? To protect them?

As Nero's hateful gaze pierced me, I couldn't keep the tremble from my voice. "What must I do?"

"I want you to tell me *everything* about Olmdere—their armies, their provisions, their plans for attack. Start with that, and you will *begin* to prove your loyalty to me today and every day for the rest of your life, do you understand?"

I wanted to look away, but his hand gripped my chin so tightly it was sure to bruise. His pupils were far too wide for his eyes. He looked at me and through me all at once, both here and not.

"Yes, Your Majesty," I whispered.

He swept a thumb across my cheek, inspecting my skin, my lips, my eyes. Each glance burned my skin like a brand.

"Good," he purred. "It would be such a shame to scar up a face as lovely as yours." His grip tightened again to the point of pain. "But understand, I don't trust you to be a good Wolf yet," he said, finally releasing me and returning to the dais. I wanted to droop in relief but remained standing tall. "And also understand, Crimson Princess—*no one* is coming for you. Not your sister and her humans, not even the one you once called a mate."

My eyes flared as I looked up at him. *What did he just say?*

Nero cocked his head at me, looking all too pleased with himself. "You didn't know, did you?" The pack laughed, the sounds pealing off the vaulted ceilings. "The Moon Goddess sought to rectify that ill-fated bond between the two of you once and for all." Nero lifted his hands up to the stained glass window high above him—the one that many moons ago had filled with the holy light of the full moon that blessed Maez and I as mates. Dread coiled in me like a snake as Nero continued, "Maez thought it was a good idea to get mixed up with a human magician, thought she could best the King of the Onyx Wolf pack with her dark magic." He tsked. "Luo should've been better prepared for it. I always thought his younger brother would've made a better king—he knows what needs to be done to keep a pack in line. Luo was too lenient. I would've never let such an attack happen to my pack."

The group grunted their agreement, a few even clapping at their King's words, but my mind had frozen on one thing he said.

"Dark magic?" My brows pinched. I still didn't understand. I knew I shouldn't ask, especially now of all times. My position was already precarious and this line of inquiry could result in more pain for me, but I *had* to know what he meant. Maez was my everything, and I would damn myself to further suffering at the hands of these evil Wolves just to know of her fate. "You say Maez got mixed up with a human magician . . . I don't understand. What does that mean?"

Nero's smile broadened as if it gave him a great deal of pleasure to deliver one final blow. "Your mate as you know her is gone, Briar," he said. "She took that dark magic into her heart. She's a sorceress now."

My heart stopped beating.

SIX

CALLA

WEARING A MASK OF CONFIDENCE WAS EXHAUSTING. I TRIED TO keep my back straight, my chin high as we toured the new mill at the center of the little village of Hanstock. Half a day's ride from Olmdere City, the town had been hit hard by Sawyn's reign. The blight had only eased in the last year. Magic was returning to the soil, the earth was healing, but still, the scars upon the town were clear.

I moved with the keen sense of being watched by the hundreds of townspeople who followed me through the village, being guided by their village elders. Grae stood close to my side, closer since I told my guards to stay with the carriages. Grae had protested but I'd insisted. These people—*our people*—were traumatized and barely healing. The last thing they needed was a show of force. I was there to serve them, not the other way around, and if another war was coming, I needed their good favor. We might be staring into the face of lean times again.

"The stonework is lovely," I said mildly to the elderly woman who walked beside me.

"It is, Your Majesty," she replied, looking proudly at the spiraling stone mosaics. "It is thanks to your trade with Taigos that we were able to build it. The rations have been keeping us going during the rebuild. It has been a long time since we haven't feared for an empty belly."

I tried to conceal my pained expression, wishing I had some of Briar's talent for hiding her unease. The rations from Taigos had been supplied before Queen Ingrid betrayed us . . . before I *killed* her. I doubted there would be any such supplies coming from the Ice Wolves in the future.

But instead of voicing any of those fears, I smiled and said, "I'm glad of it."

Soon the fields would be bountiful with crops again. Soon we wouldn't need any alliances to fill our bellies. Soon . . . I prayed it would be enough. But that was if the Ice Wolves didn't bang down our door in retaliation. Let alone Nero, who had already vowed to claim Olmdere for himself.

Meanwhile, more and more humans found their way to our shores . . . the ones who survived their passage from Damrienn. And I knew there was a whole mountain of dead bodies still lying on its beaches and littering its waters. Nero seemed content to wipe out the humans completely. Our enemies were only growing, and every day I wondered if I should blockade the golden forests of Sevelde just as Sawyn once had. And if I did . . . was I any better of a ruler for these people than a sorceress?

My eyes drifted through the crowd, finding some of the Damrienn refugees amongst them. Many had stayed close to the city, but others with agricultural skills had settled farther from the capital. More mouths we needed to feed and potentially many more coming. What good was this safe haven I promised them if I couldn't feed them? All of the things I wanted to be and all of the things I was had never felt so incongruous.

"I think we should go out for a hunt tonight," Grae murmured beside me so quietly only I could hear.

I let out a little hum of agreement. We'd donate a few stags to the village after our visit. It would feed the people *and* get some of our aggression out.

Grae's hand found the small of my back and I lowered my shoulders at his touch.

When we finished the tour of the grain silos, we stopped at the steps of the mill that looked out over the town's population. Everyone waited in silence, looking at me, and I knew I was expected to say a few words. If only Vellia had taken some time to teach me to string a sentence together during all of our fight training.

I cleared my throat.

"I never knew my parents, the late King and Queen of Olmdere," I began, much to the surprise of the crowd. "But many of you did." I searched the weathered faces that nodded knowingly as I spoke. "It is said they were good people, just and fair people. But those stories were taught to me by Wolves."

The crowd looked confused as I continued.

"I am only now beginning to learn who my family was outside the stories we tell amongst ourselves. Much of what I see in my past brings me pride and much brings me shame. And all I'm left to do with that is forge a new path ahead," I said to the murmurings of the crowd. "Many of you know of what I am, many of you also claim this word 'merem.' It is, after all, a human word. *With the river, carving its own path.* That is what we all must be now. Finding a better way into the future than our predecessors. One in which we are all given a chance at safety and comfort and joy. One where ambition isn't only for those who sit on thrones with coffers filled with gold." The crowd voiced their agreement louder now and Grae took a step in toward me. My voice rose to be heard over the buzzing din. I unbuttoned the top three buttons of my tunic, baring the golden scars across my chest, knowing that they spoke louder than any uttered promise. "I will fight for that future with my life!" I shouted to the cheers of the crowd. "I vow that we will *all* know that future within our lifetimes. I will give everything to make it so." The crowd erupted into cheers.

"For Olmdere!"

"For Olmdere!" they shouted back, touching their fingers to their chests, lips, eyes in prayer before lifting their chins skyward—an amalgamation of the Wolf and human prayers, a prayer for us all.

I stood there, letting their cheers and prayers wash over me, trying not to cry. I felt unworthy of it. I knew I could show no fear, no emotion, just the confidence that we would succeed. Right then, I needed to be the symbol these people were so desperate for, the parent who hid their own fears, the guard dog who protected the flock. But one day I hoped I could be Calla and not just the symbol of the crown. Once wars were won, once borders were safe, maybe then I could find a way to be both true to myself and true to them. But there was still a fight ahead. There could be no room for doubt. I was determined my promises for peace and prosperity wouldn't be hollow.

"You're too good at that, little fox," Grae murmured from the corner of his mouth as we wandered back through the village, shaking hands until the crowds thinned. We arrived back to the awaiting carriage circled by bored-looking guards.

I paused at the open door and turned to Grae. "I think it's time to send Ora southward," I said. "If I'm to protect our people without bringing violence to their doorstep, we need the Songkeepers. Ora will do more good helping their sect than comforting me anyway."

I knew it had been selfish, keeping Ora with me as a courtier when the leader of Galen den' Mora was born to roam. Sensing how much I needed them, Ora had stayed, holding that space for me with their quiet songs while they recovered from their Damrienn imprisonment. I wanted their counsel—the most well-traveled human to have ever existed, the most magical too. They had insights unlike any others. But Ora was healed now. It was time to let them go.

Grae made a grunt of agreement. "I have been in contact with a fisherman who will give them safe passage to the south of Damrienn to meet up with Sadie and the others," Grae said. I gave him a skeptical look and he shrugged. "I knew you'd reach this conclusion eventually. Ora is needed with Galen den' Mora." He leaned in and brushed a kiss to my temple. "But I didn't want to rush you, Your Majesty."

The way his lips lingered on my skin had my eyes fluttering closed. I took a decisive step away and he chuckled.

"We have much to do," I declared, finally stepping inside the carriage.

"One day," my mate murmured, "we are going to have a honeymoon."

I glared at him. "One day, we'll have the wedding and the fanfare and the time to be just you and me," I vowed. "But we have to save the continent first."

Grae let out a slow breath through his nose, one cheek dimpling. "Oh, is that all?"

THERE WAS NOTHING QUITE LIKE THE STEADY WARMTH OF ORA'S hugs. I didn't want to let go. Salty brine misted the air as the choppy waves slapped against the weatherworn docks.

Ora cupped my cheeks, a smile on their painted red lips. They looked at me like they saw all of me, like they saw who I was and who I would become and were just patiently waiting for me to arrive there myself.

I didn't want to give that up, the assurance I felt when they were near. But I knew I could do it on my own now. I knew who I was. And as much as I hoped I'd always have Ora's guidance, the world wouldn't pause long enough for me to be strong, so I had to be strong now.

"Safe journey," I croaked, trying to keep my eyes from welling, but I could no sooner cut a river with a sword.

"Be well, my Queen," they said with a little bow of their head, finally releasing me. "Let us sing a better world into existence." They took a step back toward the awaiting fishing boat, their eyes dipping to the lightning scars and then back to meet my gaze. "Let us bathe the future in gold."

I could only nod; any more words would make me blubber. Ora turned and passed their hefty fabric bag to the captain and then took a gruff sailor's hand to lift their heavy velvet skirts and climb aboard.

Grae was by my side in an instant, pulling me into his broad chest with a squeeze, knowing exactly how hard it was for me to say goodbye.

Ora began to sing as the boat pulled away from the docks. Watching me with a soft smile, "Sa Sortienna" filled the air between us. "Above the golden trees"—a song that meant they would miss Olmdere, that they would miss me. I watched with tear-filled eyes, voicelessly mouthing the words until I couldn't hear their singing anymore.

Sweet Moon, protect them. I'd paid the captain a sizable amount of gold to steer far from Damrienn shores until they'd passed Highwick and the leering Silver Wolf eyes.

"The Silver Wolves don't have a naval force," Grae said in a low, rough voice, reassuring me for what felt like the hundredth time. "If they stick to the horizon, they will be fine."

"But what if there's a storm? What if—"

Grae pulled me tight again. "They will make it. Their songs are more powerful than we know. Navin survived falling from the sky with the power of song alone."

I squeezed my eyes shut and prayed to the Moon Goddess to fight back any storms, to grant that boat safe passage. We needed Ora to be with the Songkeepers, needed their guidance and wisdom to pull them through this war. If they could control a fleet of monsters . . . It would have to work. After my latest contact with Sadie, I knew the humans of Damrienn wouldn't survive much longer if we didn't move fast. The longer Nero gained a foothold in the other courts, the longer he let them unravel into disarray, the easier it would be for him to take the whole continent.

We stood there, wind whipping our hair and salty air lashing our faces until the boat turned into a blur on the horizon. I blinked and blinked, trying to find it again.

Grae let out a long sigh. "One day," he murmured, kissing my hair.

And I knew all the things he wanted to say before he even said them. One day these goodbyes wouldn't be so hard, one day we wouldn't have to fear if we'd ever see each other again, one day there would be peace, one day we'd live in the future I had fought for with all my soul.

"One day," I whispered back, gripping on to my mate just as tightly.

SEVEN

BRIAR

I'D HAD A FEELING, A TERRIBLE INTUITION, THAT SOMETHING was wrong with Maez, but this . . . My body was weak with exhaustion as I sobbed, too broken to care if the guards outside my door could hear me. With every gasping breath, the will to live pulled away from me like spoiled meat from the bone. There would be no saving me now. Maez wasn't coming.

My mate was gone.

I had never thought it would be possible—to lose a mate. I thought when she died, I'd die, too, neither of us ever having to live without the other. What sick, twisted fate had been dealt to me? To be given the briefest love and hope and happiness and then have it be yanked away just as fast. It felt like my heart was being shredded to ribbons. I wanted to cut my chest open just to see its tattered remains.

Trays of untouched food sat sickly sweet on the table beside my bed, but I felt no hunger. I no longer felt anything at all except deep, unrelenting sorrow, like I was missing a limb.

No, like a part of my soul had been torn away.

I hadn't realized the sky had grown dark or the moon rose high in the sky until the door to my bedroom opened and Evres strolled in. If he'd knocked, I hadn't heard it, but I was certain he hadn't bothered. He paused at the foot of my bed, his lip curling in disgust at my sorry state. I was too broken to even be afraid. I knew what was going to happen.

"Get up," he commanded and I had just enough shreds of self-preservation to do as he said.

Although a voice inside me asked what was the point now? What was I stalling for? There would be no escaping, no rescue attempt right around the corner. Nero was right. Calla and Grae were the only Wolves left in the Golden Court now, and after Taigos's betrayal, Olmdere was entirely alone in this battle.

Olmdere needed Calla more than ever. My twin would want to storm off into the night to rescue me as they had in the past, but that was before they were a queen. And Calla and I were trained from birth to put duty above all else, even those we loved. Was there even any Wolf left in the Golden Court to send to my rescue now? Grae? As much as he loved me like a sibling, he would never leave Calla on their own—for which I was grateful even to my own detriment.

The list in my mind dwindled with every passing heartbeat. Hope faded. With Maez gone . . . that meant there would be no rescue at all.

As I walked around the bed and stood before Evres, my soul shriveled into nothingness. Should I even try to flee? Should I ram a blade into his throat before dragging it across my own? Or should I just fling myself from the window and end this life before he could take everything from me?

The latter felt so appealing. Because everything *had* already been taken from me . . .

Evres's fingers trailed featherlight up my jaw, smearing a tear down my wet cheeks.

"If you think these tears will stop me," he murmured, his wine-laden breath hot on my lips. "They won't."

I watched him through thick, wet lashes. The words were bitter on my tongue as I said, "Yes, Your Highness."

"You won't miss her," he told me as if he could command

me to just forget the love of my life. "Once you've been properly fucked by a real Wolf, you won't remember her at all."

He moved so quickly I didn't have time to react, grabbing me and shoving me on the bed. His bruising, frantic hands grabbed me by the knees and yanked me to the edge of the bed. I was numb, not even able to quite process what he was doing—what he was *about* to do, even though he'd said as much aloud. That's how thoroughly I was already finished with this semblance of life.

That's when a deep rumbling laugh echoed from the corner of the room. We both froze, turning toward the shadows that seemed to cling to the corner, so impenetrable even our keen vision couldn't pierce through its veil.

The figure took a purposeful step forward and the shadows dissipated like clouds on a windy day. She stood there like wrath incarnate. An apparition that couldn't possibly exist.

Maez.

Her eyes were filled with a violent green light, reflected from the skitters of emerald lightning zapping from her hands and flashing through the air. Her short-cropped hair was slicked straight back, new scars upon her lip and brow. She wore all black—fighting leathers and a flowing obsidian cloak that seemed to eat up the last of the candlelight.

She was the most beautiful thing I'd ever seen.

"Am I interrupting something?" Maez asked, her voice deeper than I'd ever known it to be.

I hesitated. I wanted to run to her, to call out to her. But while it *was* her—I was certain of that—it was someone else entirely, too.

"You," Evres seethed, taking a step toward her and reaching for the dagger strapped to his hip.

"Me," Maez said, and held up a hand. Evres froze, his face contorted as if he battled some invisible grip to get to her.

"Maez," I whispered, my voice cracking. Fresh tears welled in my eyes. To see her here—so whole, so real.

But then her shadowed eyes turned toward me and there was

nothing behind her stare—no love, no relief—no *Maez*. Only cold indifference. It shattered me like a frozen lake fracturing under a careless footstep.

Maez returned her attention to Evres. Her hand hovering in the air squeezed and Evres's hands jerked, wanting to go to his throat, as if that would stop his face from turning scarlet, as if he could untie the invisible noose around his neck.

"You think you can toy with what is *mine*, puppy?" Maez's voice was laced with lethal vengeance as she squeezed tighter.

I stood, rushing to her side and putting a hand on her arm. She stepped out of my touch. Unsheathing the dagger belted to her thigh, she flipped the blade over and proffered the glinting black hilt to me.

There was a taunting desire in her words as she asked, "Do you want to kill him?"

I did, and yet warning bells clanged through me at the twisted allure of her words. I felt the intoxicating pull of her offer, but it was tainted by my fear. What would taking the dagger of a sorceress mean for me? For us? Was she tempting me into her darkness? A knot formed in my throat, and all I knew was that this wasn't who I was supposed to be.

My hand stalled halfway to the dagger, my wary gaze shooting looks between the obsidian weapon and Evres's bloodshot eyes. I'd sworn that he would die by my hand and here was my chance. But instead of reaching for Maez's outstretched blade, I dropped my hand back to my side.

Shame burned through me along with my gutless anger. "Why don't you kill him?" I asked, unable to meet Maez's cold eyes. I hated the meekness in my voice, the timid little lamb felt grating to my own ears.

"He's your kill." Maez offered the hilt out one more time, and when I didn't reach for it, she shrugged. "Fine, then." She turned her attention to Evres. "Consider your life a fair trade," she said as he choked. "If you come to reclaim her, though, know that it will be forfeit."

With a snarl, she released her grip on Evres and he crumpled to the floor.

When her dark eyes turned to me once more, I rocked back on my heels. Because as much as I'd hoped it had been a trick of the light or my own shock, it was both my mate and a stranger glaring back at me, a cursed look in her eyes. But of all people, Maez and I knew a thing or two about breaking curses. Before I could think better of it, I grabbed her by both cheeks and pulled her into a kiss. She tasted different, tangier, like fresh blood. Yet she also didn't miss a beat. A heady, rough laugh escaped her mouth as she smiled against my lips. Her arms wrapped around me, pulling me in possessively to her as her tongue plundered my mouth. But I felt no golden rays of magic, no reversing of fates, only her carnal need for me.

Hunger, not love.

I pushed on her chest and stepped out of her greedy hold. Reluctantly, she let me.

Her grin was taunting and wicked. "So sentimental. A magic kiss, hmm?" she asked with a shake of her head. Her eyes swept over me, lingering on each curve of my body before stalling on my mouth. "Oh, sweet Briar, this isn't some curse you can break with your honeyed lips . . . though I wouldn't mind if you continued to try."

She moved toward me and I took a step back, hating that traitorous step. I shouldn't be retreating from my mate. But when it came to Maez, I never could be a good actress. My chest rose and fell in anxious breaths, panic lancing through me. This predator before me was far more dangerous than the one crumpled on the floor behind me.

All at once I knew: this wasn't a rescue. It was just a different kind of death sentence.

"You'll get used to it," Maez said, flourishing a static-covered hand down herself. "Come on, let's get out of this Gods forsaken place. The princeling smells like piss."

She reached out toward me and I just stared at her hand. In

the pit of my stomach, I had a feeling she wasn't taking me back to Calla, that I was simply trading one prison for another. Maez's eyes slid to Evres kneeling on the floor, still trying to catch his breath.

"Unless you'd like me to leave you here and you two can pick back up where you left off?" My eyes widened, fear gripping me tighter at the thought, and Maez chuckled. "I didn't think so." She stepped in, not waiting for my permission, and gathered me tight to her side as tingling zaps covered my skin. "Hold on tight, Princess."

I didn't have time to even register what she'd said before the world bottomed out.

EIGHT

SADIE

I SHED MY JACKET, THE MIDDAY SUN WARMING MY SKIN AS I SAT perched on the edge of the whispering well. As we waited for Calla to contact us, I enjoyed the reprieve from the constant jostling of the wagon. I took another deep breath as the meadow air swirled around us.

"How much longer until the temple of knowledge?" I asked as I plucked a seedhead from the overgrown wildflowers surrounding the well.

"I don't know." Folding his arms, Navin leaned against a tree across the small clearing. "But we're getting close or so the map says."

"The *map* is a booklet of sheet music," I muttered. "It would be helpful if you drew it out so I could read it."

"It would be helpful to our enemies, too," he countered. "Maybe I should just teach you to read the songs."

"Maybe." I stretched my neck side to side, my muscles stiff from the constant sitting. "Goddess, I hope it's tonight." I groaned as Haestas circled overhead like a burgundy vulture. "I can't take another night in that wagon."

"Eager for a real bed?"

"A bed, a cot, an earthen floor—I don't care as long as it is stationary," I grumbled. "More, I want us to be able to go somewhere that isn't within earshot of all your Songkeeper friends, too, especially your brother."

Navin coughed out a surprised laugh. "That is something I've been quite eager for myself." A yearning, desirous look crossed his face as he studied me, and he let out a frustrated sigh.

"What are you thinking about right now?" I spread my knees wider from where I sat and arched a suggestive brow at him.

"*Don't* look at me like that," he warned. "If you spread those legs any wider, I can't be held responsible for what I will do next."

"Here we are, alone," I goaded, delighting in his torment, "waiting for my Queen. Whatever shall we do with this time?"

"You better think carefully about what you're willing to let your Queen hear," Navin countered. "Because once I finally get to have you again, I'm not stopping, not even if your Queen is listening through the well."

I released a groan of frustration and Navin nodded in agreement. We'd managed a few stolen moments in the quiet of the night, wedged into a bunk in the wagon where our positions were limited. I didn't want to bury my face in a pillow any longer. I didn't want to stymie my cries of pleasure. I wanted him to make me howl loud enough that it rattled the trees.

I let out another growl, my lust-filled thoughts torturing me right along with him.

"Surely there are enough bedchambers in the temple to allow us some privacy at last?" I squinted up at the midday sun and the winged shadows tracing circles around it. "Preferably without your dragon waiting outside our door."

"I'll send her away."

"You should be sending her out with more purpose," I said pointedly. "See what else you can make her do. Command her to go catch us dinner at the very least. There's only so long we can survive on rodents. There's better game up the mountains."

Navin let out a whistle and the circling pattern above changed. The rock beneath me wobbled as his dragon soared down to the edge of the clearing, kicking up dirt as she skidded to a landing.

A dust cloud of floating dandelion seeds plumed around her as she came to a halt.

"Her landings are improving," I called. Haestas's warm breath whooshed past my face as I spoke. "She didn't knock anything over this time, either."

"Don't listen to her," Navin said to Haestas as he reached out and stroked her scaly snout. She released a pleased chittering sound and nuzzled further into his touch.

"She isn't your pet," I pushed bitterly, *definitely not* jealous of the fact that I hadn't been stroked by him in weeks. "Need I remind you, she is a manifestation of dark magic. She is a weapon, a war winner. She is the difference between our life and death." Navin's mouth pinched at that, but I knew I was finally getting through to him. "I know you care for her and I know she's still young, but the situation is too dire to not test her abilities thoroughly."

He hung his head as he gave Haestas one last sweep down her cheek. "You're right."

He started to sing to her and her pupils widened. At first, she tilted her head in curiosity; then she started stomping her legs like an eager dog ready to chase a bone. With a final chanted command, Haestas eagerly took flight again, heading out over the pine forest . . . and only smacking the tops of three trees during takeoff.

"What did you bid her do?" I asked.

Navin frowned at the bright sky. "I'll tell you if she succeeds."

My sharp retort died along with a sound echoing up from the well—a violin. Mina played through the reverberating hollow, the sound growing louder, and Navin sang back to her, the two speaking in a language I'd never learned. It was a quick back-and-forth, but Navin smiled and gave me a look as if to say, *I'll tell you later.*

"Sadie?" Calla's voice echoed up the well.

"Calla," I replied, my lips curving. "Are you well?"

"We are," their voice was strained. "And you?"

I missed when our time spent together was more than just relaying information. My mind flickered back to the dinners that stretched into the wee hours of the morning, the rowdy laughter and tales told. I hated these simple exchanges, wished I had more news to share and that we had time to make conversation that was more than transactional . . . preferably round a warm fire and with copious amounts of drinks.

"We still haven't found the temple of knowledge," I ground out. "But Navin promises we should arrive any day now."

Grae's voice sounded amused. "The wagon getting a little crowded for you?"

"You have no idea," Navin replied.

"And your dragon?" Calla asked, clearly ignoring the exchange. I had a feeling my Queen was making a silencing motion to their mate right now.

"We are testing its abilities," I said, giving Navin an equally sharp look. "Our hope is her hunting prowess can be extended to our enemies in time."

"Good."

"Yes."

Nerves coiled in me at the stilted words. I wished I had more rousing enthusiasm to share but that had never been my strong suit. I knew how badly Calla needed this hope. If Haestas wasn't the weapon we promised she could be, if we couldn't get more monsters to join in our battle, there was no hope of getting Briar back, let alone defeating Nero and stopping his human slaughter.

"We will keep working on it," I promised, needing to fill the silence. "And once we find more songs at the temple of knowledge, we will be able to double our efforts."

There was a long pause before Calla spoke again. "Any word from Rasil or the rest of the Songkeepers?"

"None," Navin replied.

"We can only hope that they have decided to stay close to the Onyx Wolves and their new King," Calla lamented. "But I fear that with the eternal songs in their possession, they will be pulled into this battle one way or another."

"Rasil craves power, Your Majesty," Navin said. "He wants praise and acclaim, too. And I do believe that he wants a world without Wolves and to position himself as the hero King for all of humanity."

"Is that all?"

"But he is careful not to put himself in harm's way," Navin continued. "If he's wise, he will stay out of the Wolf battles and wait to use his magic on whoever comes out victorious."

"We will need to come up with a contingency plan to handle Rasil in the event he decides to ally with yet another Wolf King," Calla said. "Right now, Taigos and Valta are too busy with their own infighting, but if Nero manages to pull either of them into a war against the Golden Court . . ."

They didn't need to finish that sentence. There were very few paths to success and a hundred to failure.

"Has Ora arrived yet?" Calla asked.

Grae's laughter sounded. "They only just left. The fishing boat isn't due for another week."

"Soon enough," I said, trying and failing to sound comforting. "We will be prepared for their arrival." *Soon*, so many things on the precipice but nothing solid. I hated to ask but forced myself to anyway. "Any sightings of Maez?"

I looked skyward, wishing I could see streaks of emerald lightning, wishing she would find her way back to us. I'd never gone so long without my best friend beside me. I couldn't accept that she and I would never be standing side by side again, howling up at the full moon.

She had to come back.

"No sightings," Call said, defeated. "And we are still working on a plan to rescue Briar. Highwick has yet to respond to any of my correspondence trying to negotiate for her safe return."

I heard the pain lancing Calla's voice but felt helpless to ease it.

"Right," I stated, unknowing what else there was to say. "We will contact you when we reach the temple with any more updates."

"Be safe," Calla said.

Mina's music faded away until only the wind sang across the opening of the well. We remained frozen in silence for a minute, our momentarily buoyed spirits struck low again.

"I hate these half-hearted communications," I muttered.

"And I," Navin agreed. "But neither do we have the capacity for joviality at times like this." He rubbed a hand to his weary eyes. "I had hoped for better news, both to give and receive."

I was about to reply when I heard a rustle in the forest just behind him. A beating human heart. A stick snapping under a heavy boot. Before I even gave it a conscious thought, a knife was unsheathed from my bandolier and thrown. My weapon whizzed through the air, embedding in a tree trunk . . . right beside Kian's head as he emerged from the forest.

"Kian?" Navin blustered. "What are you doing here?"

Kian looked at the knife a hair's breadth from his ear. "You missed."

"I don't miss," I snapped. "That was a warning. Don't sneak up on a Wolf if you care about your life."

"And I thought us musicians were dramatic." Kian laughed as he plucked my knife from the trunk and tossed it at my boots.

I curled my lip at my now-muddied weapon. "Did you follow us?"

He threw his head back and let out a mocking laugh. "I followed the map." Producing the leather-bound songbook from his breast pocket, he waggled it at us as if in evidence.

"Why are you here, Kian?" Navin said tightly.

"Are you the only ones allowed to use whispering wells now, oh fearless leader?" Kian asked his brother incredulously. "Some of us have our own personal messages to send."

The muscle in Navin's jaw flickered. "Personal messages to who?"

"An old friend." Kian shrugged. "She's always been sweet for me, but alas, our timing has never worked out."

I narrowed my eyes at him, about to spit more vitriol his way when a shadow appeared overhead. With a rush of wind, a large object fell from the sky and collided with the ground. Kian leapt backward, narrowly avoiding impact. The object splatted onto the overgrown grasses, smoke curling up from its sizzling form. My nostrils flared as Haestas let out a clicking rumble from above that I swore sounded *pleased*.

There, in the center of the clearing, was the charred body of a dead mountain goat.

"What in the Gods' names is that?" Kian balked, lifting his tunic to cover his nose.

I grinned at Navin in congratulations. "*That* is dinner."

AS THE DINNER TABLE CONVERSATION TURNED INTO DRUNKEN song, I let out a groan.

"Sweet Moon, spare me," I muttered, dropping a quick kiss to Navin's lips and excusing myself from the table. I'd heard these melodic songs too many times over the last few weeks. I swore I could hear them on the whistling wind, in the crunch of leaves, and the low of the oxen.

With a bellyful of dragon fire–roasted goat, I went to go sit at the front of the wagon. I craved the sight of the evening sky as we rolled farther into the vast southern forests of Damrienn. I was almost halfway through the window to the front bench before I realized Kian was sitting there.

"Too much singing?" he asked knowingly.

"Something like that," I grumbled as I climbed the rest of the way onto the bench. I'd debated retreating at the sight of him, but that would've seemed weak and I didn't show cowards like him weakness.

He chuckled, the sound so similar to Navin's own. I hated that there were any similarities between the brothers. "I'll admit,

I missed the sound," he said, and it took me a moment to realize he was talking about the music, not his laughter. "But I'm more comfortable with silence than song now."

"No cheery battle songs amongst the Rooks?" I snapped and he slid his gaze to me.

It still lingered there between us, unspoken. The whole journey we'd exchanged hateful looks but neither did we acknowledge the last time we'd met at the tip of each other's blades. A few weeks didn't change that. Maybe a lifetime wouldn't, either.

"I think my brother believes that becoming a Rook was the easy way out," Kian mused, craning his neck back to stare up at a strip of stars peeking through the pines.

"Was it not?"

He let out a bitter laugh. "I traded one danger for another," he said with a shrug. "I was a child when I pledged my sword to Sawyn. A hungry, scared child pledging myself to a sorceress who I knew thought I was as disposable as an insect. No one would mourn my death. No names carved above the mines. No altar to say goodbye."

"Poor you," I said tightly.

"Poor *him*," he echoed bitterly. "Whoever that child was, I didn't get a chance to know him long. It didn't matter which tune he'd choose, they were all sad songs after that decision."

I shook my head. Despite his choices, he still spoke in lyrics and riddles just like the rest of the Songkeepers. Studying his shadowed expression, I watched as his mind traveled back to unspoken horrors. "Then why? Why choose her?"

He let out a long, weary breath. "It's amazing what you'll do when your stomach is empty and your hopes are worn raw. Sometimes the only choice is to survive or not. I didn't think I'd survive the mines. So many didn't . . ." His voice trailed off and I knew he was thinking of his father. Navin had told me so much of their father that I'd built an image of him in my mind. He seemed like a good man. One his sons both mourned, but unlike Navin, I could now see Kian radiated guilt along with sadness.

"I suppose I can't entirely hate you for that," I muttered.

"Entirely?" Kian asked with a rueful smile.

"I hate you very slightly less." I held up two fingers so close together they almost touched. "Only slightly."

"I'll take it." He smiled at the stars. "If it matters at all, I wish I could go back and choose differently. If I'd known what my life would become. The things that sorceress would make us do." His breath curled in a whorl from his lips into the cold air. "The world was better the day she died. I could feel it, like a rift starting to close, a wound starting to mend."

"You can take the boy out of the Songkeepers," I muttered at his poetic nonsense.

"And now there is that rift again," he continued. "Another sorceress to take her place."

It was like someone had stomped their boot directly on my throat, clogging it, the pain radiating down through my limbs in panging waves.

Maez—my best friend since we were pups—was a sorceress. She'd saved my life with that power. She'd saved a lot of lives from Luo, I would wager. But at what cost? How many more would she take? How long until she turned just as dark and twisted as Sawyn was herself?

"I don't know if we'll survive this war," I said, pulling Kian's gaze. "But if we do, I won't stop until I find a way to free her from that magic."

"You seem stubborn enough to do it," he replied, sounding very much like his older brother then. I opened my mouth to reply when I caught sight of something through the trees. "What?" Kian asked, suddenly alert, straining to see farther than his human eyes would allow.

"I think we've arrived," I said, mouth falling open as I took in the shadowed buildings circling a central spire. "The temple of knowledge."

"Is anyone there?" Kian asked, voice dropping to a whisper.

I sniffed the air, trying to hone my sense further, grateful for the breeze greeting us face on. I couldn't see any movement, nor fires, nor flashes of light or reflection off steel. The place seemed long deserted. I closed my eyes to focus on the scent—nothing but old wood, dried pine needles, and dusty tomes.

"It's abandoned," I replied. At that assurance, Kian let out a sharp whistle that had me covering my ears with a scowl. "A warning would've been nice."

"It was a warning," he said. "But for everyone inside." As he said that, the songs from within the wagon abruptly stopped and Navin stuck his head through the curtain.

"What is it?" he asked, gaze darting from Kian, to me, to the knives still safely tucked on my belt. I rolled my eyes. Did he really think his brother was sounding the alarm because I'd stabbed him? I smiled at Navin with feigned innocence. If I wanted to stab Kian, I'd make sure he couldn't make a sound. Navin narrowed his eyes at me.

But Kian didn't seem to notice the silent exchange between his brother and me as he said, "We're here."

NINE

BRIAR

I COULDN'T COMPREHEND WHAT I WAS SEEING. THE GROUND whooshed away, and then suddenly we stood in a cold, austere room, flurries of snow skirting by the frosted windowpane.

"We're not in Olmdere." I said it more like a question, my eyes searching the sumptuously appointed room of heavy furs and fabrics in silver and blue. *Are we in Taigos?*

Maez folded her arms and leaned against the bedpost, shadows still clinging to her. "I don't think the people of Olmdere would much appreciate another sorceress on their doorstep so soon after Sawyn."

I turned to look at my mate fully—at the emerald flashes of lightning reflected in her eyes, at the wisps of darkness swirling around her legs. "You're not a sorceress," I said as if I could will away the dark magic from confidence alone. My statement clearly amused her.

Maez lifted a hand spitting with green static. "Am I not?"

"No," I breathed, begging. "You're a good person, Maez. I know who you are. You are funny and brave and loyal and loving. You . . ."

Maez cocked her head, cold eyes narrowing at me. I wondered if she felt anything for me at all anymore—or was it only this possessive need to have me like everyone else? It was a sadistic fate to lose someone and still have them standing in front of you. No. I couldn't accept it. We'd have to find a way to get her out of this.

There must be a way to break this curse. A cure.

"What happened in Valta?" I asked shakily, not yet ready to confront what there was—or wasn't—between us.

Maez's magic flared like liquor to a flame. "We were ambushed, attacked in Luo's castle." Her eyes grew brighter with menace and I shuddered at the pure power. She looked like an inferno ready to erupt, and I tried not to add any more kindling to her flame. "There was no way we'd have made it out alive. The look in Sadie's eyes . . . like she knew it was the end. But then Navin conjured a monster—a *dragon*—and unleashed dark magic into the world that was just there hovering, waiting for someone willing to take hold."

"But . . . why did *you* take it?" My voice cracked.

Maez looked at me like she loathed me, like I was a pestering insect with a nattering question rather than the moon in her sky. "They told me Nero had taken you, that they were going to marry you off to Evres, the little snake," she growled. "I couldn't have that."

My throat bobbed. "Why? Why couldn't you have that?" My eyes pleaded with her, beseeched her to say because she loved me, because we were mates, because there was no world—dark magic or no—in which she wouldn't come back to me.

But Maez just studied me for a long moment, her steely eyes contemplating something I did not know. Finally, as if a spell was broken, she blinked and looked away. She tipped her head to the bed. "It's late," she said. "You should get some rest. You'll be safe here."

I reached out for her. "Maez, please."

Faster than a snow snake, I was in the air, pinned to the wall by an invisible hand. My legs dangled just above the carpet, and I clawed at my throat, wondering if she'd brought me all this way just to kill me herself.

Maez frowned down to where my fingers had skimmed her

elbow before looking me in the eyes. "I don't think you're ready to play with this kind of power, Princess." That vicious green blaze in her eyes made my hands drop to my sides and stop fighting her invisible grip. She angled her head. "Are you afraid of me, Briar?"

She loosened her grip enough to allow me to croak, "No."

"Liar," she purred.

"I'm not afraid of you," I said, even as my voice betrayed me.

"Then you haven't been paying attention," Maez snapped. She gave me one last disdainful look. "Sleep or don't; I really don't care." She gave me one last appraising look. "If I decide to keep you, I will teach you how to kill dogs like Evres."

If I decide to keep you?

With that, she walked off, the door magically shutting behind her, and I crumpled to the floor.

My heart lodged in my throat as tears welled in my eyes. My mate would've never harmed me like that. That monster wasn't Maez. On shaky legs, I went to test the door and found it was unlocked. I decided to latch it anyway, knowing that it would do nothing to stop Maez from entering my room at night if she wanted to. But maybe the snick of the lock turning would give me enough time to wake at least.

I collapsed onto the carpet, sobbing, my last vestiges of strength giving in. I had been holding out hope, but now I had none. Part of me wished both of us had been taken in that battle in Valta, that my soul had been snatched up along with hers, without ever knowing this kind of heartbreak. There was never meant to be a world where she didn't love me, when I didn't feel safe in her arms. I knew it as certain as I knew the sun in the sky, me and her were always meant to be together.

The devastation was so vast I couldn't summon the energy to get up and into the bed. I fell asleep in a puddle of moonlight on the lush carpet.

When I awoke in the hours before dawn, I was in bed. I blinked as sleep clouded the realization. When I lifted onto my elbows to survey the dark corners of the room, I swore I saw Maez's shadow. I knew her shape better than I knew my own. I grabbed the candle flickering beside my bed and held it aloft, but when the light touched the shadows, it was only a lumpy curtain. My mind was playing tricks on me.

I lay back down, unable to summon the will to care about anything other than this utter hollowness inside. I pulled the sheets over my head and cried myself back to sleep.

TEN

SADIE

WE HUDDLED IN THE MAIN LIBRARY, PULLING BOOK AFTER book from the shelves. The temple of knowledge was actually a labyrinth of several buildings, some little more than underground hovels, others beautiful silver and gold temples dotting through the forest. Some areas were delineated by genre and theme; others were haphazardly arranged. We encountered piles of tomes everywhere—in doorways, in antechambers, even built into the walls of an underground bathhouse. The wilderness had reclaimed this place, but I could imagine humans from long ago darting between the many dwellings.

At first, it felt like a fool's errand trying to find the secret songs amongst a city of books. But then we found it: an unassuming little outbuilding barely larger than a closet with a shelf half shifted off the wall. Perhaps the secret passageway was left open in haste, perhaps the wind blew the shelves covering the doorway askew, but once we followed the spiraling stairwell underground, we found the main library. A catacomb filled with tomes, the place had been abandoned to a thick layer of dust and musty air. At the very top of the walls, holes of mounded earth revealed overgrown windows that allowed light to filter in from aboveground.

When we'd entered, there was a collective knowing, something like magic in the sense of rightness: this was the place. From there, we set to work, hunting amongst the vast space for the secret songs foretold to be hidden here.

The Songkeepers split into two groups—half canvassing the library and pulling books with any mention of music and the other half checking those books, sorting the magical from the ordinary. When I carried my latest pile of books down the narrow aisle, I was perturbed to find Navin had abandoned his post and Kian had taken his place checking over the dusty titles.

I dropped the books on the table with a heavy *thunk*. "Here." Folding my arms, I waited for his assessment.

Within a heartbeat, Kian passed the two books back to me. "These are children's rhymes," he said tightly.

I rolled my eyes at him. "If it has musical notes in it, I'm pulling it." I snatched the books and wandered down the stacks to return them.

So much of the Songkeepers' legends of monsters was hidden amongst these old songs. It wasn't as robust or well-kept as the library at the Songkeepers' refuge, but still, Kian had a whole stack beside him that he and his comrades were poring over.

Asha kept diligent notes of each of the songs they thought would be powerful enough to try on Haestas. But in the end, we all knew we'd need to go hunting for some new monsters—ones we needed to see if they could control with the power of song.

As I shelved the books, Svenja appeared beside me. "You look grumpier than usual, little storm cloud."

I glowered back at her, making her laugh as she returned another three books to the dusty shelves. A window had blown out on this side of the library, probably during a storm, and the pages were damp and faded, the ground caked in mud and pine needles.

"I just want to murder Kian," I replied. "Nothing out of the normal."

Svenja chuckled. "He does have a sort of slappable disposition, doesn't he?"

"I was thinking of using something a little sharper than my palm."

Her laughter faded into something more contemplative. "I like what you do to Navin."

I quirked a brow at her. "That is a very odd thing to say. Have you been spying on us in the bedroom?"

She placed her hand on her belly and laughed louder. "Not like that," she said through fits of laughter. "I mean, he used to be this forlorn, wistful thing. He was dyed the hue of melancholy."

"What a very musician-like way to describe it."

She looked at me sideways. "It's a lyric from a popular Valtan song? 'Vanek Grisada'?" I shook my head. "I'll play it for you tonight," she said, waving off the thought. "Anyway, that's what Navin always reminded me of, but not anymore. He seems steadier, happier, than I've ever seen him before."

A burst of pride bloomed in me at the thought, but I was loathe to say it. "The happiest he's ever been, trying to find and control monsters . . ."

"Yeah," Svenja said tentatively, brushing a stray curl over her shoulder. "He must be really happy to be this calm amongst all of this chaos and uncertainty." She wrung her hands together, moving her weight side to side.

"You seem about as confident in this plan as me," I muttered.

"All I can think about is all the ways this could go wrong," she said, lowering her voice as she peered down the row to where the others gathered. She spoke as if it was sacrilege to question the power of the songs. "Once we find these songs, we're going hunting for monsters. *Monsters.* I'm used to singing healing songs, songs for protection and wellness and sleep, not luring monsters through the forests like a siren. Don't you think that's crazy?"

"I do," I confessed. "But after all that I've seen these past few weeks, I don't think it's impossible, either."

I felt the confidence in me growing at Svenja's doubt, a subconscious reaction as if I knew we couldn't all be afraid, so let it be her turn.

"If we lose that sliver of control on them or if we never get it at all," she said with a shudder, "then they will kill us. And what if we *can* control them, what then? Do we bring them back here and start a farm of beasts? How are we meant to keep them under our control even when we sleep? Forever? We are not fighters—not like that."

I put a hand on her forearm, steadying her. "I am." I squeezed, both firm and gentle at the same time. "Hey," I said, making her blue eyes lift to meet mine. "If there's one thing I can promise you, it's that I'm always ready for a fight. I may not have this magic, but I have a power all my own. I will protect you."

Her throat bobbed and she nodded.

Kian leaned down the aisle. "Where are those books?"

"The ones you told me to put back?"

"Yes."

I glared back at him, gritting my teeth.

"Do you want *me* to slap him for you?" she muttered out of the corner of her mouth.

"I'm starting to warm to the idea."

NAVIN LIFTED HIS CANDLE HIGHER, HIS EYES TRAILING THE light to find me in the darkness. "How are you doing that?" he asked, tipping his head to where I stood reading by the light of the moon.

For me, the slivers of silvery moonlight were enough to illuminate the pages. "Wolf, remember?"

"How could I forget." He set the candle down and wandered over.

"Couldn't sleep?"

"The others are all asleep at the cabin," he said, tipping his head to the window and the ring of outbuildings that surrounded the temple. "But I sensed someone was missing in the night." His arms banded around me, and he kissed the top of my head. "And when I realized she was gone, I also realized wherever she was would be far from the others, and that perhaps we would find ourselves in a quiet place alone together. At last."

I shut the book in my hands and hastily shoved it back on the shelf. Navin chuckled as I lifted on tiptoes and slung my arms around his neck. It was all the invitation he needed. His mouth was on mine in an instant. Hungry. The last week had been a torture of wanting looks and taunts, brief touches promising more, and now we were finally here.

We devoured each other, the frenzy building in us instantly.

Navin scooped me up by the ass and roughly pinned me against the bookshelf. I moaned into his mouth, loving the way my sounds unleashed him. He nipped at my bottom lip as I scrambled for his belt buckle. He spun us around, dropping me on a table covered in dusty old scrolls. With little care, he swept them off the table and onto the floor. I loved his maddening desire for me, loved every single way we joined—soft and sweet, fast and rough, and everything in between. The multitudes of our relationship each brought their own unique satisfaction.

But we both knew what this moment was. Perhaps if we weren't interrupted, we'd go slow on the second or third round, but right now I needed him to fuck me fast and bring me to the climax that had been edging me for days.

Navin seemed to read every thought in my lust-filled mind as he shucked off my boots, hooked his fingers in my trousers, and yanked them off. My knives clattered to the ground, and he chuckled, shaking his head.

"What?" I balked. "You know I'm always prepared."

"I would expect nothing less." Navin stooped and picked up one of my knives, trailing the blade up my leg in sharp tingles. My chest heaved as he pushed in ever so slightly, nicking my skin. I let out a little groan, lifting my head to watch him lick away the bead of blood, something so incredibly lupine about the action.

"You would make a very good Wolf," I panted as his tongue swirled and moved, tasting my skin all the way to the mound of my pussy.

When he licked my sex, I saw stars, my back bowing off the table. My needy little clit was so desperate for him as he sucked and swirled, making my inner walls clench around nothing. It made me even more rabid for him, desperate to be filled.

I reached down and yanked him by the collar, pulling him up from where he laved my swollen bud with his tongue.

"Fuck me," I begged. "Now. I need you inside me."

Navin let out a pleased sound that caught in the back of his throat, sliding down his trousers and freeing his rock-hard erection.

I lay there, bare from the waist down, legs spread wide, waiting for him. Navin's eyes dropped to my glistening core, taking me in for one breath before he prowled over to me, grabbing me around my knees and tugging me to the end of the table. He hooked my legs over his broad shoulders, hoisting my ass off the table as he positioned himself at my entrance and slowly pushed in.

My eyes rolled back as he filled me, the sensation so all-consuming, like stepping into a hot bath after a long day of training, like free-falling. I moaned, crossing my ankles to hold myself up as Navin grabbed both of my hands and pinned them over my head. I completely surrendered to him as he rocked into me. Each rolling thrust made me moan out a cry of pleasure.

"Did you miss my cock?" He panted as he picked up a punishing pace, driving into me over and over.

"Yes," I cried out.

"Gods, I missed your tight, wet pussy," he groaned, fucking me harder until my thighs were shaking.

There was no way I was going to be able to hold on, not in this position. When my sounds tinged with mania, ratcheting higher, Navin released my hands. He unhooked my knees from his shoulders and pulled me up so my ass rested on the edge of the table. My legs hugged around his hips as he kissed me. He pulled almost all the way out and slowly slid back in, making me feel every delicious inch as his tongue caressed mine.

He swept his hands down my back, our frenzy turning into something slower and deeper.

"I love you," I murmured against his lips.

Navin pulled back to meet my eyes. "I love you, Sadie." He moved in and out in slow, rolling thrusts. "My Wolf, my song."

He dropped his forehead to mine and just held me there, our foreheads pressed together, our souls intertwining just as much as our bodies.

When he pushed back in again, the feeling was so overwhelming that even the slightest movement was going to topple me over the edge. Navin began to move faster again as if reading my mind. No slowing down now. Each pump of his cock sent me spiraling higher until I was coming undone.

I cried out his name, shattering, as my pussy clenched around him, pushing him over the edge of his own release. He battled my tight channel, getting three more thrusts before his hand circled to the back of my head and he guided me back down to the table, both of us collapsing in a breathless heap.

A blissful calm swept over me. Even with everything on fire all around us, surrounded by monsters, here we were, together at the end of the world.

I knew then I'd do anything to make sure we were never apart again.

ELEVEN

BRIAR

I STAYED BENEATH THE COVERS FOR MOST OF THE DAY, ONLY pulling the blankets down when I scented smoke in the air. I peeked out into the too-bright room as creamy daylight seeped through the frosted windows. The burgeoning flames growing within the freshly lit fireplace made me frown. The little acts of kindness only made fresh pain blossom anew. Better for the sorceress to be wholly heartless than to have heart enough to keep me from freezing to death.

"Are you going to keep yourself trapped in this room?" that rough voice asked before I even spotted her.

The sound of her voice was like a long-lost song etched upon my soul, but it wasn't mine anymore. That voice didn't belong to me.

A fresh wave of grief hit me all at once as I sat up and rubbed my swollen eyes. Haunted by a ghost who still lived.

"You look terrible," Maez said, staring at me coolly from the corner of the room. "You'd think being rescued from a dungeon would have brightened your spirits."

That was when I had something to live for, I'd wanted to say but refrained. If anything, she probably would've enjoyed my suffering.

My Maez would've never hurt me, not in body and not in

words. With this person standing before me, I had no such assurances. She might have dragged me all the way here just to kill me at one wrong move. Dark magic was senseless. There was nothing I could put past her, no assumptions I could permit myself to make.

"This is just another kind of dungeon," I muttered, pulling my knees up to my chest.

Maez threw her head back and let out a rough laugh. "Shall we send you back to Evres for a few weeks and see if that changes your mind?" She raised her eyebrows, but her amusement disappeared when she saw the utter fear on my face. Would she do it? She might? "There are no locked doors here, Princess," she continued. "You can go wherever you please, do however you please. I'm surprised that you haven't run back to your twin yet. Perhaps you need a bit of food to gather some strength for your journey; then you can rid yourself of this *dungeon*."

In a blink, a tray appeared beside me—a fresh scone still steaming from the oven and little jars of jam and whipped butter beside it. A teacup swirled with sage-green liquid, wafting the telltale scent of peppermint tea, my favorite. I looked between the food and Maez warily and she scoffed.

"It's not poisoned," she said with a shrug. "Eat, don't eat. It doesn't matter to me."

"Why do you want me to leave?" I asked, seemingly surprising us both with the question.

"You want to leave," she said flatly.

"I never said that." Even if I did, I'd never voiced it.

"You want to stay? *Here?*" Maez asked incredulously, waving her static magic across her obsidian leathers. "You can't be serious."

Did I? Did I want to stay? Did I still carry some hope that maybe Maez's curse could be broken, that she would find her way back to me? If the roles were reversed, I knew she'd never give up trying to reach me. I think I was questioning all this because I was still reeling from the knowledge of her turning to dark magic, still grieving her like she died even though she stood right in front of me. I *should* want to leave. I should be fleeing for the hills. I suspected her of trying to poison me for Moon's sake!

And yet it still chafed to think she wanted me to go. She was practically ushering me out the door, and while my mind told me to go, my heart urged me to stay.

I held her stare as I grabbed the teacup and took a fortifying sip. Her wicked grin widened as I licked a lingering droplet from my lips.

"What happens now?" I asked.

Maez's eyes lingered on my face for a moment too long before darting to the frosted window. "Now you do whatever it is you want to do, Princess," she said, crossing her arms tightly across her chest. "Your life belongs to you again."

"Just leave me out of it."

When she pushed off the doorframe, I leapt out of bed. "Leave you out of it?" I growled, the words wounding me even as I spoke them. Just when I thought she couldn't tear me open any further, she twisted the knife deeper. "And what if I don't want to leave you out of it?"

Maez took a step toward me. "Then you'd be making a grave mistake, Briar."

I blinked. So rarely now she called me by my name and not "Princess," and yet every time she did, it seemed more like a slip of the tongue, one that made traitorous hope bloom within me. "And what will you do about it? Pin me against the wall again? Choke the life out of me?"

Maez huffed, her shoulders rising and falling with a twisted sort of joy. "Don't pretend you wouldn't love it," she said with a wink. "I know your heart, Briar Marriel, darkness or no."

And with that she vanished, leaving nothing but glittering emerald stars in her wake. My heart battered against my chest as I stared and stared at that vacant space she'd left, wondering if it would be worth taking whatever she threw at me next just to keep her close.

MAEZ DIDN'T RETURN FOR THE REST OF THE DAY . . . OR THE next. Whatever glimmers of hope there were from our last interaction quickly faded again and I had the distinct sense she was avoiding me, as if maybe I could sway her back into the light.

I'd awoken with a half-hearted resolve to leave for Olmdere, but when the icy whiteout gales started blowing across the window, I thought better of it. I could travel in my furs across Taigos, but if I was sniffed out by any Silver Wolves—or Ice Wolves for that matter—I'd definitely be killed. And the only way I knew was the roads, which was the worst way to go. I could end up lost in a snowstorm or stuck up a mountain, and now that Maez wouldn't die if I died, there was no incentive for her to help me survive the trek.

But I knew it wasn't the snow nor the threat of enemy attack that kept me from lacing up the new snow boots by my bedroom door—it was the hope that I could find a way to bring Maez back to me. She wouldn't have given up on me, so I wasn't going to give up on her. As much as I wanted to go back to Calla and Olmdere and the quiet little life that we were just beginning to build, I knew there was no way I could move on without her. Maybe Maez could survive losing me now, but I couldn't say the same for myself. Whatever was left of her was still mine.

After that heartbreaking thought, I was determined to stay in bed all day when someone cleared their throat and I sat up, finding Maez standing exactly where I thought I saw her figure the other night.

"You need to get up," she said. "You need to bathe. You need to eat."

I frowned at her. "If you want me to eat so badly, why don't you just conjure food to appear magically at my feet."

"I could," she hedged. "But I think it would be good for you to eat outside of your room."

"You care what's good for me?" I asked, hopeful. "I thought sorcerers didn't have feelings."

Maez's lip curled. "Feelings are a weakness, Princess," she said. "It is power that fuels my magic—*death*—not feelings."

For all the distance she seemed to be trying to create, I liked the hint of sarcasm to her voice—it sounded a little more like her normal cavalier tone.

"If you want death, why don't you go kill Nero, then? You were so close to ending Evres, why stop?"

I wondered if she had the strength to kill only one or would she be like a shark in chummed water. Would the next kill create a blood frenzy? That's what I heard happened to sorcerers. I wondered if killing Nero would make her insatiable. Right now, she seemed so close to the Maez I knew and loved, but what would happen after a decade of killing. Two? Would she even be recognizable to me anymore? Would she turn her bloodlust onto me one day, too?

"I told you before," Maez replied, seemingly unaffected by my line of questioning. "Evres is *your* kill." She studied me intensely. "I could bring him here right now, you know. Let you run him through with my blade." A smile curled her lips as she licked her canine. "I could help you. It could be fun."

Fear gripped me. "No."

"No?" She seemed smug at my response, as if it had proved something to her. "You can't bring yourself to do it, can you? Because in your heart of hearts, you are pure goodness."

"I'm not so sure of that anymore."

Fear mixed with a strange envy. I wished I had a small spark of that dark magic within me to make me say yes, to seduce me into going through with it. What was the point of goodness if it allowed beasts like Evres to live?

"Cast Evres from your mind, Princess." Maez swirled her

hands wreathed in brilliant green. "He's nothing more than a fearful coward. He won't cross me again."

"I should kill him," I admitted, finding more resolve in my voice. Maez's magic seemed to flare in response. She *wanted* me to kill him. Clearly her magic delighted in the thought. A scintillating desire coiled in me to see how else I could provoke it. "With a flick of your hand, you could do it now," I pushed, trying to lure out her magic like a siren's song. "You are *powerful*. You can protect me. You can protect everyone. You can end this fight before it even begins."

Apparently, though, that was the wrong tack.

"I can spot your manipulation from a mile away, Princess." Maez shook her head in disappointment. "I am no longer interested in fighting any battles but my own. If you're too afraid to kill Evres yourself, then let him live. You think you can just pick and choose who I kill for your own ends?" she asked with a bitter huff. "That some killing is somehow good and just if you say it is? I don't believe in that anymore. I am not a hit man for hire. I am not a dog for you to command."

"I wasn't asking for myself. I was asking for all of us, all the Wolves and all the humans."

"What do I care about all of anyone?"

"So even with all this power, you won't use it to help us?"

She cocked her head like a curious lioness. "Who's *us*? You and your court? No. Me and you? Always."

A flicker of excitement flashed through me at that. She was still willing to fight for us. I still meant something to her, even if it wasn't the same. But if she had no loyalty to anyone outside of me, then she wasn't the same person I knew at all.

"What about Olmdere?"

"What about Olmdere?" she echoed. "It seems to me your twin has bit off more than they can chew." It both surprised and comforted me that Maez still used Calla's correct pronouns, unlike Sawyn. Even filled with a magical bloodlust, Maez was no monster. "Nero is prepared to destroy them, the Onyx Wolves have a pack to avenge, and now even the Ice Wolves are after Calla since they stabbed the Ice Wolf Queen in the heart in this very castle."

I sat up ramrod straight at that. "Here?" I pointed to the floor. "This is where the battle happened? This is where I was taken?"

Maez nodded. "It's safe here now," she said. "Everyone is far too busy pulling their courts back together after the chaos that *your* twin instigated."

"They didn't instigate it. They only reacted to what Nero is attempting. Calla only wants to be a good ruler to Olmdere," I protested and Maez looked annoyed at the statement. "Is there really no hope that you will help them? You used to be loyal to the Golden Court..."

"Used to be. Now I am loyal only to myself," Maez replied, and I waited, hoping she'd say and also to me. But she didn't.

I shoved the covers off and stood, my hands balling to fists at my side. "You can't expect me to just stay here and play house while my twin *and my Queen* could be going to war."

I moved forward, and instead of retreating, Maez took a step toward me, her proximity a rush. "I told you: you're free to leave. I don't expect anything from you," she said. "Although a little gratitude for saving you from Nero's dungeon would be nice."

"Thank you," I gritted out, and Maez laughed, the laugh I knew so well and wondered if I'd never hear again.

It was killing me. She was right there, right beneath the surface, but I couldn't reach her, couldn't pull her back above water.

"Calla hasn't lost the Ice Wolves yet if they play their cards right," Maez offered, following me out the door. She kept her hands in her pockets, casually strolling after me as I stormed down the hallway, not knowing which direction to go. "Then again, the Golden Queen may not need them at all if Sadie and the Songkeepers learn how to control those monsters."

I paused and looked back at her. "What does that mean? What monsters? And what are Songkeepers?"

Maez's lip tugged to one side as her static eyes looked me up and down. "Have breakfast with me and I'll tell you everything," she said. "Then if you still want to brave days of solo travel through the court that your twin just killed the reigning monarch of, I'll gladly conjure a horse for you."

I blinked at her. "You'll conjure a horse for me?" I asked incredulously.

Her eyes sparkled with electric green again. "That isn't even a speck of my true power, Princess," she said with a wink. "If you come eat breakfast, perhaps I'll show you some more."

I COULDN'T FATHOM IT. I STARED OUT THROUGH THE SNOW-covered window, my mind whirling with all the information Maez had shared with me over the past few days. There was a whole secret sect of humans—ones who used the power of song to conjure monsters and cast smaller magics. It seemed farcical, like something out of a storybook. I wondered if Maez had just dreamed it up on the spot.

I needed to talk to Calla, needed to figure out what I could do to help my court. Help my *twin*. I felt Maez's looming presence watching me as I stared at the cloudy sky. The best way to help Calla was probably standing behind me right now. If I could get Maez to use her new magic for us, the tides of this war would surely turn in our favor. Dare I say, it would be an easy win.

If Maez would fight, maybe all wouldn't be lost. Maybe we could find a way to rid the world of tyrants like Nero with a sorceress on our side. The irony of that wasn't lost on me, but if we were already trying to harness monsters . . .

No. She's not a monster. She's powerful, yes, but she's still Maez. Or at least, she still could be. And Maez would help. She just needs to be convinced.

If anyone could sway her, it would be me.

I'd spied the spark of intrigue in her before. She *wanted* me to play her games. Maybe if I knew the right way to tempt her, she'd be willing to play mine, too.

"Time for that horse?" Maez asked, misreading the way I stared out at the snow-covered stables. Was that . . . eagerness? Was she still trying to push me away?

I didn't turn to look at her, my breath fogging the glass as I asked, "You're not worried about me going alone?"

"You're a big girl, Briar." Maez let out a derisive snort. "You don't need an escort."

"What about the snow snakes and the Ice Wolves?"

"I don't know, you fight them and win, or you die," she said, bored.

I finally turned to look at her. Clad in all-black attire, she cut a menacing figure, but one that still sent a thrill down my spine, my eyes clinging to muscled curves. "Why won't you die if I die anymore?"

"I found a way to get rid of that stipulation, like weeding out nettles. I'm not anchored down by any moon magic."

"So . . . we're no longer mates?"

"Would you still want us to be?" Maez let out a maniacal laugh as she waved a hand up and down herself. Magic spit from her fingertips like a hissing cat. "You'd want to be mated to a monster?"

"Yes," I replied instantly. Something like disappointment flashed across Maez's expression at that. "Don't you want us to still be mates, too?"

Nothing in Maez softened to my question. "For what reason? Because the fucking moon said we were meant to be? Give me one good reason why I should care about you more than anything? More than riches? More than safety? More than *power*?" When I didn't reply, she simply laughed.

"So that's it, then?" My chest heaved. "We're not mates anymore?"

Maez crossed the distance to me. Standing only a hair's breadth away, she lifted her hand and tucked a strand of red hair behind my ear.

"I didn't say that," she murmured. "But I don't think you have it in you to be my mate now. You will always be mourning *her*." She crouched down slightly to meet my gaze, looking me dead in the eyes. "And I'm telling you now, Briar, there will be no going back to what we once were. This magic cannot be undone; there is no curse to break. I can still see that flicker of hope in your eyes, and I promise you now, it will kill you."

She bent her head, leaning in closer, and I instinctively pulled away.

Maez let out a rough laugh. "That's what I thought," she said, turning and striding off. Before she vanished around the corner, she called, "Let me know about that horse."

TWELVE

CALLA

ICE WOLVES WERE OVER OUR BORDERS.

I sat anxiously on my throne, rolling my shoulders back as if the act alone could prepare me for the envoy from Taigos. When scouts reported five Ice Wolves traveling through the Sevelde Forest, I'd rallied my soldiers and put the city into a state of high alert. I didn't trust that this was simply a messenger's visit. Perhaps they thought five Ice Wolves would be all it took to fell the Golden Court once and for all.

A little snarl escaped my lips at the thought.

"Steady," Grae said from the throne beside mine. His hand landed on the knee I bounced up and down.

Mina played her violin from the corner—a song I knew was meant to soothe. If the Ice Wolves had any unfavorable plans, her magic would come in handy. They would have no clue that the most powerful weapon among us was the musician in the corner.

"Another declaration of war," I muttered, adjusting my crown as I stared at the golden doors at the far end of the great hall.

"We don't know that. We haven't heard anything about who has taken Ingrid's place yet. How is Taigos rallying for a war against our court without a ruler?" Grae adjusted his fur mantle, both of us equally uncomfortable in the regal garb.

"Stop fidgeting," I snapped.

"You're fidgeting, too."

"Well, you've had a lot more practice wearing these ridiculous garments than me so I expect you to be better at it."

Gods, we sounded like children.

Grae reached over and squeezed my hand. "Whatever happens, we will find a way through it together."

The giant doors rumbled open and Grae reluctantly dropped my hand.

Through the opening doors, we found five heads of ash-blond hair and five sets of cool blue eyes staring at us. They moved as a unit, the one at the front clearly their leader. She appeared to be in her mid-forties, a true beauty but with sharp, predatory features. She wore the finest clothes of the five, her eyes keen, her mouth tight as she marched to the end of the dais and dropped into a deep bow. Her packmates followed suit.

"Your Majesty," she said, staying in her bow. I raised an eyebrow at the reverent gesture. *Hopefully*, this meant she wasn't about to try to kill us or declare war. People didn't usually graciously bow to their enemies. "I am Verena Baliczech, second cousin to the late Queen Ingrid. I believe you knew my older brother, Klaus."

I had to bite back my scathing retort. Klaus had been an arrogant courtier, one that neither respected my gender nor my sister's mating bond. He deserved his bloody end.

"Rise." The group stood as one and I met Verena's pale gaze. "Yes, I remember your brother."

She smirked at me. "He was a piece of shit, wasn't he?" Verena said. "I'm glad someone finally put a blade through him."

My eyes widened as I took her in. She didn't seem to speak in jest. "I suppose on that, we can agree."

"I think we could agree on a lot of things, Your Majesty," she added coolly. "Like how Olmdere and Taigos could both benefit from the support of the other. Like how a war is coming with the Silver Wolves, and if either of us want to keep our kingdoms intact, we need to set our differences aside to do it."

I narrowed my eyes at her. "Differences? I killed your Queen."

"Semantics." She shrugged. "Ingrid didn't truly want change, she just wanted power for herself. Much like the sorceress you ousted off your own throne. Either way, me and my ilk forgive you for Ingrid."

"Who are these ilk you speak of, Verena?" I asked curiously. "Why have you come all the way to Olmdere to wax poetic about forgiveness? Let us speak plainly."

"Right." Verena straightened her shoulders, clearly knowing I wanted her to cut to the chase. "As you probably have assumed, there is infighting amongst the Ice Wolves since our Queen's death. Three front-runners have each splintered off with their own packs, each claiming their rights to the throne. My cousin, Djen, is one, as is our army general, Hestoff."

"And you?" I guessed.

She bobbed her head. "And me, Your Majesty," she said. "Djen and Hestoff are both claiming that it was a mistake to let a woman rule, a mistake they're not willing to make again. Hestoff has all the war strategy in the world but could not win one friend to save his life. Djen is a pathetic weakling who will roll over and show his belly to Nero in an instant. Still, they have garnered the most allies just for what lies between their legs, however small."

I couldn't help but smile at her. She was certainly intriguing to say the least.

"And how many Wolves have followed you, Verena?" I asked, wondering if it was just the four behind her.

"Fifty-two," she said, and I raised my eyebrows, impressed. That was a considerable amount of the original pack. That put her at only at a slight disadvantage to the others. I was impressed more that she admitted her lagging numbers to me outright. "My second-in-command has our forces gathering in the northwestern part of the court, waiting for Djen and Hestoff to pick each other apart before we go in and strike them at their weakest."

"Nero will encourage this infighting," Grae said. "Play both sides. He will sweep in and take Taigos while you're all too busy chasing each other's tails."

Verena nodded her head. "I know. Which is why I've come to seek an alliance. I am the only one of the three who would consider siding with Olmdere again," she said. "But with your backing, I know I will pull more votes to my side. You have gold, you have resources, you have a human army, and—if rumor is to be believed—one of your courtiers has a dragon?"

I pursed my lips, considering whether I should answer her fishing questions. Finally, I decided it was better she think I had a dragon than not. Wars had been won from perceived fighting power alone.

"I have all of those things," I confessed. "And I'm guessing, as an ally, you will want access to all those things. What is in this alliance for me and my court?"

"Besides a friendly ruler who won't sell you out to Nero?" Verena chided.

"Those promises are easy to give and hard to keep."

Verena paused, considering me. The sparkle in her eyes gave me the feeling she was about to lay down a winning hand before she even spoke. "What if I vowed to help you get your sister, and only once she's safely returned to your court would I ask anything of you?"

I leaned forward in my throne. That certainly got my attention. "How do you plan on breaching the dungeons of Highwick?"

"Your sister isn't in Highwick."

My eyes flared and my heart galloped in my chest. "What?"

Verena tilted her head, smiling at me. "See, this is but one example of why an alliance with a Taigosi Queen would be so fortuitous."

"Where is Briar?"

"She's at the former Queen's castle on the border to the Stormcrest Ranges."

I furrowed my brow. "The same castle she was taken from?"

"It seems her sorceress mate has claimed the castle as her current abode."

My hands gripped the wooden armrests tighter. "Maez saved her?"

Verena tipped her head back and forth. "Saved, abducted, who's to say? That is beyond my purview."

My hope soured at that, wondering why Maez would bring Briar to an abandoned castle in a foreign kingdom instead of their own cottage home in Olmdere City. New anxieties began to cloud my mind. What if Maez was just as bad as Sawyn now? What if she was hurting Briar? Was Briar even *safe* with her mate now?

"How do you plan on helping us retrieve her?" Grae asked, filling in for me as my mind spiraled.

"My cousin used to take us to vacation there every year," Verena said. "I ran through all the corridors, found every servants' passageway as a child playing hide-and-seek in its halls. There are many secret ways in and out of that castle. I can help you get your sister back."

I wanted to say yes immediately, but Grae jumped in first. "We will, of course, need time to discuss this privately with our council."

"Of course," Verena replied with a bow.

I wanted to scream and pull my hair out with frustration even though logically I knew Grae was right. I was willing to do anything to get Briar back, make any allegiances necessary, sell my soul all over again for a little more magic to help me. I didn't know if I trusted Verena, but whatever her terms, I would take them. For too long Briar had been a trophy, a pawn taken by every power player in our realm, and I refused to leave her behind. We were destined for better lives now. Both of us.

Grae snapped a finger and two guards came forward. "Why don't you have a tour of the gardens while we discuss this privately. We can finish this conversation over lunch."

"Wonderful, thank you." Verena turned, leading her miniature pack back toward the far doors.

"Your brother," I called, making them all stop and turn back to me halfway across the room. "Why did you think he was a piece of shit?" I knew I had my reasons, but I wasn't his family. I needed to hear the truth directly from her.

Verena's eyes darkened. "He felt entitled to do whatever he pleased. He would use and hurt and take from anyone just because he knew he could—a trait he shared with many Wolf rulers." I knew from her tone there was more to her words than what she was saying, hated the thought he had taken from her and everyone with impunity.

"And Ingrid?" I asked. "Why do you hate her?"

"Because she let him," Verena said. "Ingrid's belief in supporting women in power stopped at the tip of her own nose. The only person she wanted to save from the cruelty of our rigid world was herself."

I inclined my chin. "And you won't be the same?"

"I know what it feels like to give someone a leg up and to have them then turn around and pull the ladder up behind them," she admitted. Her eyes dipped to the golden fissures that snaked over my collarbone and up my neck. "I believe you and I are here to break the curses of evil men and the women who uphold their tyranny. I believe you and I have the courage to be different than our predecessors. I believe you are like me, merem. I don't see worlds of men and women, Wolves and humans. I only see one broken world that needs mending and I'm not prideful enough to believe I know how to mend it alone."

With that, she turned and followed the guards out, and it took all I had not to follow her and pledge our support there and then.

THIRTEEN

BRIAR

WHEN I SPILLED THE FLOUR OVER THE COUNTERTOP, I CRIED. Then I burnt my fingertips on the stove and laughed as tears streamed down my cheeks. With no one to bear witness to it, I let the storm take me. My emotions seemed to swing violently back and forth between hope and sorrow, shock and grief. I hadn't requested that horse. I hadn't left despite my fears. This strange determination was growing in me that maybe if I remained stalwart, Maez would find her way back to me.

So far that glimmer of hope hadn't killed me as Maez promised, even if it festered. I would be of no help to Calla as a crying mess on the castle floor. I wasn't a war strategist nor a soldier. But if I could put a crack in this sorceress's armor, that would be the most good I could do for my court.

So I busied myself in the kitchen, crying over spilled flour and laughing at the ridiculousness of my runaway fate. The castle kitchens were enormous, rooms upon rooms, nothing like the cozy one we'd made for ourselves at our cottage in Olmdere. I had to rifle through three different pantries to fetch the salt and return it to the stove, but still, it gave me something to do.

Cooking had always been a surefire way to Maez's heart . . . well, that and something else, but I wasn't about to *sleep* with this newfound person—someone who didn't even see the point in having a mate.

I swept the flour off the table and into my cupped hand, placing it back in the bowl. The kitchens were incredibly well-stocked for a holiday home that was frequently empty, and I wondered if Maez had magicked the food there just for me. When I found a punnet of fresh blueberries in the second pantry, I swiftly snapped them up, knowing that I would make Maez's favorite blueberry muffins with brown sugar crumble on top.

It felt strange to have seasonal berries on hand with the frozen winds lashing the windows. I wondered if they'd even go bad—if Maez's magic would hold them frozen in time until we were ready to eat them. Could she do that for us, too? Frozen in this liminal space between enemies and mates, stalling until we could decide which we would be to each other.

There was so much I still didn't understand about this dark magic. Dark magic . . . that felt like a bit of a misnomer. Conjuring blueberries in the winter didn't seem like dark magic, but then again, maybe she was just trying to lure me into submission, maybe this wasn't a kindness but rather a game. I'd always known exactly what Maez was thinking, and even if I didn't, if I asked, she'd have told me. This new person—this stranger—was opaque to me, just as hard to see through as the frost-covered glass surrounding me. I tried, I strained, but I couldn't see beyond it, and yet I knew it was there just beyond my grasp.

I toiled away with my thoughts hanging over me like an ominous storm. I needed the work, something to do with my hands. It kept my mind from completely spiraling out. When I finished the muffins, I put them on a ceramic serving platter and went in search of Maez.

The castle was an absolute labyrinth of gray and white stone. I knew it would take me a lifetime to memorize the layout. Door after door, floor after floor, I searched for the sorceress, but she was nowhere to be seen. Had she left? Was she magicking herself to new corners of the realm for new misdeeds? Did her power compel her to?

I resigned myself to go sit by the already lit fireplace in the sitting room on the third floor. In some ways, this magic felt strangely familiar. I'd grown up with faery magic. Vellia had made our meals appear with the flick of her fingers. We never had to wait for a bath to be drawn or a fire to be lit. But unlike Maez, Vellia had loved us; this . . . this felt more like being a magician's pet.

I was about to sit on the armchair by the window and stuff my face full of muffins when the door behind me creaked. I turned and found Maez leaning against the doorjamb, watching me with sharp hawklike eyes.

My mouth went dry at her intense stare. When her eyes dropped to the tray in my hands, my cheeks flamed. I'd been a silly heartsick fool to think a tray of muffins would do anything to the sorceress standing before me. The way she carried herself, the stillness with which she moved was entirely new. My Maez had been playful and boisterous and heroic; this sorceress seemed cold, aloof, reptilian, more of a beast than even the most feral of Wolves.

"Hi." I felt incredibly pathetic the moment the word squeaked out of me.

Maez raised an amused brow. This wasn't me. I was supposed to be poised and regal, not a helpless puppy. I cleared my throat, rolling my shoulders back and lifting my chin, trying to mold my body into the picture of the queen I was trained to be. "I have decided I will extend my stay until the storm has passed," I announced. If Maez was surprised by this statement, she didn't show it. "I would like to send a letter to Calla, though, at your nearest convenience."

"At my nearest convenience?" Maez asked, a slight curve to her lips. She jutted her chin to the side, and I looked to see a stack of paper upon the low table along with a quill and inkwell.

"And a pigeon to deliver it?"

Maez's smile stretched. "Or with a flick of my wrist it could appear in their palace, hmm?"

"Oh," I said. "Right. Yes. That please." My words were choppy and slow. This new person put me on unsteady footing. I never knew what to expect from her. She was both kind and cold in equal measure, surprising me with offerings and then taking them away just as swiftly. "Calla will be worrying sick about me, probably hatching some half-cocked plan to spring me out of the palace of Highwick." Maez nodded but didn't comment. "Thank you for the paper." I was rambling now, desperate to keep her here, to figure this thing out. "I still don't understand how your magic works."

"Nor I." I was surprised Maez offered me that much. She seemed so closed off to sharing any of her inner thoughts. "It is not the bottomless well it seems. There are lesser and greater feats; some like transporting myself across the realm require a lot of power. Afterward, I'm left feeling depleted."

I inclined my head. It was a surprising act of vulnerability to share that with me. I wondered if she trusted me to keep that secret or if she simply didn't care who knew.

"And how do you refill that well of power?" I asked. Faeries' magic was fueled through dying wishes, Wolves' power came from the moon, and the Songkeepers' magic was fueled by song. What did sorcerers need to keep their massive amounts of power?

Maez looked up at me from under heavy brows, her eyes telling me I should already know the answer. "Death," she said, as if it was as simple as listing an ingredient in a recipe.

Death.

That was what fueled her magic. How many people would she have to kill to conjure quill and paper and fresh blueberries? How many lives would need to be taken? How long until her lust for killing became an addiction like it had for every sorcerer past? And the worst question of all, the one that plagued me from the moment I heard Nero tell of Maez's fate: Would I be strong enough to stop her? Or would I stay even as she contorted herself into darkness just to cling to the shadow of who she once was?

We stood there for so long, my mind spinning with heartbreak and fear. I thought I had been trained for everything, but nothing could prepare me for this. Maez's eyes dipped back to the serving tray in my hands, and I realized I was still holding the platter like a fool.

"You made muffins," Maez said, her tone so steely, I couldn't tell if she was mocking me or amused or bored.

"I did." My voice was more breathless than I'd intended. *Come on, Briar.* I was trained to deal with all manner of people. But I was never trained for this—for opening my heart up completely to someone and then forcing myself to close it again. "Would you like one?" I asked, holding the tray higher. When Maez didn't move, I lowered it back down, deflated. "Do you even need to eat?"

Maez's shoulders rose and fell in a small huff. "Do I need to eat?" she asked, pursing her lips. "I suppose I do not. I don't think I need anything at all anymore." Her smile stretched wider as mine fell.

She took a step forward and then another, and it took everything in me not to back away this time. Power radiated off her like a living thing and my Wolf senses wanted to shift to protect myself. Maez's eyes flickered at the way my shoulders bunched at her proximity, like a raising of my hackles. It was such a small look in her eyes that anyone but her mate wouldn't see it, but I knew that flicker of mischief, knew it so well that the slightest widening of her pupils told me multitudes.

Maez reached out and took a muffin from the tray.

"I thought you didn't need to eat?" I asked.

She tilted her head. "I still have desires, Briar," she said. "Even if I don't *need* to satisfy them."

My eyes were transfixed on her lips as she opened her mouth and took a bite.

Her eyes closed for a second as if relishing the taste and my throat bobbed as she licked the crumbs from her lips. We'd been parted for so long before I was taken, before she became a sorceress. If I had thought the last time we made love would truly be the last . . .

When Maez's eyes opened again, they flickered in emerald, her stare finding mine instantly. "I'd ask what you're thinking about, Princess," she murmured. "But I think we both know the answer to that."

I swallowed thickly, ears tingling. "I don't know what you're talking about."

"No?" Maez taunted. "Shame. I think you and I would both enjoy seeing where that line of thinking took us."

My legs trembled at the rumble in her voice, my body yearning for her touch. But the magic that swirled around her zapped the air. The arm's length with which she held me . . . no, I couldn't be with this version of her. I needed the old Maez. I needed my mate back.

Maez seemed to notice the transformation of my lust to sorrow, but she didn't comfort me like she used to do. Instead, she grabbed a second muffin off the tray, turned, and left without so much as a parting word, leaving me with a strange mixture of confusion and longing. An unwelcome question tumbled through my mind:

What would it be like to be with a sorceress?

FOURTEEN

SADIE

THE TASTE OF INK FILLED MY MOUTH AS IF I'D LICKED EACH OF these bloody pages. So many books, in so many languages, some that didn't even exist anymore.

We hunted for any mention of the songs hidden amongst the shelves. Determined to turn over every page of every book in the entire library, we had yet to find anything of particular use. There were lots of vague mentions of the magic of song, poetic enough that you wouldn't know it meant anything if you weren't a part of the secret sect. Songs of love and of healing, of family and friendship—all the usual themes one would find in music. But nothing of monsters or great power. No mention of the sacred songs nor the word "eternal." I now knew too much about things I never wished to learn.

Curse this temple, I never wanted knowledge again.

At least it was almost over—we were on the very last shelf. But we had yet to find what we were looking for, and if we didn't succeed here, we'd have to seek out other refuges in other kingdoms—more treacherous journeys that might be just as fruitless. I heard the telltale swoop of Haestas's wings overhead. Maybe we could just train her in tactical warfare and leave all this monster-training business behind us. If she could be trained to hunt goats and deer for us, surely she could learn to hunt Silver Wolves. I didn't want to spend another month in the wagon, crammed to the hilt with Songkeepers. And if I was being truly honest with myself, I didn't want to leave Damrienn, either.

The smell of the pine forests, the birdsong, the constellations overhead . . . I missed this place, even if I didn't particularly miss the pack that resided within its borders. No matter how I tried to reconcile it, Damrienn still felt like home. The floating mountains of Upper Valta, the snowfields of Taigos, the golden trees of Olmdere . . . Now that I'd seen every court, I knew this was still the one I longed for.

"Nothing," Asha declared, her voice squeaking despite her foul mood. She slammed the book shut and shelved it, taking a bracing sigh before grabbing the next.

I paged through the linen-bound tome in my hands, searching for music notes or words like "song" or "magic." My eyes snagged on a word and my flipping paused.

"Please for the love of all the Gods, tell me you found something of note."

I chuckled, glancing at Asha sideways. "I think you're spending too much time with me, tiny one," I teased. "Give it another week and you'll be throwing daggers just like me."

"If you teach me how," she said, intrigued.

"Deal."

She leaned over to look at the book. I tapped on the Valtan word for "power." "Fire magic," I read, scanning through the lines of scrawling text again. "What is fire magic?"

Asha studied the page for a second before she shrugged. "There are some old Rikeshi songs that talk about fire wielders," she said. "There's a song called 'Afa Adauri'—*the healing flame.*"

"That's just a love song."

She eyed me sideways. "All this time with us and you still think it's just a song." She let out a derisive exhalation. "Such a Wolf way of thinking."

I wanted to tease her with my bared teeth but that would only further prove her point. I was *mostly* used to the jibes by now.

They would never let me forget for long that I was the only Wolf amongst them.

"How does one wield fire?" I asked, grateful for the reprieve in our hunt for information.

"All types of magic are formed from others, like a transference of power, one morphing into another over time." She stretched her neck from side to side. "I suppose it's an old kind of magic that has since disappeared."

"Disappeared?" My brain was muddled from so many hours of staring at nonsensical words on faded pages. "But where did it originate?"

"All magic is born out of need," she said. "Out of desperation. Dying wishes, songs, even the Wolves. Something was needed so badly it was created."

"I desperately need a drink right now," I muttered. "And yet one doesn't magically appear in my hand."

"I think the Gods might debate the merit of that request." Her chuckle was so high-pitched, she sounded half mouse, half fairy. "I imagine there will be many more types of magic in the future, just as many current ones will disappear."

"Like the Wolves," I said, rubbing my tired eyes. "There're so few of us left."

"Us, too," Asha added. "The Songkeeper magic was almost lost in the annals of time. And that was before your king started killing us off."

"Nero is not my king," I corrected. "I am a member of the Golden Court."

It was a strained sentiment, one I wished I felt more confident in. Calla was my Queen, of that I was certain, but Olmdere? I remembered idling there as the Queen's guard, bored out of my wits, before I was whisked away on an adventure with Navin. I didn't think I could return to that humdrum life, but to travel in Galen den' Mora forever? Crammed into a wagon with an ever-changing rotation of musical strangers? I didn't know if I could stomach that, either.

So what, then? Where did I belong?

I was saved from dwelling on that unanswerable question by a shout and then a mild cheer coming from down the stacks.

"You found it?" Asha called, dropping the book in her hands and running down the long row of old tomes.

Navin appeared, scroll held aloft in triumph. "We found it!"

I returned the book in my hands, swinging my arms back and forth to stretch the tight muscles between my shoulder blades. "Time for a celebratory drink, then?" I asked hopefully.

"Aye," Timon agreed, giving me a wink.

"One," Navin cut in, holding up a long finger. Kian tried to pluck the scroll from Navin's hand and Navin swatted his brother away. "We'll need our wits about us for what comes next."

"What comes next?" Asha asked.

Navin's smile widened. "Now it's time to find some monsters to test them on."

Asha took an instinctive step into me, and I slung my arm around her shoulder. "Perfect time to learn to wield a dagger."

She gaped at me, and I winked back.

"But first—we drink!"

FIFTEEN

CALLA

"WE WOULD GET THERE FASTER IN OUR FURS," I MUTTERED, staring at the silvery moon illuminating the carriage curtains.

Grae let out a long-suffering sigh. "We are not running in our furs alone with five Ice Wolves," he repeated again.

"What if we stick close to the soldiers?"

"You and I both know the second you are on all four paws, you will be shooting off faster than they can keep pace with."

I gave him a mirroring frown, tracing the crease of his forehead with my finger. "I don't necessarily know that."

"Your lupine drive to run at the head of the pack could be used against us," he countered. "It could be an ambush; it could be a trick to lure us away from the palace and slaughter us. We are not going anywhere without enough guards to take on whatever tricks they might have up their sleeve."

"I don't think they are fooling us," I said, even though I knew it was naive to trust them. "I think Verena needs us just as badly as she says. I think she would make a good ally for the future."

Grae's mouth tightened, and I already heard all his arguments before he even said them. I knew he was right. Knew it was illogical to go chasing after my sister at the cost of everything else. I was a ruler. It was important I didn't put myself in harm's way or make an already difficult time worse for my court, and yet something hotheaded and wild came through me when it came to my family. I would do the most foolish things in the world if it meant saving them.

Grae folded his arms and leaned back against the bench across from mine. Our slow convoy of carriages trailed through the Sevelde Forest.

"Maez will keep her safe," Grae said, already knowing the fear in my mind.

My throat bobbed. "We don't know that."

"We do." He nodded and I didn't know if this display of confidence was to comfort me or because he really believed it, but Gods did I need his calm reassurance. "The skies could fall and the mountains erupt and the seas boil, but Maez would never hurt Briar even if her heart has rotted to ash."

"I cannot imagine it," I murmured. "Losing a mate."

Grae leaned forward and took my hand in his own, linking our fingers together as he swept his thumb over the back of my hand. "Nor I." He lifted my hand and kissed it. "When we go, we go together, to whatever end."

"To whatever end," I echoed, staring back out the window as if I could see Damrienn all the way from here.

I felt the war brewing like it was building in my body, the urgency making my heart beat faster, my mind race quicker. If Verena spoke true, we could attack from the north with the Ice Wolves in tow and Sadie and the Songkeepers' monsters from the south. We could circle around Highwick, take the castle, kill Nero . . . and then what? What would happen to Damrienn then?

Grae's hand squeezed mine, making my gaze drift back to his. "Do you want to run through it again?"

A sad smile crossed my lips. Of course he knew that I was running through every possible scenario and eventuality, knew I needed to talk through a plan for every outcome. We ran it again and again, dissecting each way our plans could go awry, every "what if?" And still my mate knew I needed to talk it through again.

"I love you," I said instead of "yes."

A surprised smile ghosted his lips. "I love you, too, little fox." He kept smoothing those soothing circles over the back of my hand. "I have faith in us, too. From the very moment I met you all those years ago in the forests of Allesdale, Calla," he said, "I knew you would make my life an adventure." He fiddled with my engagement ring—the protection stone he'd once given me as a necklace when we were still kids. I knew seeing it on my finger still brought him comfort. "We've been through impossible straits before and come out the other side unscathed." He lifted his other hand, fingertips trailing the golden scar down my collarbone. "Well, mostly unscathed. I don't think I will ever truly shake the image of you lying on that floor from my mind." Grae's haunted eyes lingered on my face. "Which is why I won't let you run off with some half-baked plans. My soul couldn't take it."

I leaned forward, resting my forearms on my knees in mirror to Grae. "Together. We'll get Briar. We'll ally with the Ice Wolves. We'll kill Nero. And we'll rule Olmdere until we're very, very old, surrounded by two dozen of our brave and cunning grandchildren." Grae chuckled as I tried to will those words into existence. "What?"

He toyed with my ring again. "I'm going to hold you to that, little fox."

SIXTEEN

BRIAR

THE SHIMMERING CRYSTALLINE NIGHT WHORLED WITH MY steaming breath as I huddled beneath my new fur cloak. I wondered how many lives would pay for it.

It took me hours to draft my letter to Calla. I kept getting choked up writing it, as if putting ink to paper would finally resign myself to the fact that it was true: Maez was a sorceress. And she still wanted me, in her own way; I knew from that look in her eyes she did. But did that make it any better? She had no reason for a mate, but she'd keep me as a lover? Would I bed her while I watched her kill and slaughter to keep our stolen castle warm? Was this the life I resigned myself to if I stayed by her side?

I hadn't shared all those fears with Calla, but I knew my twin would be thinking them all the same. Calla had always been too perceptive for me to keep any secrets from them. I wondered if they would hate me for it, choosing to stay with someone who was by all accounts now evil. Sometimes I thought my twin put me on too high a pedestal. Sometimes it seemed like they saw me as the personification of good. How would that idealized version of me compare to this—someone willing to love a killer? Someone who was beginning to realize she carried her own darkness?

When I'd given the letter to Maez, she'd flicked her wrist and the letter had disappeared. She said she left it on Calla's bedside table. My anxieties eased at that. At least Calla would know I was safe.

Maez cleared her throat, pulling me from my thoughts and back to the frozen balcony. She appeared without even opening the door and I was beginning to suspect she was always around, lurking in the shadows, ready to be summoned.

"These aren't the furs I expected you in on the full moon," she mused, ambling over and leaning on the railing to survey the moonlit tundra.

I'd felt the pull of the full moon like the heavy undertow of a mighty wave. I'd walked almost mindlessly out to the balcony to gaze up at the Moon Goddess.

"Doesn't the Goddess call to you still?" I asked Maez. "Doesn't she pull you out of your skin to run in the moonlight and howl at her beautiful glow?"

"I am beholden to no magic now," Maez said, pride in her voice. "No Goddess can control me." Her eyes dropped from the sky onto me. "Nor person."

"Is that what you thought I was to you?" I silently cursed myself for being unable to hide the pain lancing my words. "Was I a shackle? You thought I controlled you?"

"You put a target on my back the moment the moonlight touched me," Maez said, her bright magic even more vibrant in the dark. "I'd finally found my place, my safety as a guard for Grae. You plucked me out from those shadows and brought the eyes of all of Aotreas upon me."

I swallowed the lump in my throat. I hadn't really considered what a burden it would be to be tied to the Crimson Princess. To be mated to someone that everyone wanted for their own gains. Within hours of our bonding, Maez had suffered for it.

"I'm sorry Sawyn took you to keep me cursed." I said it like I hadn't a hundred times before. I'd forever feel guilty for what Maez endured at Sawyn's hands while I was under that sleeping curse. Weeks and weeks she was starved and tortured before Calla and Grae saved her.

I scrutinized her with new eyes.

"What?" Maez asked, seeing instantly the flash of a question on my face. I hated that she could read me just as easily as ever even when I couldn't do the same.

"Nothing," I said, shaking my head.

"No," she corrected. "Say it."

"I only wondered . . ." I took a deep breath and blew it out, the steam curling like pipe smoke. "I wondered if all that you suffered at Sawyn's hands was one of the reasons you grabbed for that dark magic in Valta." Maez went stock-still. "When you heard that I'd been taken, had it been out of fear that I would bear the same fate as you?"

"So close and yet so far." Maez chuckled and I shuddered at the bitterness in her laugh.

"Tell me."

"Like I said"—her eyes darted back to the moon—"no one controls me anymore."

"I'm sorry," I whispered, voice cracking. "I'm sorry I brought all of this upon you. I'm sorry I am who I am, my own kind of curse."

My hand slid across the balcony to cover her own and Maez instantly yanked it away.

"Oh bleeding heart Briar," she scoffed. "Save your apologies. I've never felt more free."

Tears welled in my eyes. I knew she'd chosen the darkness because of me, to save me, knew the old Maez would stop at nothing to get me back. But now that the magic had taken hold of her, I knew she wouldn't make such sacrifices again.

When I sniffed, Maez glanced at me and rolled her eyes in annoyance. "Go," she said. "Run in the moonlight. Pray to any Gods that control you."

She turned and I reached out, without thought, my hand landing on her forearm. "Wait." Maez paused and looked down to where my hand touched her flowing black robes. "Come with me." I knew she was going to make another sniping comment, knew she'd make another jibe about control, so I switched tack. "Can you even shift anymore? Or did you lose that power for a different one?"

"I can shift," Maez said defensively, and I knew I had her hooked.

I quirked a brow at her. "Do you think you're faster than me now?"

"Without question."

"Prove it," I challenged. "You run this pack. Lead the way; show me the land of your new domain."

Oh, she liked that. Her lips curved into a catlike grin. Perhaps I could find a way to work my charms over this version of her, too, goad her into spending time with me, growing closer again. I asked her to lead the way, a fun, distracting game of cat and mouse, but really my heart was screaming out to her. Maybe the run would put a dent in her newfound armor. This was one step in the right direction, and I had to try.

I bowed my head to her and gestured to the door. "After you."

She let out a little huff. "Are you sure you can keep up?"

My eyes twinkled with the challenge. "You may be a sorceress, but I'm a Gold Wolf." With that, I turned to the door and ran toward the stairwell, Maez laughing, hot on my heels.

THE MOONLIGHT ON MY FUR WAS SUCH A GLORIOUS RELEASE. I didn't realize how much I needed this after being cooped up in the castle. Maez's silver fur was a gleaming flash through the white snow, but I stayed close, nipping at her legs and making her push faster. As she weaved across the snow dunes, I tracked that black tip of her tail, keeping her locked in my sights. No magic seemed to spark around her Wolf form. She seemed almost back to her normal self, howling at the moon, playfully swirling back to snap at me.

When we dropped low enough down the mountain, we hit the

tree line and plunged into the dark forest. Spindly pines and shrubs gave way to more and more robust trees until we were in the sweet-scented pine forests that made me giddy. Running through the forest was so much more enjoyable than a frozen tundra. There were logs to jump over, brambles to dodge, rivers to breach, animals to scent and hunt. We ran and ran, my soul singing.

When we reached a powdered meadow, Maez slowed her pace and spoke into my mind for the first time on the run. "All right, Princess," she said, her voice warm and crystal clear. "You've proven your point."

It felt so good to sense her in my mind, to feel that connection between us so strongly. This was Maez. She was still here. She still existed. A flutter of dangerous hope sparked in me.

"Do you admit defeat?" I asked.

Maez's head turned back toward me. She had beautiful amber eyes, rimmed in black fur that faded to silver. "Never."

She pounced on me, playfully trying to pin me. I let out a yip of delight, rolling out from underneath her, and trying to get my teeth to grip the back of her neck. She dodged out of my strike and pounced on my again, using her barrel chest to pin me down.

"Shift."

"What?" I asked, laughter in my unspoken voice.

"*Shift*," she commanded, her voice tinged in desperation.

Without thought, I did as she said. Maez shifted at the same moment I did and all of a sudden it was us—her bare skin on top of mine. I didn't feel the burn of the snow on my back as her dark eyes hooked into mine and she smiled for a split second before she dropped her head and kissed me.

This kiss was all her, all my mate. My body reacted on instinct, my hands sweeping around her bare skin and pulling her tighter to me. I could feel the magic tying us together, like a flaming rope I could reach out and grab on to. My lips tingled as her mouth worked over mine, kissing me with a passion and hunger as if she'd been starving for weeks, gorging herself on me. Her thigh slid between my legs, spreading them wider as her hand dropped to cup my ass and rock my hips against her.

Electricity sparked between us, crackling and zapping the air.

Maez gasped and pulled back, her eyes now filled with that eerie green.

And just like that, my mate was gone.

Her mouth tightened into a scowl.

"Maez." I reached for her, but she leaned out of my touch.

She shoved backward onto her knees. "You don't want this, Princess," she said, her voice still husky with lust. "You don't want what I've become. You are too sweet. Too good."

"I am not so good," I spat.

Maez threw her head back and laughed bitterly to the full moon. "If ever there was a portrait of goodness, Briar Marriel, it would be you."

There it was again, the accusation chafing against my inner thoughts. I was not as sweet as all of them seemed to think. The urge to prove her wrong crested in me like a wave. Maybe I'd have to absorb some of her darkness into my soul to pull her back into the light. Maybe we could both become a mixture of the two.

"No," I muttered, sitting up and gathering my knees to my chest. "I am not that person. Not anymore." The bite of the cold came rushing over me, stinging my vulnerable skin.

I wouldn't give up, not now that I knew she was still in there. If we had to live our entire lives in Wolf form just to be together, then so be it. A part of her was still mine and I would cling to it with everything I had.

Maez frowned, seemingly reading all that determination on my face.

"Time to go home now, Princess." And with a swirl of her magic, the world disappeared.

SEVENTEEN

SADIE

"THIS IS A REALLY, *REALLY* BAD IDEA," ASHA SAID AS WE HIKED through the pine forest. "Never in my life did I think I'd be *searching* for monsters."

"These ones should be fairly harmless," I said.

"'Fairly,'" Timon muttered.

"Can that even be a thing?" Asha asked.

"They will be good practice to see if the songs work," I countered. "Unless you'd like to go hunt down a crishenem and pray the songs work before we're impaled with one of their stingers?"

Svenja shuddered. "Do we even know if any will be there?"

"They say the visturong dwells in the hollows beneath the giant oaks of the southern valley," I said, remembering the folktale from when I was a pup. "It was said that they surrendered to the Silver Wolves and promised to never leave their giant oaks again and the Wolves let them live."

"But we all know how Wolf stories get twisted to their own arrogant beliefs," Timon muttered.

"How about you stop muttering and just talk to us?" I snapped, and he flushed. "And to answer your question, this one was corroborated in the temple of knowledge."

Nostalgia warred with shame. There were parts of my childhood that I'd loved and missed—the unique scents of the Damrienn forest, the food and clothing, Gods, even the jokes. I missed the way the language felt on my tongue. We mostly spoke Olmderian now, and while I was fluent, there was something about the word formations that still felt like I was performing—pretending to be someone else.

I knew deep inside that if we survived this war with Nero, I couldn't just go back to Olmdere with Navin and live out my days there. I didn't know if I wanted to stay in that wagon for the rest of my life, either . . . I hadn't expected I'd fall in love with a human, and now that I was, it still left a heap of unanswered questions: Where would we live? What did we want out of the life we'd been given? I didn't know. Ever since leaving Highwick, everything still felt up in the air and I couldn't figure out where I wanted to land.

The mission kept me going. I just wasn't sure what my destination actually was . . .

"You okay?" Navin asked, coming to match my stride.

I realized I was practically running and slowed, the anxiety of my thoughts pushing me to a faster pace than the humans could keep up with . . . except for Navin with his incredibly long legs who easily always seemed to meet me wherever I was.

"I'd feel better if Haestas was here." I'd come to find comfort in that red shadow.

"One monster at a time," Navin said. "The songs might confuse her. She's a weapon we can't afford to lose in an accidental visturong battle."

"If this ends in a battle," I said tightly, "I think I would like your giant dragon to be here."

Navin waved the crumpled song sheets in his hand at me. "It won't end in a battle."

"I just need this to work." I paused at the top of the next hill to let the others catch up. "Olmdere needs this to work. The world hangs in the balance."

"No pressure, then?" Navin joked. When I didn't laugh, he continued. "This is just the first of many trials. Calla is headed to Taigos to make new allies, and the Silver Wolves haven't left their borders; we have time to figure this out."

He swept a comforting hand down my back. I was all fire and sharp edges, while Navin was as smooth as a lake on a windless day. I brought out his spark; he quelled my storms. I leaned into his touch for the briefest of moments until the others caught up to us, and then I pressed on, leading with my nose. I sniffed out the oak trees, the shifting of the pines to a deciduous forest, and led us straight as an arrow toward them.

When the last of the pine trees gave way, we paused at the line of low brambles that bisected the forest. The giant oaks were ringed with shrubs and thorns as if fences to protect the monsters that dwelled within.

"There," I said, pointing to the peak of a hole in the earth. Like the air hole of a crab buried below sand, I knew this little opening did nothing to show the true size of what lurked under the earth. "Who's going to try first?"

"I will," Kian declared, his tone carrying its usual arrogance. I rolled my eyes as he pushed through the group to the front. He plucked a reedy wooden flute from his trouser pocket and played three notes before his older brother muttered, "Wrong key."

"Please don't get us all killed because you haven't memorized the sheet music," Asha mumbled from behind us. She stood a single pace behind me like a child hiding behind their mother's skirts.

Navin offered out the sheet music in his tight grip, but his younger brother swatted it away.

Kian quickly switched his key and started playing again. At first, we thought it wasn't working; nothing was happening. But then the leaves of the closest oak started to rattle.

"Holy Gods," Svenja whispered.

I was certain nothing holy was about to happen.

The ground started to tremble, and Navin instinctively

reached out to steady my arm. The ground split, the little hole tearing open to reveal two bloodred eyes from the shadows. An ashen paw, covered in scaly skin like the bark of the tree, reached out. It had a catlike face and razor-sharp claws, its skin coated in that flaky white bark as if it might disintegrate at a strong wind. But the way the ground trembled when it prowled out of its hollow told me this was nothing to trifle with. From my childhood stories, I had been prepared for something weak and timid, but this beast was something else.

Kian's song grew light and shaky as the giant creature fully emerged, standing twice as tall as the rest of us. It towered above us, watching with hateful eyes, but neither did it strike.

"It's working," Navin whispered with a disbelieving shake of his head. "Try to get it to sit."

Kian's tune changed and the creature let out a growl that had us all leaping backward in unison. But its back legs bent; slowly as if fighting off the spell, it sat.

"Sweet Moon," I murmured. "This might actually work."

Kian's music stalled for a second as he crinkled his nose.

"No, no, no, don't!" Navin called, racing past me to get his brother.

It happened all at once: Kian sneezed, the music stopped, and the earth around us exploded.

I SCREAMED, WET EARTH FLYING INTO MY MOUTH AS FIVE visturongs flew up from their hollows, snarling and snapping their jagged teeth.

Shit.

I shifted instantly. Knives alone weren't going to save us. Kian commenced playing again and the others started singing the accompanying tune, but by now, it was no use. There were too many of them to control, the sounds of trees cracking and earth tearing crowding out the sounds of the songs.

I launched forward at the first visturong that aimed for

Navin. I sunk my teeth into its giant forearm, the taste of its flaking ashen skin making bile rise up my throat, but I tore and tore until bitter black blood came oozing from its wound. The creature squealed and retreated.

I howled and the creatures seemed to freeze at the sound.

The pact.

The visturongs had made a pact with the Silver Wolves to stay in their hollows, to never harm the pack in exchange for their lives. Perhaps they remembered my ancestors and the agreement they had made thousands of years ago. Maybe they would bow to my own songs.

I howled again and the front three retreated another step, but the last two still battled against the pull of the magic.

"Don't stop," Navin shouted to the Songkeepers, leading them in their trembling tune, growing stronger at the sight of three of them held at bay.

I prowled forward toward the nearest one, howling and snapping. Those scarlet eyes landed on me and then past me, searching the forest. My stomach sank when they found no pack behind me—a lone Wolf. I didn't know what they communicated to the others, but one minute they were retreating and the next, they were screeching, launching forward at us.

I growled and yapped, trying to pull the beasts' attention on only me. Maybe I could lead them through the pines and away from the others. But the creatures scattered in every direction, chasing down the musicians.

The Songkeepers broke rank, turning and fleeing into the forest. I heard Navin shout my name as a spindly limb collided with my side, sending me flying. The ground shook, jostling me over the uneven terrain as the visturong skittered toward me, its bloodred eyes hungry. I scrambled to get my feet back under me.

Then more music came flying through the forest. It was the sharp trill of a metal pipe. I whipped around to the sound, my eyes landing on a figure on the hill.

Ora.

Their power was immense, clearly greater than the other Songkeepers, the sound so hypnotic, it pulled me in, too. I moved forward, entranced.

"Go home," the song told me. "All is well. There is no danger. Go home."

It was an impossible sort of calm. My racing heart instantly slowed. I started moving toward Highwick, feeling the overwhelming urge to go back toward the city of my birth.

"Sadie?"

Home. I needed to get home. All the sounds faded to that one notion: go home. I faintly heard Navin shouting for Ora to stop.

When the song stopped, I felt like a puppet with its strings cut.

Navin appeared in front of me, unfazed by my Wolf. He held a hand to my chest. When I snarled, he retracted it. He whipped off his coat and wrapped it around my shoulders.

"Shift, Sadie," he murmured just for me to hear. And his voice cut through all else as if he knew how to speak directly to my soul.

I shifted. Bones popping, muscles stretching, and then I was there, crouched in my skin with Navin's coat draped around my shoulders. Navin stood close, shielding me from the others while I buttoned up his coat. When I was covered, I gave him a nod. Only once I reassured him I was okay did he turn and embrace Ora.

They hugged for a cathartic moment, two long-separated friends reunited once more. "It's good to see you in one piece," Navin said, clapping Ora on the shoulder.

"You have no idea." Ora chuckled. "I'm not sure what was worse, the Damrienn dungeons or being stuck on a fishing boat in choppy waters."

Ora still looked a little green, eyes weary. They didn't wear their signature painted lips, but their clothing was just as colorful as ever—a mishmash of fabrics and patterns that made them look ready for any stage, as if their entire life was one long show.

I would've been more relieved to see the leader of Galen den' Mora, though, if they hadn't just had their claws in my mind. That song still had a hold of me, and I still felt its echoes, my feet wanting to steer me toward Highwick of their own volition. I wiggled my toes into the earth, trying to feel more firmly planted and less likely to be taken away by my mind. The visturongs had all returned to their hollows, nothing but upturned earth left in their wake.

The rest of the Songkeepers waved from the distance, calling out to Ora as they wandered over to us on shaking legs.

"The journey here was not exactly restorative," Ora quipped, their warm eyes finding mine. "But I'm glad to be back home."

"That song," I said, looking around the woods. "It was as if I'd been hypnotized. I . . . all I heard was 'go home' over and over in my mind."

"Gods," Navin said, his eyes going wide. "I had never considered it before." He looked between Ora and me. "What if these songs can control Wolves, too?"

Left unsaid as I stared at him in horror was the question "What if Wolves are monsters?"

EIGHTEEN

BRIAR

AFTER OUR MOMENT IN THE FOREST, MAEZ SEEMED TO DISappear. I didn't even know if she was still in the castle or if she'd left me there. The magic still flowed easily through the house—food, warm baths, clean clothes, as if a bunch of invisible maids had been tending to the place—but Maez was gone.

I wondered if I'd spooked her. Did she fear that moment we kissed as much as it excited me? She was like a wild animal, one whose power had been threatened, and now she fled from me, and I wondered if she was afraid she'd lose more of that dark magic to me. It's what I'd hoped for—that I could spool her back into herself and away from the darkness. It seemed her Wolf form was a conduit for that change. I wondered if she'd never shift again.

I sat on the settee with my head in my hands, losing all manner of hope when she didn't return one day and then the next. I couldn't just bake and read and pretend everything was normal. I didn't want to be cooped up in a castle alone.

When I heard the rustling sound of movement, hope reignited in me. Maez had finally returned. But when I lifted my head, I saw six soldiers spilling from the stairwell and fanning out over the room. My heart leapt into my throat as I spotted their fawn leathers, inky black buckles, and the bursting suns carved onto their hammered bronze armor.

Onyx Wolves.

I shot to my feet, eyes widening with alertness as I held up my hands. They didn't even try to hide their approach, knowing I was outnumbered.

"What is happening?" My frenzied voice trembled as the soldiers circled me.

"Where is the sorceress?" the head one, judging by the crest of his helmet, asked.

I shook my head. "I don't know." My eyes darted between the six of them. They had curving metal blades, scythe-like, that I was certain were sharp enough to cut my head clean from my body.

"Well then, we'll just be taking you," he said, lifting his blade to point it at me. "The Crimson Princess. Her mate." His eyes scanned up and down my body with a hunger that made my stomach curdle. "You will make an excellent little piece of bait to lure the beast back out of hiding."

"No."

"No?" He balked. "You might be a royal, girl, but this isn't a negotiation."

My lip curled and I wondered if I could take on six soldiers on my own. I bet Calla could. I bet they were fierce enough to take on ten times the number. But I was given only the basics of fight training. I was taught how to use my wits and looks to get what I wanted. And I had a feeling I wouldn't be able to charm my way out of this one.

"Let's go," the head solder said, beckoning me with his sword. When I didn't move, he smiled. "Or we could do this the hard way?"

It was clear which one he preferred.

My mind spiderwebbed out, thinking of every possibility. I had three exits from this room—four, if I counted the window. It was a steep fall, but we'd just had a snowstorm, and as long as the powder wasn't too iced over, I could make it . . .

Too risky. I'd just as likely impale myself on an icicle as I would escape.

The upper stairwell led to a long hallway where these soldiers would probably outpace me before I could lock a door behind me. The stairwell the soldiers came up was narrow and twisting and currently blocked by a hulking soldier. If I could lure them away . . .

No, that would have to be the backup plan.

The best option was the bathing chamber to my left. I could lock the door and then climb out the window. The soldiers would certainly be able to knock the door down, but it would give me enough time to escape.

I licked my lips and swallowed, knowing this could end very badly for me, knowing the Briar before would've bowed her head and played the part of a good little puppy in order to be treated more kindly by her new captors. But I was done being a puppet, let alone a puppy. What had it ever got me? First Nero, then Evres, now the Onyx pack wanted me for their own plans—first as a bride and now as bait.

No more.

"Let's go," the head soldier said again as his comrades at my back pressed in closer. I looked to the grand stairwell. "Don't," he warned.

The guard behind me was almost within reaching distance now.

I smiled at him, the sickliest, sweetest smile. "I won't," I said with a pout. Then I did what I thought Maez would do in this situation—something brave, and bold, and cheeky.

I winked.

He paused, uncertain, while I whirled, kicking the closest soldier square between the legs. When I feigned to the right, the rest of the soldiers all went in the same direction to head me off even as I sprinted to the left. I just managed to skirt past their grasping hands and out of the circle of their blades, my blood pumping so hard I could feel it pulsing behind my eyes. I made it to the chamber and slammed the door, barring it with the surprisingly sturdy lock before whirling to the window, the wood behind me thundering under the pummeling fists.

I raced to the window. From here, I could drop down to the balcony below, and from there, I could climb down the frozen trellis into the snow and make a dash for the forest in my furs. Once I shifted, there's no way they could outrun me. I just needed to beat them to the ground.

I climbed out of the window too hastily and my foot slipped on the icy balcony. I went tumbling sideways, cracking my ribs onto the frozen stone and scrambling to cling on. My cheek slammed hard into the railing, and amazingly I didn't topple over the side. I tasted the copper tang of blood in my mouth as my chest heaved. Each breath stabbed into me.

I'll heal if I can shift.

If, if, if . . .

I heard the door above me give way and the soldiers spilled into the bathing chamber above.

Shit.

I scrambled to the trellis, my body screaming at me as the soldiers shouted orders to one another from up above. I just had to get down, just had to shift and I'd heal and be fine. Three more steps and I'd jump, even if it was too high, the shift would make me survive the fall . . .

A hand grabbed the back of my dress and roughly yanked me upward. I screamed, losing my grip on the trellis. I dangled by the fabric of my dress, the thin fabric ripping. That sound was my savior, letting me focus. I tucked my chin in, lifting my arms, lace scraping against my skin as I fell out of the dress and plummeted to the snow below.

I thanked all the Gods that I had been right about the fresh powder. I stumbled, disoriented, to my feet in nothing but a thin cream slip. The world spun, a voice shouting in my mind to shift, but I couldn't control my limbs. I was tackled to the side before I could regain my senses.

Snow seared across my raw skin.

"I got her!" a soldier shouted as he scrambled on top of me and pinned me into the snow.

I scratched at his face, feral, as he laughed. I couldn't buck him. He didn't even bother to grab my wrists or restrain me, just used his weight to hold me down so tightly I couldn't take a deep breath, already tough because of the injury to my ribs. He crossed his arms, a smug expression on his face as he arched a brow at me.

"What now, Crimson Princess?" he mocked, wiggling on top of me and squeezing the air from my lungs. "Go on, shift. I dare you." With each laugh it compressed my stomach more, the ice crunching and snow groaning beneath us. I bared my teeth at him, and he chuckled. "What are you going to do?"

"Show you why there's crimson in my name," I gasped out.

Confused, he didn't perceive the threat. Fast as a striking ostekke, I grabbed the lowest knife from the bandolier that crossed his chest and lifted up to drive it into the side of his neck. I twisted, raking the blade in an unclean cut across his throat until rivers of steaming blood poured down on me.

His hand flew to his throat, grasping and choking on his own blood. He toppled sideways, shifting into his Wolf form, trying to save himself, but the wound was fatal.

I kept a white-knuckled grip on the knife as I pushed up from the snow. Heaving, I prepared for more attackers, but there were none. Someone slowly clapped from behind me, the sound eerily jovial amidst the carnage.

I turned to see her standing there—Maez.

Her eyes were so filled with violent green I couldn't see their true color anymore as they darted to look at the five decapitated bodies circling her. I hadn't even heard their deaths, so quick, so silent.

Her gaze dipped down to my slip, coated in steaming blood. "Crimson Princess indeed," she mused, something akin to pride in her voice. A thrill ran through me at the look in her eyes. "You fight well, mate. I didn't know there was bloodlust in you."

I turned and stared at the dead Wolf in the snow—the one I had killed.

I had killed.

And she'd called me *mate* for it.

"The Onyx Wolves have made their move, it seems. They're taking Taigos," Maez said. "I can't stay here anymore."

All the blood drained from my face. "What?" Taigos couldn't fall to the hands of the Onyx Wolves; Calla needed them as allies or, at least, not as staunch enemies. How could the Golden Court manage to wage a war against the rest of the entire continent?

Maez's eyes narrowed at me. "Do you want to stay here or come with me?"

It struck me that even now she was giving me a choice. But in my letter, I'd told Calla not to come for me, which meant I was safer by Maez's side, and after that kiss in the forest, I wasn't giving up on her, either. I eyed the dead soldiers ringed around her. She might be the key to Olmdere's salvation, too.

I met that flickering green gaze. "With you," I breathed.

Maez blinked at me and oh the hundreds of warring emotions I saw in just one blink. One split second that told me so much. She seemed relieved and heartbroken and terrified that I still wanted to go with her.

But instead Maez just extended out a hand zipping with green static to me. "Then it's time to go, Princess. We've got a detour to make on our way."

NINETEEN

CALLA

I FELL ASLEEP TO THE ROCKING OF THE SLEIGH, MY HEAD slumped on Grae's shoulder. We'd traveled through the night, only stopping to change over from carriages to sleighs as we ventured further into snow-laden Taigos. The moon was high in the sky, begging for our shift. But I would shift when I saw Briar, when I knew she was safe; until then we had to press on.

When the sleigh lurched to a stop, Grae's arms instinctively flung out and grabbed me to stop me from hurtling forward. When he was certain I wouldn't go flying across the sleigh, he released me and hopped up to look out the window.

"Just some snow snakes," Verena called from up ahead. "We've got to clear them off the path for the horses to pass through. Won't be a minute."

Grae waved a hand and ducked back into the sleigh.

"Bloody snow snakes," I muttered, staring out into the shadowed forest.

We were halfway across Taigos, which meant we were only halfway to Briar, not nearly close enough, and I prayed we wouldn't need to stop again until we reached her.

Grae gathered me into his chest and rested his cheek back atop my head in the same position we'd been in before our jarring wake up. This was the only position I seemed to be able to sleep in; like a babe startled in the night, I needed Grae's warm arms to swaddle me from waking to the nightmares plaguing my every sleep.

A howl cut through the night and Grae and I both straightened to the sound.

"Was that one of ours?" he asked, wiping a sleeve across the fogged window. When his forearm streaked across the pane, we saw them dotting across the dunes of snow: Wolves.

"We're under attack!" Verena shouted as she started barking orders to the other Wolves in her retinue.

Grae and I leapt from the sleigh, shifting instantly to protect ourselves from the line of Wolves cresting the hills.

Ice and Onyx alike stood shoulder to shoulder, looking down on our caravan—at least twenty of them. The Onyx Wolves were in Taigos? I barely had time to register what that meant, too busy calculating defense strategies in my head. Seven Wolves against twenty wasn't great odds, but I had a battalion of human guards surrounding the sleighs, too.

We'd prepared for this. We'd expected this even.

Judging by Verena's wide lupine eyes, she *hadn't* anticipated this attack, especially not with a foreign pack in tow. My guards moved in front of us, blades drawn, as the opposing Wolves snarled and advanced.

I wondered which of the two other Taigosi factions this was: Djen's or Hestoff's. Whoever it was, they'd managed to ally with the Onyx Wolves with stunning swiftness. A second row of another dozen Ice Wolves crested the hill, and my stomach plummeted as a whine escaped my maw. I shook off the remnants of my shredded clothes and darted a look to Verena.

If these Wolves broke through the human line, it would be hard to tell friend from foe in their white furs.

"We can handle them," I said into Grae's mind, not sure if the confidence was meant to calm him or me. "We've faced worse odds before."

"So long as victory doesn't come from another bloody dying wish," Grae replied.

Like a soldier sparring before a contest, I nipped at his side and he snapped back, snagging a tooth on my fur.

"We can take them."

"We can take them," Grae echoed.

My senses narrowed; my breathing slowed. I was ready.

The Wolves sprang forward, a clash of teeth and fur as they battled the human guards. A few breached through the front lines, and Verena and her Wolves were swift to pounce upon them and rip out their throats. At least we knew they were truly on our side of this battle—the last time I trusted an Ice Wolf Queen, it had not gone so well. Blood stained the snow as the night filled with snarling and shouts and screams of pain.

We cut through the attackers spilling through the two guards stationed directly in front of Grae and me. My mate and I worked as a team—me distracting them as Grae pounced and snapped their necks. Quick, ruthless, efficient. There was no time for honorable kills when we were so vastly outnumbered.

I was grateful for every day we trained, every day when I was tired and weary and Grae would still drag me into the ring and not hold back. His fighting skills were still sharper than a knife and I knew something about having a mate to protect made us both even more lethal.

The panic that was gripping me tightly began to ease. We were winning.

I stole a fateful glance at Grae when the snow erupted in front of us. I shook off the powder, a keening note cutting through the air. It was the sharp, trilling sound of a tin whistle. I looked up the hill to see a human standing there—a thin metal pipe held to his mouth. Was that one of Ora's ilk? The ones who wielded song magic . . . a Songkeeper? Whoever he was, he was clearly our enemy.

I only had a moment to study him, when my eyes darted to

where the snow was exploding, leaving a giant pockmark in the earth. And in that hole? My eyes flared, my heart booming. A creature emerged from the snow—dozens of translucent white hands and spiky rows of teeth. It grabbed one of my human guards and brought him to the central ring of sharpened teeth, chewing and shredding as the guard screamed. Blood sprayed everywhere as the beast shredded through its prey.

The lines broke, soldiers fleeing at the horrifying sight.

I heard scrambling behind me and turned to find Mina climbing atop the roof of her sleigh, violin in hand. Her limbs trembled but her violin sang over the sounds of fear and death. The beast seemed to pause for a second to her music. The Songkeeper on the hill stopped his playing to laugh and shake his head.

Even with keen hearing, I could only barely hear him say, "You think you can control my creature, Mina?"

My gut clenched—they knew each other.

I didn't have time to dwell on the exchange as I was bowled over by another Wolf. I scrambled back to my paws, fighting and snapping my teeth. The sleigh rocked with the force of the rushing Wolves and the music stopped from behind me.

Mina!

Grae scruffed the Wolf atop me. "Go!" he shouted in my mind. "Protect her."

I was already moving, twisting onto all four paws and leaping over the toppled sleigh. I jumped in front of Mina, catching one Onyx Wolf in midair as they leapt toward her. The Wolf yelped as I knocked them back.

Blood misted the air as the monster behind us shredded through the group. I had planned for a Wolf attack, but monsters? That I hadn't bargained for. We'd only heard of one from Sadie—Rasil—the one who betrayed them, the head of the Songkeepers. Was that him on the hill? Had he and the Onyx Wolves allied with the Ice Wolves? Were they moving to take Taigos?

Four Wolves of white and black started inching forward toward us. I stood in front of Mina, guarding her from the attack, but I knew, no matter how I calculated, we wouldn't be able to take them. I frantically looked around, seeing if there was a path of retreat—

A flash of blinding emerald light exploded all around us. Lightning cracked, a white-hot bolt striking one of the advancing Wolves. The others paused in horror, taking in the sight of their comrade's sizzling body.

I knew that magic, felt as though that lightning bolt had carved its way through my own body once. But Sawyn was gone, which meant . . .

I looked to the east. At the head of the caravan stood a cloaked black figure—green lightning dancing around her fingertips as she shot bolt after bolt at our attackers.

Maez was here. Maez had come to save us.

But all the relief flooded from me when I saw who cowered next to her, covered in blood.

TWENTY

BRIAR

I SHIFTED AND STARTED RUNNING THE SECOND I SAW THEIR rust and gold fur. Calla. I darted through the snow, practically bowling my twin over.

"You're alive!" Calla exclaimed into my Wolf mind.

"I'm alive. I'm okay," I replied, scrambling for my words. "Though as much can't be said for you." I followed Calla's line of sight and spied the Songkeeper on the hill running away, his monster in tow. Even a monster was no match for a sorceress. "It seems the tides are turning . . ."

"Coward," Calla spat, turning to look me over and studying the bloodied nightdress shredded in the snow beside me. "We came to rescue you."

"And yet here I am, rescuing you."

"Where are you hurt?" they said, ignoring my joke, their eyes frantically searching me, sniffing my fur for blood. "What happened?"

"I'm okay," I reassured my twin. "It's not my blood." The sounds around us began to morph from panicked orders to calmer ones. The battle was over, not a single Wolf having been permitted to retreat. In one blaze of Maez's power, the attackers lay dead, sizzling smoke rising from their bodies.

So many bodies.

Horror flooded through me at the sight of so much carnage.

"It's time for me to go, Princess," Maez's voice called from behind me.

Calla snarled and took a step in front of me. "You do not touch her."

Maez huffed. "Or what?" Her eyes delighted in the challenge.

"Stop," I commanded, stepping between the two of them. I didn't know to whom I addressed the order. I looked at Maez. "Give me one minute."

"One," she said tightly, stalking off into the snow, away from the others.

"Maez," Grae tried to call to her, but she ignored him and kept walking. His face fell. His cousin, his best friend since childhood, acted as if he was a stranger to her—no more than a ghost.

"Briar what is going on?" Calla asked. "What has she done to you?"

Done to me? The question nettled the edges of my mind. Would Calla even believe me if I told them I was coated in the blood of the person *I* killed, not Maez? That I slit that Wolf's throat and it felt *good* to finally not be waiting for someone else to defend me? Maez believed I was capable of it, proud even, of my newfound courage to fight for myself.

Trying to force that courage into my voice, I looked at my twin. "I'm going with Maez, Calla." They opened their mouth to protest but I pushed onward, "She's still there, underneath it all. I saw it the last time we shifted. I think . . . I think there's still hope, and I can't give up on her."

"Briar." Calla shook their head. "It's too dangerous. That magic is unpredictable, you don't know if—"

"She won't hurt me," I said with such assurance that I suddenly realized I believed it. Maez wouldn't hurt me, at least not intentionally, but I wasn't about to say that while my twin was panicking.

"Don't go with her," Calla pleaded. "Stay with me. I need

you. Olmdere needs you. Our family's court is falling apart and . . ."

"Look around you, Calla," I said. "Maez's power is a weapon we can't afford to lose, let alone get into the wrong hands. She could win us this war."

"If you can find a way to control her," Calla said. "Which you won't. Dark magic isn't to be trifled with, Briar. She could turn it on us the second Nero is dead."

"We've got to try," I begged, trying to urge my twin to understand. "Please."

"I know it's hard to let her go," Calla said, a desperate look in their eyes. "I know you loved her."

"*Love* her," I corrected. "Gods help me." Emotions constricted my throat. "I love her even still. I love her *always*."

"Briar—"

"If it were Grae," I cut in. "If it was *your* mate. Would you ever give up on him?"

Calla's golden eyes guttered. "No," they said, resigned. "Never."

I knew they understood now that I was never going to let this go, never going to move on. I felt it, too, like a claiming. I couldn't go back to Olmdere and just live my life as a passive participant in someone else's story. I was sick of being a doll. I had a life, a purpose, and it began and ended with the cloaked figure at the edge of the forest.

"I love you, Calla," I said, getting choked up. "I love you and I will write every day and keep you updated and do everything in my power to keep you on our family's throne, but don't ask me to leave her, because you know I can't."

We looked at each other and both shifted, instantly hugging each other, our twin telepathy still as strong as ever. They hugged me so tightly I thought they might crack a freshly healed rib, and I hugged them in return just as fiercely.

"I love you, too, Briar," Calla murmured. It was all they needed to say.

I hated releasing Calla from that hug, but finally I did, stooping to grab a discarded blanket from beside the sleigh. I wrapped it around my bare shoulders, encasing me with warmth and stalked off through the snow toward that cloaked spot in the distance.

Maez didn't turn to greet me. "I suppose this is goodbye," she said. "You've found your people again. Time to go home."

"No," I replied, and she looked over her shoulder. "I already told you: I'm coming with you."

Her brow arched in surprise, something in that darkness clearing, and I saw how desperately she needed me to say it. "Why?"

I held her flashing emerald eyes and said, "Because there is no home without you."

TWENTY-ONE

SADIE

I WAITED UNTIL THE MOON WAS HIGH IN THE SKY TO UNTANGLE myself from Navin's warm arms and creep from my bed. The waning moon welcomed me as I padded on bare feet through the cool earth. I loved her in every form, but this . . . here beneath the pine trees of Damrienn was my favorite way to view the Goddess.

I heard the soft hum long before I spotted them. I walked through the woods, following the sound until I spotted Galen den' Mora. Ora sat on the back steps, watching as the oxen grazed through the forest undergrowth. Haestas had taken off on her midnight flight to scour the southern forests for deer to eat—hopefully she'd bring some back for us. I still wasn't sure if Navin had to command it from her every time or if it was an ongoing order. I pondered the magic as I wandered. The nighttime forest was a quiet whisper apart from Ora's song.

"Don't you ever sleep?" I asked, surveying them from head to toe. They wore a deep purple dress embroidered in giant sunflowers and evergreen sprigs. Beaded earrings hung from their lobes and silver and gold bangles ringed their wrists. Their face was fully painted, making them look more like they were about to attend a ball than sit in the forest by themself.

"I missed this," they said with a shrug. "I wasn't able to dress myself how I like for a very, very long time when I was a prisoner. I'm enjoying my freedom now."

I hadn't considered that. How simple it felt to me to be able to rim my eyes with kohl and wear my favorite knife belts. How so much of one's identity could be stripped away with the control Nero was imposing on the humans of his court.

"Not to mention I'm a nighttime creature, much like your kind," Ora added, their eyes crinkling with warmth. "I'm used to keeping all sorts of hours in this job, performing until the sun rises."

I grunted an acknowledgment and wandered closer into the pool of moonlight that filtered through the tall trees.

Ora kept their eyes fixed on the oxen as they said, "I already know what you're going to ask me."

"Then you already know I won't take no for an answer," I countered, folding my arms around me and smoothing down my pebbled cold skin.

Ora chuckled, a smile tugging at their ruby lips. "You are exceptionally fierce, Sadie Rauxtide."

"I'm also exceptionally right," I pushed. "We need to see what these songs can do. We don't need to hunt monsters across the desolate regions of Aotreas. We don't need to master every species. We just need to learn to control one."

"You're right," they said with a shrug. "If Rasil gets even a whiff of this knowledge, though . . ." Their eyes grew vacant, leeching their warmth. "Like so many of the magics we protect, we protect them for a reason. I am afraid if anyone besides us learns of the bounds of this power, it could destroy us all." They slicked their obsidian hair off their face, their jewelry tinkling at the movement. "I never wanted this, you know—humans versus Wolves. Songs versus howls. It should have never been this way. But people who want peace and harmony are often too placid to fight those who want power. I'm afraid we're going to need to be more fearsome if we're going to bring this world back. We'll need to make sacrifices."

Their eyes finally lifted to mine and I met their gaze. "Which is why we need to figure out how to do this. Just you and me," I said with a nod. "If you could control Nero . . ."

Ora's throat bobbed. "Too long the Wolves have controlled the humans, but I do not like the idea of the humans controlling the Wolves, either." They sighed. "This power cannot go unchecked. I love my people, but there's a reason these songs were hidden from the hungry eyes of people like Rasil."

"Do you see our cause as the same as his? If ever there was a time to use these songs, it is now," I urged. "This moment in time is why they weren't destroyed completely. Humans might not exist at all if we don't stop Nero."

Ora hung their head, and I knew I'd won. "I don't know how far we can push this, but we can try."

"Thank you for trying."

With even that small sense of relief, I stepped behind a tree and tugged off my nightdress. I shifted, the change taking me quickly as I relished the delicious feeling of being in my furs under the swollen moon. I prowled back out and stood in front of Ora.

They shook their head. "It will never stop being miraculous, seeing you do that." They pulled their wooden pipe from the bag beside them. "You ready?"

I nodded.

Ora was about to lift their instrument to their lips when Navin stormed through the forest. "Stop," he growled, sounding wolfish and predatory in his own right.

He was shirtless, only in his light linen trousers, his hair still mussed from sleep. I swore he grew an inch with each step, reminding me just how tall and formidable he truly was.

He glared at Ora. "How could you do this?"

Ora didn't look ashamed, just calm and a little forlorn. "This is bigger than either of us, Navin," they said. "I know you love her."

"I don't just love her," Navin spat. "She is my song, Ora. Have you forgotten what that means? What she means to me?"

Ora's eyes bracketed with sorrow. "I know exactly what it means. And I know you will lose her, Navin. We will all lose each other if something isn't done."

"I don't like this," Navin ground out, standing in front of me and crossing his arms.

I darted back to the tree, shifting as I ran, and yanked back on my nightdress.

"*I* wanted to do this," I said, even as my throat was still reforming. "*I* asked them to do this for me." I stood in front of Navin with my arms crossed.

"There's death in the air. Monsters with a vendetta against us." He glared at me. "You snuck out of bed. I woke up and you were gone. I—"

"I'm sorry," I said, placing a hand on his chest. And I was. For someone who had been alone for so long, it was strange to have to consider another when making a decision. I hadn't, and I realized how much that must hurt.

His hand instantly lifted to cover it, holding me to his warm bare skin. His head dropped, his eyes closing for a second to ground himself in my touch. I knew he was trying to win the battle with his anger.

"I don't want you to be controlled by anyone," he said. "The idea that someone could get into your mind, could make you do things against your will . . ." The muscle in his jaw flickered as if the very thought pained him. "I can't bear it." He looked back at Ora. "This magic needs to be destroyed. We cannot use it. Not every Songkeeper is as trustworthy as the ones in our retinue."

"The songs are already being used, Navin," Ora stated calmly. "If Rasil teaches even one of his brethren to use the sacred songs and summon more monsters into existence, it would mean more sorcerers, too. And we both know it's only a matter of time before Rasil uses the power of those songs again."

"Which is why you need to use magic of your own." I stepped between them again. "One that doesn't summon more dark magic, only controls it."

Navin's eyes dropped to me. "Where does it end?"

"These questions would make you a good ruler," I pointed out. Ora hummed in agreement. "It ends when the Golden Court is safe, when the humans of Damrienn no longer live in fear of Wolves. It ends when everyone is as free as I am right now, asking that you train this magic on me."

I lifted on my toes and kissed him. He softened into my touch. "Not fair," he murmured against my lips.

"You see?" I said. "I have a magic all my own. We all have our ways of controlling the other."

He chuckled and then pulled me back in to kiss me again.

A twig snapped from behind me, and I whirled to the sound.

I spotted him instantly.

Icy dread curled in my gut at the sight of those eyes, that face, so similar to my own.

"Hector."

My brother held my gaze for one second before he turned and ran.

"We're under attack!" I screamed and three Silver Wolves came shooting through the forest.

I KNEW IT WAS MY FATHER AND UNCLES INSTANTLY, BEFORE I even had a chance to study them in their furs. I'd wondered when Nero would send them to find us. My family and I had unfinished business.

"Go warn the others," I shouted, shoving Navin behind me.

"Ora, you go," Navin called, moving to stand by my side again. He grabbed two knives, one from each of his boots and passed me one. I lifted my eyebrows, impressed. "I learned from the best," he said with a wink, turning so we were back-to-back as my father and uncles circled us like vultures to a carcass.

I resisted the overwhelming urge to shift at the sight of them circling us. I wanted to be able to call out warnings and directions to Navin in the melee if needed.

Navin whistled out for his dragon, but Haestas had taken to hunting in the evenings and was probably too far away. We'd have to keep her closer now that we had this target on our back.

That was, assuming we had a second chance . . .

Ora shot through the forest back toward the library when Hector ran out of the woods, shifting into his Wolf form as he chased after them.

"No!" I screamed, my hand reaching out as if I could stop my brother.

With a barked command from my father, Hector paused and turned back to the clearing. I was equally relieved for Ora and terrified for Navin and me—four Wolves against the two of us—all of them warriors, all my family.

Hector stood stock-still, neither moving to my father's aide nor turning away and I wondered if my father commanded his son to stand there and watch how real Wolves fought. *Watch as I teach your sister a lesson*—the memory of my father saying that phrase so many times flashed in rapid succession in my mind. More, I remembered all the times I was bade to watch as my father took out his aggression on Hector under the guise of "teaching."

Countless years and training sessions in our youth until I had no more lessons to learn—apparently, they hadn't stuck for either of my father's children. I swore the same thought crossed Hector's mind as his eyes flicked to me and widened, his fear a warning that made me whirl back to the Silver Wolf prowling closer.

As my eyes landed on him, my father shot forward, his powerful maw snapping around my forearm and yanking me down. I cried out in pain as I fell to the ground, swiping at him with my blade.

Fuck this.

I shifted, rolling and snapping at my father's side.

"There's my girl," my father goaded, speaking into my mind.

"I wondered if you even remembered how to be a Wolf, you filthy skin chaser."

"I'm most certainly a Wolf, while you're still Nero's lapdog I see," I snarled back.

"He is your King!" my father seethed. "I will drag you back there, Sadie, even if it's only your pelt. He will wear you like a stole, daughter. Your bones will be buried in Highwick where they belong."

"I thought I belonged in Rikesh?" I countered. "You were so quick to sell me off like a broodmare to Prince Tadei, hmm?"

"You—"

I didn't wait for his response. I feigned left, then shot right, landing my jaws in my uncle's rear leg and biting until the bone snapped. He yelped, scrambling on three legs to pull himself away. He'd have to shift back to his human form to heal that break, which would at least buy Navin some time.

But my eldest uncle, Pilus, didn't shift and heal himself, instead turning on Navin. His prey drive blew his pupils wide as he limped toward Navin's exposed back as he squared off with my other uncle, Aubron. I tried to shout a warning to Navin, but it came out as a garbled yowl as my uncles attacked him from both sides.

Distracted by Navin's peril, I didn't notice the flash of movement until it was too late. My father bowled me over, knocking the air from me.

Before I could move out of his way, he landed on top of me, his jaws landing around my neck and squeezing but not enough to break the skin. We had trained this maneuver so many times when I was a pup. He'd always taught me: tear out the throat, don't choke, don't waste that time when another enemy could be at the scruff of your neck at any second.

But my father didn't do that; he squeezed just enough to bring on panic. I writhed beneath him, trying to suck air back into my lungs but couldn't. He wanted to kill me slowly, wanted me to regret all the things I'd put him through, all the ways that I'd failed him. This was the most personal kill he would ever make—ending his daughter's life—and it made him blind to everything else.

Like the large mass that hit him square in the side. His jaws released me, and he growled, scrambling to his feet as I regained my own footing and looked to see who'd tackled him. I blinked at the Silver Wolf with the curled and snarling maw, his chest heaving—Hector.

"We were meant to bring her back alive," my brother snapped.

"*You betray me even still?*" our father shouted so loudly that my temples pulsed. "Shameful children. Neither of you deserves to carry on our family name." He looked at Hector. "You help me kill her now or you will be next. I can't bear another day seeing you strung up behind our King's throne, making all of our pack hate me for siring such a traitor."

Hector just stood there, neither coming to my defense nor turning to attack me. "You could have stopped Nero," he spat. "You could have cut me down."

"This is how I spared you, Hector," my father seethed. "The only reason you were cut down from your comfy perch at all was because I told King Nero you would come with us to reclaim Sadie. This is your chance to never be strung up again, to bring honor back to our name, and *still* you choose the path of a traitor?"

That sentiment made Hector pause. Neither did he charge my father again nor turn his attention to me, just stood there rooted to the spot as if trapped in his own terror. What had Nero done to him that had made him so immobilized with indecision? I could see the cogs in my brother's mind turning, caught between two opposing loyalties.

My father's expression was so riddled with disappointment. These weren't the faithful, unwavering Wolves he'd raised us to be. In Wolf society our father's will was only superseded by the pack leader, and in this moment, we were defying both.

I used that moment of heartbroken shock to launch myself at my father. I pinned him in one swift move, knowing exactly how he liked to attack, which side he was first to defend. I outmaneuvered him easily, and when *I* went for the throat, I didn't wait.

I sunk my teeth in and tore, ripping out his throat as hot coppery blood spurted into the air and coated my fur. I watched his wide, shocked eyes as they met mine, the connection between our minds severing as he gasped for air but choked on nothing but blood. His body twitched and spasmed, and he shifted back and forth, human and Wolf, again and again as if one form would save him.

When his blood-soaked body finally stopped writhing, he was in his furs. My chest rose and fell in heaving pants, the world spinning out from under me.

I'd killed him.

I'd killed my father.

In my grief, I shifted. Naked and bloodied, I knelt beside my father's corpse.

I'd killed him.

Through bleary, tear-filled eyes, I looked around me to find Hector, but my brother was gone. My uncle's bodies lay on either side of Navin, his back to me as he stared down at them. Blood dripped from his knife, his light brown skin splattered with it.

When he turned to me, his venom disappeared in a flash, and he raced toward me as a broken sob escaped my lips.

Navin's warm arms banded around me, and he pulled my blood-slick skin against his own. He cradled me to him as sobs racked through me.

"I killed him," I cried, a keening broken sob.

Every moment of my childhood flashed back through me between one gasping breath and the next. My father had loved Hector and I once. He had been strict, like any good Wolf father, but he had been proud of us—always bragging of our accomplishments, always watching each of our competitions and fights. We had been his legacy. Even when he wanted to sell me to Prince Tadei, somewhere deep down I understood. He was doing what he thought was right not only for the pack, but for me, saving my soul from the traitor I had been, giving me a chance to redeem myself in the eyes of our pack. Never in a million years did I think it would end like this, with us fighting to the death. Never did I think I could kill him so swiftly, my training taking over.

Navin held me tighter, crushing me against him, fusing us into one. Any lighter and I might shatter into a thousand pieces, but he held me together with such ferocity as if he knew his arms were the only thing keeping me from slipping away and never coming back.

My father and uncles were gone. Hector had stopped my father but did nothing to save me, either.

I lifted my face from Navin's skin, staring out to the shadowed forest as tears carved through the coagulated blood on my face. I knew by the end of this I'd have to kill Hector, too, and I knew once I did, I'd never be the same.

TWENTY-TWO

BRIAR

WHEN THE GROUND FINALLY FOUND MY FEET AGAIN, THE change in climate was a shock. The air was balmy, scented with citrus and jasmine. Warm tiles greeted my feet, and I craned my neck up to see the atrium of a cream- and teal-tiled room. Potted trees billowed in a humid breeze. Bright orange and yellow birds flocked overhead. I dropped my gaze to look around the room, mesmerized as I stared out the windows to endless blue sky beyond.

"Where are we?" I asked as Maez shook off her cloak and hung it on a hook beside a fountain.

"Upper Valta," she said.

"Valta?" I choked out, my eyes bugging wide. "This seems like the worst place in all of Aotreas to be after you just killed a bunch of their comrades in the snow."

"Not just me," she reminded pointedly, and I remembered the soldier whose throat I'd slit.

I stalked to the open doorway—teeming jungle toppled down, down, down a steep cliff and then nothing but open air. The sand was a sea of beige so far below, the warm desert air whooshing up to greet my face. I felt like I was flying and falling all at once, my stomach dipping as if the floating mountain we were on might suddenly plummet.

At the sight of the sheer drop, I reeled backward, my arms wheeling and practically falling to get away from the ledge.

"The Onyx Wolf pack is in tatters," Maez said. "Half of them were slaughtered the day . . ."

The day I turned.

I knew it's what she wanted to say. She rolled up her sleeves and began to wash her hands in the fountain, splashing fresh water on her face.

"Another good chunk of their force was just decimated in Taigos," Maez continued. *Also by her hand.* "I don't know how much of an army they have left at this point. It might just be a few pups and Prince Tadei hanging around." She shrugged, the V of her black tunic dipping lower. "Valta might be the safest place to be right now."

I stared out through the open doorway again. "Where in Valta are we?"

"A little remote island floating just past Rikesh," she said. "There's no rope bridge here anymore. It was wrecked in a sandstorm a few years ago, and since it only housed this abandoned castle, no one saw the point in rebuilding it."

"How do you know that?" I asked, watching the beads of fresh water trail down her muscled neck and dip between her cleavage. I cleared my throat.

"It's amazing what you can learn when you have no need for sleep and the ability to be a shadow in the corner of any room," she mused, her eyes dipping to take in my body.

It was only then I realized I was naked apart from a rumpled blanket caked in gore. Normally, I wouldn't have thought twice about being naked in front of my mate, but this predatory gaze—this was someone else entirely.

I shrunk backward, ducking behind one of the leafy trees that had sprung up through the cracks of the abandoned palace. Maez chuckled at my sudden act of modesty.

"You look good in nothing but the blood of your enemies,"

she said, taking a deep breath as if scenting the blood on me. "It makes me want to take you right here and now."

I pressed my thighs together, my cheeks heating. This was not something that should turn me on. But the heat in her eyes promised that I would very much enjoy the way she devoured me. I wondered how different it would be now with her—deft skill with her new edge . . .

I cleared my throat, shaking the thought from my head. "I just killed someone."

Her glinting smile widened. "You will see a lot more die if you intend to stay with me."

"I can't do that."

"You can," she said with a confident nod. "Perhaps you'll come to enjoy it as much as me. Maybe I need to help you sharpen those claws."

"No." My protest wasn't convincing even to my own ears, but it felt like the thing I *should* say.

"Or maybe you just need the right person laid at your feet," she said, considering.

It made me uneasy to hear her say it. To not only think I was capable of murdering again, but that I would enjoy it. A thought crept up before I could push it away: *I bet I would enjoy it, too.* The idea had my mind reeling. Where was the line between acts of strength and acts of evil? I wasn't so certain anymore.

"So no rope bridges," I said, trying to redirect the conversation away from my swirling thoughts. "I suppose I won't be running away, then."

"You should've run before," Maez said. "But if you want out of here, you know you only need to say the word."

She gave me a choice time and time again and I wondered what madness drove me to pick this one. Why was I able to believe in this fleeting hope that we could find our way back to each other somehow?

Maez seemed to read it all on my face as she shook her head. "You don't want this, Princess." She said it firmly, but I could still see the question in her eyes. "I am not the person you once knew."

I opened my mouth to protest, and she closed the distance between us, gripping me by the upper arms. "Briar. Hear me." She crouched to meet my eyeline and repeated, "I am *not* the person you once knew. And I will never be her again." She studied that truth as it hit me like an arrow, but I'd come too far now; I refused to hear it.

I shook my head. "I can't believe that." My voice broke. "I won't give up hope."

Her eyes darkened as she released me, disgusted as she stalked away. "Then you are a fool," she shouted over her shoulder. "Go clean yourself up."

And like a fool, I did exactly that, looking to my next chance to prove her wrong.

TWENTY-THREE

CALLA

WE WALKED THROUGH THE PALACE WITH NEW EYES, THE grounds in utter disarray. Blood speckled the walls, portraits were torn out of their frames, glass shattered across the dirt-streaked carpets. Once they had been so perfectly silver, not a single stain or spot in the fabric; now the ransacked castle looked like a war zone.

We moved silently, following Verena's guards who guided us to her location. After the siege in the snow, Verena had hastened to secure the castle with the bulk of her remaining retinue while Grae and I hung back to burn pyres to our fallen Golden Court soldiers. Only a few short hours had separated us, but I was relieved to return to our joint forces again.

As we stalked into the throne room, the space was vacant apart from Verena who stood frowning at the throne upon the dais as if she was afraid to sit upon it.

"What happened here?" I asked, looking around the room that had once held glittering balls and lavish parties and now looked like a juvleck had been set loose.

"Before Hestoff came to meet us on the battlefield," she said, lifting her chin to the sky like a Wolf howling at the moon—a prayer for him, "he and Djen fought to seize control of this place.

All that was found of Djen and Hestoff were tatters of gore-coated pelt, barely enough of them to burn on a pyre."

"Looks like they didn't care if there was any pack left by the end of it," Grae said as we closed the distance to her, "let alone a palace to house it."

She looked up at us with sad, weary eyes. "No more of this," she said with a solemn shake of her head. "Our pack is done killing each other. I've spoken to what remains of both parties"—she let out a huff—"barely any adults. Terrified pups, that's all that's left of my pack."

She rubbed a hand over the back of her neck, and I could see the weight of it all crashing down on her—a burden I felt all too keenly. Becoming a queen was an honor, but it was also a terrifying responsibility, the lives of so many were squarely placed in our hands.

"It never gets easier," I said, moving to stand beside her and stare down at her throne. "But the work becomes more bearable, putting one foot in front of the other. Knowing it's for your people and not for yourself."

Verena sighed. "We've all agreed we've lost too much already. If we keep going, there will be no pack left." She glanced sideways at me. "And then who will stop Nero from knocking down our doors?" She looked at Grae. "Or Valta for that matter."

"That monster," I said with a shudder. "Sadie had told us of it before, but to see it in the flesh . . ."

"I'm guessing that is Rasil, then," Grae noted.

"If that sorceress friend of yours hadn't shown up . . ." Verena clicked her tongue.

It hurt to hear her still called our friend. Whoever Maez was now didn't seem like the person we used to know. The way she hadn't even acknowledged Grae, the hurt on my mate's face, made me want to wring her neck. She'd always been a soldier, but now she just seemed like purely a killer. And Briar had still chosen to go with her . . .

A fresh wave of fear washed over me as I thought of my twin, hoping she was okay, wherever Maez had taken her.

"Do you think we can rally her to our cause?" Verena asked.

I shook my head. "I don't think she's within our control."

"What about in the control of your sister?"

I swallowed the lump in my throat, thinking of the danger Briar had put herself in. I knew it was hopeless to try to dissuade her. My sister and I were as obstinate as they came—a Golden Wolf trait. Briar was either going to save Maez or let Maez destroy her, and there was nothing I could do about it.

"Briar will do whatever she can to get through to her mate, but on that front all we can do is hope. I think we will have better luck turning our attention to Sadie," I said diplomatically. "Songkeepers against Songkeepers. We have a dragon now. And the possibility of controlling more monsters. If Rasil shows up again with that creature, we will need them all in a battle."

Verena nodded.

"Unless," Grae said, "Rasil and his lackeys make more monsters."

Verena's eyes widened. "What? They can *make* monsters?"

I sighed, rubbing the back of my neck. "There is much we still have to tell you."

Verena turned from the throne and gestured to the far door on her left. "Not here," she said. "The council room is relatively unscathed. We can discuss there."

We all gave one last look to the untouched throne sitting stalwart amongst the ruin and debris, and turned to go plan our next moves.

I FOUND MINA OUTSIDE THE MOON PRIEST'S CHAMBERS. A ROW of bodies had been lined up along his outer wall, each one being taken into his open-sky chambers in turn and burned along with his moon prayers. It was more than they deserved, the traitors, but Verena was determined to have the pack be united in their grief. There was no room for vengeance amongst the dead.

When she spotted me, Mina quickly recovered the face of the dead Wolf with the white burial shroud. I knew at once she was looking for Hector's face amongst the dead.

"I didn't see him," I signed to her when she looked up at me. "I don't think he was there."

"I didn't see any Silver Wolves either, besides Grae," she signed back. "But I had to check."

"What would you have done if he had been there?"

She shook her head. "I don't know."

I let out a long sigh and sat upon the stone bench carved into the far wall—a place for mourners to gather and wait. But there would be no mourners this time; anyone bold enough to openly mourn these Wolves was lying dead beside them.

"I hate him," Mina continued, her throat bobbing. "I hate him so much for what he did. But I miss him, too. He was the only thing holding me together after Malou died." I was reminded once again of the pain of her loss. I couldn't imagine losing a twin. Even having Briar leave with Maez felt like my soul cleaved in two. "I just needed to know if he was truly gone."

I scrubbed a hand down my face. "I hate him, too," I said aloud. "And yet I miss him in equal measure."

"Do you think he'll go south and try to find Sadie?"

"I don't know."

"I think she's why he betrayed you." She grimaced as she signed the words. "He would do anything for his sister, no matter how misguided. He made the wrong choices for her, but I can't bring myself to blame him for it. The way he looked at me when he held that sword to my chest, the way it faltered . . ."

"Everything is in tatters," I said, dropping my head in my hands. "This is not how our court was meant to be. We were supposed to all be together. We were supposed to all defeat Nero together and live out our happily ever afters in Olmdere. Now Sadie is hiding out in Damrienn training monsters, Briar and

Maez are Moon knows where, and we are *yet again* in a foreign kingdom trying to build allies."

Mina wandered over and sat beside me, placing a hand on my back and rubbing. She waited until I lifted my head to sign, "Briar went with Maez?"

It didn't surprise me she already knew which of those three things I was most fretting over—only a twin would truly understand. Of course I was worrying about Briar. Maez had practically snapped her fingers and killed an entire pack, and my twin was still so desperately in love with her, she couldn't let her go.

"I hope she's okay."

"I have to believe Maez will protect her."

"But she must be hurting. Maez isn't the same person she fell in love with. That darkness will twist and warp her and maybe Briar will one day realize it and want to get out and it'll be too late."

We sat there in silence for a long time, both of us staring at the row of endless shrouded bodies.

"What Maez did on that battlefield . . . ," I said, staring up at the ceiling. "We could definitely use that in a battle with Nero. His 'friends' are dropping like flies. The Onyx Wolf pack is practically extinct, and the Ice Wolves are now our allies."

"Finally," Mina signed.

"Finally," I echoed. "And at a terrible cost. Do you think we can trust Verena?"

"I don't know how much trusting I'm going to be doing from now on."

I huffed. "Agreed."

"But if we can use her," Mina signed, "we should."

"I don't know if she's willing to storm Damrienn with us. Not after losing so much of her pack, but I will endeavor to convince her nonetheless. I think between us and the Songkeepers we might have a chance." Mina's face pinched. "What?"

"That monster."

"The one with the many hands?"

She nodded. "It's called a samsavat. Rasil is its master."

"I can't believe Navin was married to someone so cruel," I said, shuddering.

"He wasn't always as he is now," Mina signed. "Not that he was ever particularly likable. He believes it is our sect's cause to defeat the Wolves and return the land to one ruled by humans. But there are many of us who believe our calling is to return to a place of harmony between humans and Wolves."

"Like Ora?"

"Like Ora." She nodded. "But now that Rasil knows the eternal songs . . . he could create an army of monsters and sorcerers. Maez's powers could be the least of our problems. Each day I wake wondering if he finally decided to do it."

My shoulders drooped at the thought. It felt like our battles were innumerable; perhaps Nero was the least of my future problems as Queen. "I don't want to kill humans."

"Let us handle them," Mina signed. "The Songkeepers should deal with our own."

"And how do you do that?"

"We need to lure them all to one place—Highwick."

My eyes flared. "The Silver Wolf capital?"

"We can't afford to split our resources fighting Nero in Damrienn and Rasil in Valta. We need to get Rasil to come to Damrienn. We need to have our force from the north and Navin's from the south close them in. Both targets in one place. We won't beat Nero or Rasil without all of our manpower."

I arched a brow at her. "You've turned into quite the military strategist." She grinned at me. "So how do you propose we get Rasil to Highwick?"

"I may know just the person to lure him out. An old friend. Leave it with me," she signed, then patted me on the leg and stood. "I have a plan."

TWENTY-FOUR

BRIAR

I SAT ON THE LEDGE OF THE THIRD-FLOOR WINDOW, MY FEET dangling in the open air. I didn't even flinch when Maez appeared beside me. She wore a black cotton undershirt and her normal black leather trousers. Stripped of most of her weaponry, this was probably the most dressed down she would be.

"You're not jumping now, are you?"

I let out a half laugh. "No." My bare feet swung out over the open air, feeling light and tingling as I stared down at the massive drop. "And I know you would catch me."

I felt Maez's eyes on me, the weight of them skittering across my skin. "Always."

"What does it feel like," I asked, "flying through the air like you do?"

"I can show you," she offered. I pursed my lips, not sure if I would find that exhilarating or terrifying. When it came to Maez it was usually both. "Already bored in this little place?"

I chuckled. "I wouldn't exactly call this place little." I looked up at the several stories towering above me and the two more below. "I don't think I've explored even half of it yet. But . . ."

"But?"

I finally looked at her. Those dark pools of obsidian stared back, unblinking. "What are we doing here, Maez?" I asked, shaking my head. "Why have we buried our heads in the sand . . . or up in the clouds, as it were? Sweet Moon, do I wish that nothing existed outside these castle walls, but they do. We can't pretend otherwise."

Her eyes dropped to my lips for a split second and then back out to the floating islands far in the distance and the sea of desert sand below, staring so far as if she could almost see Damrienn.

"When I heard that Nero had taken you . . ." Her voice drifted off as her expression grew more severe. Most would only see the anger there, but I saw the fear beneath the surface, too. "I think sometimes you forget that I had a life before we met," she said. I swallowed the lump in my throat. That wasn't what I had expected her to say. "I knew Evres as a pup. I knew what a bastard he was, his penchant for violence, his lust for control . . . but he is nothing, *nothing* compared to Nero." She let out a long breath as if it pained her to release it. "I had so many reasons why I grabbed that power from the air, grabbed that dark magic with two hands and didn't let go. And I would make that same choice a million times over to make sure all of the fears I had for you never came to fruition. I would damn my very soul to keep you from being hurt by him the way I have been."

My heart plummeted. "What?" I practically choked on my words. "What did he do?"

Fear coursed through me like white-hot lightning. Why had she never told me this story before? Why was it only in this darkness and with this power that she finally felt she could speak these truths aloud to me? I was her mate. But I knew the answer: some things are too terrifying to even admit to yourself. Maybe only now she could.

Maez took another steeling breath. "Being the niece of a king is a precarious position," she said. "I think you know the roles we are given as highborn Wolf women better than anyone, the sacrifices we are forced to make."

I was practically shaking, quivering with fear. I didn't dare speak.

"Nero had plans for me," she said, and bile rose up my throat.

"The greatest benefit I could give him was for me to be sold to another. He had plans for all of us since the moments we were born. He used you to get Olmdere, Calla to get Valta, and me to get Taigos."

"Taigos?" I breathed, panic gripping me.

"Ingrid's uncle, Stellan."

"But didn't he die when you were—?"

"Thirteen," she added. "Yes, he did. But not before . . ."

Ice filled my veins, my hands coiling into fists.

"Nero told him I was his, that he could have me whenever he wanted me," she said and tears misted in my eyes, my heart cracking open. "Nero watched," she added, half chuckle, half growl. "The sick bastard. I was lucky Stellan died before he could ever visit again."

"Lucky . . ." I whispered as tears rolled down my cheeks.

"Grae was already away, studying in Valta," Maez said. "I never told him. The only person who knows other than Nero is Sadie." Maez swallowed thickly, her voice still an even steel. "And I'll never forget what she told me. She said that I had to be the very best soldier. So undeniably powerful with my blade that Nero could not say no when I pledged my sword to Grae. And even after Stellan died and Ingrid's claim to her throne was further cemented, I never forgot that. I had to be a warrior that Nero couldn't lose to a foreign army. I had to be worth more to him through my power than my body. But I always lived in fear that he could take that away from me again. And no one would stop him."

"You can stop him now," I whispered, voice cracking. "When you took on this power, why didn't you kill Nero straight away?"

"Because even monsters have ghosts, Princess," she murmured, hanging her head. "I don't want to face him. I don't want to feel stripped so bare. Even with this power . . . I don't want to feel like I'm thirteen again."

I swiped at the tears on my cheeks. "Everything seemed so . . .

fine," I choked out. "You seemed so happy, carefree even when I met you. I knew your past was challenging; I knew from the stories you'd tell me, but this . . . You never told me this before."

Maez held her head in her hands as she looked down at the straight drop. "You were too pure, Briar." She swept her hair back and sat up to look at me. "I didn't want to stain your beautiful soul."

"I'm not pure anymore," I whispered, looking at my hands as if I could still see the blood on them. "I don't *want* to be anymore. I want whatever we are to be one and the same." More tears spilled from my eyes and Maez reached out and wiped them away as if she couldn't help herself. "And I want to be the person who helps you kill him."

"I don't want to make you a villain." Her eyes bracketed with pain. "But I will if you let me." She wiped one more tear and moved to leave.

"Don't," I begged, reaching out for her and grabbing her elbow. "Please."

She looked down at where my hand gripped her elbow. "The moment I grabbed for this magic," she said, green streaks of lightning hovering over her skin and tingling over my fingers. "I felt strong. I *feel* strong, I feel unafraid, for the first time in my life." She swallowed. "Don't ask me to come back from the way I feel now. I never want to feel powerless again."

"I won't."

"This is a road you can't follow me down, Briar," she said. "I've been waiting for you to realize it. In your heart of hearts you *are* good; you wouldn't choose to be a monster, a killer. I would. I *have*. And I'd choose it every time if it meant protecting you from the things I've seen."

"Stop this." I swung my legs back around and pushed into the room to meet her face-to-face. "I am not as good as you think I am."

Maez's eyes crinkled, endless amounts of heartbreak hiding

behind those mirth-filled eyes. "Ask me to take you back to Calla."

"No."

"Ask me because I don't have the strength to do what's right for both of us on my own," she said. "I will keep you here forever, destroying your sweetness just like the beasts I tried to save you from. You deserve so much more than this, than me. Please. Ask me to take you back."

I couldn't even make out her face, my vision was so blurry from tears. "No," I cried. "I won't go. I won't leave you."

Maez gently held me by the cheeks and dropped her forehead to mine. "You deserve to be happy, Briar."

"I deserve you, only you," I sobbed.

"Nobody deserves *this*," she said vehemently.

"*Exactly.*" I squared my shoulders, meeting her frustration and anger with my own.

"You say that so easily. But you aren't listening to me. *This* is who I am. *Forever*, Briar. I will not change, not even for you."

"Forever, Maez," I confirmed, ignoring the fact this wasn't what she was saying. "You and me. I meant it then, and I mean it now. I know what I'm committing to." *I'm committing to you*, I kept unspoken.

"You don't. But you will."

I pinned her with a defiant look, feeling a growing promise building within me. "I'm yours even in darkness. I *will* prove that to you."

She pushed away from me and wiped a single stray tear from her eyes. "Then so be it," she said and stormed away.

TWENTY-FIVE

SADIE

I TRUDGED THROUGH THE DAMP MORNING FOREST WITH MY shoulders bunched around my ears. Navin followed a pace behind me like an early morning shadow. Clearly he had no respect for the hours that Wolves kept because this was the most cursed time of day to be awake. I didn't know if I was angry at him or Nero or the Gods . . . all I knew was I was angry.

We hiked out toward the sea, Haestas trailing us like a ruby in the cloudless sky. We headed straight east from the temple in the hopes of tracking down a water monster to practice Navin's magic on. This time, I insisted no one else join us. The last thing we needed was to die because of a poorly timed sneeze.

"We are wasting precious hours with this nonsense," I muttered. "Need I remind you Highwick is a landlocked capital. What use is a water monster?"

"It's to practice," Navin said just as tightly.

"You can practice on me."

"No."

I threw up my hands in exasperation. "We should be packing up the wagon with the others," I snapped. "The sooner we get out of this place the better. We've gotten what we've come for and one of our attackers escaped."

"Even on four paws, your brother won't make it to Highwick before we move camp," Navin assured me.

The thought stung. I knew Hector had saved my life during the attack from my father and uncles, but that didn't mean he hadn't betrayed us before . . . or wouldn't do so again. But to who and to what end? Whatever his loyalty, it was still unknown. Maybe he would tuck tail and run, roaming the edges of the forest as a lone Wolf forever.

My father spoke of Hector being strung up by Nero, tortured by him. Surely Hector wouldn't return to Highwick to face more of Nero's wrath? But maybe he saw that as his only means of survival now . . .

It was all so up in the air. I'd thought I'd known my brother's motives before. I wouldn't be foolish enough to think he wouldn't make another bad decision and turn himself back in to Nero for more punishments. It was what we were raised to do after all. And while I tried to only hate my brother, I feared for the punishments Nero would mete out upon him if he made such a foolish choice.

"And how long before Nero realizes they haven't returned?"

"Long enough for our wagon to be far away," Navin replied. "Our songs will keep us hidden and cover our trail."

"When they attacked," I said, unable to call our attackers by their names. They weren't my family now. "I almost lost you. When my father pinned me, that left you alone and outnumbered. You had a more powerful weapon than a single knife. You should've used the songs."

"No." I was getting real sick of these monosyllabic responses.

"No?" I whirled on him. "This isn't funny, Navin."

His dark eyes pierced into me. "I'm not laughing, Sadie."

Sweet Moon, why did he have to be so attractive when he was angry? I wasn't sure if I wanted to throttle him or fuck him . . . or both at the same time. *Now that would be interesting.*

I balled my fists and turned, storming faster through the forest, hating the feeling of the morning dew clinging to my boots and trouser legs. It was doing nothing to help my mood. I lifted a low hanging branch, and instead of releasing it gently, I pulled it farther so that it would snap back like a whip. Navin's grunt was the only confirmation I needed that I'd hit my target.

"Listen," I grumbled, "you might be strong and skilled for a human, but—"

"But?" I heard him take a decided step forward, closing the distance between us until his chest was at my back. I turned to look at his tight expression. "I killed them, without the aid of the songs," he pointed out. "If I had used the songs, it would've controlled you, too."

"It would've been worth it to save your life," I hissed. His anger softened a little at that. There was no way for him to go toe to toe with me when it came to anger and we both knew it. "I can handle it. Promise me if there is another Wolf attack, you will use the songs to protect yourself."

I waited for a long time, but Navin didn't respond. "Sweet motherfucking Moon," I gritted out, spinning and pushing through the last of the trees to the sloping pebbled shoreline.

The gradient was steep, the dark water beyond choppy and roiling with angry white foam. Sea mist sprayed the air, coating my already damp skin, and I let out another grumble. I folded my arms and sat on a lichen-covered rock.

"Go on," I muttered. "Sing your bloody songs."

Navin strolled around to face me, hands in pockets. "We have to wait for one to come."

"You brought me here at dawn to *wait* for a monster?" Oh, I was really going to kill him now.

"They are known to stick close to this shoreline."

"This is a very long shoreline," I spat.

"One will come," he said with a nod. "Be patient."

"I'm sorry, you must've mistaken me for someone else. When have I ever given you the impression that I can be patient?" I picked up a handful of stones and started chucking them out to the water one by one in the hopes that if a monster lurked in the waves it would come. But none emerged. "This is ridiculous. We don't have time to wait," I said, crossing my arms tight across my chest again. "We don't have time for you to stumble across beasts to train when you have one right here."

"I won't do it." I almost wanted to laugh at his deeply serious tone. "I won't take control of your mind. I won't take that freedom from you."

"Your chivalry is noted and currently very unappreciated," I muttered. I tipped my chin up to the sky. "Practice on Haestas while we wait for this great sea creature, then."

"What would you have me do? Make her bring you another goat?"

"Tell her to bring me a Wolf," I suggested. "One with silver fur. Alive. One we can interrogate. *That* would actually be a good use of our time."

"Why do you think I spend every evening poring over sheets of music? I have been *trying*, but the more involved the command, the more intricate the song." Navin mused up at the clouds. "And since no song exists to command a monster to fetch a living Wolf, I must write it myself. It will take more time to uncover the right notes, if it can be done at all."

"Practice something else on her now, then," I grumbled, ignoring his mounting frustration. "Don't make my sleep exhaustion be in vain."

Navin let out a long-suffering sigh. "Fine."

"Fine."

He let out a sharp whistle and Haestas came shooting like a carmine arrow through the sky. She tucked in her shimmering iridescent wings until within striking distance of us and I thought for a second she might crash into the rocky shores, but at the last second, she opened her wings like a sail to a strong wind and slowed to a graceful landing. Her clawed feet sunk into the pebbles under her enormous weight and she let out deep growling clicks as she stalked closer.

She was incredible and lethal and yet I knew by her posture and the brightness in her eyes that she wasn't a danger to us.

Navin started his low, guttural song, making Haestas do all the things I'd seen him have her do a hundred times before: sit, lie down, even breathe little streams of fire.

"Is she going to light a candle for us? Doing parlor tricks won't help us in an actual battle," I said, rubbing the crusted sleep from my tired eyes. "She needs to be trained to *kill* on command. I know songs have been written about that at least."

Navin shot me a look but acquiesced, his song changing, morphing to something faster. Haestas sat alert, her pupils narrowing to slits, and then she took flight. With a whoosh, she shot out toward the sea, circling the tall waves a few times before shooting down toward the water. Talons bared, she snatched a writhing creature from beneath the roiling waves. It had the claws of a crab and the long reptilian body of a crocodile with rows upon rows of sharp sharklike teeth as if the three animals were sewn together into one foul beast.

"I'm never swimming in the ocean again."

Navin ignored me, too focused on his dragon. He let out a whistle and Haestas tore at the monster with her talons, ripping it limb from limb before dropping its shredded remains back into the sea.

"Was *that* the creature we were waiting for?" I asked, looking at the burnt orange remains bobbing on the surface.

"Yep," Navin said.

"Great." With a groan, I stood. "If you can have her do that a few hundred times in rapid succession, we may very well have a chance." Navin's expression soured. "Let's head back to camp, then—there's only one beast you're going to be training today." I smiled at Haestas as she flew higher above the clouds again, released from her deathly performance. "Unless you'd like to try on me?"

Navin turned and scowled. "No."

"Aw, come on," I said, sidling over to him. Well, my attempt at sidling. I needed Briar to teach me how to swish my hips in that alluring way she did. I was never one to be seductive, but judging by the heat in Navin's eyes, it was working all the same. "It could be fun." I ran my hands up his arms as he arched a brow at me. "It could be a lot of fun—you trying to control me, making me do whatever dark ideas are floating around your head."

The desire in his eyes betrayed that frown and I knew I'd *finally* found my in. Navin wasn't one for playing games outside the bedroom, but oh the fun we had inside it. If I could get him to practice this new power *and* get a wickedly fun night out of him, then so be it.

"Never mind," I said, reeling him in like a fish on a hook. I waved away the thought. "We could just let Ora practice with me—"

"No." Navin stepped into me, his hands sweeping around my waist and gathering me to him. His possessive fingertips pressed into my leathers. "If anyone trains you, it will be me."

"Good." Plan hatched, I rose on my tiptoes and brushed a chaste kiss to his lips. He tried to pull me closer, to continue the kiss, but I pulled away and patted his chest. "Save it for tonight."

"Tonight?" he asked as I started back toward the forest. I heard the crunch of his boots beneath the pebbles as he followed. "Tonight we'll be on Galen den' Mora heading northward."

"Ora still has that tent, don't they?"

I heard Navin's light laugh from behind me as I stalked back toward the temple. "Do I even want to know what you have planned?"

I flashed him a catlike grin over my shoulder. "You really, really do . . .

"But there's no way I'm going to tell you unless you *make me*."

TWENTY-SIX

BRIAR

FIRELIGHT FLICKERED IN MY BEDROOM WHEN I ENTERED, THE nights surprisingly chilly in the balmy tropical atmosphere. When the door fully opened, I screamed.

A body lay in a heap at the foot of my bed. Shining silver eyes stared lifelessly up at the ceiling. That perfectly carved cold face, the royal garb . . . Evres.

Maez appeared from the shadowed corner of my room. "Do you like my present?"

She asked it like a cat bringing me a dead mouse, so utterly pleased with herself.

I gaped at the body on my bed. "You killed him?"

"No," she sang, and my eyes narrowed to the rise and fall of his chest. "He is under the very same sleeping curse that you were once subject to. Although I'd imagine you looked much more of a beauty," she said, roughly grabbing Evres's cheeks and shaking them back and forth. "And less of a dead fish."

"What are you going to do with him?" I breathed, unable to hide the horror in my words.

"I'm not going to do anything with him," Maez said, producing a dagger from her cloak and flipping it to offer me the hilt, just as she had the day she first rescued me. "You are."

I took a step back, banging into the now-closed door that Maez must've magically shut.

"I can't," I said firmly, shaking my head.

"You said you wanted to prove you could handle this darkness, handle *me*."

"I know, but—"

"Enough! I'm not talking to the Princess right now," Maez cut in. "I'm talking to *you*, Briar. I don't care what you were taught to be. What is it you *want* to do to him?"

Drawn in by the undertow of her empowering words, I found my true voice. Not the sweet affected one I'd been taught, the real one pulled up from below the surface. "I once vowed to myself that I'd be the one to kill him."

"Good. He was going to *torture* you," Maez pushed, gesturing at Evres with the dagger. "He was going to breed you and break you in body and spirit until you were nothing but a shell of the vibrant person you once were." Her voice was laced with a promise of violence. Static filled the air as if it angered her magic, too, as if every ounce of her being wanted to exact revenge. "He was going to do much worse than kill you swiftly. But these powerful men have never known a power like mine." She took a step forward and placed the glinting black hilt of the dagger in my hand. "A power like *yours*."

I gripped the warmed hilt, taking a step forward even as I said one last time, "I can't do this."

"You can," Maez urged, leaning into me until her mouth was only a hair's breadth from my own. "You can be every forge and fire, Briar. You can be vengeance."

When she stepped away again, I stared at Evres, knowing that if the roles were reversed, he wouldn't hesitate. His only sorrow from slicing a blade across my throat would be that he'd bleed me out in minutes instead of decades. And yet I couldn't bring myself to take another step.

Anger mounted at my own inaction. How long would it take me to fully grant myself this permission? How long would I be untangling my truth from the facade? Would I forever be leashed to the person I was told I should be?

"Is it because he is asleep?" Maez asked with a cock of her head. "Because if you could hear all the sick things twisting through his mind, you wouldn't hesitate." When I didn't move, she sighed and snapped her fingers. "Fine."

Evres shot up, gasping. His hand went to his throat, and he searched the room.

"Maez," I warned as Evres started to realize what was happening. His cold eyes landed on me, a sneer on his lips as he said, "You." He looked like he wanted to kill me, like he wanted to drag me back to Damrienn and strangle the life out of me.

I gripped the dagger tighter. "Maez," I pleaded again.

"You can do this," she said. "You are stronger than you know."

"I . . ."

My whole life I'd done the right thing, done exactly as I was told, and look where it got me. Maybe it was time I stopped looking to others to save me. Maybe the right thing wasn't patience and calm and kindness. *The right thing.* I was beginning to wonder if that concept was one of the many lies taught to women to keep us chained. My soul sang with the realization: maybe the *right thing* to do was bring this bastard to a violent and bloody end.

As if hearing my inner thoughts, Maez stepped to my side and dropped her mouth to my ear. "Come on, Briar; show me your thorns."

When Evres shot forward, hands out like he wanted to strangle me, I ducked under his arms and kicked out the back of his leg. It was a move I'd watched Calla perfect over hundreds and hundreds of hours while I practiced the waltz and the dainty way to sip tea. Bitterness roiled in me that I'd once been so thoroughly declawed. *Not anymore.* Sweet Moon, it felt good when my fist collided with the side of Evres's head. Even the pain of my knuckles lit me up inside.

"You bitch!" Evres shouted as if shocked by the audacity I had to defend myself. He scrambled to his feet, launching to attack me again.

Maez could've easily stepped in, but she didn't. This was *my* kill and we both knew it.

I'd once coached myself to remain calm around Evres, to not provoke him. Calm no longer existed in me, only bright, burning fire.

No more hiding behind my title, and Calla, and Maez. I will fight my own battles.

Evres grabbed a fistful of my dress and yanked me toward him. "You're nothing but a pretty little whore, Briar Marriel," he hissed. "You're no solider. You don't even know how to use that dagger."

His other hand fisted in my hair yanking it to the point of pain. My eyes watered as I held his hateful stare.

"Maybe I don't," I rasped, tightening my grip on the dagger. "Will you help me practice?"

I drove the blade up into his chest with all my might, the blade so sharp it slid into his belly like slicing through warm butter. Evres gasped and staggered backward, his eyes bugged as he held a hand to his bleeding gut. A glorious, dark satisfaction zipped through me at the shock on his face. I shot forward, not giving him another second to contemplate what I'd done before I stabbed him again.

And again.

And *again*.

Chest, shoulder, arm, cheek. I tore him apart with my blade, the blood driving me to a frenzy, spurred on by the look of utter disbelief in his eyes as if even as I ended him, he couldn't quite believe I had the courage to plunge a knife into him. I smiled wickedly. *Yes, me. The pretty, little whore. I am your executioner.*

I grabbed him by his bloody cheeks, prying open his limp mouth. With my blade I delved beyond his teeth and cut out his tongue, the one he had once forced into my mouth. Blood sprayed as I threw the wet piece of flesh across the room, and it hit the wall with a sickening splat. Never would it touch me again.

Evres's eyes rolled back, his body limp, but I didn't stop. I screamed, releasing my fury on him, punishing him for everything I was put through, for everything he wanted to do to me, for every way I was made to feel lesser than, weak, meek, pathetic.

It wasn't until Maez's powerful arms hauled me off him that I dropped the blade. I tried to struggle against her, but she whirled me and pinned me to the wall, her mouth instantly finding mine. Her burning kiss was so all-encompassing that everything else flew to the back of my mind. She kissed me like my blood-splattered lips alone sustained her. She consumed me, her body pushing into mine, her mouth working over me until all my rage had simmered into lust.

When she pulled away, her eyes were filled with pride as she said, "I knew you were hiding under there, my vicious Briar. My mate."

Heat bloomed in my belly at her claiming words.

She clicked her fingers and Evres and all the blood coating the floor disappeared, though I remained slick with gore.

"What have you done with him?"

She grinned. "Sent him back to Nero with a little note from us." She winked. "Nero is losing heirs faster than he can name them."

Maez turned toward the door.

"What now?" I asked and she paused, her hand hovering above the handle.

"Now you bathe and then you sleep," she said but neither did she move.

"And if I don't want to sleep?"

"Oh, I like this new you," she crooned, stalking back toward me. "Or should I say, the real you?" She studied me. "I could make you feel so, so good, Princess," she promised, but then her eyes darkened. "But this isn't what you want."

"What I want is for people to stop telling me what I want," I snapped, finding my voice again. Each time I did it, it became easier. I hadn't come this far for her to push me away again. I wouldn't let her.

I grabbed her by the back of the neck and pulled her lips to mine. She moved instantly, her mouth crashing into me as she hoisted me up, grabbing my ass as I wrapped my legs around her lean waist.

She tasted of copper and rust, Evres's hot blood still dripping from my hair and clothes as I clung to her. Maez carried me backward, dropping me onto the mattress, uncaring as we soaked the sheets crimson. Swiftly she stripped me until I was bare before her.

"I told you before, mate. You look good in nothing but the blood of your enemies." My chest heaved as her hungry eyes took me in. "Gods, I missed this body." She studied every inch of me as she unbuttoned her shirt, letting it fall open.

I feasted on the sight of her smooth muscled skin as she slid her trousers down and stepped out of them.

"I need you," I panted, and a smile tugged the corners of her lips.

She prowled forward, crawling up my body, lighting up my skin with every inch she touched. She kissed me fiercely, pressing me down into the mattress. Her touch was so different, her mouth more demanding than she'd ever been before, but I relished it. My desire overriding everything else. I needed to be fucked, needed her mouth and tongue and hands, needed her naked and dripping for me so badly I might implode.

My hands dove into her hair and raked down her back, touching her rougher than I ever had before. She let out a little groan of pleasure as she nipped at my lips. I rocked my hips into hers angling myself to rub my clit against the rock-hard muscle of her thigh.

She moved lower, angling herself so her own wet pussy met mine, rocking in rhythm to my own feverish tempo. This heady union made me moan, chasing my pleasure against her slick sex. Maez broke our kiss to drop her mouth to my hardened nipple. She sucked the peak into her mouth, swirling her tongue around it twice before testing it with her teeth—hard.

I cried out, pain and pleasure mixing in equal measure as her hand dove beneath me to grab my ass and rock me harder against her. I let her take control, moving me in just the way she wanted, her hips jerking against me as her lust drove her wild.

"More," I moaned and Maez moved, rolling and pulling me on top of her, the hand gripping my ass dropped to my core and she pushed two fingers inside of me, hooking them and massaging my inner walls.

With a cry of pleasure, I pushed back against those fingers as they thrust in and out, taking me faster. My hand slipped between us, and I found her throbbing clit. I circled it with my fingers as she fucked me with her own.

"Harder," she groaned, and I pushed down on her swollen nub harder than she'd ever liked it before. "Yes," she panted, grinding against my hand. "Yes. Fuck, Briar."

Her fingers worked me faster and I gasped, struggling to catch my breath as the pleasure crested in me like a violent wave. Her other hand rolled my nipple in her fingers as she lifted her head from the mattress and claimed my mouth. At the brush of her tongue, the tug of my nipple, the thrusting of her fingers, I exploded.

My orgasm took me by surprise, roaring through me so wickedly that I saw stars. Maez followed after me as I circled her clit, bring her to climax right along with me. Our sweat-slick bodies slid against each other as we moaned in unison—the sweetest harmony.

When we finished, I rolled off her and lay tucked into her side. She didn't reach for me. Didn't brush a loving hand down my arm. Didn't kiss the top of my head. Didn't tell me I was beautiful or incredible or that she loved me.

The come down from that euphoric high was brutal.

I could embrace Maez's strength and violence, but I still needed her softness, too. She unspooled me, revealing more of my true self to her, but something still held me back—the hope that we could reverse time, the inability to let go of what we once had in order to form something new. One hand still gripped on to the past. I knew I'd need to release it and free-fall into this unknown to ever truly have all of her again.

A sudden bout of tears welled in my eyes, a knot forming in my throat. I didn't want to let that hope go. Not at all.

Maez looked down at me with a frown. "Delightful," she muttered. "Go to sleep, little puppy," she snapped and shoved off the bed. "You're not ready to play with this kind of power." She stalked out the door without even opening it, disappearing in an emerald haze.

I curled onto my side, hugging the pillow into me and sobbed. I knew then for certain—Wolf or no—I was never getting the old Maez back.

TWENTY-SEVEN

CALLA

VERENA PROPPED HER BOOTS UP ON THE STONE TABLE, FOLDING her arms and leaning back in the only chair. Her bone white crown slid back on her head until it rested upon the upholstered velvet behind her. It was far too big. A new one would eventually have to be made. But I had a sneaking suspicion that she was waiting until after the attack on Highwick. It would be bad luck indeed if she had a new crown made only to die a few days later.

The Ice Wolf Queen still hadn't sat on her throne for the same reason, existing in a constant balancing act between rebel soldier and newfound royalty. I wondered once her claim was cemented and her borders protected, if she'd finally accept her new title fully. I still grappled with mine. Perhaps it would never fully sit right with us. We'd live forever in a state of trying to prove our worth to our citizens and to ourselves.

"Here," Grae said, stabbing his finger to a point on the map, "is the best point of entry. This end of the castle is all servant's passageways. No Wolf would stoop to use them, not even the guards."

"And *why* wouldn't they guard every exit?" Verena asked. "Especially during such tumultuous times?"

"It's beneath them," Grae replied. "They don't fear human retaliation, nor do they care to protect the humans in their employ.

And a Wolf attack is meant to take place on an open field of battle, as is custom. Nero thinks we will show decorum and respect for the Wolf ways, even when he does not."

Verena let out a long whistle. "Three cheers for Wolf arrogance, I suppose. Only a king would believe he can crush people under his boots and then expect the courtesy of an invitation to their revenge." She looked around to her advisers who circled the table. "Make note of it."

One of them began jotting down the details on a piece of paper to relay to the rest of the pack. Grae had drawn a detailed map of Highwick castle from memory—floor after floor with little notes and suggestions of where guards would be stationed. We planned our attack on the castle from every angle. We'd need our Olmderian soldiers and Verena's pack to be on the same page, having memorized each passage, dead end, and dogleg.

"What is this?" I asked, tapping what appeared to be a window in the center of the third-floor hallway that bisected the western wing.

"That is a portrait that hides a doorway to the library balcony," Grae said. "A painting of three white stallions being chased by a Silver Wolf. I used to sneak into the balcony and listen as the tutors taught lessons on art and poetry."

Verena snorted and I shot her a death stare. She held up her hands. "I just wouldn't think of a Silver Wolf prince as someone who wanted to learn about art and poetry."

"Hence my need to sneak. It was a nice reprieve from war and politics," Grae said tightly. "It was also an excellent spot to hide from my sword instructor."

"Ah." Verena chuckled. "Now that I believe."

I leaned into Grae until my jacket brushed his sleeve, a little silent acknowledgment. Verena didn't know all he'd endured as Nero's only child. No one did. Although with the Silver Wolf King's recent behavior, I was certain people would believe him if he spoke truthfully about his childhood. What Nero had done to Grae's mother . . . what he would do to so many more—

"We move out tomorrow, then," Verena said wistfully, pulling me from my haunted thoughts. "We'll get to the foothills of the Stormcrest Ranges and regroup there." She moved her carved wolf paperweight to the map of Aotreas in front of her. "It will be too far from the capital to raise the alarm and give us some time to rest and gain our strength before the final push to Highwick." She glanced up at me, her blue eyes narrowing. "Your friends will be able to make it in time?"

"They are already moving northward," Mina signed, stepping up to my side. She had been staying in extra close contact with the Songkeepers during their stay at the temple of knowledge, but now that they were on the move again, their communications would become less frequent. "Three days from the full moon, they know to be ready."

"I think we have them take the front gate," I said, looking between Grae and Verena for their agreement. "Have their dragon torch the eastern wing, flush them out, and take down any marksmen on the rooftops, while we enter from the western side." I looked at Mina. "Let's just make sure that dragon doesn't destroy the palace with us still inside, okay?" She nodded.

Verena let out a groan, grimacing at me. "Can such a beast really be so controlled? One lash of its tail and it might topple a tower upon us or cave in a wall."

"So long as it stays to the east and us the west, we shall be safe," I insisted. "The only Wolves being crushed by crumbling walls will be fleeing Silver Wolves."

"All the better, then," Grae added, supporting my claims.

Verena rubbed her thumb contemplatively across her bottom lip. "So much could go wrong," she said. "If one piece of the puzzle doesn't perfectly align, your entire plan may crumble."

"That's the nature of battle. It is a sound plan," Grae cut in, seemingly growing an inch in anger.

I put a hand on his forearm. I could handle the criticism; we needed every plan to be fully scrutinized. "We have three alternate plans of attack should something go amiss," I said confidently.

"Our biggest concern is making sure all our soldiers know them forward and backward." When the tension in Verena's face didn't ease, I added, "I get it: this isn't the way Wolves battle. This is a siege. We corner them from all sides in the middle of the night, we block every exit, we split up the force of their army into smaller, controllable factions, and then we end them.

"I know this is different—it's different for all of us. But it's the way we win."

She held my gaze for a long moment before nodding. "In only a handful of days, we'll know if your plans were sound."

"Thank you," I said, softening my harsh tone, making sure all the rest of her pack heard me as well. "For fighting beside Olmdere."

"It is I who should be thanking you, Queen Marriel," Verena said, rising to stand. "You may very well be able to close off your borders, unaware of a world beyond your golden trees. Your court may survive the reign of Nero, but mine won't." She looked around to her advisers, adjusting her ill-fitting crown. "Together, we shall prevail." She waved a hand to her head councilor.

"Ready the troops—we leave tomorrow when the moon rises."

TWENTY-EIGHT

SADIE

WE'D SET UP CAMP A GOOD TEN-MINUTE WALK AWAY FROM THE wagon. Clearly Navin didn't want anyone seeing or hearing me in a controlled state. And while I relished his protectiveness, I needed him to put his concerns to the side. We only had a few more weeks to practice this magic before we had to be ready, and yet Navin insisted we only practice in a tent far from the others.

Calling it a tent felt as much of a misnomer as calling Galen den' Mora a wagon, for inside it was so much more. A lush carpet covered the tarping, soft upon my bare feet. A leather-bound chest served as a low table holding a copper tray of dripping candles. And in the center of the room sat a bed. The interlocking posts that created the frame were rudimentary but easy to disassemble. And the bedroll and blankets that covered it seemed just as plush and comfortable as in any home. It was a magical feat that such a cozy space could be created out of the single cart of supplies that we hauled through the forest.

"Are you sure you want to do this?" I asked, eyeing Navin as he tied shut the flaps to our tent, double-checking each of the knots.

"Unless you want to abandon this ludicrous plan?" he asked again.

I gave him a flat look. "Controlling Wolves in battle seems a far safer plan than hunting monsters," I said for what felt like the hundredth time. "You saw how well the encounter with the visturong went. We can't let the balance of this war be tipped by a sneeze. We have Haestas and soon we will have control of Wolves and that will be all we need."

Navin huffed, rubbing his eyes. "I don't like this."

"You've made that abundantly clear. So let Ora do it. Not everything has to fall on you." I moved to push past him, and he grabbed my elbow, smoothing his thumb across my skin. I bit my lip as I looked down at where he touched me.

"When it comes to you, Sadie, I don't trust anyone else," he murmured. "Only me."

I sighed, sliding my hand up his chest and up to cradle his face. "Only you."

Navin released me and reached for his lastar propped against the bed frame. He perched on the bed and began tuning the instrument. I started undressing, not wanting to tear up my clothes just for the practice. I set my knives belt and weapons on the dresser, slowly unbuttoning my trousers.

"You have to resist me like our enemies would," Navin said as he plucked the strings. "If it gets too much, shift and I'll stop."

I nodded, letting my clothes pool on the floor and shifting straight away. I knew if I stayed there naked for too long, we wouldn't get any practice done.

Navin rolled his shoulders, his eyes narrowing at me as I stood across the cabin in my furs.

"Ready?"

I didn't respond and he started playing that familiar tune. I was starting to pick apart the intricacies of it. I wasn't a musician, but I knew that different notes corresponded to different words, different types of communication that when woven together could make instructions like when Ora had told the visturongs to "go home."

It started off as a beautiful song, just like any other, but then I felt it—the hooks in my mind, like someone's dirty paws digging through my thoughts. A voice both foreign and known started speaking to me—not of any pitch or gender—just a deep-seated knowing.

"Come to me," it said, and I was met with the overwhelming urge to crawl forward.

My jaw clenched, my paws digging into the threadbare rug beneath me. I leaned backward against the force as if I could fight my own body. Sweat beaded on Navin's brow as if the magic infused into the song drained him as well. His expression was tense as he watched the way I struggled against his magic.

"Come to me," the voice insisted, pushing harder.

One paw moved, then another, the effort of trying to stay put was splitting my brain in two. It felt like being dragged by the strongest force, being tied to a weighted-down cart tumbling down a cliffside. I moved, unable to resist, even as my muscles strained and fought.

"Stop," the voice said, and I froze, my muscles shaking.

"Stick your tongue out," it commanded.

A snarl curled my maw. This was so degrading. I tried to fight it off, but the music pushed me harder and harder. My vision began to spot with the exertion, my survival instincts finally kicking in, and I shifted, crumpling to the floor.

The music stopped all at once. The claws in my mind retreating with such speed it left me reeling.

"I'm sorry," Navin said again and again as he dropped to the floor.

I pushed him away, trying to regain my senses. "Keep going," I said. "Try to see if it'll work in this form."

"Sadie—"

"Keep going," I urged, shoving him back toward the bed. I rose up on my knees, naked before him, and I saw the way his eyes lingered over every inch of my exposed skin. "Go on."

"What—?"

"Who says we can't have a little fun with this?"

His brow arched in mirror to my own, his cheeks dimpling as he picked the instrument back up.

I brushed the hair out of my face and placed my hands on my hips, waiting, bracing as his music started again. Navin went slower this time, the tune more soft and melodic but still forceful. I felt it more distantly than I had in my Wolf form. It was more playful and taunting like this, more of a suggestion than an outright command. I knew then for certain that the Wolves wouldn't be as easily controlled in their human forms. They needed to shift for the Songkeepers' magic to truly take hold. I kept my gaze hooked on Navin as I listened to the unspoken wills of his song. When it finally became clear what he was asking me, a smile split my lips.

"Touch yourself," the music instructed.

Navin's eyes were filled with heat as I cocked my head, my hand trailing down my side and to the apex of my thighs. His music picked up speed, the feeling more insistent in me. I could break away from this control in this form, but it was still compelling, like I wanted nothing more than to perform for him.

"Touch yourself," the music pushed more, and I felt myself falling under its spell again.

Parting my sex, I circled my clit, my eyes hooding as I watched Navin. His gaze was transfixed on my core, his lips parted.

"Faster," his song commanded, and I picked up speed, touching myself faster.

"Add your fingers."

I did, fucking myself for him while he watched. His gaze lifted to meet mine and he looked like he wanted to devour me. The pleasure of his song, my touch, of him watching me with those wanton eyes was building me higher and higher.

Then another command came.

"Come for me."

And I did, the orgasm taking me without warning. I moaned,

dropping onto my side, stroking myself through the last of my release. It was a sharp sudden burst of pleasure, one that quickly ebbed when Navin released the lastar and dropped to the floor beside me.

"Gods," he cursed. He scooped me up from the floor and pulled me onto the bed, cradling me in his strong arms. "That was . . ." He swept the hair off my sweat-stained brow and lifted my chin to search my eyes.

"Incredible," I panted, dropping my forehead to his chest. "Gods I thought I was going to pass out."

"Passed-out enemies would certainly be helpful on a battlefield," he murmured into my hair. Navin trailed his fingers down my bare back.

"As long as you don't make them pass out like that," I added with a chuckle.

"You are so breathtaking, Sadie," he murmured. "I love the way you move to my music."

A blush crept up my cheeks, a reignited heat pooling in my core. "We are too easily distracted, you and I." I let out a light laugh. "We should keep practicing," I said, pulling away from him, but his arms banded around me tighter.

"Later," he said, dropping his mouth to mine, his kiss searching and insistent. "You just collapsed. I need to know that you're okay first. That we're okay."

"We're okay," I assured him.

"Thank you for trusting me," he said, kissing me more fervently. Heat flooded my veins once more.

"If you could use your song on me right now," I goaded, pulling back to meet his eyes. A mischievous smile curved my lip. "What would you have me do?"

A little rumbling sound caught in his throat. He swept his thumb across my bottom lip and tugged. "Does that idea turn you on?" he asked. "Me controlling you?"

He already knew the answer, his eyes lit up with lust.

I pulled away, climbing off his lap and back to stand before him again. He reached out and I took a farther step, tsking. "Try again."

"Sadie—"

"Use your magic." I flashed a toothy grin. "Make me do all the things I know are swimming around in your head right now."

Navin's jaw clenched, the muscle popping out as he stared at me, anger warring with desire, but I knew I had him right where I wanted him now.

Navin tossed the lastar onto the pillows in the corner and dropped his head into his hands. But when he looked up, I could see the heat in his eyes, the gauntlet I'd thrown down being picked up. He started singing, so low and deep it rumbled through me. A tingling flush burned across my skin as I started to feel the pull of his song.

"Oh, Sadie," the song seemed to call to me, singing my name like a prayer.

My lips parted at the sweet, heady lure.

"Get on your knees."

My pussy fluttered at the sheer command, but I was fully given over to his song now. I dropped onto my knees and looked up at Navin with lust-filled eyes as he rose from the bed and stalked over to me. His song continued as his hands drifted to his belt.

"Open your mouth."

My mouth fell open of its own volition, my pulse ratcheting higher as he pulled out his hard cock from his trousers.

"Suck me down like a good little Wolf."

And I did.

Navin's song paused on a heady groan as I sucked him into my mouth, laving my tongue across his shaft and hollowing my cheeks as I took him deeper. His hand dove into my hair to steady himself, his head falling back.

He could barely get out one more desperate line of his song before he was lost to the sensation. "Don't stop until I come."

My skin rippled with gooseflesh at the power and command

in his voice, knowing that he was all mine, knowing I was the only one who would give this to him—a control I knew he craved and needed. I took him deeper until my eyes watered. He started moving, fucking my mouth as he got closer and closer.

"Sadie." He groaned my name. Not a song but a warning. I didn't stop, just as he commanded, as he spilled down my throat.

When he finally pulled back, I licked my lips and flashed him the most satisfied smile. "Your power is getting stronger," I said.

He shook his head at me between panting breaths. "That is one way to get me to use my magic."

I rose and he grabbed me by the hips, pulling me into him and onto the bed. He rolled us until he was laying on top of me, pinning me into the mattress.

"And what if *you* were in control of me, hmm?" he murmured against my skin as he kissed down my neck. "What would you have me do to you, Sadie?" His mouth hovered over my nipple, his eyes lifting to meet mine. "Something like this?"

When he sucked my nipple into his mouth, my head dropped back into the mattress. His hands roved my bare skin.

"Not fair," I moaned. "I was meant to be playing out your fantasies and now you're determined to meet mine."

"They are one and the same," he said as he skimmed his lips lower. His breath skittered across the planes of my stomach, and I writhed beneath him. "Don't move," he commanded. "Or I'll tie you up to feast on you just as I like."

A little amused hum escaped my lips. I loved when he got possessive. He kissed his way to the inside of my thighs, hands hitching at my knees to spread me wider. His mouth hovered over my throbbing sex. At the first lick of his tongue, I arched back, chest heaving, too exhausted from the training to fight against the waves of pleasure that crashed over me.

Navin laughed against my wet core, clearly pleased with my response. "Perhaps this training won't be so bad," he purred, giving a soft taunting lick to my clit again.

"I'd train every day if you keep doing this to me afterward," I moaned as he started working his mouth over me again.

His fingers circled my entrance and slid into me, stretching me, making everything he was doing with his tongue all the more acute. I reached over to grab his hair, to ride his mouth, when his hand snapped out and pinned mine to the mattress.

"I said don't move," he taunted, and my chest rose and fell faster, loving the command in his voice. He knew just what I liked, the way he took control in the bedroom, one less thing I had to be in charge of. But I liked to push him, too.

When my other hand reached for him, he stopped and rose up to meet my eyes. I looked at him with a defiant smile, a goading one that I hoped would taunt him into handling me rougher. His smile matched my own as he shook his head.

"That's how you want to play this?" he asked and my smile widened.

He flipped me over roughly, his hand in my hair holding me down as I heard him fumble to grab his discarded belt. He quickly tied my hands behind my back, tight, the leather of his belt biting into my wrists. He yanked at my hips, pulling me back until my ass was high in the air and then brought his hand down on a cheek, stinging my skin. I moaned at the sensation, my skin buzzing.

"Yes," I groaned as he repeated the action, spanking me again. My ass seemed to move toward his strikes. Gods, I hoped I'd have the perfect outline of his hand on me when we were done.

As I panted and writhed, he slid the head of his cock up and down my center, spreading my wet heat over myself.

I moaned, trying to push back like I had with the spanking, but the hand gripping my hair held me in place.

"Is this what you really wanted, Sadie?" he purred as he positioned himself at my entrance. "For me to fuck you hard?"

"Yes," I panted. "Yes—"

My second begging word was cut off in a gasp as he slammed into me, making my vision glaze over. He was so big, but the angle with which he took me was hitting *that* spot inside me and had my toes curling. My fingers clutched at the belt binding them together. It was already too much. My orgasm sitting just below the surface as he fucked me hard, slamming me into the mattress with each of his powerful thrusts.

I cried out with each piston of his hips. His hand in my hair tightened with a bite of pain that had my eyes welling and I shattered. The pain and pleasure so overwhelming I came as I screamed his name.

Navin battled my clenching channel, my release only aiding him with thrust after thrust until he was spilling into me, chasing my orgasm with his own. I was completely wrecked by the time he stopped moving, my breathing ragged, my body pulsing with the intensity of my climax.

Navin untied my hands and gathered me back into him, kissing me soft and tender as he smoothed over the sore spot on my ass. I loved this, loved how he could push me to the edge and bring me back, the dichotomy of his ferocity and his tenderness, so very wolflike himself.

"Only you," I whispered and kissed him again, completely forgetting that we had come out here to practice magic. But when it came to Navin, I fell under a spell sweeter than any song.

TWENTY-NINE

BRIAR

I PICKED AT THE BLOOD BENEATH MY NAILS UNTIL THEY WERE so raw I couldn't tell if it was Evres's or my own. The day was silent, Maez gone to some part of the castle—or somewhere else entirely—I had no way of knowing. Either way, I didn't dare go looking for her. Not now, not after everything.

I studied my warped reflection in the water of the fountain—long red hair spilling over my shoulders, bright blue eyes shining back at me. I wore no paint on my face, no kohl lined my eyes nor rouge on my cheeks. There was something tougher in my gaze than its usual softness. No longer was I the perfect little doll. Maybe this was truly who was there under all the smiles and faux pleasantries, maybe I'd always had this darkness lurking in me and I just needed someone to pull it out—to be more than what I was expected to be.

That I might *want* to be something more.

Ever since Calla claimed merem . . . ever since I saw them bloom into this confident leader, into the very best and truest version of themself . . . I began to wonder.

Maybe I could let myself be more, too.

I knew something for certain: I could be more than the doll, the puppet, the vixen. And rather than taming the rulers of the world with my smiles and looks, I was more suited to tame them with my blade, my teeth, my claws. I thought of the way I'd attacked Evres, of his mutilated body, of the way I threw myself at Maez still coated in his blood. Of how much it delighted me to play into both her and my darkness.

It terrified me and liberated me in the same breath.

I dipped my hand back in the water, breaking the reflection, and kept scrubbing.

When I heard the scuffle of feet behind me, I knew Maez wanted to be heard. I looked over my shoulder and found her holding out a letter toward me.

"From Calla," she said. "If you'd like to reply, I'll make sure that it actually reaches her this time."

She was guarded and unsure as I rose from where I perched on the fountain and took the letter from her hands. Her intense, dark eyes studied my face.

"Is it hard being parted from her?"

"Yes and no," I said. "We were all each other had for so long." I turned the letter over in my hands. "But the plan was always for us to be parted, me remaining in Damrienn while Calla led an army to fight Sawyn with the allegiance of Silver Wolves at our back, and while those plans have irrevocably changed, I always knew our lives would take us farther from each other. It's time we carve our own paths. Calla has truly shined since stepping out from my shadow."

And I'm finding I might like *the shadows.*

"When we were in Olmdere," Maez said hesitantly, and it hurt to hear the delicacy with which she remembered those times as if they were so far away now. The sorrow panned through me as I remembered our little cabin and how she and I were so giddy, interrupting our everyday tasks for bouts of lovemaking, delighting in the fact we had the chance to be something more than the soldier and the Princess.

Maez took a step toward me. "When we were in Olmdere,"

she said a little more confidently, "you said that you didn't want to rule."

"I don't," I replied with a shake of my head.

"You said you wanted a little house at the edge of the world," she continued, tipping her head to the open window and the jungles that dropped to open air all around us. "You said you wished we could be in a sanctuary of our own, where no one was knocking on our door, where we could just be together."

My chest tightened, making it hard to take a deep breath. She remembered. I'd been lying in our bed, tangled in her arms, drifting off to sleep with my head rising and falling with each of her deep sleepy breaths. I'd thought she'd already let sleep take her, but she remembered.

"It was a careless, selfish wish," I said. "Our court needs us; our family needs us. We all need to fight to protect Olmdere."

"And then?"

"What?"

"Will it ever be enough? Would your life and service always be to your twin's crown? Because the world will never stop, it will never be perfect, and while we can do our best to make it so, at the end of the day you have to decide to give yourself over to the things you need, too." She scrubbed a hand down her face. "But perhaps it isn't the place, but the person you spend it with," she said, defeated. "And I am not the woman you wanted to run away with." Her eyes dropped to the paper in my hands. "I'll leave you to read your letter."

When she turned, I called out. "You had me kill Evres to prove a point not to me but to yourself." She paused, and I knew my words connected. "You are stronger than you know, too, Maez. Help me kill Nero. Then maybe we can talk about our home at the edge of the world."

"An ultimatum." She paused and looked over her shoulder at me, bitterness on her face. "If I'm your weapon, then I can be your lover, hmm? If you can have my magic, then you will consider my heart?" She kept walking and threw over her shoulder, "You will have all of me or none of me, Briar Marriel."

All! I wanted to shout.

All . . .

I wanted to believe.

I PACED BACK AND FORTH OUTSIDE MAEZ'S BEDROOM DOOR, adrenaline filling my veins.

All of her or none of her. I knew the moment she said it which I would choose and yet it still took a great force of will to bring myself to her doorstep. At every challenge, she expected me to turn and run, and I knew now that I never would. And that probably made me a terrible person. It probably stripped all the good I'd ever done . . . if I ever had done any. It was Calla who was truly the good one. They had saved our homeland while I'd been a cursed damsel. Maybe I'd never be all the things I'd been raised to be. Maybe I needed to finally shed the skin of that pointless potential.

I balled my hands into fists and let out a growl of frustration. I was sick of overthinking this. I was tired of trying to find the morality in a relationship where there was none. But I knew I wanted Maez. And I knew she'd have me if only I asked.

Finally, I stopped pacing. I planted my feet decidedly in front of her door and banged on it like I was threatening to break it down.

When Maez opened her door a second later, her eyebrows were raised, her expression intrigued.

"You want a lover?" I asked. "Then take me."

Her eyes sharpened as she shook her head. "This isn't what I meant," she snarled. "I don't want you to treat me like another one of your men. I don't want you to fuck me just to get me to do your bidding. Don't use your body as a weapon with me."

I arched my eyebrow, full seductress now. "And what if I just want you simply because I'm sad and lonely and it feels good to have your skin against mine."

She shuddered, eyes dipping to where my hands slid up my legs and under my skirt. I slid my undergarments off and let them pool at my feet before kicking them away. I lifted a hand to her chest, pushing her back to step into the room and shut the door. Maez's eyes guttered as I held her gaze.

She shook her head. "This will just be one more thing you regret in the morning."

"Or is it something *you'll* regret?"

"I don't regret anything."

"If I do, I'll deal with it then. Because right now, I don't care."

Her eyes widened with intrigue, the dark hair falling across her brow. "What?"

"I don't care anymore," I said. "I want you right now and I don't want to think about the world and our mating bond and forever. I want you to touch me. I want my body to belong to you again."

Her smile turned wicked. "And if this once again ends in tears?"

"It doesn't matter," I cut in. "Who cares if I cry afterward—you certainly don't. You want all of me? Have it. Fuck me."

She cocked her head, lust morphing her face. "You're starting to sound a lot like me, Princess."

"And you love it, mate," I purred, watching her smile widen as I prowled closer, stopping when my skirt brushed the leather of her trousers. "So are we just going to stand here, or—"

Maez's hands shot out and she grabbed me by the waist. Stumbling backward toward the bed, she hastily sat, yanking me into her lap. Her mouth collided with mine, barely having time to close her smiling lips before our teeth knocked together. She moaned against my mouth as her hand skimmed up my leg and squeezed my bare ass. She was so damned pleased with herself.

So was I.

I rocked against her, enjoying the friction of her rough leathers as her tongue explored my mouth.

"I fucking love your body," she said, hands roving up and down my curves as if they couldn't decide where to settle. "I love every dip and curve and dimple."

Her kiss was so deep and all-consuming that every other fear drifted to the back of my mind. As she kissed her way down my neck and started kneading my breast with her rough fingers, I threw my head back.

"Yes," I whispered like a prayer to the Moon Goddess high above us.

There was not a shred of doubt in me now. I wanted this. I wanted her. Desperately.

"Briar." She groaned against my lips, balling handfuls of my dress in her grip and guiding my hips against her.

I loved the way she said my name, like she spoke to the deepest part of me, the part beyond the roles we played, just one soul to another, however dark and twisted—it was just her and me now.

Maez leaned back, dropping into the soft pillows behind her. Her tight grip on my hips guided me forward farther and farther until I was straddling her head. I gasped, rising up on my knees, afraid I was going to be too rough with her. But her grip just tightened on me, and she pulled me down against her open mouth.

I cried out as her tongue lapped at my clit. The feeling from this position was so overwhelming I keeled forward, needing to grip onto the headboard to keep from shattering.

My thighs trembled trying not to suffocate Maez as her tongue lashed over my sex, but she was having none of it.

"Sit." Maez pulled me down against her mouth harder until I was well and truly riding her. "I want to drown in you."

A gasping moan escaped my lips at her heated command. And damn if I didn't want to drown in her, too, to lose myself so fully within her that all I could feel was *us*. The ending and the beginning. Shredding to ribbons every barrier between us, tearing down the last vestiges of doubt until we were consumed by an equal power everlasting.

A deep groan pulled from my lungs as I dropped my forehead against the upholstered headboard, biting into the fabric to keep myself anchored as Maez worked my clit. My whole body pulsed with pleasure as she sucked my swollen bud into her mouth, caressing it with her tongue, feasting on me as if I was her last meal on this earth. I felt weighted down with lead and featherlight all at once, the only thing holding me to the world was her mouth on my body.

I started moving against her, rolling my hips, pushing harder, bolder as I chased my pleasure. Her hands kneaded my ass, encouraging each movement. When she moaned against my throbbing sex, I came, a fierce orgasm tearing through me and I screamed around the fabric gagging my mouth. It was so world-shaking that every cell in my body felt like it ruptured into fizzing wine, melting like candle wax until I was nothing but sensation.

Wave after wave of pleasure rolled through me until I was shuddering, my muscles still beyond my control. My high-pitched gasps slowly ebbed to deep lungfuls of air as I tried to find my way back down into my body and my mind.

It had never been like that before. It had been good—Gods, had it been good—but this was something else, something sacred, something so consuming that it eclipsed anything else.

I crumpled forward, dropping on top of Maez. I propped my chin on her chest to look at her as she wiped my release from her lips with a wolfish grin. I wasn't crying, I wasn't running. I was here, and if she didn't want to kiss the top of my head and hold me, then I didn't care. I would hold her. I would be everything I needed.

I held her gaze, wanting to see the impact of my words as I said, "I will never regret that."

She chuckled, her eyes zipping with emerald delight. "Maybe there's hope for us yet," she said, letting it linger like a suggestion between us.

"Maybe," I taunted. "If you keep doing that to me, I think so."

She propped up on her elbows, her hands encircling my waist. "Oh sweet, little Briar," she crooned. "That is only the beginning."

Then she rolled me and pinned me back down into the mattress.

THIRTY

SADIE

EACH DAY WE TRAVELED NORTHWARD, KEEPING TO THE craggy shoreline and densely packed forests where no human trails existed for miles in any direction. It was slow-moving, often having to cut a path large enough for the wagon to travel through, but we needed to get as close to Highwick without detection as possible . . . which was particularly challenging when we had a giant red dragon in tow.

In the evenings, Haestas took to the sea to hunt upon Navin's instructions, bringing back everything from squid to massive fish to whales. And when the dragon was feeling particularly benevolent, she would share her kills with us, taking the onus off me as the primary hunter of the group.

As we sat around the midday campfire, drying out our rain-sodden clothes, Navin sang a little tune to Haestas as she slept curled up in the clearing, tucking her snout under her leathery translucent wing. I wasn't certain if dragons were nocturnal by nature or if Navin had made Haestas that way. It was much easier to travel covertly with a dragon who hunted at night. No more taking to the skies when the sun was high.

Svenja perched on the log beside me and Timon plopped down beside her. They each ate a bowl of steaming fish stew.

"Not long now," Timon said through a mouthful of food. "We'll be rolling up into Highwick in less than a week."

"Do you think your Queen is ready?" Svenja's eyes darted to mine and then back to her bowl.

I let out a long sigh. I was constantly being peppered with questions from the whispering wells. Calla and I would commune frequently through them. Whenever we stopped at a well, Navin would sing the magical songs, and we'd connect. But so far, Calla's news had been incredibly bleak. The Ice Wolves were a third of their original size, recovering from a civil war that had shaken their pack. They were not the robust military we needed against the Silver Wolves. Even with our natural fighting instincts, the Silver Wolves had been trained since infancy in strategy and formations. We didn't just hunt as a pack, we learned to destroy our enemies as pack, and in a battle of sheer numbers versus skill, skill would win, especially in the home territory of Highwick.

Pressure mounted every day. I knew Calla was counting on the Songkeepers and Haestas to be key players in this attack. My overly confident promises were beginning to feel like lies.

"I think Calla will do everything in their power to secure their throne and help the humans of Aotreas."

"How diplomatic," Svenja replied with a huff. "I don't know why a Wolf queen cares at all whether the humans have a good life or not. No Wolf has cared about us before. Let alone to the extent of being willing to fight a superior foreign power just so humans had freedom."

"No Wolf has ever been like Calla," I said softly.

Svenja snorted. "I've heard that before."

"No, you haven't," Navin cut in.

"The other packs need Nero neutralized just as much as the humans," Asha added, her words confident even with her high squeaky voice.

"Aye. There's more at stake," Timon retorted. "Olmdere can't just shut its borders and watch the rest of Aotreas fall to Nero. Half of the kingdoms on the continent are in disarray while Nero sits pretty on his throne waiting for the world to crumble and seize the ruins. The Golden Court Queen must do something."

I was about to open my mouth to reply they *were* doing something when a scream rang out through the forest. We were all instantly on our feet, Navin's singing cut short. I turned in the direction of the scream and ran.

"Sadie!" Navin shouted after me, muttering a stream of curses, but I didn't care—I kept running.

I narrowed my focus, scenting them in the air: humans. Not good. I prayed the cause of the scream was anything other than Nero's Wolves.

It was only over the side of the next hill that I found them—a group of scraggly-looking humans. One had slipped into a ravine between the hills and was desperately clinging to the clumps of grass on the steep slope to keep them from falling in. I appeared through the trees on the other side of the ravine and judged the distance across—not too far.

The humans all looked at me in unison and froze. I didn't know if they could tell just from the sight of me that I was a Wolf, but if I jumped across the ravine, they surely would.

Still, the slope was too steep for the humans to climb down and rescue the girl. I'd been trained my whole life to make quick decisions, that even the wrong one was better than stalling, and so I decided there was no other choice; I leapt. There was nothing but open air under me for a brief, gut-wrenching second and then I landed on the other side.

The humans gasped at the death-defying jump, but I was focused on reaching the girl before she lost her grip. I grabbed her by the back of her belt and hauled her up into the awaiting arms of an elderly woman. She scooped the girl up and held her tight to her chest, whispering soothing words of comfort.

The Songkeepers started appearing through the forest on the other side of the ravine, shouting at one another to go around and cross closer to the shore. I didn't look back, though, not as I climbed up the rest of the way to flat ground and came face-to-face with a dozen sets of wary eyes.

I had a sudden terrible feeling like I might be shoved back into the chasm.

"Are you one of the Silent Blades?" an elderly man asked. He looked me up and down, his mouth set firmly as he pushed a child behind him.

My brows knit together, and I shook my head. "I am not."

"Don't believe her," another said.

"Why would I save you if I was trying to harm you?" I growled, which only made them all retreat another step. Fucking Moon, I had no finesse in these situations.

Fortunately for me, the Songkeepers finally reached us. Navin practically collided into me, holding me at arm's length to check me for injuries. "Are you okay? What were you thinking?"

"I was thinking I wasn't going to let a child fall to her death," I said, stepping out of his grasp and adding more mildly, "I'm fine."

The humans watched, darting wary looks between us.

"I know you," one of the humans said, pointing to Navin and then spotting Ora in the distance crossing over to them. "Yes. You're part of Galen den' Mora."

"We are," Navin replied, his heavy breathing slowing as he realized the humans weren't going to attack me. "We are traveling northward."

He was met with a chorus of "nos" and admonishments.

"The north isn't safe," the woman who held the girl said. "Nero's Silent Blades are patrolling all of the human towns now. Controlling our food, our words, our prayers. Any dissent and . . ." She looked down at the girl and decided not to finish her sentence. But we knew. We'd seen Nero's destruction when we crossed the border and found Rockford reduced to ash. The stench still clung to me even now. "We cannot survive in Damrienn anymore, but neither are we allowed to flee."

"They told us we could seek refuge in Olmdere only to burn our boats once we were at sea," another said. "We've come from Allesdale and are fleeing to the south, hoping the Wolves won't follow us."

The old man eyed me and lifted a knobby, crooked finger. "Is she a Wolf?"

Navin moved to stand in front of me and I rolled my eyes. "She saved that child's life," he said.

"She will rat us out to her King the second she gets a chance. I knew we weren't safe coming this way."

"We couldn't stay in Allesdale, Fredrick," another replied.

"Nowhere is safe anymore, Alice," the other said. "Not while the tyrant King lives."

"I am trying to kill Nero," I said, stepping out from behind Navin. I could see him cringe at my words. "I would love nothing more than to see him pay for all he's done. I'm Sadie Rauxtide, member of the Golden Court."

Their eyes flew wide at that. "The Golden Court," they whispered amongst one another as if I spoke of some paradise beyond their borders.

"The land of the golden trees," said the elderly woman. "Where humans sit on the Queen's council."

My soul ached at the hollowness in her voice. "It should be that way here, too," I admitted, throat constricting. "You shouldn't have to leave your homeland to be free."

"And who will lead us, then?" the man asked. "What Wolf would take the throne of Highwick? Who could we trust to keep such promises."

"Maybe there shouldn't be a throne at all," I muttered.

I thought the humans would cheer, or at least agree with me, but instead, they all seemed disconcerted by that idea. Did they still want the Silver Wolves' protection even now after they'd had generations of anything but? Or did they want human royalty in the Wolves' stead? I didn't know. I was a soldier, and all of this was beyond me.

Ora pinched their side as they hustled over to us. "Come, come, we have a fire going and plenty of stew to share," they said, beckoning the people over. "We will help you find your way to the temple of knowledge. It's hidden in the forest. It will be a safe place for you."

The group murmured their thanks, following Ora's encouragement. They all looked so exhausted they might drop where they stood. Relief crossed their mud-streaked faces at the mention of food and fire.

Ora in their ever-welcoming way started to lead the group to the safer ravine crossing when they paused and looked over their shoulder. "Oh—I should mention." They looked at Navin and then back to the group.

"It's nothing to worry about, but we have a dragon traveling with us."

THIRTY-ONE

BRIAR

THE GROUND SUDDENLY ROSE UP TO MEET ME AND THEN I WAS standing in a giant room, vaulted ceilings of marble and midnight pennants rimmed in gold. High stained glass windows cast the glittering floor in a rainbow hue. I dreamed of one day traveling to the floating palace of Rikesh, but I had never imagined it abandoned.

"You see," Maez said, gesturing around the empty echoing space. "There's no one here anymore. He's defenseless."

I was still wobbly on my feet as her black boots clicked across the floors. The place seemed frozen in time, like the stillness after a hurricane.

"You think Tadei is the only survivor? They can't *all* be gone," I murmured. "The whole pack? They didn't leave anyone behind to guard their King? Surely some survived."

Maez's eyes roved the walls. "Where do you think the King of these ruins is now? My guess would be hiding in a tower," she said, not really listening to me.

My trailing footsteps paused. "Are you going to kill him?"

"I'm debating it," she replied coolly. "It would certainly help the Golden Court for him to be gone."

"It would help the Golden Court more if we joined them in their fight," I pushed. The urgency of the looming battle of

Highwick made my nerves spike. "Let's kill Nero first. And once we win, *then* I will happily watch you gut Tadei." Maez shot me a look, clearly annoyed we were having this argument again. "If not for that, then why did you bring me here?"

"You said you've always wanted to see Rikesh." She flourished a hand down the dusty hallway. "Welcome to Rikesh, Princess."

We wandered the vacant halls, spilling into an atrium. The doors to the gallery beyond were thrown open, the walls bare and the pedestals empty. Shattered glass covered the floor, the place clearly looted. The eerie stillness made the hairs on my arms raise.

"I'm glad the humans got to take some part of this place," Maez mused, staring up at a splintering hole in the trellis that looked like a rock had been thrown through it.

"I'm surprised they haven't taken up residence here," I said. "There must be dozens of rooms—"

Maez swept her foot through a pool of dried blood, smearing the burgundy stain across the tiles. "Why would they want to live in the location of a massacre?" Maez asked. She spoke of it as if the massacre were a long time ago, as if it didn't happen recently *by her hand*. "This palace is cursed. Better to level it, I think." She flicked her wrist, and her emerald magic appeared. "Do you think I should help them?"

"Wait!" I said, holding my hand up to her. "Listen."

I tipped my head to the far hallway where I heard the scuffle of sandals. Maez and I followed the sound to a dead end with only a single door beside it, buckets and crates stacked on either side. Probably a closet.

Maez moved toward it first, but I grabbed her by the shoulder and pulled her back.

"Let me handle this," I whispered. "I'd like to get some answers without anyone pissing themselves."

She looked absolutely smug, her static magic crackling around her as she said, "Am I really that scary?"

I rolled my eyes. "That wasn't meant to be a compliment."

"I'll still take it as one."

I held a hand to her stomach, trying to hold her back. Maez scoffed and took another step, my sandals skidding across the tiles as she easily moved me just to prove that she could.

"Okay, you're a very scary sorceress," I said mockingly. "What if I promise to let you murder them if they're an enemy? Then will you stay put?"

"I have a lot of ideas running through my head right now about ways to change that tone," she said, her eyes hooding with lust. She nodded to the door behind me. "But go be the diplomat first, Princess. Then I'm going to pile together every last bit of treasure in this abandoned palace and fuck you atop it."

My mouth went bone-dry, my cheeks burned as my body filled with heat at that promise, one I was suddenly desperate to fulfill. She made me ravenous and wild. It took me several moments to regroup enough to turn back toward the door and my original mission. Maez snickered at me as I smoothed down my dress. Gods, she loved to rattle me. I put an extra swish in my hips to make sure she felt equally as rattled and was rewarded by a little groaning sound lodging in Maez's throat.

I turned and sauntered to the door, trying to contain the wild version of myself that Maez pulled out of me.

The second I opened the door a human woman appeared on her knees, her hands clasped and pleading. "Please, please don't hurt me," she begged. Ice doused my libido at that. "I will take you to the pups. Please."

I held up a gentle hand and lowered it, moving extra slowly so she knew I meant no harm. "I'm not going to hurt you."

Her wide saucer eyes darted over my shoulder and then back to me, my blue eyes, my red hair. "Are you . . . the Crimson Princess?"

"Wow, that name has really stuck, huh?" Maez muttered from behind me. "Tell her what it means now, love."

I offered the woman a gentle smile, ignoring the comment. "I am," I said. "Please stand. I won't hurt you."

I would probably need to say it at least a dozen more times

before she started to believe me. Then I remembered something else she said.

"The pups?" I asked. "Where are they?"

"Are you going to put them with the others?" she asked, trembling. "Are you going to hurt them?"

"No," I said, cocking my head at her. "You . . . you are protecting them?"

She nodded. "I am, Your Highness."

Maez appeared beside me and the woman cowered again. "Why?" she snapped. "Why help the Wolves?"

I rolled my eyes and turned toward Maez. I put a hand on her side and forced her backward, hissing, "Let me handle this, please?"

"They're only children," the woman was responding. "They aren't responsible for the evils of their parents."

"And the parents? Where are the rest of the Onyx Wolves? Have any survived?"

"All those old enough to fight are gone," she said. "Broken up into two factions by order of King Tadei."

"How do you know all of this?" I asked.

"I worked in the nursery, Your Highness," she answered. "The walls have ears in this place and the staff likes to talk. Well, that was before . . ."

"And where are the pups now?"

"Most of them gone, the staff took them, left to their homes in the city and on other islands." She looked embarrassed as she added, "They took what treasures they could carry as well and left."

"Two factions, you said," I continued. "We know of the one going to Taigoska. The other?"

"West," she said. "They are sweeping up toward Highwick to join King Nero's war."

"Gods." I swallowed thickly. "The pups?" I asked, my mind snagging on something the woman had told us. "You asked if we were going to put them with the others—what others?"

Her eyes flared and she pointed a shaking finger to the ceiling. "King Tadei has taken them." Her voice cracked. "They're barricaded in the southern tower with him."

My stomach curdled and Maez took a decided step toward the stairwell. I grabbed her by the wrist to stall her.

"Go back to wherever it is you came from," I told the woman. "And send word. There will be more young ones to look after soon."

The woman scurried past, keeping her eyes locked on Maez until she was far down the hall.

"Let's go find the tower," I said, pulling her wrist from my grip. "We'll rescue the pups and then we head to Damrienn to join Calla's fight."

"Damrienn?" Maez sidled over to me and swept her hands up my curves. "I've made other promises to you."

"You can't be serious." I looked at her like she'd grown two heads. "Those promises can wait," I muttered. "I know you don't want to face him, but we must help in this fight."

"We have no business in Damrienn."

"Maez," I snapped. "Grae is your cousin. Sadie is your friend."

"I don't have friends anymore," she said. "I am not so weak. I have told you I won't intervene in this, Princess. I will do what I can from here and be happy of it. It is more than any sorcerer has done before.

"I am *not* fighting for the Golden Court."

"But you have to!" I blustered. "People we love could die."

"People *you* love could die," she countered, then sighed, almost weary. "How many times do I have to tell you all this?" She shook her head. "Do you want me to go drop you off on the battlefield like I did in Taigos? I offered you a chance to join your twin and take up arms against Damrienn and you chose to stay with me. *This*," she said, gesturing up and down her body, "is *me*."

It was. And yet despite everything, it wasn't. I was changing, yes. But not so completely that I was a whole other person. I didn't think it was the same for her, either. The darkness she embodied—

the darkness I was starting to embrace—could be strength and bravery and justice, too. The righteousness of a sharpened blade. This power didn't need to equate to indifference. I just needed to make her see it.

"I chose you," I said. "I *still* do. But damn it, Maez, we need to go help them!"

"I am never returning to Damrienn again," she said definitively.

"You returned to save me," I countered.

"Because you are mine, Briar," she said. "And I would go to the ends of the world for you. But don't ask me to return again."

I rocked back on my heels at that. She would go to the ends of the world for me. That should be enough. It had to be enough. She loved me, even if she didn't have the words to say it. I was hers and she was mine, and still . . . *still* I needed more from her.

I tried to hide the pain of it, the fear, that she was unwilling to help them. Maez was so powerful, so strong, she could annihilate the Silver Wolves just as she had in Taigos. There was nothing to fear except the ghosts of her past. But she chose not to go, and I had no control over that decision. It had been foolish of me to think I could sway her. I knew I could push her forever and she wouldn't budge.

"To the tower, then," I said, holding her gaze. "At least we can end one evil king."

"That's a plan we can agree on." Her eyes alighted with mischief, and she held out a hand. "Lead the way, Princess."

WE CUT THROUGH THE ROOMS IN SEARCH OF THE NEW KING. The top floor of the palace was a twisting labyrinth of doors, hard to navigate. And in each room, we found more maids and young pups, the children surrounding the King's chamber like rings of a tree, protecting their King with his most vulnerable.

"Who uses their young as shields?" I growled, looking around one of the anterior rooms where a human servant wrapped her arms around three cowering pups.

"Sick, evil men," Maez growled back. "I'm not going to hurt you," she added tightly to the Wolf pups who flinched at the shooting sparks of her angry magic. "My lightning will carve up a much more appropriate host."

"Get them out of here," I said to the human servant. "Take them and whatever gold you can carry into the villages. Raise them better than the ones before them."

I said it over and over to every carer who'd listen. Sending them from the squalor of the beautiful rooms that had rotted under their confinement. The farther from Tadei, the better.

Maez had told me the way the King had leered at Sadie, of the failed marriages and wives who'd barely escaped . . . and of those who didn't. And I knew then why when she swore she didn't care for anyone but the two of us, she was determined to put an end to this King: she'd lived through this story before.

We got to the last antechamber. This one only filled with mountains of treasure like a dragon hoarding its wealth.

"He uses his young to protect his gold," Maez snarled. She grabbed a burlap bag and began stuffing it with jewels and coins.

"What are you doing?"

"I'm taking a souvenir."

"You've come for treasure?"

"I've come to kill the Onyx Wolf King," she said. "But stealing his treasure is far more satisfying than pissing on his grave. He will have no need of these riches now."

"We don't need this treasure," I said. "Let the humans keep it."

Maez shrugged. "I'll leave most of it to them, just a token for me."

"Maez—"

But Maez wasn't listening. She dropped her bag of spoils at the last door and kicked it in. A pathetic yelp sounded when the door banged open.

The place looked ravaged by a madman. The bed upturned like a barricade, shredded open with feathers strewing from the spilling guts of the stuffing. It reeked of piss and shit, the windowless room unable to throw the excrement out. A lone candle was burnt nearly to the nub.

Two bloodshot eyes peeked up from behind the overturned bed frame. Pupils blown so wide that they nearly consumed the sockets, hollow faced, the effects of the mountain flower evident even without its sickly-sweet cloying scent filling the air. Drugged half out of his mind, Tadei watched us.

"Come to finish the job, you monster?" he asked, but his voice was only filled with fear, no heat of venom left in it without his many guards to protect him.

"Everyone uses that word as if there's only one definition. Take a look in a mirror, *King*. Look how pathetic you've become in only a few short weeks," Maez said with a click of her tongue. "Only babes to protect you now."

"You can have them," he said all too quickly. "Take them, they're yours. A trade for my life."

I let out a little snarl, and Maez took another step forward, the brightness of her magic illuminating the shadowed room.

"You are truly loathsome, *Your Majesty*," she said.

"They—they're all gone," he whispered. "All of them. My pack dead or stolen by Nero to fight his own battles and not for their King. He convinced me to send every last one somehow," the King rambled, his voice tinged with madness. "I don't know what spell he cast over me to compel me to do so. The power he wields now . . . But what about me? What of my power? He's going to steal my crown, isn't he? He's going to take my gold."

"Your gold should be the least of your concerns," Maez growled.

"I-I'm all alone now. Please. Please don't kill me."

"You're begging me?" Maez asked, cocking her head.

He instantly dropped to his knees. "Yes, yes, please. I beg you. Spare me."

Maez threw her head back and laughed, the sound making

Tadei flinch again. "You know, I've heard many things about you in my time, Tadei," she said. "I heard you were quite fond of making people beg." His eyes grew even wider at the accusation. "Tell me, did you ever show them mercy?"

"Please—"

"No," Maez cut him off as bile rose up my throat. "It turned you on, didn't it?"

"Mercy, please—"

"You don't know the meaning of mercy."

Tears streamed down Tadei's face as he blubbered, begging and pleading that Maez spare him.

"Silence!" Maez shouted and Tadei abruptly stopped. She wandered over, nose wrinkling, and she stooped in front of him to meet his watery eyes. "One day, Tadei, your death will feed my power. Your soul will give me enough magic to end another dozen just like you." His whole body trembled violently. "But I will spare you today."

My mouth fell open in surprise as Tadei collapsed in relief, sobbing his thanks.

Maez turned and looked at me, and there was nothing but hatred in her eyes as she said, "Let's go."

"But—"

"Let's. Go." Low and lethal. She stepped back to let me go first, stooping to blow out Tadei's candle as she went.

I walked out of the room, and she closed it behind us, leaving the sobbing pathetic King in the dark.

"I don't understand . . ."

Maez ignored me as she picked up the bag of treasures and slung it over her shoulder. She surveyed the walls. "You know it took hundreds of years for builders to place each of these stones," she said, and I turned to her with a questioning look. "Hundreds more for them to paint every tile. And yet with one flick of my wrist, I can undo what took hundreds of years with a single burst of power."

She turned her hand over, emerald sparks shooting out so

bright I had to shield my eyes. And when I lowered my hand again . . .

The doorway was gone. Only a smooth wall of beautiful, intricate tiles, not even the slightest inconsistency or crack to denote old from new. It was as if the door to the King's chamber never existed.

I gasped—not at the result, but at the show of power. At the ingenuity of her actions. This was vengeance. Not only was Maez killing an evil king, this was one small ounce of retribution for what had happened to her so many years ago.

"Briar," Maez rasped my name, and I looked down to see the hand she offered out to me.

I looked back up at the wall in surprise as I heard the faint screams and bangs from the door beyond. But instead of gaping in horror, a smile curled the edges of my lips.

Maez held my harsh gaze, but I didn't shrink from this darkness. My surprise morphed to glory until I basked in it. How many more would be saved by her—my Goddess of Vengeance? I knew I would never blame Maez again for taking that dark magic, for using it like this. If anything, I wanted her to use it more. A rueful smile split Maez's lips as I stepped into her side and took her hand, leaving the King of the Onyx Wolves to die in his pitch-black tomb.

THIRTY-TWO

CALLA

I SAT WITH MY BACK TO THE WHISPERING WELL, FIDDLING WITH a tattered sprig of fallen holly. I'd told Mina to head back without me, that I just needed a moment, and a moment turned into several. My legs were numb from sitting on the bare ice by the time Grae found me.

"I'm guessing the conversation with Sadie didn't go particularly well?" he asked as his shadow rose up my legs.

Unlike me, Grae had been smart enough to wear a thick fur-lined cloak. My mate spread the cloak out beside me and crouched, wrapping one arm around my waist to slide me across onto the fur lining. I let out a little hum as he pulled me into his side, and I leaned into his warmth. I hadn't realized how cold I was until he arrived. I was so stuck in my head, I'd forgotten to live in my body.

"They found a group of humans seeking refuge in the south," I said, feeling the weight of each human victim stacking atop me like a poisoned stone. "It's only getting worse. I fear Nero won't stop until there are no humans left." Grae's grip on me tightened as I cleared my throat, trying to push away the haunting images Sadie had left conjured in my mind. Every time I felt like we might have a pause to regroup, to strategize, I was once again reminded of Nero's boot on all our necks. "How was the training with Verena? Do you think they'll be ready?"

Grae let out a long sigh, which did nothing to assuage my worries. "They will be as ready as they can be," he said. "They weren't trained like the Silver Wolves. No amount of practice now will replace a lifetime's worth of skill . . . But it will have to be enough."

My stomach soured. It was not the news I needed. We were leaving the following day to start our journey toward the Stormcrest Ranges. We had orchestrated with Sadie that our attack would take place three days before the full moon in the hopes that the Silver Wolves were waiting to take advantage of the full moon to reinvigorate their powers. We'd been shifting every night, getting our strength, preparing for battle, but normally, the week before the full moon was when Wolves were at their most diminished . . . which was why we were bringing more than just Wolves.

"It will have to be enough," I echoed. "Surely a dragon will help?"

"Surely." Grae chuckled beside me. "And my father's arrogance. I doubt he thinks we will go on the offensive and strike first this time. No one dares attack Highwick. We have the element of surprise."

"And the songs," I added with a shake of my head. "We have the songs. I can't believe the Songkeepers found a magic that can control Wolves. Imagine our soldiers cutting through a line of Wolves who are unable to fight or move."

"I'm happy to imagine it . . . so long as we stay far, far out of earshot."

"Agreed." I laughed lightly. I leaned into Grae farther, letting him take my body weight as he reclined against the well. "It is a concern, though. If Rasil and those other Songkeepers learn of that power, it could destroy the Wolves."

Grae squeezed my shoulder. "One worry at a time, little fox."

"First Nero, then the rest of it," I said wearily. "The humans of Damrienn can't wait another moon for us to save them. There may be none left."

Grae kissed my temple. "You are incredible, you know that?"

"I feel far from it," I admitted. "But we can't stop now. We can't hide and wait for Nero to pick us off one by one, so we must fight."

"Together, we will succeed." Grae swept a comforting hand up and down my arm. "Especially if Maez joins us."

My heart sank a little on hearing that. "I've received another letter from Briar." I let that sentence linger in the air between us as I pulled the crumpled letter from my pocket. It had magically appeared there only moments before we communed through the well and I was still processing the message.

"Will they come to our aid?" Grae asked and I hated the hopefulness in his voice. Maez would've never left him in doubt before she took the dark magic. The only blood relative he still had, and his cousin was a stranger to him now. It made me want to skewer her for making my mate feel that way, let alone my twin.

I looked up at the sky and shook my head. "I still don't know," I said. "What are they even doing, hiding in the mountains of Valta?"

"Valta?"

"Her letter makes it seem like they won't be joining the battle in Highwick, but it's strange. She said they intend to visit Rikesh, that we don't need to worry about the Onyx King anymore at least . . ."

"I don't even want to know what that means."

"Nor I, but if Tadei is dead, that's one less enemy to worry about." I sighed and leaned my cheek against Grae's shoulder. "It brings me some comfort to think that if it all goes poorly, Briar is safe, that she will live on. The last Gold Wolf in all of existence."

Grae squeezed me tighter. "Perhaps we should work on rectifying that." I looked at him and he hastily added, "If we survive."

"Pups," I said with a little smile. "I could see a miniature version of you tearing up the castle, pink nose and ink-dipped tail."

"And fur of bright gold." He let out a laugh, his steaming breath curling into the frozen air. "It feels like an impossible dream right now," he murmured. "But maybe one day it won't."

"Maybe one day," I said, curling into him. "Maybe one day we'll permit ourselves to dream of our little pack running beneath the golden trees." I let out a grumble as I untwined myself from Grae's arms and stood, extending my hand back to him to help him up. "But first we've got to start a war . . . and win."

THIRTY-THREE

BRIAR

THE SCENT OF JASMINE RAMBLING THROUGH THE WINDOWS greeted me first.

Home.

This castle in the sky was everything I wanted it to be—a sanctuary, an oasis, a reprieve from the horrors of the rest of the world. It lulled me in, making me forget the land below and the responsibilities beyond it. Maybe I could be like Maez. Maybe I could forget the world beyond me existed. Maybe with enough time and practice, I could just be selfish and have something just as good.

"Going back to your room?" Maez asked from where she lounged on the bed, sifting through the mounds of treasure she'd spread across it like a gilded blanket.

It was only then I realized that I was staring at the door, unmoving.

I put a hand on my hip, the fabric already crumpled from our escapades around Rikesh. I turned back to Maez. "I don't want my own room," I announced.

Her eyes lit up at that, green magic sparking around her.

"What do you want?" she asked, a catlike grin stretching over her face as she studied me.

"I want to stay here with you," I said, defiantly squaring my shoulders and firmly planting my bare feet on the tiled floor. "Will you move my things in here?"

She snapped her fingers. "Done."

I leaned my weight side to side. "That's okay, isn't it?" My bravado wavered. "Me being here?"

This is what I wanted—to be selfish, to claim what I wanted, to surrender to this little world we created and pretend nothing else existed.

Maez's smile widened. "It is more than okay, Princess."

She prowled off the bed, grabbing me by the hips and spinning me so I landed on the treasure. Coins jingled and jewels clinked together as I bounced on the mattress.

"Look at you," she said, taking me in. "You look good splayed out on a bed of jewels."

"Better than in the blood of my enemies?" I taunted.

"With some minor adjustments," she purred, leaning forward and unclasping the shoulder pins of my dress. She yanked the fabric down leaving me bare before her. "Better."

My chest rose and fell at that hungry look in her eyes.

She grabbed one of the pearl necklaces and lifted it over her head. She draped the beads over my naked body, trailing them over my breasts and belly and down toward my core. When she got to my pussy, she grabbed the other end of the necklace.

I rose on my elbows. "What are you doing?"

She looked up at me with a wicked grin and commanded, "Lie back down."

She parted my sex with the taught strand of pearls, the smooth round balls dragging over my clit. That rolling rhythm made me gasp. She moved them faster, making me vibrate with the feeling of them.

"Do you like that?" she asked as I grabbed handfuls of silken sheets for purchase.

"Yes," I moaned as she pulled the necklace over me slower

and faster and slower again, torturing me. My back arched off the bed, the sensation so different, so all-consuming it was already pushing my body toward an orgasm. "That feels so good."

At my words, Maez stopped, and I let out a whimper. I rose back on my elbows to watch as she lifted the pearls to her mouth, cleaning one bead with her tongue and then another, sucking along the string. She hummed.

"Delicious," she crooned. Her eyes drifted past me and her smile widened.

She prowled onto the bed. Kissing me, her tongue sweeping over mine and letting me taste my own desire. I took advantage of her position, unbuckling her belt and yanking down her trousers. She barely had time to kick them off before I sat up and dropped my mouth to her pussy. My hands wrapped around her legs, kneading her ass as I pulled her sex against my tongue.

Maez's head dropped back as she grabbed my hair, rocking her hips into me with a groan. Her knees leaned into the bed frame as if the feeling was too good and she couldn't hold herself up. I licked her in quick circles, knowing exactly what made her come undone. I laved my tongue over her clit as she rocked into my mouth.

I had thought I would bring her to the edge and leave her wanting, just as she had done to me, but as she tightened her grip on my hair, I knew I wouldn't. I wanted to feast on her, wanted to make her unravel and come against my mouth, wanted to hear her sweet moans as I brought her a pleasure no one else could.

I worked her in that steady rhythm—not too fast, not too slow—letting her take the lead as she pressed into me harder. All at once, she climaxed, coming against my tongue, her ass tightening under my grip as she thrust against my lips. The sounds she made had my own pussy fluttering, wet heat coating my legs.

When she pulled back, there was a black fire in her eyes as if she knew how aching and desperate I was for her. She grabbed me by the waist, flipping me over so I was belly down across her gold. Maez spread my knees wider across the bed, pulling my hips back and my pussy against her waiting tongue. She gave me one long lick and hummed.

"You're so wet for me, Princess."

I could only let out a strangled sound of agreement as she plucked a long smooth emerald from the bed. She trailed the gem down my back, tracing it across my spine as I trembled in anticipation. When she pressed the tip of the precious stone to my core, I swallowed thickly, and when she started to push it inside me, I clawed at the bedsheets.

"That's it," she purred. I felt her kneel on the bed behind me, her thighs hitting mine as she pushed the stone deeper. "You take my treasure like such a good girl."

I moaned as she pulled it out and thrust it back in again faster. "Maez," I panted, desperately clinging to bed as she began to fuck me in earnest.

"Yes. Say my fucking name."

Her thighs slapped against mine and I wondered if she was holding that stone to her clit, fucking me while pleasuring herself with it. My pussy dripped, my thighs slick with the sensation of her pushing in and out, pumping that gemstone into my eager body. When her other hand snaked around to rub my clit, I cried out. The feel of it was so overwhelming.

"What am I to you?" She panted, rubbing faster. "Say it."

"My mate," I moaned. "You're my mate."

Maez bent forward, curling over my back, her breasts rubbing against my bare skin, and I could hear in her ragged breaths that she was close again, too. She thrust the emerald into me, holding it there deep inside of me, stretching me until my eyes were rolling back. She moved against it, rubbing herself again and again against the rounded edge of the oblong and the heel of her hand gripping it. Her fingers kept circling me as my inner muscles squeezed against the stone.

I felt so light and weighted with lead all at once, my vision spotting.

"Yes," I groaned as her fingers worked me faster.

Maez's breaths grew more sharp, her breathing frantic as she began moving again, fucking me through her own release. The feeling of that stone pumping in and out again had me toppling over the edge.

I screamed, my eyes going dark as I bit down into the silken sheets and let her ride me through the most explosive orgasm I'd ever had in my entire life. My soul seemed to tear apart and reform, the sensation so overwhelming that Maez's hand on my clit was the only thing keeping me from collapsing back down onto the bed. Wave after wave she pulled out of me, one orgasm colliding into another, feeling like I might never come back down.

My mind was blank, my body jelly, when she finally released me and I dropped against the coins and silk sheets, panting and ecstatic.

"I take back everything I said," I panted into the sheets. "We definitely, definitely needed this treasure."

Maez chuckled, slowly pulling the emerald out of my happily sore pussy and tossing it onto the bed. She dropped beside me and gathered me into her arms, and the feeling of my skin against her own soothed me. *She was holding me.* She hadn't done that in so long, and Sweet Moon, it felt so good. It was like its own homecoming the way her fingers trailed down my back.

Yes. Maybe I could be selfish. Maybe I could have this. Maybe nothing else mattered. I'd turn my soul into her same shade of darkness until we were once again one and the same.

THIRTY-FOUR

SADIE

WE MOVED BY THE LIGHT OF THE MOON, NAVIN DRIVING THE oxen while I hopped off the wagon every few minutes to clear the path northward. We had three days to be in Highwick and ready to battle. Every night was filled with those hypnotic songs. Navin and Ora had begun teaching them to the others, but still, Navin refused to let anyone control me but him. And I, for one, didn't mind. He and I had always made the most sense when we were tangled up in bed together. A human and a Wolf. A magician and his song.

And oh the songs he made me sing when our bodies were intertwined.

Our love existed in this singular moment, the future not promised. And if we did survive the next three days, what then? Would I spend my life traveling, never planting down roots? Would I even be able to grow those roots in Olmdere, bored and idle? The training for this battle provided a much-needed reprieve from such questions.

"Those humans," I said to the moonlight, shaking my head. The words hung in the cool night's air. Navin's chin bobbed from where he sat on the wagon bench beside me.

We'd had to quicken our pace northward after taking the humans to the temple of knowledge, but doubling back for them had been the right thing to do. They were so shaken up; they needed our guidance and the soothing songs sung around campfires that healed them of wounds we could not see and lulled them to sleep.

"I know," Navin murmured. "I won't forget the looks on their faces for a long, long time."

When we arrived at the temple, they were all so relieved, some even burst into tears. Others just warily surveyed the place, too broken and hollow to ever trust they'd be safe again.

"I'm going to gut Nero myself," I hissed. "You sing him still and I'll plunge my knife into his belly."

"Not your teeth?"

"No. I don't want him to die like a Wolf."

Navin nodded. "Deal."

I rubbed the back of my neck and stared down at my shadowed boots. "Do you think the Songkeepers are ready?"

I knew the weight of leading his people into battle was heavy on him. So few Songkeepers existed, and now they were battling between themselves, along with the Wolves, the humans collateral between them. No beings in Aotreas were safe anymore.

"They know the songs."

"Why does that not actually comfort me?" I muttered. "If they manage to control the Wolves to our advantage, great, but what if one of them goes rogue and decides to join with Rasil? Or decades from now decides they want to use that magic for their own gains? Wolves could be ended forever."

"Not ended," Navin countered. "Maybe they'd have to stay in their human forms more often, though. Even with all of my force behind it, you cannot be easily controlled by my magic in your human form—well, not unless you want to be," he added ruefully.

"And oh how I want to be." I released a sultry chuckle.

Navin's hand landed on my knee and slid up to the top of my thigh before squeezing it.

The oxen stopped, and I sighed, wishing we could have a

little more time to let Navin's hand explore up my leg and down into the waistband of my trousers. But our life was nothing but a constant string of interruptions.

I grabbed the sword from under the bench seat and prepared to hack away at the vines and underbrush blocking the trail. But when I climbed off the wagon, I found there was nothing in our path.

I searched the darkness, sword aloft. "What is it?"

The oxen seemed firmly planted where they stood. I blinked, trying to hone my vision to make out shapes in the shadows. To our right was the dense forests of northeastern Damrienn and to our left was the rocky cliffside that dropped to the ocean far below. The moon glinted off the rolling sea, but I saw nothing along the cliff's edge.

"Is everything okay?" Navin called.

I strained my ears, attuning to the nighttime sounds. "I don't know."

I heard a twig snap and then rustling leaves. Could be a deer, or maybe a bear, judging by how spooked the oxen were?

A black shadow shot out across the path and a set of luminous eyes reflected the moonlight back at me. My stomach dropped to my boots.

Shit.

"Wolves!" I screamed. "We're under attack!"

The last word died on my lips as I shifted.

I shot forward, plowing into the first Wolf as howls rent the air. The Wolf yelped and dashed back into the forest before I could get a good look at him. My fight training took control as I assessed the attackers and terrain. I circled, searching the darkness. How many of them were there? Gods, I scented at least a dozen.

Fuck. A dozen? That wouldn't be good.

I heard Navin scramble back into the wagon behind me, shouting and waking the other Songkeepers.

"Well, you wanted to practice your song on Wolves, Kian,"

Navin barked as he and his brother emerged out the back of the wagon. "Now's your chance."

Another Wolf flashed past me, and I launched forward, bowling into it and sinking my teeth into its side.

A chorus of instruments—string and brass and wood—all rose up from behind me as I dug my teeth into the scruff of the Wolf underneath me, shaking my maw and tearing fur from flesh. The Wolf yowled as my mouth filled with the metallic tang of his blood.

The song rose in volume, echoing through the night. The pull of the magic was a familiar tug to me now. I had strengthened my resolve against it, but still, the power of so many Songkeepers pulled me under.

"Jump off the cliffs," it sang to me.

I looked to the left, to the jagged cliffs that dove down, down, down to the sea. The smallest Wolf stood no chance, immediately bolting over the side while others dug their paws into the earth and tried to resist the command.

"Jump off the cliffs," it urged me.

I started to rise on shaking legs before catching myself and shifting back to my human form. The relief was instant. I rose, returning to where my shredded clothes were on the path. But I wasn't in search of modesty.

I was in search of my knives.

Another Wolf, then another, jumped over the side like bolting deer running straight into the jaws of a waiting lion.

But eventually some had the instinct to shift. Except when they did, I was there. Bringing my knives down on them, I didn't give them a chance to get their whereabouts before I slit their throats. Blood sprayed the air, the night filled with violent song. Unfortunately there were too many Wolves, and even with the powerful song, it was clear I was soon going to be overrun. Navin's song broke from the others. He dropped his lastar to the ground and ran out to join me in the fray.

Shadowed bodies converged on us as we tried to battle them

backward. I swiped one's side as a fist collided with my jaw. I staggered back, my leg sweeping out. There were too many of them. Someone in the group must've spoken into their minds, must've warned them to shift. The sharp trill of Navin's whistle cut above the chaos, desperately calling for Haestas, but as a press of bodies towered over me, I heard Navin cry out in pain.

I screamed as a bare foot stomped hard on my chest, knocking the air out of me. Blinding pain shot through me as my rib cracked and ligaments snapped. If I shifted to heal, I'd be overcome with the Songkeepers' commands. I curled onto my side, trying to find a less vulnerable position from the ceaseless onslaught of blows.

Get up. Get up. Get up!

Arrows whizzed by me and I knew Asha had moved from her lute to her bow and arrow. My attackers paused at the deluge of arrows. I managed to get one arm under me, unable to breathe with the crushing pain lancing through my sternum. Then I heard Asha's high-pitched scream, and the arrows stopped flying.

I took in a stabbing breath, trying to shield my face from the renewed attack of pummeling fists. The world spun as I clung to consciousness . . .

A fireball erupted in front of me, snapping me back into reality. My skin sizzled, the heat whooshing over my bloodied bare skin. The light was so bright I couldn't see. I held up a hand against the flaring illumination as all of a sudden the night was engulfed in flames.

And then I heard her.

Haestas screeched overhead, burning a protective circle of fire around us. Navin rushed to me, one limp arm hanging grotesquely by his side. With his good hand, he hauled me to my feet. "Are you okay?"

I nodded, holding a pained hand to my side. "Nothing shifting won't fix. You?"

"I think I broke my arm," he said, wincing as he held the limp appendage. There was no thinking about it; it was a clean break.

Navin looked up into the night sky and I followed his line of sight to where Haestas circled overhead. Her ferocious golden eyes glowed like violent stars as they tracked the carnage below.

"One got away," Navin gritted out.

He whistled to Haestas, the tune unfamiliar to my ears, and she let out a rumble, seemingly wanting to disobey his command. He whistled again, and with a final chuff of curling smoke, she flew out over the forest in the direction of the fleeing Wolf.

My eyes dropped to the ebbing wall of flames, and I searched the destruction all around us. So many charred bodies, the trees and brambles still ablaze . . .

"Only a single Silver Wolf survived," I whispered.

"Those aren't Silver Wolves," Navin replied.

I gasped, studying the bodies more keenly, the tatters of inky black fur. "Those are Onyx Wolves. In the middle of Damrienn." My mouth fell open as I surveyed the carnage. "That explains why they didn't keep to any formation. If they had been Silver Wolves, I don't think we would've won so easily."

"Easily?" Navin groaned, holding his arm.

I turned back to Galen den' Mora. The Songkeepers all stood gaping at the destruction Haestas had wrought. If she hadn't come . . .

Finally Kian's eyes drifted from the bodies to me, and he let out a low whistle.

Navin instantly stepped in front of me, blocking my naked body from view. I rolled my eyes. I was so covered in dirt and gore there was barely anything to see.

The wind whipped up around us as Navin craned his neck skyward. "Look out!"

With his good arm, he shoved me out of the way as Haestas arced back across the sky. A giant form plummeted from the spot where Navin shoved me: the last Onyx Wolf.

He collided in a heap of brambles, moaning and clutching his side. His face was contorted in pain, blood trailing from his mouth and nose. I knew the look in his eyes, knew he was on the precipice of death.

He screwed his face up. "Just kill me," he begged.

"Why are you here?"

He didn't answer, shifting into his Wolf form to try to heal. With a groan of frustration, I shifted right along with him. The relief was instantaneous, my wounds healing along with the change. Not so for the Onyx Wolf in front of me, scrambling legs and twitching maw battling the throes of death.

"What is an Onyx Wolf doing in Valta?" I pushed again, towering over him and snarling.

"King Tadei commanded us." His eyes shot frantically to and fro. "We were on our way to Highwick when we caught your scent."

My pulse raced. "Why has Tadei sent you to Highwick?"

"To join King Nero's army," the Wolf whined. "I don't know why he did it. He's terrified of Nero. Tadei feeds us to the hungry beast that sits atop the Highwick throne." His frantic movements slowed; his eyes stopped searching. "I knew when I stepped foot in this haunted place, I'd never see my homeland again. This place is covered in a pall of dark magic. I never thought I'd see a dragon . . . never thought I'd die under these strange skies . . ."

The life faded from his eyes before he could finish the thought. Reeling, I shifted back to my human form. Confusion clouded my thoughts as Navin pulled me into his side, hiding me once more from view.

Haestas screeched overhead before flying back out toward the sea.

"You figured out the command," I murmured, staring as her shadow disappeared beyond the clouds.

"I didn't." Navin's voice was strained. "It just came to me."

"Well, we know the songs work," Svenja called, glancing out at the cliffs.

"But we still needed the dragon," Timon countered. "The songs aren't enough on their own."

Navin wrapped his coat around me, and I shrugged it on, stepping out from behind him.

"And what if something happens to the dragon?" Kian cut in. "What if all the Silver Wolves stay in their human forms and Haestas decides she'd rather hunt for deer than turn our enemies to ashes? What then?"

Ora worried their lip, looking out to sea. "We need both," they said, distracted as they repeated what was already said. "And we need all of our songs . . ." Their words died off as they looked at each of us in turn.

"What is it?"

They whirled, searching more frantically. "Where is Asha?"

And then I remembered her scream.

THIRTY-FIVE

BRIAR

I SAUNTERED INTO THE OFFICE IN A SHEER GOSSAMER GOWN, wearing nothing beneath the translucent fabric apart from a thigh belt and a scabbard. Maez sat atop a stool in the corner, sharpening her dagger. I knew blade sharpening was something she could easily do with magic, but I guessed the methodical action was more out of habit than necessity.

Shick, shick, shick . . . The sharpening stopped when she lifted her gaze and saw what I was wearing.

"I want you to bring me someone," I demanded, placing my hands on my hips.

"*Bring you someone?*" she repeated, confused.

I pointedly pulled open the high slit of my dress and stuck my leg out, more prominently displaying the belt holding a single knife against my bare thigh. "Someone deserving of my knife. I need to practice."

"You temptress." Maez's eyes filled with green sparks, her magic delighting in my request. "Whatever tricks do you have up your sleeve?"

"I don't want your magic depleted, darling," I crooned, speaking directly to Maez's power. Lust clouded her gaze at my tone. "Bring me someone to replenish you with. Let me feed your power."

Wicked gratification filled her face as a smug expression crossed mine. I wanted her to see how well I knew her, *all of her*, how well I embraced that darkness, too.

"So you want to play, Briar?"

I licked my canine tooth, knowing how much I was turning her on. "I do."

Maez stood, stretching her neck side to side, before sheathing her sharpened dagger. She wandered to her desk and perched, gripping the edges tightly. "Then let's play."

With a crack of green lightning, a tall, stout man appeared in the space between us. He landed on his feet, hands wide, knees bent as if catching himself from falling.

I sniffed the air, assessing my prey. "A Wolf. Ice judging by the blond hair and the frost still clinging to his boots," I announced to Maez. The man looked between us, dumbfounded, clearly wondering if this was real or a nightmare. My eyes dropped to the weapons on his belt. "A soldier." I scented the ale seeping off him. "And a drunkard. Possibly a defector." My playful gaze slid to Maez. "Was he a bad man?"

She cocked her head. "Does it matter?"

Before I could reply, recognition sparked in his eyes and then a moment later in mine.

"You," he said, brows pinching. "You—you're the Princess. You're supposed to be dead. Nero said—"

"You're one of the soldiers who took me from Taigos," I recalled, remembering his thick blond beard and ruddy cheeks, the same stale breath as in the carriage I was tied up and brought to Nero's castle in. "You delivered me to Highwick."

"He fled to the mountains after Ingrid's death," Maez said mildly. "Now he serves no throne, only the bottom of every barrel of ale. Too cowardly to fight in the Taigosi civil war, hmm? Care to apologize to my mate?"

"Let me handle him." My voice was colored the shade of death.

Maez's smile stretched wider. *Oh how she loved when I*

played her games. Oh how I would have her playing mine all night long once I finished off this man.

The Taigosi drunkard was either too stupid or too arrogant to be fearful. "You can't fault a soldier for following orders," he said, looking between us.

I reached for the blade on my thigh. "I think you'll find I can do whatever I like."

The man's gaze dropped to my bare skin, trailing up to my breasts visible beneath my dress. I laughed with vicious glee as he took me in, and his leering gaze grew wary.

"You know," I hedged. "I always thought of my body as a weapon." Confusion crossed his face, but he continued to stare, drinking in my nakedness. "I thought I was meant to use it to persuade, to suggest, to seduce. But better yet, I can use it to distract."

The blade had left my hand before his eyes ever lifted from my breasts, too hypnotized to dodge my strike. My knife embedded in the meat of his thigh, and he bellowed out a curse. Ripping the knife from his flesh, he threw it to the side. He balled his hands into fists instead of wisely attempting to stop the loss of blood. Clearly, he'd already lost his senses to the ale.

"You fucking bitch," he seethed.

I shot Maez a look, showing the man I wasn't afraid to take my eyes off him. "I love it when they call me that."

"Indeed," she replied with a laugh.

On swaying feet, he charged me. I ducked and weaved out of the reach of his lumbering arms. He pawed at my shoulder, but my oiled skin slipped from his grip, and I laughed.

Too cavalier.

He moved faster than I expected, and before I could decide my next attack, he backhanded me across the face. My cheek stung, my vision blurring at the periphery as I dropped and grabbed for my discarded knife.

With a sickening crack, the man cried out, the hand that had struck me now twisted at a nauseating angle. I glared at the flicker of magic. Maez was like a mother Wolf maiming a deer for her pups to practice the hunt. But I was no pup.

"Let me handle this myself!" I barked and Maez held up her hands, a smile still stretching from ear to ear.

"Sorry, love," she said mildly. "He's your kill."

"I . . ." the man searched the air around him, panic rising. "I can't shift."

"Another little spell of mine," Maez added with a shrug. "I much prefer to watch you fight in this form."

Focusing more on my approach, I charged at the man again. He squared off on me and took another swing that I darted under, raking my blade across his side. It took a surprising amount of effort to pierce through his clothes. I learned more with each movement, how hard each blow needed to be to inflict damage. There could be no timidity. I sliced him again, cutting a little deeper.

"That's my girl!" Maez cheered. "Use his size against him, the oaf. He is a bull, and you are a snake, Briar. Strike fast."

With that encouragement, I repeated the action, attacking from the side of his injured hand, using more force to stab him between the ribs.

His cry of pain was belabored and watery, the sound telling me I'd pierced a lung. The mountain of a man held a hand to his side as blood wept between his fingers. A glazed confusion slowed his responses.

When I attempted the same tack a third time, though, he'd learned my approach. He grabbed for my throat, his hand too slick with his own blood to grab hold, but his leg stuck out and tripped me, sending me colliding cheek first into the wall.

"Gah!" A tooth cracked, piercing my tongue. My mouth filled with the coppery tang of blood.

"Bring him down, love," Maez whooped, clapping her hands.

I groaned, spitting blood and tooth shard onto the floor as I lifted my knife again. I felt Maez's magic swirling around us. A buzzing pall hung in the air. A power begging me to reach out and toy with it, use it. My resolve grew, my hands clenched, until I was filled with the same burning fire.

The man's chest rattled with the exertion of a deep breath, but still he glared hatefully back.

Fear me, I silently demanded as I ran at him head-on.

To my great satisfaction, his eyes widened in fear as I skidded across the wet stones. He lifted his good arm to clock me, and I crouched, impaling my knife in his groin—deep.

He howled out in pain, blood spraying faster than I'd ever seen before, coating the room in a scarlet mist. Dropping, his kneecaps cracked against the stone. I didn't wait. I punched him, hearing the satisfying crunch as his nose broke. He fell like a stone, eyes rolling back as his life finally drained away.

I toed his lifeless body with my bare foot. Towering over him in victory, I smiled. I was no longer a pawn in a world ruled by men. Between Maez and I, we were now moving all the pieces on the board.

Maez slowly clapped. "Impeccable, darling."

I stooped to the body on the ground, freeing my knife with a wet splat, and wiping it across my dress. Painting myself in blood, I sheathed my blade. Maez's eyes tracked each movement—a carefully choreographed dance just for her, reeling her in.

I held her gaze as I lifted a dripping finger and licked the blood clean.

With that action, Maez moved, storming across the room and pinning me against the wall.

"I am going to be the one to lick every inch of blood off you," she growled, eyes hooded with lust.

I pursed my bloodied lips, taunting her. "I'll allow it."

"You are magnificent." She took a step back to take me in, her hand skimming down my dress and cupping my breast before sliding down my curves. "As if the Goddess carved you out of moonlight to be perfectly mine."

I lifted a hand to trail Maez's sharp jawline and down the column of her neck to wrap my fingers around her throat. I leaned in and kissed her, relishing the sharp pain of my injured lip. She released a rumbling sound, trying to kiss me deeper, but I pulled back, teasing her.

"*This* is who the Goddess wanted for me," I said, flicking my tongue across her bottom lip and pulling away again before she could kiss me. "Just as you are now. Vicious. Bloodthirsty. *Mine.*" My hand constricted around her throat in warning as her lips parted with desire. "Now fuck me until nothing exists except you and I."

Her eyes flashed the most beautiful emerald as she grinned. "As my mate wishes."

THIRTY-SIX

SADIE

THERE WAS NO SUCH THING AS A BEAUTIFUL GRAVE. NO AMOUNT of flowers could be laid upon the freshly turned soil to make the sight sting any less. My heart filled with steel and ice as I stared at the mound of earth under which Asha would forever remain. I never taught her how to wield a dagger. Maybe if I had . . .

No. I knew following that line of thought wouldn't do anything to resurrect her. I also knew it wouldn't have made a difference. She was a human, half my size, facing off against dozens of Wolves. If Haestas hadn't arrived when she did, many more of us would be dead. Perhaps all of us.

We gathered in a circle, each taking a turn to share some murmured words. I hadn't known the smallest Songkeeper very long and still I ached with her loss. She had been timid and shy at times, but underneath was a strength and magic enviable to all. She had stood in battle with us, her arrows flying, and had done so until she was cut down. With a little more practice and a few more years, she could've been mighty.

No, I thought again. *She* was *mighty*.

"For Asha," Ora said, lifting their cup to the cloud-covered sky.

"Asha," the others repeated as we all took a drink.

"We will listen for her song in the afterlife. May she sing us to her so that we may sound again as one."

We all took another long drink, liquor burning fire down our throats. I was about to turn toward the wagon when Navin started singing, then Ora, then the others. It was a song I'd never heard before, though the language in which they sang was that of my homeland. Wolves didn't sing burial songs. Our remembrances were never so beautiful.

I huffed, trying to push away the morbid thought. By rebuking human traditions, Wolves didn't only miss out on so much in life, but also in death.

I listened from where I leaned against a nearby tree, unable to participate in their mournful song but needing to bear witness to it. Once again, I was reminded how different I was to the rest of them, not only as a Wolf but also as a person who'd lived most of my life in one place. These Songkeepers were an eclectic mix of cultures, languages, beliefs, and traditions—a blended harmony that made something unique only unto them, something I would always be an outsider to.

When the songs finished, Ora announced we'd stay the night to sing Asha's soul into the afterlife.

As the group disbanded, I felt restless and uneasy. Needing something to do with my hands, I left to fetch Navin's and my tent. A gloom settled over the campsite as I found a barren patch of ground to erect our tent and I began solemnly staking the wooden spikes into the cold earth. When Navin found me, he silently started working on the other side of the tent.

What was there to say? It felt wrong to break into idle chitchat and I hadn't the stomach for strategizing in the aftermath of an attack. And if I spoke of Asha . . . I might very well cry and that was just unacceptable.

When we finished, Navin and I just stood there, staring at the canvas structure.

"She will be missed," I whispered when Navin didn't move.

His throat bobbed. "I fear we will be missing many more still, even if we survive this."

My eyes saddened. "One more day and we'll be in Highwick."

My breath curled into the cool night air. "One more day after that, and we'll know if we've survived."

Navin's shoulders rose and fell on a mirthless laugh. He closed the distance between us, pulled me into his side, and kissed me.

"I wish I didn't have to ask this of you all." Regret filled my voice as I lowered from my tiptoes. "I wish I could tell you all to turn and run back south, but if you don't join in this fight . . ."

"Don't carry that guilt," Navin said, rubbing a hand down my arm. "We would've been here whether you were with us or not. The Songkeepers can't sit this fight out. There might not be another dawn for our people if we continue to let Nero annihilate us one by one." He threaded his fingers through mine and tugged me toward the tent. "Come. Rest."

I didn't budge and Navin turned to give me a questioning look. "I don't belong here." I swallowed thickly. I waved back toward the firelight behind us. "Not in Galen den' Mora. Ever since we stepped foot back in Damrienn, I knew it deep down in my bones. I am not a Songkeeper, Navin, and I never will be. I can't travel the realm with you like this."

Navin paused for a long moment before turning back to me. "I know."

My brows pinched together. "You know?"

"I see every part of you, Sadie," Navin said, making me feel stripped bare in a way only he could. "Every form. You were never meant to hide in the footnotes of someone else's song."

I shook my head. "So what, then?"

"If the world was different," he asked, "if you could have any life, where would it be?"

I didn't know why emotions constricted my throat. Perhaps it was the funeral and the generous cup of liquor, but the thought of being able to pick any life had tears filling my eyes.

"If the world could be anything," I said, "I would flatten Highwick to the ground and build another Damrienn city anew, one on the very outskirts of Damrienn, in the heart of Aotreas. A place where people from every corner of the continent would be welcome. I would run through the mountains of pine forest every full moon, I would swim in the streams in the summer, and curl around fires in the winters. Not in Olmdere, not in Valta, not traveling town to town on an endless adventure. I would choose to plant down roots here." My eyes lowered to meet his storming gaze.

"And you would be there with me, in this make-believe world. And we'd be happy and love each other deeply forever."

Navin's cheeks dimpled and he dropped his head, his hand sweeping to the back of my neck and pulling me into a soft kiss.

"But that world doesn't exist," I murmured against his lips. "And even if it did, it isn't one you'd choose for yourself."

"You make too many assumptions, love," Navin said, licking into my mouth once more before pulling back and resting his forehead against my own. "Ask me what I want."

I took a step away to look into his eyes. "What do you want?"

"You," he said instantly, simply. "The easiest question of my life. The answer will always be you." He held up a hand as I opened my mouth to protest. "Asha's death has made things so crystal clear in my mind. Tomorrow isn't promised, Sadie. And whatever time we have left in this life, I want it to be by your side." He fished in his pocket and produced a velvet box.

"What is . . . ?" My hands flew to my mouth as he got down on one knee.

"I've been carrying this with me since Valta. I thought I'd wait until this journey was over, but the truth is one adventure always collides into another when it comes to us. And if the only time we have is now, I don't want this question to go unasked." Navin lifted the box aloft, a smile on his face as he revealed an opal ring on a thin silver band. "Sadie Rauxtide, will you marry me?"

I gaped at him. "Navin . . ."

"Sadie," he gently mocked with a smile. "You are already everything to me. You light up every corner of my soul. Let me be yours in every way. Be my wife?"

I was so overcome I could barely get out the word "yes."

When Navin rose and pulled me up off my feet, a chorus of music began playing through the trees. We both looked through the dense forest to where the lights of Galen den' Mora gently flickered.

"Did they know?"

Navin chuckled. "They might have suspected," he said. "But no. This is how we celebrate Asha, with music and memories swapped round the fire until the dawn light breaks. When a human dies, we use it to remind us all to celebrate life. To not wait to act as we feel."

"Many an engagement happens at a funeral in your culture then I take it?" I asked with a laugh.

"Indeed," he said, pulling my mouth back to his. His hands roved up and down my body, fusing me to him.

We broke our kiss only long enough for him to slide the beautiful ring onto my finger. I grabbed him by the hand and tugged him toward the tent.

"What are you doing?" he asked with a laugh at my eagerness.

"I'm keeping with human tradition," I said as I shoved him to the ground and straddled him. "I'm not waiting to act as I feel."

THIRTY-SEVEN

BRIAR

WE NEVER MADE IT ONE STEP FROM THE OFFICE FOR THE REST of the sleepless night. Maez had taken me in ways I didn't even know existed. She brought me so much pleasure that I thought I might implode from it and yet still I begged for more. She was already a sex goddess before, but now . . . now I was pleasantly appreciative of her newfound wicked streak . . . and mine.

When exhaustion had finally overtaken our lust in the wee hours of the morning, we ambled to the bedroom and I left my sorceress to sleep. I'd found a robe in her wardrobe and padded off down the silent halls to find water. I desperately needed to hydrate after the last night. Peeks of early dawn filtered through the windows as I steered my way to the kitchen and found a pitcher.

I poured myself a glass and walked along the hall, studying the tapestries that hung along this wing. Beautiful woven art of gardens and castles, before stopping at the one on the farthest end. A knot formed in my throat when I saw it. I knew this story.

The Sleeping Queen.

In the piece was a forest of golden trees and floating above in the clouds was depicted my mother. She was so young, laying on a tomb, her hair spilling over the sides and a bouquet of white flowers in her hands. And standing over her was my father, strong and heroic, bending as if about to kiss her and break her sleeping curse.

I'd never known my parents—more myth than reality in my mind. They died at the hands of Sawyn the day Calla and I were born. And my mother's dying wish was that I may live to marry Grae and save our court—a wish ultimately fulfilled by my twin. My twin who was about to run off into battle without me.

At that thought, all my daydreams came crashing down. The glass illusion of the life Maez and I could have, uncaring of the world outside, shattered into a thousand heartbroken shards. Even high in the clouds, I couldn't forget who I truly was.

The pendulum of fate swung sharply back in the other direction, reminding me I was neither sweet nor wicked but something perpetually in between. I could embrace the darkness, but I couldn't hide within it any longer, either.

I looked out at the nearly full moon dipping below the horizon as the sun rose. My mother would never know that I shared her curse. Nor that I fell in love with a sorceress like the one who had killed her. Not only had I abandoned my parents' cause to save our people, I'd abandoned my only living relative to save them without me.

Would they have hated the person I've become as much as I did in this moment? Would they feel the same shame that had taken me by surprise?

My eyes welled. It didn't matter. My parents would never know me at all. I'd lived so much of my life as an idea, as a symbol, I'd never been given the chance to be my own flawed sort of person. I liked the wicked edge that Maez brought out in me and being more complicated than the perfect Crimson Princess. I liked that my bleeding heart had now been ignited into flames.

I liked all of who I was becoming . . . apart from one thing.

Maez appeared silently beside me, but I didn't so much as flinch. I could feel the weight of her eyes on me before I even spotted her in my periphery. And I knew then for certain, I could be fierce, I could be hers, but I couldn't bury my head in the sand anymore.

"I'd give everything to be with you," I said as a single tear streaked down my cheek. "Every last ounce of my soul, but—"

"After all that we've been through . . . Why are you saying this to me again when you know my response?" Maez's voice rasped with sleep, her face solemn. She seemed just as saddened by the statement as me. "You know I will do terrible, terrible things for you, Briar. I will be loyal. I will love you in the most fearsome ways, but I can't be the mate you once knew. I can't be everything for you."

"You don't understand." I sniffed. "You already are." Maez's eyes widened, her thumb lifting to sweep away my tears. "I would kill for you, Maez. Die for you."

"Don't stay that. I don't want that." She shook her head. "There is no choice for you."

"There are many choices and I'm making one of them right now." I faced her fully, watching her with bleary eyes. "And I choose *you*. I need you to understand that before I tell you—"

"Briar—"

"Hear me! Know that I speak true. You told me to give you one good reason to care about me," I choked out. "And it's not because I'm rich or beautiful or poised. It's not because I'm a princess. Sweet Moon, it's not even because we're mates. It's because every time there is a fork ahead, I will choose the road you're on, Maez. Always. It's because even at your darkest I will never stop fighting for us.

"If you become a monster, then I will become a monster, too."

She was so damn still but I saw the tears in her eyes, the rise in color in her cheeks.

"But I would die for Calla, too."

I watched as her face fell when it finally clicked why I needed to repeat my love and loyalty to her now: because I was leaving her, and if things went sideways, I might never return. I needed her to know that come what may, my heart would remain here with her.

"I am going to Damrienn," I said. "I am fighting alongside my twin, my court. And I am not asking you to come, but I *have* to go." I cupped her cheeks in my hands, my heart cracking open as one tear spilled from her welling eyes. "And I will come back for you when we win because you are mine and I choose for my heart to always belong with you, but you have to let me go. I will be your Goddess of Vengeance when you cannot."

Her throat bobbed. "I love you," she whispered. "I choose you. Always, no matter what I become."

My lips crashed into hers, and I kissed with all the desperation in me, all the words I couldn't voice. Her fingers pressed into my flesh, holding me to her. I gave her one last all-consuming kiss and pressed my forehead to hers.

"Send me to Calla," I whispered.

"I don't want you to go," she cried, the last of her walls finally breaking down, finally letting out all those raw feelings she'd been bottling up for decades.

"I know," I said, soothing a hand down her back. "But I need to be a part of this fight."

"I can't come with you." She practically trembled with the fear she finally allowed herself to feel. "I can't. I just can't. I can't come—"

"I'm not asking you to."

"Briar." The desperation in the way she said my name—it was almost enough to break me. But I had some darkness, too. I had the right to be selfish. And this was *my* choice.

"I love you," I said, kissing her salty lips. "I will be brave enough for the both of us. I will be your courage just as you are mine. My sorceress, my mate, my everything." I gave her one last kiss, one I wanted to remember forever and into the afterlife. "Now send me to Calla."

The ground dropped out from under me, and I disappeared to be with my twin.

THIRTY-EIGHT

CALLA

THE VALLEY WAS SLICK WITH RAIN, THE SLOG DOWN THE STORM-crest Ranges a miserable tramp through knee-high muck. We camped in the rolling forests halfway to Highwick. The army of Olmderian soldiers were exhausted trying to keep pace with the Ice Wolves and I was glad we'd allotted extra days in our journey west. I hadn't prepared for the brutality of the terrain. When I'd traversed it before, the ground had been dry, and most of my journey through the mountains had been traveling in Galen den' Mora. I was grateful for Verena's suggestion to budget for a day of rest before the attack.

One more day.

One more day and we'd live or die, succeed or fail. It filled the air of the campsite, the many fires circled by stony-faced soldiers. I felt a deep responsibility for each and every one of those faces. It weighed on me more with each passing hour. As did a single question:

Was I leading them to their deaths?

I trekked to the edges of the campsite and into the forest. Each town we'd passed had been either abandoned or burned to the ground. Western Damrienn was a graveyard, not a single inn open, not a single beating heart or human alive. It reminded me with an unsettling familiarity of Olmdere under the reign of Sawyn.

How had it gotten so bad so quickly? This was the work of generations, not months. With Damrienn's borders closed, we only heard glimpses of what life had become like within Nero's rotten kingdom, but this . . . this desolation was beyond even my comprehension.

It gave me a newfound resolve, an unwavering acceptance, that the only thing to do was move ahead. There would be no world left if we didn't. Someone had to be willing to stand up and fight.

I swept my hands through the dew-covered seedheads, plucking one from the stem and scattering it across the wet earth. Not so many moons ago, I had knelt in a meadow just like this, thinking I had been cursed to a mate who would never love me back, thinking my life was over. I wished I could go back in time and reach out to that fearful soul. I wished I could tell them all of the love they would soon feel, all the beautiful things they could become. One day they wouldn't live in the boxes and titles of others. One day they'd flow with the river and feel free.

A spitting crack sounded like a wet log bursting on a fire, and I whirled to the noise. I found her standing in the meadow, a few paces from me, staring down at the black battle leathers she wore along with a surprised look on her face.

The other side to my coin. My twin.

"Briar!" I shouted, racing forward and enveloping her in my arms. Her arms banded around me, and she dropped her head into my shoulder, our embraces like a well-practiced dance that would never be forgotten. The two of us just always perfectly fit. "You came back."

She smelled the same, of the lavender and honey lotion she'd massage into her skin, but different, too, like shoe polish and steel and the coppery tang of blood. She smelled like a princess and a warrior, like the two parts of herself that I always knew existed had finally fused into one.

My throat constricted, tears pricking my eyes as I squeezed her tighter. "You came," I said again, disbelief in my wobbling voice. I hadn't realized just how much I missed her until she was back in my arms.

"I'm here," she said, her arms holding me with greater force than she ever had before. I wondered if she'd gained some muscle during her time away, her movements more determined and gruff than practiced and lyrical. "If you're going into battle, Calla, then so am I. I won't ever let you fight alone."

"Look at you." I held her at arm's length to survey her impressive fighting attire and glinting weapons. "You look like a warrior."

"I've been practicing." She wore a cheeky expression that reminded me so much of Maez.

"Do I even want to know?"

"Probably not."

I let out a light chuckle, unsure when the last time I made such a noise was. "Fighting prowess or no, I'm glad you are here."

"I may still be a novice at wielding a sword," she amended, "but in my furs there's no faster Wolf around, apart from you perhaps. But teeth or steel it does not matter, if Nero's blood is being spilled, I want to be a part of it." Her lips curved up at my surprise.

"Listen to you. You wear this newfound conviction well." She was bolder and brasher than I'd ever known her to be, more confident in her stance, as if she'd stolen some of her mate's bravado and turned it into something more.

She nodded down to her garb. "Courtesy of Maez."

I released Briar and looked around the meadow. "Where is Maez?"

My twin's eyes bracketed with sadness, and she shook her head. "She's not coming."

It felt like a punch to my windpipe. Maez wouldn't come. I had all but given up hope of it, but upon seeing my twin, that hope bloomed again. Maez could have won us this battle without even trying. Even Nero couldn't compete with a sorceress's power.

I put a hand on her shoulder. "I'm still glad you're here. We were in need of a runner to convey my commands to the back line archers. And no one is swifter than a Gold Wolf," I added with a wink. "But promise you'll keep behind me, and I'll promise to paint the castle red with Nero's blood."

"Agreed." She looked through the trees to where we knew the castle of Highwick stood far in the distance. "I wouldn't miss this." She flashed another tight smile, but this one was tinged with pain. "Nero's reign would have been my prison and ultimately a living grave just as it almost had been yours. I want to be a part of his end."

"Come," I said, leading her back toward the camp. "Eat, rest. We leave this evening for our final approach."

Briar stalled me with her hand and pulled me back into another fierce hug. "I missed you."

Tears welled in my eyes as I hugged her familiar form to me, her presence a comfort like no other. "I missed you, too." I swallowed the lump in my throat. "I don't know what tomorrow brings, Briar, but I hope by the time the sun rises, Nero and his pack will no longer threaten to make anyone's life a prison again. Thank you for fighting by my side."

She released me and sighed. "People don't understand, not even our mates. We battled our way into this world together, Calla," she said, looking up at the glittering stars. "I know now that there is a magic to every bond but no more so than the ones we choose. I feel the heat of it, roiling inside of me. You tore your way across the continent for me. I couldn't sit this out." She slung her arm around my shoulder as I wrapped my arm around her waist, the two of us standing like we always did when the other needed comfort. "I will see you secure our family's throne. *Your* throne. And perhaps I have just enough darkness in me now to bring vengeance upon those who'd threaten it, too."

THIRTY-NINE

SADIE

WE CREPT TO THE EDGES OF THE FOREST AND LEFT GALEN DEN' Mora hiding in a copse of trees just outside town. The capital city of Highwick was not at all as I'd remembered it. What had once been a teeming metropolis was now a wasteland of derelict buildings.

What had happened to my hometown? Where were all the humans? Had they all fled the city under Nero's wrath? Or had they been culled by that same wrath?

The only humans I spied from our vantage point were peeking behind boarded-up windows and cowered behind broken crates in the alley, barely alive. They hid from us as if at any moment we might turn on them. Did they even know that it was humans who sat in the shadows, waiting to help them? How badly had they been tricked by Nero's guards before to be so untrusting? But I already knew the answer, had seen it etched on harrowed faces and molded onto rotten corpses. The fact any humans remained in Highwick at all was a miracle.

We cut westward along the outer streets of the city, circling out toward the forest just beyond the castle. Calla and the Ice Wolves would be crossing Nesra's Pass and down into the valley of the forest. We'd wait until nightfall, and when the swelling moon reached its apex in the sky, we'd attack. I kept looking to the sky. Dusk had already settled on the land. It wouldn't be long now. Soon we'd be storming the castle of my former King.

In a few hours, for better or worse, everything would change.

We set up a makeshift camp on the outskirts of the city so that Haestas could hide amongst the undergrowth of the forest. Sitting in a circle of cobbled-together logs, we didn't dare light a fire as we ate our dinner. Ora had emptied the cabinets of Galen den' Mora, making a veritable feast for us with all the leftover rations, but we couldn't help the ominous undertones of such an offering.

This might be our very last meal. The oxen had been unhitched and turned out to graze through the forest. I noted the way Ora shed a tear as they rubbed a hand down each of their backs and kissed their snouts. It was clear they were saying goodbye.

My stomach was a mess of tight knots.

Navin passed me a bowl of stir-fry, but I just held up a hand and waved it away. His lips curved down as he passed the bowl to Timon and grabbed me by my hand, tugging me in the direction of the forest.

"Where are we going?"

He pulled me farther into the forest until I could barely see. "If you're not going to eat, you need to shift one more time. You need to be at your full strength for tonight."

"I shifted yesterday." I let out a grumbling curse. "I am strong enough."

"Sadie—"

"Navin," I countered. "Your worrying for me is misplaced. Go fret over someone else."

"No."

"No," I rumbled in a mocking version of his deep voice. "If all goes amiss, this could very well be our last night alive," I said, watching as his shoulders tightened. "I don't want to spend it chasing bunnies."

"Shift," Navin commanded, occupying his jittery hands by starting on the buttons of my tunic.

"If it'll be one less thing for you to worry about, then fine." I swatted his hands away. "I can do it myself."

He swayed side to side, and I knew he was just as much a ball of nerves as I was. Probably more so. And I needed him to be okay just as he needed to know I would be. That was the smallest gift I could give him before we launched our attack.

I slinked out of my tunic, kicked off my boots, and then my trousers. I slid off my ring and passed it to him for safe keeping. Navin circled his finger around the delicate silver band. Normally, I wasn't one for jewelry. Wolves who wore jewels tended to leave them broken in the dirt in all sorts of random places when they had the sudden need to shift. One of the benefits of tying my heart to a human, I supposed. He could always hold my ring for me.

I shifted, prowling around the forest in a circle, sniffing the air and stretching just to prove to him I was making the most of it. The tension didn't ease from Navin's expression like I'd expected, though. He started walking toward me and I watched him carefully. What did he think he was doing? But then I saw it—the hunger in his eyes—the need for me to show him I would be all right in every possible way.

I shifted back, standing bare before him as he continued stalking forward. He grabbed me without stopping, hoisting my legs up around his hips and pinning my back against the nearest tree. The bark bit into my skin, igniting my senses. We needed this release so keenly, a little relief to take the edge off the promise of imminent battle.

He held me aloft with his one good arm, his broken arm still trapped within a sling. With a lust-addled yet resigned grumble, he moved us, taking me down to the forest floor. My hair splayed out across the fallen leaves as he lowered himself, his body covering my own.

"If it is our last night alive," he murmured against my mouth, "then I want to spend it buried inside of you."

I frantically unbuckled his belt, freeing his already hardening cock. There would be no slow lovemaking. We may never have all the time in the world again. But if the world was going to end, then I needed the love of my life to fuck me one last time before it all came undone.

I positioned him at my entrance as my mouth collided with his. He pushed into my wet core, letting out a groan as he filled me to the hilt. He licked into my mouth, his tongue battling mine as he started moving inside me.

"I love you, Sadie," he said, his proclamation dying on a groan.

"I love you," I cried out, angling my hips for him to take me deeper.

He fucked me hard, driving me into the loamy earth with each brutal thrust. I was lost to the frenzy and sensation as he gave me everything I so desperately needed. My sounds spurred him on. Feral, he took me with wild abandon. My orgasm roared through me, catching me suddenly. My clenching inner walls pulled Navin over the edge, and he started spilling inside me. I clamped around him, milking his release, as we came just as fast and rough as we started.

My lips found his as I took deep sips of air.

"We will survive this," I murmured against his mouth. He didn't reply and I pulled my head back to meet his eyes. "We *will* survive this," I repeated, finding strength in all the ways we joined, body, mind, soul. I would be his lighthouse in this storm. "We will win."

FORTY

BRIAR

I WAS MEANT TO BE HERE. IT WAS THE ONLY THOUGHT THAT kept me moving forward. I wouldn't stall long enough to be afraid.

We crept forward through the nighttime forest, all in our human forms so the Silver Wolves wouldn't catch our scent. Just as Calla had suspected, the Wolves weren't running through the forest so close to the full moon. They were saving their shift for the holiest of nights. Maybe it was part of a sadistic tradition, maybe it was to heighten the pleasure of the change, although now I was beginning to suspect it was yet another way that kings controlled their packs, just another arbitrary rule to keep us in line.

I kept looking up at the sky, checking to see if the moon was directly overhead. But I'd be lying to say I wasn't checking the sky for those glittering emerald stars as well. I couldn't seem to let it go, my eyes playing tricks in my periphery. I swore I saw flickers of that brilliant green light.

With each passing hour, I hoped more and more that Maez would change her mind, that I would see her violent lightning streak across the sky. But hour after hour, she didn't come. It was the most wicked thing she'd done, more than killing even: letting the ghosts of her past be more important than the love of her present.

But if Maez wouldn't avenge herself, then I would do it for her. Fighter or no, a promise rose up in me like its own kind of curse: Nero would die at my hands for what he'd done to her.

We reached the back entrance to the castle, undetected, and waited in the shadows as the moon rose higher. *Any minute now.* I prayed Sadie and the Songkeepers were on the other side of the castle, ready to attack from their end. I prayed I'd see the infamous, bloodred dragon that Navin had conjured during the battle that turned my mate into a sorceress.

I prayed it would all be enough.

Rolling my shoulders back, I waited, and waited, watching my twin for the signal. Calla observed the moon as it crested to the apex of its trajectory across the sky. I saw in the way their chest rose and fell, the coiled fear coursing through them. Their eyes fell to Grae, and he nodded and then Calla looked at me, one final glance, and I knew everything that was being said in that one expression. We never needed to speak to know each other's minds. I swallowed thickly and bobbed my head at Calla, watching as their face morphed into that of a ruler, one that would have made our parents proud.

The Golden Court Queen lifted their hand to the sky, holding it there for a split second to ensure every Wolf and human soldier behind them saw, and then dropped it to the ground. Everyone moved at once, three of the back doors being breeched simultaneously. I followed Calla and Grae through the central one—a servant's passage that led straight to the grand hall.

Calla picked the lock to the anteroom door and moved in, funneling quietly through the pitch-black and up the stairwell under Grae's murmured guidance. In a single line, we moved through the eerie stillness, Grae's back inches from my face and another soldier's chest directly behind me. The stone floors were uneven here and we had to pick up our feet higher so as not to trip. The servant's passage was dank and musty, the underbelly of a well-appointed castle, feeling more like the prison cell I'd been caged in than a space for staff to move through. Being a servant was just another kind of trapped, I supposed.

My ears tingled as I tried to listen for any sounds up ahead, any scuffle of boots, or fighting from other distant corners of the palace, but I heard nothing. It made acid rise up my throat. This all felt far too easy. Was the whole castle truly asleep? Not even a guard alerted to the hundreds of enemies now swarming through the palace?

My anxiety grew even sharper when we reached the first floor, readying to pick off the guards normally stationed along the main hallway, but we found it empty. The sconces were lit, casting the corridor to the grand hall in a bright glow, but no one guarded the doorways. No boot prints marked the burgundy carpets, no scent of blood, no sounds at all. We looked up and down the halls but saw no one. Calla and I exchanged wary glances, a chilling expression rising on Calla's and Grae's faces.

Our army spilled onto the first floor, tiptoeing down the plush carpet, a feeling of dread mounting in my stomach with every step. At the far end of the hallway, the doors to the grand hall were shut, not a single glimmer of light coming from underneath the doorway. I held my breath as we crept to the towering doorway. Pressing my cheek against the smooth wood, I listened but didn't hear a sound.

Calla's throat bobbed from where they listened beside me. They nodded to me in silent command, and in unison, we held our hands to the door and gave the gentlest of pushes.

We opened one side of the heavy doors inch by inch so as to not make a sound. It took several heartbeats to fully open before we began filtering into the grand hall. Still no sounds from the windows beyond. Where were the Songkeepers? Had something happened to them? Had they been delayed? Was the entire force of the palace manning the front of the castle while we crept through the rear?

Gods, it would feel good to see a dragon right about now.

We took in the shadowed room, the moon partially obscured through the stained glass windows. The space was vacant, but it still flooded me with memories, of the day of my failed wedding, of the way the moonlight hit me. Back then all I saw was Maez, knowing with unfailing certainty that she was mine and I was hers. Then the memory was violently replaced by another one: being brought before Nero the last time, Hector hanging in the corner, and Evres's hungry, possessive stare.

The shadows around the throne seemed to twist, black nothingness pulling in on itself. Upon the throne was a void darker than night. Calla and I froze when we saw it.

The shadows finally pulled back to reveal a lone figure lounging upon the throne, and when they did, what I saw made my heart stop. I knew those shadows, more solid than natural. I knew that inky black abyss . . . but this magic didn't belong to who I'd hoped.

The silhouette upon the throne stood and stepped from his swirling darkness, revealing himself upon the dais. Emerald magic filled the air, spitting and sparkling with vicious promise, as the Silver Wolf King lifted his violent green eyes to us.

Nero was a sorcerer.

FORTY-ONE

SADIE

MY PULSE DRUMMED IN MY THROAT, ECHOING OUT THROUGH every inch of my body, making every cell vibrate as we tiptoed through the silent capital streets. But if any guards were stationed within the greater regions of the city, they didn't spot us. Our passage through the human quarter was eerily smooth; not even a rat skittered upon the midnight streets.

We approached the palace gates uneventfully, which only made my heart thunder louder. I'd expected at least the castle would have candles in their windows or the warm glow of a fire flickering between half-closed curtains, but apart from the two guards stationed at the gates, there was not a single sign of life.

The Songkeepers' tricks had already come in handy, though. They'd hummed a quiet tune that had made the two guards at the front gates fall asleep, dropping like heavy stones. I quickly shot out of the shadows and grabbed their keys. I unlocked the front gate of the palace, and we zipped into the silver stone courtyard and barreled toward the front door.

What an odd sort of army we were—me with my knives and the Songkeepers with their instruments. Haestas circled the castle high overhead, her shadow peeking from between the clouds. It was only clear to those who knew to listen for it, but the whoosh of her wings brought me great comfort. I reminded myself again and again of the way she shredded that sea creature, the way she captured that Onyx Wolf. We would be okay.

But when we got halfway to the door, Navin froze, his hand shooting out as I collided into his leather-clad arm. The air was knocked out of me by the force of my abrupt stop.

I looked to the threshold. "You've got to be fucking kidding me," I snarled. "What is your ostekke's asshole of a husband doing here?"

Rasil stood, his arms folded across his barrel chest and a rueful smile on his face.

"Hello again, Navin," he said, pursing his lips and looking Navin up and down. "You're looking well." His hawklike eyes roved over the group. "So that's where you all disappeared off to? You even got Timon to join your suicidal plan." He tsked, shaking his head as twenty more humans appeared behind him, fanning out. They held neither instruments nor weapons, but their presence was foreboding nonetheless. The last many weeks we'd spent preparing to battle *Wolves*, yet here was a line of human magicians, looking like they wanted to tear us in two.

"Siblings, family," Ora called to them. "We are gladdened to see you."

"Save your pleasantries for someone who actually buys them, Ora," Rasil spat. "You've undermined my authority with your softhearted nonsense for the last time. Wagon or no, it is *I* who is the Head Guardian of the Songkeepers, not you."

"You defend the castle of a Wolf king?" Navin called. "First you betrayed us in Rikesh, now this? Are you loyal to the Wolves now?"

Rasil let out a deep laugh. "That's rich coming from someone who's fucking one."

The Songkeepers behind Rasil curled their lips in disgust, and I bared my teeth back at them. A few had the good sense to school their expressions.

"What is your plan, Rasil?" Navin asked, shaking his head. "This is the opposite of everything you once believed in. First helping the Onyx Wolves, now the Silver? Why come here to ally with a Wolf king?"

"We've come to collect one of our own," Rasil said with a devious smile.

My brows knit together in confusion as Kian broke off from our group and wandered over to Rasil's side. "I'm sorry, brother," he murmured under his breath, unable to meet our eyes.

"You absolute motherfucker." I shot forward and Navin barely had time to grab me by the belt to hold me back. "You betrayed us? *Again?*"

"Sadie," Navin grunted out my name as he struggled to hold me back.

"I'm going to rip out your throat with my teeth!"

"I promise you can kill him," Navin groaned as my elbow collided with his side, "but not right now."

I eased up but Navin kept a grip on my belt just in case. He knew me too well.

"Your brother has been telling me all sorts of stories, Navin," Rasil mused. "About your travels, and your discoveries, and most importantly about a song—a song that can control Wolves no less."

His eyes filled will delight as my stomach dropped to my boots. "Gods."

"So you see," Rasil said. "I haven't come to defend a Wolf king. I've come to take his crown. In fact"—his smile widened—"I hear there are three Wolf crowns in Highwick this night. Perhaps I will take all of Aotreas for our kind while I'm at it. I always thought I would make a good king."

"We won't let you do that," Navin shouted.

"And how exactly are you going to stop us?" Rasil asked.

The Songkeepers behind him parted and the samsavat skittered out, its body rippling across the ground toward us, its mouth open and gnawing at the air.

I grabbed my knives, dropping into a fighting stance as the beast charged, but Navin beat me to the attack.

He let out a whistle and Haestas dove from the clouds, eager. The opposing Songkeepers ducked, retreating farther into the doorway as the dragon scorched a trail toward the samsavat. The creature squealed, making my ears ring as it was eviscerated, trying to flee Haestas's flames. Bile rose up my throat at the burning, writhing monster who quickly crumbled into ashes before my very eyes.

Navin looked through the flames at Rasil, victorious, only for a fleeting second until he saw the look on Rasil's face.

"That beast was getting old." Rasil shrugged. "Thank you for putting it out of its misery." He let out a whistle, then said, "I've conjured myself a new one actually."

The air fissured, a whiplike crack as giant black wings appeared. The creature was larger than Galen den' Mora stood tall. With snapping mandibles and a hardened black shell, the beetle-like creature took to the sky in a deep, drumming rumble of beating wings. Haestas roared and shot her fire at the creature, but the flames just rolled over its hard exterior. The dragon's eyes flickered, flashes of gold in her gaze as she turned tail, arcing out toward the sea as the monster chased her through the night sky.

"No," I gasped, horrified as I watched our best chance at victory flee. My eyes dropped to Rasil and Kian. "Can I kill them now?"

Navin grabbed a dagger from his belt and choked up on the grip. "Let's go."

The Songkeepers laughed as they turned and ran back into the castle, making way for the row of Silver Wolves guarding the doors behind them.

"Shit!"

Already in their furs, the Silver Wolves didn't wait for any signal, they just lowered their heads and charged.

FORTY-TWO

BRIAR

Nero was a sorcerer.

His terrifying smile was lit up by his green magic, a magic I had come to know so well over the past few weeks, a magic I now understood the intricate workings of. Even Maez wouldn't be enough to save us now. I saw our violent end unfurling before us. Nero would feed off each and every one of our deaths to make himself stronger and, unlike her, wouldn't even consider hesitating.

I braced for it, waiting for one single flick of his emerald fingertips that would obliterate us all. This was no idle conjecture, either—lightning zipped overhead, threatening to strike us down at any moment.

But no such strike happened—not yet. Rather, Nero clicked his tongue, and my stomach lurched, acid rising up my throat as his gaze briefly lingered on mine before landing on Grae.

"I should've done a better job teaching you what greatness truly is, son." Nero's smile stretched as he returned to his throne. He sat slowly, so even-keeled, the eye of a hurricane that belied the magic encircling us now. "*This* is what true power looks like."

"You're not even a true Wolf anymore," Grae rasped. "Look at you. What have you done?"

"What you didn't have the strength to," Nero said coolly,

static circling from his fingertips up to his shoulders. "What is right for my people.

"I saw what happened to Evres with this dark magic," the King continued. "One moment he was sitting at our banquet, the next he was gone." Nero's cool gaze slid to me, and I straightened my shoulders. I wouldn't shrink from that magic anymore. "Hours later his body dropped from the sky, splattered across this very floor. You can still scent his blood with every deep breath. That's when I knew I would not let such power take me next."

Grae's lip curled. "So you became a monster to spare yourself from one?"

"He was carved up until there was barely anything left!" Nero roared, his eyes holding mine. The unpredictable oscillation between calm and rage made me further attuned to his every movement, unsteady in my predictions of what he might do next. My silent promise of vengeance bloomed hot in my belly, zipping with its own static energy. "The work of your sorceress, I presume?"

"The work of my own hands," I growled, glaring back. "I enjoyed driving my blade through him, you moon-forsaken tyrant." I could feel Calla's eyes on me, warning me. But what did such a warning mean? Now wasn't the time for poise or flattery; now was the time for last utterances before we all perished. I knew I probably shouldn't admit such things, but since these were my last moments alive, I decided to speak true. I decided my last breath would be one filled with all the power I'd denied in myself for so long. I glowered at Nero and said, "I enjoyed making sure Evres knew he had no power over me anymore. He saw only what I had allowed him to see—someone weak. A fatal error. He underestimated me just as you underestimated me, Nero."

The King threw his head back and laughed. "You underestimate *me*, Marriel princess. I was being lenient on you before because I needed you to legitimize my claim on Olmdere." His eyes scanned me up and down. "I couldn't break you beyond mending, not before you produced an heir. Though once you whelped, I would have enjoyed it." His gaze slid to Grae. "Did your mother ever tell you the way I liked to snap her finger bones under the dinner table?" Grae snarled and launched forward. Calla and I barely had a split second to grab him and haul him back. "She got so very good at hiding her pain. I wonder if the Crimson Princess would've been able to do the same." He smiled at me as he tapped his temple thoughtfully. "I bet you could've endured a great deal, girl," he said. "But I know what would've sealed your fate. Not the promise of your own pain, but that of your children—"

"I will gut you!" Grae shouted and his father laughed again.

"You never understood, Graemon," Nero mused. "You and your mother *belonged* to me. My property to do with as I saw fit. Such is the Wolf way."

Nero clicked his fingers and one of his bolts of lightning struck the chandelier above us. We only had a heartbeat to dive out of the way before it came crashing down. Glass shattered, the booming sound filling the cavernous space. Our group fractured in two to stand on either side of the wreckage. A few soldiers at the back started inching away, but with another flick of Nero's wrist, the doors slammed closed, trapping us in the room.

"Alas, I don't need anything from you anymore," Nero said, his faux sadness both terrifying and infuriating. "Not you, Graemon, not you, Princess, and certainly not that *thing* that you call a twin."

My lip curled and I reached out with my hands as if I could choke Nero from this distance just as Maez had once done to Evres. No one insulted Calla. Flames of anger grew within me.

"I don't need anything from anyone, and that is what truly makes me dangerous," Nero continued, so pleased with the sound of his own voice. I almost wanted to throw in his face the fact that truly dangerous people don't need to say they're dangerous. But there was no lie in his words.

That said, if Maez were here, she would've never let him drone on in hateful monologue even if it killed her.

"All of Aotreas is mine now." Nero's laugh was tinged with madness as he added, "I don't need an heir at all. With this power, I shall live forever."

I remembered Sawyn's face, still seemingly younger than my own as if frozen in time. But despite her long life, she *hadn't* been invincible; Calla *was* able to kill her. We would have to do the same.

Somehow . . .

"Sawyn didn't live forever," I said, exchanging looks with Calla. My fingertips twitched by my side and I saw them take note. It was all we needed to say. If we all charged the King at once, we might be able to overpower him. If he hadn't grown his power too strong already, we might be able to fight him from sheer numbers alone.

"Sawyn made a grave mistake from what I heard," Nero said, smiling at me. "She let you get within striking distance."

Before I could even reach for the hilt of the dagger on my belt, the room exploded in bright green light.

FORTY-THREE

SADIE

"THE SONGS! NOW!" I SHOUTED AS I HELD MY KNIVES UP.

I dropped into a fighting stance and braced for the onslaught of Silver Wolves barreling toward us like a pewter tidal wave. I remained in my human form, standing at the front of the group as the musicians behind me frantically began to play. Their music was more powerful now, the attack on the Onyx Wolves and the vengeance for Asha laden upon every note. I felt the heady tug of it even in my human form.

"Stop," the music commanded. "Don't move an inch."

The line of advancing Wolves slowed, some stalling entirely, while others battled forward against invisible hands. Navin seized the opportunity, breaking from the songs to attack. For a split second, I watched, impressed as he moved his dagger with lethal efficiency.

"Sadie!" Navin shouted and I fought against the pull of music, snapping out of it. I ran forward to join him in cutting down our frozen foes.

Some Wolves dropped before we even had a chance to reach them, the music commanding them in more and more violent ways: "Don't move. Don't breathe. Die."

How horrifying must it feel to have your own heart betray

you, to stop beating at the command of another? But right now, we needed all the brutality we could get.

Some Wolves didn't have the fortitude to do anything but obey, while others fought the commands. None were a threat to us, though, their movements slower than swimming through mud. A few Wolves had the good sense to shift back and flee into the palace with their fingers in their ears. But a naked human soldier with their ears covered was still an easy target.

When each and every one of the remaining Wolves was cut down, the music stopped. Blood coated the silver-flecked stones, trailing between the cracks and crevices.

Navin turned to survey the rest of the Songkeepers. "Everyone okay?" He quickly examined them one by one, but none were harmed. They didn't seem all that particularly rattled and I gave them approving nods. Once again, they reminded me how formidable they truly were. Even with the dragon being chased off into the night, perhaps we were still at a great advantage.

That thought was bolstered when a flare of green magic beamed through the far windows and my heart soared further. Maez was here. She came. I would get to see my best friend again. Victory was well and truly in hand now.

"Let's go!" I called, my spirits buoyed as I waved the Songkeepers onward.

We ran into the castle and turned toward the great hall, when the doors flew open and the screams erupted. I locked glances with the horrified faces of Calla and Grae who dragged an unfamiliar soldier between them. A bolt of green lightning hit him square in the chest, carving a hole straight through him. The mates dropped the body and continued to dash forward.

"Nero's a sorcerer!" Calla screamed. "Run!"

I didn't have time to fully process what they said; I was too busy moving. When my Queen shouted "Run!" I ran.

The soldiers pouring from the great hall scattered in every direction, through corridors and leaping out windows.

We whirled back in the direction we came only to be greeted with a fresh retinue of Silver Wolves guarding the door and blocking us in. Svenja lifted her violin, but I held up a hand. We might be able to fight these Wolves, but not with a sorcerer headed our way.

Moreover, my friends hadn't had the chance to inure themselves to the song, so they could be vulnerable as well.

"Stairs!" I shouted, grabbing Timon by the arm and shoving him toward the staircase. One by one, I ushered the Songkeepers up the steps with Navin and I taking the rear. Calla, Mina, and Grae closed the distance and followed hot on our heels as screams and cracks of lightning filled the air.

We circled up to the third floor and sprinted down the hallway.

"Here," Grae shouted, grabbing the corner of a painting and swinging it open. "Quiet."

We rushed inside the room, the dozen of us cramming inside. I could see the shadows of the Silver Wolves rising up the stairwell as we pulled the painting back in place.

"Quiet," I hissed at the panting, whimpering breaths of my comrades.

I listened keenly, pressing an ear to the canvas, but upon not seeing us, the Wolves didn't even bother stalking down the corridor. With their heightened senses, they should've been able to smell us, and they certainly would've heard our thundering hearts. But instead they turned tail. Why?

The unknown was truly frightening.

I found Grae's gaze in the darkness and he shook his head—he didn't know, either. Everything had turned upside down. And the worst, most horrible part of it all was that Maez *wasn't* here. She hadn't come to our aid. I'd traveled through the most unforgiving lands, forsaken my court and king, was beaten to near death on my quest to rescue her from Sawyn's imprisonment. I would've died trying to save her all over again . . . and she didn't come.

"This way," Grae whispered. "We can find our way out through the library."

He pushed a door open to the other side of him, another portrait, and I realized then that we were hiding between the walls.

I gave Grae a look and he rolled his eyes. "Later," he mouthed silently to me, and I had to bite back on my laughter.

He knew me too well. He knew I was going to chastise him for not sharing this secret hiding space with me. My whole life I'd spent roaming these halls with him and he'd kept this place to himself. But that momentary lightness disappeared when we heard voices echoing up from the library below.

With a finger to my lips, I locked eyes with the other Songkeepers, and we crept more carefully forward. I was one step through the portrait to the library balcony when Calla's panicked whisper stalled my foot.

"Briar?" Calla whirled, their eyes combing through the group of us crammed into the small space. "Briar? Where is she?"

My gut plummeted as I looked around the press of faces and found Briar missing.

FORTY-FOUR

CALLA

I SWORE I SAW HER FOLLOW US, A FLASH OF RED HAIR ON THE periphery. She was right there. She was with us. She . . .

My arms flew out as I tried to move through the tight cram of bodies. "Briar?"

Grae grabbed my arm. "Calla—"

"We have to go back for her." I pushed back toward the hallway as panic flared within me. "Didn't you see her follow us? She was behind me, wasn't she? She . . ." A panicked warble caught in my throat. "She was right there and then . . ." I combed back through the frantic memory of the explosion and our run. Had my mind played tricks on me? Was she separated from the group somehow? Had someone taken her?

My mate's arms banded around me, squeezing until I couldn't breathe as if he was afraid I might evaporate. "Calla," he panted. "She was barricaded by the rubble in the side corridor. I saw her bolt through the servant's passage door. She's probably hiding there." He looked at the balcony and the light emanating up from below. "She'll be far safer there than here with us at least."

I cursed my hopeful mind, my panic conjuring the image of her running alongside us only to be woefully mistaken.

"We have to go get her!" I battled his grip and Sadie joined in holding me back.

"We *will*," she whispered. "But if she's hidden and safe, then let's first deal with the problem below our feet."

"Let me go!" My voice cracked even as my limbs resigned themselves not to battle further. "I can go after her alone."

"No," Grae and Sadie replied in hushed unison.

"Calla." Grae forced calm into his voice. "If she is barricaded in the servant's passage, she *is* safe. Let her remain hidden until the castle is secure. Pulling her from the hall now will just bring her back into danger."

I didn't know if his logic was sound. What if she was trapped under the rubble? What if Nero saw her retreat and went after her? Every part of me wished to rush back to her. But running back through the halls filled with Silver Wolves and a sorcerer king would do her no good, either. The only thing keeping me from bolting was the resolute look in her eyes when she'd returned to us. She'd always been strong in spirit, but she was hardened now, too, more resolute.

She is tough. She will *survive this.*

We continued through the portrait on the far side and crammed into the balcony. Sitting, we hugged our knees to our chests to hide from the glimpses of light from the boardroom below.

Thank the Gods they were all humans down there. At least they couldn't hear our panting breaths and rapid heartbeats.

Grae sat to one side of me, Sadie to the other. As my panic finally ebbed to a solemn determination, I tilted my head, looking at Sadie for a split second before she and I both wrapped each other up in a fierce hug. Relief coursed off us. For a second I thought I might never see her again.

But that relief was short-lived. Now we had a sorcerer behind us and powerful magicians below. Even with an army circling the castle, the odds seemed to slip from our favor.

"Sweet Moon, am I glad to see you," I signed to her.

"I wish under better circumstances," Sadie signed back.

I grabbed her hand and elbowed Grae as we both stared down at the silver ring on her finger. "Did you get engaged?"

"Now is seriously not the time, Calla," she mouthed, shaking her head even though her lips curled up. Navin leaned forward to look down the line at us, a proud expression on his face. Even under attack from a sorcerer, he looked like it was the best day of his life, so foolishly in love.

"If we survive this, I want all the details," I whispered.

"That's a big 'if.'"

A chorus of laughter circled up from below us and we all stilled to listen to the conversation.

"I knew you hadn't forsaken the cause, Kian," Rasil said. I leaned forward to see him clapping the man on the back.

"Who is that?" I whispered to Sadie.

She leaned in until her lips were an inch from my ear. "Navin's traitor brother, Kian."

"That's Kian?" I balked. "He betrayed you again?"

Sadie let out a little growl beside me.

"I will always remain loyal to our brethren," Kian said, his arrogant voice easily echoing up to the balcony.

"I'll hold his arm while you stab him," I whispered to Sadie.

Mina waved to me from the corner, catching my eyes as she signed, "Wait for it."

My brows creased as I looked from her back to the people gathered below. Then my mouth fell open in silent shock. Was this what she had meant when she'd signed, "Leave it with me"? Her plan to get the Songkeepers to Highwick? The *old friend* she needed to speak to was Kian?

Blasts of power echoed from the distant reaches of the castle. I feared it was Nero tearing into everyone who hadn't fled. How many more were still trapped? I wondered if Verena and her pack had made it out. Were the rest of our armies now dead in the castle? Had some managed to run? We had made a dozen different plans, but none of them involved Nero becoming a sorcerer. It was every Wolf for themself now.

We wouldn't have long until Nero picked us all off. He was like a cat playing with its prey. I wondered if he did it on purpose—felling us one at a time so that he could enjoy each of his kills. Maez's tactics in the snow in Taigos had been to cut down her enemies in a single strike. But Nero seemed to delight too much in the killing to make it so quick.

We needed to get him into a more strategic position, one in which we could circle him from all sides, draw him out. Even then, it would probably be a death sentence, but with the element of surprise, maybe we could get close enough to ram him through with a sword. Or . . .

I shook Sadie's arm. "Where's the dragon?"

Her mouth tightened, the muscle in her jaw popping out at she shook her head. "A new monster was created—that's how Nero took that dark magic," she whispered. "The beast that was conjured from it chased our dragon into the night. I don't know where she is."

Her words flooded me with ice. *No dragon.* We were well and truly fucked.

"Quickly, brother," Rasil said, cutting my attention back to the room below. "Teach us the song. How can we control these Wolves?"

"You mean besides with a juicy rabbit?" The group chuckled and waited as Kian leaned back in his chair, taking his time.

My heart thundered, thinking back to Briar. I wondered if I could just turn and bolt the way we came, but Grae held me tight, knowing my intentions.

"With haste, Kian," Rasil growled and the rest of the Song-keepers hiding on the balcony stifled laughs.

"Perhaps I had underestimated him after all," Sadie whispered to Navin.

"Maybe he needed us to sell the lie," Navin replied.

"Well, it certainly worked," Sadie muttered. "I almost killed him."

When Kian finally began to sing, it wasn't at all what I had expected . . . No, as I strained my ears to listen, the bodies around me started shaking with laughter.

I'd heard this song in the boisterous taverns of Allesdale. It was a lewd sea shanty. One that had even me blushing.

Kian's song was cut off abruptly as Rasil's fist collided with his face. Kian spat blood to the side, painting the wall scarlet.

"Was that not it?" he asked, wiping his mouth with the back of his hand. "Maybe it was the one about the fairy and the giant?"

Rasil punched him again, whipping his head to the side like a limp doll. *"Traitor."*

"If you're trying to insult me, try another word. That only affects me when people I care about use it." He paused to spit more blood onto the table. "People like Mina. She told me to contact you, that you'd be foolish and arrogant enough to take the bait—"

His words were cut off by another brutal slap.

Rasil lifted his fist for a third punch when Navin leapt up and vaulted over the balcony railing, landing squarely on the boardroom table. Unsheathing his knife, he pointed it straight to Rasil. "No one is allowed to punch my little brother but me."

"Finally." Sadie was on her feet in an instant. "Time to stab some people," she said, looking at us with a wink. "Good luck," she added as she launched over the railing to join her fiancé.

Another sharp crack of magic echoed from behind us, and I grabbed Grae and pulled him back the way we came. "Let's go," I said as more Songkeepers vaulted over the railing and into the melee below. "We've got to draw Nero out and away from Briar."

Grae unsheathed his weapon and nodded. "Agreed." He looked at me and raised his eyebrows.

"Ready?" I asked.

He shot forward, pulling me into a burning kiss, one that would have to say everything. Leaving me momentarily reeling and breathless.

"Ready," he said, his smile a source of light and warmth on this too-dark night, and he swung open the portrait.

FORTY-FIVE

SADIE

THE INSTRUMENTS WERE LONG ABANDONED FOR FISTS AS SONG-keeper battled Songkeeper. Blood sprayed, the magicians' training truly showing now as they grappled with one another. Even the ever-gentle Ora was walloping someone over the head with a massive tome from the shelf behind them. But there was one person I wanted to see go down above all else and Navin already had him cornered.

I leapt from the table, fighting my way through the chaos around me to get to him. Navin clocked Rasil with a punch to his chin, snapping Rasil's head back as he collided into the far wall. The Head Guardian grabbed the slender metal tube around his neck as he fell.

"No!" I shouted but it was too late; he'd already blown into it, releasing an earsplitting trill.

Navin fell backward as if punched, dropping to one knee and holding his bleeding nose. Rasil flashed a bloody smile at Navin as he started to sing. Scarlet dribbled from his lips as Rasil sang.

I pushed through the crowd faster, shoving one Songkeeper into a bookshelf and kicking in the knee of another, trying to get to Rasil.

No, no, no.

I knew this song. It still haunted my dreams. I'd heard this deep, guttural chanting once before, right before the world cleaved in two and a red dragon appeared.

Rasil was trying to summon another monster.

The air around the Head Guardian seemed to warp as I hacked my way through the last stretch. Navin's expression was outraged as he scrambled to his feet. As one, we launched at Rasil, Navin choking him and silencing his song as I drove my knife into his side. I twisted the knife, but Rasil's cry of pain was cut off as the bookcase behind us exploded. Wood splintered, pages flew through the air as my eyes tried to find the source of the explosion through the fluttering debris.

I heard it before I saw it. Screams erupted as that sickening chittering sound started. The cloud of pages cleared to reveal Rasil's beast. The beetle-like creature must've been summoned by his whistle, coming to defend its injured master.

It barreled toward us to get to Rasil, easily tossing Navin and I to the side with its armored body. I lost the grip on my knife, dropping it in the ankle-deep stacks of books that littered the ground. I quickly unsheathed another, though, driving my blade down toward the creature's wing. But my blade glanced off the hardened obsidian shell as if it was made of stone.

"Fuck!" I aimed for the creature's legs, but they were just as impenetrable.

Its body was so large, it filled the entire room. At least it couldn't maneuver quickly in the tight space, but even if we avoided its mandibles, we might be crushed against a wall if the creature turned swiftly. And the behemoth stood between us and the library exit.

I spotted one flash of white beneath its jaws, the narrow joint where its head attached to its abdomen. Ostekke fucking gut me! Of course the only part of the beast that was vulnerable had to be right next to its claw-covered mouth. I'd have to dodge the serrated knives that this creature called a face to kill it.

Navin began singing and chanting beside me, and I looked

at him as he sang the familiar song, one to control beasts. Ora joined in a shaky harmony. But the creature seemed impervious to the song, not even stalling as it twisted and grabbed Timon in its mandibles. Timon's eyes bugged in horror for a split second before the beast began shredding him apart.

Svenja screamed, running forward as Ora doubled over and vomited onto the carpet at the sight of their mutilated friend. The creature spun toward us, its pinchers snapping the air, searching for its next victim. It lumbered through the tight space, knocking down shelves and crumpling chairs under its weight as it moved. It wasn't swift or nimble, a battering ram if ever there was one. When it finally squared itself toward us, it advanced.

Rasil sat crumpled in the corner, a bloody hand to his side, his face draining of color as his chest rose and fell in belabored breaths. It wouldn't be a killing blow to a Wolf, but I hoped it would be enough for him.

If not, I'll finish him after I deal with this . . . thing.

Navin ran down the stacks of books behind us, herding the other Songkeepers to the far wall and shielding them with his body, but I knew the truth: we were trapped. Either we'd be shredded apart or trampled if we didn't do something—if *I* didn't do something.

I stayed put, facing down the creature and blocking the path to the others with my body.

"Sadie!" Navin shouted but I didn't move. I'd only have one shot at this . . .

The creature hissed and clicked, prowling toward me with an ever-quickening pace. I unsheathed another knife from the bandolier around my thigh. I waited, grabbing a blade in each hand, tighter and tighter until my knuckles were white.

"Goddess, help me," I whispered and then I started to run.

I faintly heard Navin scream my name—and my heart screamed his name back, even as I charged toward the creature. Just as I'd hoped, the beast lifted its massive jaws, ready to grab me head-on. And when it did, I dropped, sliding beneath that giant head and to the creature's unprotected underbelly. With my blades crossed, I swiped, cutting the creature's neck joint. A nauseating snap sounded, the weight of its head too heavy without that joint holding it together. The midnight black head tumbled, breaking clean from the body, and crashing into the floor, almost crushing me. The wood beneath me splintered as I moved. I only had mere seconds to scramble out from under the beast's belly before its legs gave way and its torso came crashing down.

When I rose, I quickly took in the carnage—Svenja crumpled over Timon's shredded body, the other Songkeepers cowering behind Navin, so many bodies slick with blood upon the floor . . .

And Rasil still propped up in the corner, his face drawn.

I took a step toward him when Navin's hand landed on my shoulder. I looked up at him as he grabbed a knife from my hand, his own dagger having disappeared in the fighting.

"You can't allow him to live," I said, horrified.

"That's for certain, love," Navin said, but shook his head. "I have need of your knife." He lifted my hand and brought my bloodied ring to his lips for a kiss before turning and marching toward Rasil.

The word "please" died on Rasil's bloodless lips as Navin drove my knife into his neck.

All was silent for a moment before Svenja's cries cut the air again. I looked around the room, back at the beheaded beast, and then to the thin strip of open doorway between the top of the creature's shell and the doorframe.

"What is it?" Ora asked, walking over to my side. They dropped their hands back to their knees, trying to catch their breath.

"Well, the good news is we're safe for now," I said to them, trying and failing to sound reassuring. "The bad news is we're trapped."

FORTY-SIX

BRIAR

I COWERED BEHIND A CURTAIN IN THE HALLWAY, DUCKING beneath the windowsill, trying to make myself as small as possible. I peeked out to the moonlit forest . . . too far to jump, too steep to climb. My hair was matted with gore and my skin was splattered in dirt and blood. I didn't know if it was mine. I couldn't feel anything other than the thump of my heart like a fist bashing into my sternum. I'd lost all control of my muscles. My whole body shook, and my stomach roiled as I heard the zaps of lightning and the bloodcurdling screams. Hot tears burned down my cheeks.

"Maez," I whispered, my lips trembling. "Please. Please be brave for me. I don't want to die here."

Before I could continue my prayer, the curtain was ripped back and a man with silver hair and a lined face sneered down at me.

Recognition alighted both of our expressions at once.

I knew that face. I'd seen him staring up at my window as he commanded his soldiers to disembowel those humans.

"If it isn't the Crimson Princess," he said. "I'd hoped we'd meet again." He snatched a handful of my hair and yanked me to my feet. "Such beauty was wasted on Evres. You need a wiser hand to know what to do with all of you."

"You," I spat, raking my nails across his face.

Blood beaded in neat little lines across his cheek as he cursed. He shoved me against the wall and my head cracked against the stone. "You bitch."

Before I could move, he pinned me with his body, my attempts to shove against his barrel chest all in vain.

"You think you know how to handle me?" I asked, my voice suddenly soft and sweet as I felt my way across the wall and to the loose stone I'd spied nearly falling from it. "You know, I made you a promise that day."

"Did you now?" he asked, intrigued.

Aroused?

I couldn't believe this man. That he had the audacity to smile at that, that his eyes hooded with lust. I'd just clawed up his face and now he thought I wanted to fuck him from a single pointed smile? By all the Gods, it was too easy.

"Tell me," he murmured, his eyes dropping to my mouth.

The seduction was a skill of the old Briar . . .

What came next was a skill of the new.

Another booming crash from the grand hall had him turning to the sound and the loose stone jostled farther. I gathered it into my grip as I said, "I vowed that I would be the one to end you."

I moved all at once, smashing the rock into the side of his head and spinning. I was rewarded with a satisfying cry of pain as blood trailed from the man's temple. The blow was not enough to knock him unconscious but that wasn't the entirety of my hastily laid plans. In another life, I'd dream of pummeling him to death, watching as his eyes fell from their sockets and flesh pulled from bone, but I couldn't risk his superior fighting skills against me now.

There was no sorceress to hold this one back. I felt her magic buoying me even still, but this kill would be from my strength alone.

The man before me was a high-ranked Wolf, a commander. I knew he'd use his size and brute force, try to shove me backward and pin me again. The fool. He should've been trying to run. Instead, as I stepped to the side, he charged into me, and right as he did, I twisted, kicking out his leg and sending him flying through the window.

Glass shattered and he plummeted.

As I looked out the broken windowpane, my only regrets were that I didn't have enough time to kill him slower and that my mate wasn't there to watch him fall.

Such regrets were short-lived as another crash sounded and the wall beside me began to tremble. More rocks jostled loose. Dust and grit fell from the ceiling above and my mouth fell open.

"Sweet Moon," I whispered. The wall was about to crumble, and I'd be crushed beneath it.

I looked at the door that led to the grand hall. Risk my luck with the sorcerer or submit to certain death here?

Fuck it.

I bolted to the doorway as the wall began to give way down the corridor, a zephyr of grit and debris chasing me. I ran as fast as I could before a rock hit me in the back and sent me sprawling. A dust cloud ate me up as I covered my head.

I lay there, bloody saliva dribbling from the corner of my mouth, my ears ringing, a sudden stillness to the fighting all around me. The grand hall doors were thrown open and I searched for familiar faces amongst the fighting. So many bodies and many more still on their feet, not all of them friendly. A horde of Silver Wolves had entered the battle, tearing apart the ones Nero's lightning bolts had yet to touch.

The Silver Wolf King still stood on the dais. His pupils had disappeared to churning emeralds, power flowing in and out of him in spitting sparks. He moved his fingers this way and that as if conducting an orchestra, and his magic obeyed, shooting through the air. He wore a crazed smile, lost in the frenzy of bloodlust.

My vision blotted in and out, my mind spinning. Was I wounded? *I must be*, I thought, as more of my blood spilled onto the stones. I shook my head, my fur ruffling, and it was only then that I realized I had shifted. The shift was so sudden, trying to save me from the crumbling wall. One of the Silver Wolves caught my scent, his eyes trained upon me as he prowled in his furs in my direction.

I blinked, trying to clear my double vision, and looked up beyond him to the window. Was I hallucinating or . . . was a ruby red body silhouetted through the stained glass window? Like a god of fire, it flew through the night's sky, its form growing bigger and bigger.

A dragon.

Our dragon, I thought.

The beast kept coming and coming, unfathomably large. And then I realized it had no intention of stopping. I had just enough time to curl and bury my face in my tail as it exploded through the window. Glass and stone flew all around me, rubble littering the floors of the great hall. The far wall crumbled, and the ground trembled like a drum beneath my body.

The dragon screeched and I peeked between my paws to see its glowing red eyes. Its chest began to glow, too, and I recognized what it intended to do. I felt its fire, like magic hanging in the air, before it even opened its mouth. I scrambled to a stand, bloody paws cutting across the shards of glass.

I faintly heard Calla scream my name, but I wouldn't slow to find them in the distant crowd. I prayed my twin wasn't about to watch me die.

And I thought of Maez. Glad she wasn't there to watch me die either, that our mating bond was severed and that she would live on without me. Maybe in the next life we'd have that little home in the corner of the world. Maybe in the tales they'd tell about this battle, they'd change them so that we could be together. Maybe we'd be remembered better than we lived.

"Goodbye, my mate," I whispered and ran.

I bolted, uncaring of the pain, hoping my speed would save me as the dragon opened its mouth and unleashed its ferocious flames. The blast threw me forward, losing my footing. The world was engulfed in smoke and fire and pain. I felt it now, scalding into me.

I lay there, unsure if I was alive or dead. Half my fur had been singed off in one single dragon's breath. Smoke choked my lungs, and my eyes watered with unshed tears as I blinked through the plumes of flame. The first peeks through the haze were of devastation.

Smoking Silver Wolf bodies trailed on and on and on. As the smoke slowly cleared from the dais, there was still a flicker of Nero's green magic. Utter defeat filled me as I saw him standing there, surrounded by the bodies of his pack, looking fierce and unscathed. I reached a hand up into the smoking air like a drowning person reaching above the waves, grasping for some lifeline that would pull me through this.

More green magic flickered, and I blinked, my watery eyes playing tricks on me. But as the smoke cleared, I realized the magic wasn't sparking from Nero . . .

. . . It was sparking from Maez.

Maez's eyes found mine as if magnetized to my gaze and she mouthed one single word to me. "Go."

And then the room erupted into dragon fire and dark magic.

FORTY-SEVEN

CALLA

MAEZ.

The room fell silent for a moment to take in the formidable sight.

"Hello, Uncle," Maez said, her face tight, her voice cold.

Nero only smiled at her menace. He opened his mouth to say something, but Maez's hands shot out and her magic blew him backward. Caution morphed his arrogant face as if he was surprised Maez didn't allow him to speak.

Green lightning stabbed at Nero from every direction, a zipping ball of static surrounding him, but not a single blast penetrated the swirling air that encircled him. He grimaced, opening his balled fists and pushing his hands forward as emerald sparks shot out, knocking into Maez. She growled, gritting her teeth, holding her hands out in mirror to Nero's own as her feet skidded backward toward the edge of the blood-slicked dais.

A figure stood amongst the field of corpses, so coated in gore I didn't recognize her at first. But then she brushed her red hair over her bare shoulder to tumble down her back.

"Briar!" I called.

I was only able to take a single step toward her before three Silver Wolves ran at us. Grae jumped in front of me, sword drawn as he caught a Wolf in the side and then turned to the other while I finished off the third.

As I yanked my blade from the Wolf's side, I watched as Briar turned to me, her expression pinched, her eyes bloodshot. I could tell from the way her brows knit together that she was crying. She gave me one single look, placing her hand over her heart, before turning toward the dais and limping toward her mate.

"No," I sobbed.

The ground rumbled as the dragon flew past the rubble of the now-missing wall, circling back toward us again. Grae grabbed me just in time, throwing me to the ground and shielding me with his body as the dragon barreled into the hallway, piercing another hole into the palace. Fire ignited in every direction—the carpets, the tapestries. A hole in the roof above us caved in, blocking our way to the far end of the great hall.

I scrambled to my feet, searching for Briar, but the pile of stones was too tall. I climbed up the crumbling heap of debris two steps before my feet slid out from under me and Grae pulled me back.

"We need to get out of here before that dragon brings the whole place down," he shouted.

I lifted on my tiptoes, barely getting a peek of Maez and the feral green fire that burned all around her now. Her face was tight with pain, her posture stooped, and I knew in my gut that she was losing this battle. That she was more experienced with the magic, but that Nero was simply stronger—in his madness, if nothing else.

But then I looked around and realized it wasn't madness. It was the blood—the deaths *he'd* caused. He was more powerful because he had been more indiscriminate. More ruthless.

More of a monster.

A retinue of Olmderian guards began climbing through the blasted hole in the wall to my right and I barked orders to them to remove the rubble. Despite their frightened expressions, they did as I said.

"Calla," Grae snapped, but I was already moving rubble with my raw, cracked hands. My mate let out a curse from behind me and jumped to my side to help move the debris.

We were all getting out of this together or not at all. I wasn't leaving my twin to die in this place. She had come to my aid, and there was no way I wasn't going to hers.

A scream rent the air, and I looked between the walls of rubble to see a bolt of lightning hit Maez square in the chest and she tumbled off the dais. Nero laughed, stalking forward, summoning another wave of power to end her.

Dread gripped me as I watched him lift his hands, knowing that when they fell, Maez's life would end along with any hope of us surviving.

But when Nero lifted his hands to the sky, a flash of brilliant lightning struck him from behind, not of emerald . . . but of crimson. The rest of the wall in front of me crumbled to reveal the source of the rogue dark magic:

Briar.

She stood on the dais behind Nero, a flow of churning green siphoning off from Maez and morphing into scarlet as it poured out of my twin. She was taking Maez's magic and turning it into something else entirely.

"What in the Gods . . . ," I whispered, horrified, as Briar seemed to draw the sorceress's power into her, using herself as a conduit to shoot at Nero.

Maez stood on wobbling legs, blood trailing from her nose and ears. Her magic sputtered, barely a spark, but she shot it at Nero's other side. He stood in the middle of the dais, pulled in either direction by Briar's and Maez's magic, his teeth bared, clearly in pain.

But he didn't drop.

Sweet Moon, it still might not be enough. After all the deaths by his hand, he was so fueled with dark magic, even their combined power might not be enough to fell him.

I kept moving stones, revealing another familiar face in the walls between us.

"Mina!" I tried to reach for her hand and pull her over the rubble, but she slipped. "Grae, help me!" Before he could reach her, a soldier appeared, one in Damrienn garb. "Look out!"

Mina whirled toward her attacker as he lifted his sword aloft and charged.

The blade swung down, and I screamed Mina's name, but then a flash of silver fur shot out from the melee. The soldier slashed his dagger clean through the side of the Silver Wolf who yelped and fell backward.

I knew in an instant who it was. Only one Silver Wolf would protect her with his life. A Wolf who had tried so hard to keep his sister from falling in love with a human. A Wolf who clearly loved one himself.

Hector.

Even with blood pouring from his chest, Hector righted himself and launched at the guard, snapping at his legs and toppling him over. He barely paused before tearing out the guard's throat. And then his body spasmed and he collapsed.

Mina shot forward as he shifted into his human form, so caked in blood and gore I couldn't see his wounds, but I knew from his gaunt, gray gaze that a shift wouldn't save him now.

His eyes peeked open, his lashes clumped in congealing burgundy. He lifted a trembling hand to Mina's cheek, leaving a streak of blood where he swept his thumb across her face.

She let out a silent sob, shaking her head at him. His hand wrapped around the back of her neck, and he pulled her down into a fierce kiss. My vision clouded with tears as motes of golden light started collecting around him, lifting his soul from his body and warping it in a glittering orb.

I sucked in a sharp breath.

I knew that golden light. Felt it stitch me back together with my own dying wish.

Tears spilled down my cheeks as the cloud of sparkling dust collected, and with a flash like rays of sun peeking through the clouds, she appeared. Vellia, beautiful and ethereal as ever. The silver-haired faery floated down to Hector's side.

Mina sobbed harder, shaking her head. Signing ferociously for Vellia to go away, but Vellia just calmly drifted over to Hector and crouched down so he could whisper in her ear.

Her eyes lightly drifted to Nero, to the blinding battle he was locked in with Maez and Briar, and she nodded. When her hand touched Hector's chest, his grip on Mina went slack. Mina keeled forward, gathering him into her arms, kissing him, shaking him, but he was gone.

Vellia stretched her glowing golden hands apart, stretching, stretching the final fabric of Hector's life. She gave me a single look, a stolen glance, the warmth of a mother's smile telling me everything I knew she wanted to say. I nodded back to her through watery eyes. Her gaze found Briar next, and Briar's magic sputtered to a stop as she held our faery godmother's gaze. Despite her distance, I could see the single word being chanted on my twin's lips. "Please, please, please."

Vellia nodded to Briar and then clapped the golden threads of Hector's soul together with Briar's crimson magic and Maez's emerald ether and let it fly forward, crashing into Nero and causing him to vault across the room in an arc of rainbow light.

FORTY-EIGHT

BRIAR

"BRIAR."

I heard her voice like the sweetest song.

It was the last sound I wanted to hear as I died, my name on her lips. My name, my body, my soul: hers. Always hers.

My mate called me into the afterlife. I felt her arms around me and drifted further, letting myself melt into her strong hold. I was ready to go, ready for us to finally be together at last, in another life, another world, where Maez and I were at last one and the same again.

"Open your eyes." The arms held me tighter. "Please, Briar, open your eyes." The pleading voice was tinged with panic, and I finally acquiesced, squinting open my eyes to see Maez's blood-streaked face.

Her shoulders slumped, relief flooding her as her lips curved up at the side. Tears welled in her eyes as the last walls around her crumbled.

"Hi," I whispered, my voice a rasp.

At that she broke, the tears spilling down her cheeks and dripping off her chin. "Hi."

"You came."

"I did," she said, swiping my matted hair off my face. "I'm here." She sniffed and lifted me up to sit, propped up in her strong arms. "I'm sorry I ever made you doubt it. You made me brave."

"I . . ." I realized all at once that I was naked, that my body was wounded in a thousand different ways. The pain flooded me anew as the shock began to ebb. I gritted my teeth as I balled my grip into the leather strap across Maez's chest. I screwed my eyes shut, willing myself to be healed. Fire burned behind my eyelids. With a flash of bright red sparks, the pain disappeared.

"How?" Maez gasped as I sat up farther.

I looked down at myself to see I wore black battle leathers that matched Maez's own. My hair was braided off my face, my broken fingers now straight, and my skin freshly washed. I took another deep breath and then another, no stabbing pains as I moved. I'd . . . I'd healed myself.

"How did you do that?" Maez asked, looking me over in disbelief.

"That thread of moonlight," I whispered. "The one that tied your soul to mine. I felt it in the forests of Taigos. We are still connected, you and I. One life. One power." I looked up and wiped a tear from her cheek. "It wasn't until I saw you on that dais, facing down your fears, that I knew for certain I could summon it, *use it*. I knew that I could help you win."

Maez shook her head. "But this darkness—"

"Is mine as well. It is a burden and a blessing that you and I will share together," I said, cupping her cheek. "Together. Always, Maez."

Maez looked around. "Nero, he . . ." Her eyes snagged on something as her words died off.

Whatever magic Vellia had cast hadn't been what I had hoped. Nero lay there, swallowed up in his flowing silver robes, but his chest rose and fell; his hands moved to cover his face.

Alive.

Disappointment thrummed through me as I unsheathed my blade. Had Vellia only taken away his dark magic? Was that all

Hector had wished for? Was his dying wish still not fully on our side?

I made to take a step forward, to deliver that final killing blow before Nero got his wits about him, but Maez held out a hand and stayed me.

"Wait," she said. "Scent him."

I raised a perplexed brow at my mate but did as she said. Nero smelled of blood and sweat, his rapid human heart beating faster than our own—

Human.

It hit me all at once.

There wasn't an ounce of Wolf left in the Damrienn king now.

"No, no, no, no," Nero whispered, horrified as he stared at his hands and then up to his son who watched him from atop a pile of rubble. Hatred filled Nero's eyes. "What are you going to do?"

"Me?" Grae asked, pursing his lips. "Nothing." He stooped and grabbed his father by the scruff of his cloak and dragged him across the rubble. "I think we should let your own kind decide your fate."

I watched with horrified amusement as Grae dragged Nero across the ruined castle stones, through where a wall once stood and to the entrance where the human citizens of Damrienn gathered at the gate. They looked more hollow and ragged than ever before, beaten and half starved. But they cheered at the sight of Grae dragging their former king to the gate.

"No! No!" Nero wailed, trying to fight against Grae's iron grip, but there was not any strength left in him now.

His screams were cut short as Grae threw Nero into the throng, the mass of bodies quickly absorbing him. He disappeared, swallowed into the press of humans, and I knew I'd never see him again.

Not whole, at least.

I wrapped an arm around Maez's side and tugged her tighter into me.

"An apt dying wishing," I whispered touching my chest, lips, eyes in prayer.

Maez and I turned back to what was left of the palace. From this vantage point we could see all the destruction. Only one tower remained intact, the rest dissolved into rubble apart from the far wall of the great hall and the stained glass window upon which the moon had once not so long ago revealed my fate.

I hugged my mate tighter to me, sighing up at the window like a good omen. The only thing left of this place would be from the Goddess herself.

"I think I'm ready for our little corner of the world now," I murmured.

"As am I." Maez dropped a kiss to the top of my head, moving me to look back out at the group gathering behind us. "But first, let us spend a little time sharing in this victory with our family."

FORTY-NINE

SADIE

WE TRIED IN VAIN TO SHIFT THE DEAD BEAST BLOCKING OUR exit to the library. Try as we might, the creature could not be hacked apart nor moved. Eventually we gave up and affixed a rope to the balcony to climb back up the way we came. But when we entered the hallway, we found half of it caved in, the far wall gone. The floors above were now open to the sky and the nearby trees had all been felled by the palace collapse. I stared at the moon who now dipped below the forest in the distance as the sun began to rise.

Thank the Goddess, I thought. The rest of the castle had crumbled but we had been saved.

Not that we were in any way *safe*. Our passage through the rubble was slow-moving, as each movement had ripple effects that made us fear the section we were in wasn't long for this world, either. And that was just a part of the terror.

It made my stomach turn to see hands and fur peeking up between the stones. The ground reeked of blood and piss, but we didn't see a single survivor amongst the avalanche of stones. When we finally descended the loose shale of shattered glass and silver rocks to the first floor, all was quiet.

Navin whistled and Haestas came flying through the pre-dawn sky. Tears welled in his eyes at the sight of her. Her leathery wings were tattered, a few scales bent at odd angles, and one pupil more dilated than the other, but she was still flying, still alive.

"Did you do all of this?" he murmured.

She released a snort of steaming air as if in response.

"Thank you, my firestorm," Navin whispered before singing her back out to the forests beyond.

We looked back to the path we'd carved. "She was trying to get to you, I think," I said, noting how the only part of the palace not destroyed was the location we had been.

Navin gave a sad smile as he watched the red dot fly toward the horizon for a much-needed rest.

We traversed the carnage in the direction of the grand hall, moving the right way through memory alone. Olmderian guards carried wounded comrades out to the front courtyard. A few healers wearing the Golden Court's crest swarmed through the lined-up soldiers. And I knew if they were able to start openly triaging their soldiers upon the silver stones of the ruined palace, it meant one thing: we'd won.

As I moved farther across the devastation, I spotted a familiar face and the tears I'd wanted to shed for her for many moons caught me off guard. Maez lifted her head, her eyes catching mine, a profound sadness in them as she walked toward us, Briar a few steps behind.

I had been staring so hard at my old friend, I didn't quite get a chance to look at Briar. When I did, I blinked. She was the only one who looked entirely unscathed, abnormally so, practically glowing. I gasped when I realized that's *exactly* what she was doing, spotting the flicker of flames in her eyes. I looked between her and Maez twice more before Briar smiled at me in a way that relieved some of my nerves. She wasn't a sorceress, too, or maybe she was? But she was far from evil.

Or was she?

I was too tired to care.

I ate up the distance between Maez and me, throwing my arms out wide. Maez's brows pinched, and she took a step back. "I'm sorry, Sadie," she said. "For what I did. For what I've become. For everything."

I took another step. "I don't care. I don't care if you're evil."

"Evil is subjective—"

"I don't care about a Gods-damned thing except that you're here right now." I kept going, ignoring whatever nonsense she was trying to say. I grabbed her by the bandolier that crossed her chest and yanked her forward. "Fucking hug me."

She let out a surprised laugh as her arms wrapped around me and I hugged her back just as tightly. I half laughed, half sobbed as I fused myself against her, the strength of my hold letting her know just how much I fucking missed her. My best friend in the entire world. I hugged her in a way that told her I would never be letting her go again. Dark magic or no, we were still going to be friends. I would make sure of it.

When we pulled apart, Maez's eyes immediately found the ring on my finger. "Are you engaged?"

"Is it really so noticeable? I knew this ring was a mistake." I chuckled. "There's a lot I need to catch you up on."

"And I you." She clapped me on the shoulder, and it made me want to start crying all over again. I thought the next time I saw her she'd have sprouted horns or try to carve me up with her power, but she was here, alive, still her in all the ways that mattered.

"Briar!" a voice shouted from the distance.

Calla started running, Grae beside them. I don't know who moved first but we all started running toward them, colliding in a clumsily unified embrace. We all began looking the others over, relief coating us, adrenaline flooding us. So many had died but we had made it out the other side; we were alive.

"Your cheek," Briar said, studying the slash across her twin's face. "Here."

She swiped her hand across it and the cut disappeared, but the magic that emanated from her fingertips wasn't the same emerald green as the sorcerer's magic . . . No, this was like a bloodred flame, less lighting and more blazing fire, one that healed? Why did that sound so familiar?

"What is that?" I gaped at Briar's hands. "What happened?"

Maez shook her head. "It's like a magic all her own," she said. "She's siphoned off my power and turned it into . . . something beautiful."

Briar studied her fingertips. "I don't know," she murmured. "I just willed it so and knew I could do it. I felt it hanging there in the air between us and I grabbed it."

"Do you think this power feeds on death magic?" Maez asked, a hint of fear in her voice. "Though I suppose there is enough of that to draw upon to last us a lifetime."

Briar shook her head and looked at her mate. "I think this power is fed by *us*, by the connection between you and I."

Maez's gaze softened at that as Navin let out a whistle. "A new kind of magic rising in the world," he said, looking at Calla. "One that heals and unites instead of destroys. A light to balance the dark, a heart of crimson flames to balance the emerald spark."

"Forgive him," I said. "He's a musician."

Navin chuckled and looked at the carnage all around us. "We will need it now more than ever."

"Music or magic?" I asked.

"Both," he said.

"Now we can finally go back home," Calla said to their sister. "The Golden Court. I think that 'one day' has finally come."

With a twinge of sadness, I opened my mouth to speak, to tell Calla that while their court was united again, we wouldn't all be returning to Olmdere.

"Not yet," Grae cut in, saving me from my explanations. He kissed Calla's temple. "There's one thing I need you to do first," he said, looking up to the single stained glass window, impossibly whole. The only part of the great hall still standing. The Moon Goddess's light seemed to sing from it even still.

"What?" Calla asked.

He smiled at his mate. "Marry me under the light of the full moon."

FIFTY

BRIAR

I STUDIED MY TWIN IN THE MIRROR. "ARE YOU *SURE* YOU DON'T want something a bit more fanciful?" I held up my hands when they gave me an incredulous look. "I'm not saying a gown, but at least let me replace your scuffed leathers." I flicked my hand over and red sparks emanated from my fingertips. "It's no problem."

Calla rolled their eyes at me. "You're going to be insufferable now, aren't you?"

I laughed lightly. "Probably."

"No—battle leathers, scuffs and all," they said, studying their reflection. "It seems wrong to flaunt opulence in the echoes of a bloodbath."

I hummed. "Look at you being the poised diplomat."

"And you the killer," they quipped, their green eyes finding mine. "How our fortunes seemed to have reversed. Me, the Queen."

"And me, the shadow," I mused. "I think it was the way it was always meant to be. If I hadn't cut in front of you emerging from the womb." We laughed in exactly the same way. "Maybe it would've always been this way. But I'm glad it's been rectified now. You have the heart of a ruler, Calla. I know our parents would be so proud."

Calla finally turned from the mirror to look directly at me. "I had thought it was just me," they said. "That I was the only one who didn't fit the roles we'd been given. I thought only I asked the question, but now I realize, that question that had plagued me for so long was the same one that also plagued you."

I cocked my head. "What question?"

"If I could be anyone, who would I choose to be?" A smile crinkled my eyes, emotions welling in them again as I stared at my twin. "Now it's so clear, so simple."

"Who would we be?" I asked.

"This," Calla said, waving between us. "No other definition or explanation will do. This is who we always were, who we always will be. I found my voice and you found your power."

I swallowed thickly and nodded. "Yes," I whispered.

So long the two of us had lived our lives positioned in counter to those around us. So long we'd denied our inner voices and shoved down every questioning thought to be who we thought we had to be. But I was never meant to only be an image, a moving portrait. We were never meant to exist as a person to others: twin, daughter, mate. At the very crux of it, we were so much more to ourselves than in relation to someone else: a soul, a heart, a shadow, a crown.

We breached the distance to each other in the same breath, wrapping each other up in a familiar hug, one that was well-worn into the grooves of my heart. "Who knew this is what awaited us all those moons ago in Allesdale? Who knew we were meant for so much more?"

"I think Vellia did," Calla said. "Did you see her? You were caught up in your fire magic but she—"

"I saw her," I said, wiping the tears from my eyes as I smiled. "And I think so, too."

Light knuckles rapped on the door and Maez peeked her head in. "Might I steal away my mate for a moment, Your Majesty?"

"Just Calla," my twin corrected with a wry smile. "And yes, you may."

I beamed at Maez, unable to hide the way she made me feel every time I spotted her. It was like being bowled over, the emotions overcoming me every single time as if for the first time. She wasn't the same as she used to be, but neither was she the way she had been when she first absorbed the dark magic. She was something brand-new. This raw version of her might be her truest form yet, fearless. Mine.

I released Calla from our embrace and wandered out into the hallway. The Silver Wolf townhouses that circled the destroyed castle were truly beautiful. Sadie and our group had reclaimed her family home, but the rest went to the displaced humans. More and more were pouring into town each day in preparation for the full moon wedding. With only the clothes on their backs, they'd come to see the Golden Court Queen wed the former Silver Wolf Prince. Or more, it was as if they needed to see with their own eyes that Nero was finally gone, that they didn't need to fear his bloody fist anymore. The wedding was just a bonus.

And still others came purely to see the dragon that tore down the Silver Wolf palace.

"I needed to show you something," Maez said when we reached the edge of the hallway.

"What? What is it?" I asked, searching her face.

She cracked a smile, grabbed my cheeks, and kissed me.

I chuckled, murmuring against her lips, "Is *this* what you needed to show me? Not that I'm complaining."

"Nope." She gave me one last peck and released me. "You just have such kissable lips, I couldn't resist."

"I never want you to resist." My shoulders shook with laughter. "Now show me what it is you wanted me to see."

She took a deep breath and rolled her shoulders, the determined look on her face making me wonder if she was about to do a backflip. Then she flipped her palm over, and zaps of violet-shaded lightning shot out from her hand.

"It's . . . purple?" I studied the magic, perplexed. "I don't understand." Sparkling clouds of amethyst circled her as she conjured her magic.

"I think it's because of our bond," she said. "I think your flames are mixing with my sorcery somehow . . . like pulling poison from a wound. But I feel almost more powerful, not less." She shook her head. "It's incredible, isn't it?"

I reached out and brushed my fingers through the tingling magic. "It is." I studied the color of her eyes for the magical green, but instead I found the softest amber glow to them. "Do you . . . feel different?"

Maez smiled at me. "Do I seem different?" I nodded and she threaded her fingers through mine. "It's you. As you accepted all of me and I embraced all of you, just as we are, we became *more*. I think I have taken on more than just your magic. I think it's given me your bravery, your heart."

Emotions welled within me again as I swiped under my eyes. "I just stopped crying."

"I'm making up for lost time." Maez laughed, wiping her eyes, too, as she pulled me into her. "Thank you for not giving up on me."

"Never."

"Thank you for healing all those broken parts of me," she whispered, dropping her head to kiss me.

"Thank you for unearthing my fight, my fire."

She grinned. "Thank you for making me whole."

"Always."

FIFTY-ONE

CALLA

WE WOULD HAVE ANOTHER WEDDING—A GRAND ONE IN FRONT of all the Golden Court. I'd commission Ora to make the perfect regalia, something beautiful and strong, something that expressed all the things inside of me. There'd be music and laughter and lighthearted joy, but this—*this*—would be the wedding I'd always remember.

Dressed in my battle leathers, in the rubble of a tyranny at its end, in the blood of our enemies, we'd celebrate the love that pulled us through. I strode down the makeshift aisle that my sister had once walked down, and toward the prince turned king who was always only waiting for me.

The rocks jostled beneath my boots and shattered glass clinked as Briar inched closer into her mate's side. Maez seemed so different now. Neither sorceress nor Wolf, like all her dark magic had been spent, eased by its shared weight with Briar. She was energized and jittery with excitement instead of the cold steel I'd seen in her eyes in Taigos. She seemed more settled in herself than ever before, too, as she slung an arm around Briar.

I didn't know what it would mean for them. Would they return with us to the Golden Court? For some reason, I doubted it, that something had irrevocably changed, maybe for the better even. Maybe the simple life that Briar had dreamed up for herself wasn't really the life she needed, maybe she was still destined for so much more but in an entirely different way. But as I studied the way Maez looked at her, I knew one thing for certain: I didn't need to fear for Briar's safety anymore. She would defend Briar with her life—give her the love she deserved.

And Briar would do the same.

I heard the barest subtle sniff, and I moved my gaze from Briar and Maez back to Grae standing at the top of a heap of bricks and stones—a makeshift dais beneath the light of the single intact window. Ora stood beside Grae, beaming, as if their smile alone could block out all the death and destruction that we'd faced, as if they could assure me that there would be no more.

My eyes were fixed on my mate who seemed overcome with emotion and possibly nerves? As if I would turn and run just as Briar once had? I gave him an incredulous look and that seemed to cut the tension in his body. I loved that I could make him crack a smile with a single glance.

I walked faster, eager to get to him, and his smile broadened. Let him never doubt that I was his and he was mine. That even if the moon had never shined her magic on us, even without the fates all aligning—Grae and I were always meant to be, in every reality. Briar and Maez had taught me that. That some love was greater than any magic.

Grae extended a hand out to me as I climbed the tenuous rocks to stand beside him, knowing that we were probably standing atop the blood of his former pack. It was morbid and brutal, bittersweet and beautiful all at once—a poetic end to the Silver Wolves who had tried to rule our lives and our hearts. It was the sort of thing a Wolf king might never do, but a queen would.

The Moon Goddess bathed us in her ethereal glow, filling me with that same rush of magic I'd felt the moment I knew what Grae was to me. And how he became so much more to me still than even the word "mate" could encompass.

I held Grae's hand tightly as I stood by his side, the congregation of Songkeepers, Golden Court soldiers, and my pack—my *family*,

I realized as I looked from Sadie to Mina to Ora. This entirely illogical mix of people had become my family, against all odds. And I would fight for them all over again if it meant knowing peace, but I prayed that our golden years had finally reached us. I hoped I would usher in an era of peace so that we would never have to be here again.

I looked beyond my family and soldiers to the hundreds of humans who crammed in amongst the rubble, some having traveled for the last three days to arrive in time. Word of this wedding had spread, the intimate ceremony turning into a symbol for the entire continent.

I could see Grae warring with himself as he held my gaze. Finally he relented, releasing our grip to grab me by the cheeks and kiss me. The room chuckled, such a strangely light sound after the utter chaos that had filled it days before.

"We haven't quite arrived at that part yet," Ora murmured with a laugh. "We haven't even given you your song."

I arched my brow at them. "Our song?"

"You're getting a Songkeeper wedding, Your Majesty," Ora said, looking out to the large crowd. "A *human* wedding. It is customary to gift the couple their own song—one that combines the elements of melodies of the two into a new whole."

I heard the ting of Sadie grabbing the hilt of her blade and turned to see her staring daggers into Navin. "Did you and Rasil have a song?"

Navin looked at us tightly, an apology on his face. "Can we talk about this at a more opportune time?" he whispered out of the corner of his mouth as the rest of us tried to contain our laugher.

"It wasn't a very good song," Mina signed as if that was comfort enough. "It never really sounded right." She gave Sadie a wink and my friend's steely expression fissured.

Navin plucked the knife out of Sadie's grip. "You will get it back after the ceremony." She rolled her eyes as he wrapped an arm around her. "And our song will sound much better."

She lifted her eyebrows and looked at him. "Our song?"

He hummed as he nodded his head, toying with the ring on her finger. "I've got plans for you, Sadie Rauxtide, just you wait."

"Preferably until after we finish our own wedding ceremony?" I called and they both gave me sheepish grins. The murmuration of the amused crowd echoed all the way to the edges that spilled into the courtyard. I shook my head. "Mates, I swear."

Grae smiled at me. "Go easy on them. Love makes us do strange things—break curses, fight monsters, win wars." He beamed at me with such pride I couldn't help myself. I rose up on my toes to kiss him again and the crowd chuckled anew.

Ora cleared their throat, and I turned to them. "If we keep going at this rate, we might not even get to the music."

"When did you manage to write us a song?"

They smiled. "I had quite a bit of time sitting in a cell beneath these very floors to perfect it," they said. "But from the moment I saw you two together, I started to hear it."

With that, Ora began to sing. At first it was soft and somber, but then it rose in pitch. Mina stepped forward, lifting a violin, and started accompanying the tune, and then Navin added his own baritone. The other Songkeepers joined in as well, many brandishing instruments and wearing the badges that Ora had made for them—the same ones they wore when they battled Sawyn by my side.

The chorus crescendoed, each one adding their own unique rhythm and melody to make this glorious sound. It was as if each one was gifting us a part of themselves, the way each of them saw us, so deeply that words wouldn't do it justice. It was a song that only made sense when combined all together.

My eyes misted and I looked up to see Grae's eyes welling. "You and me," he mouthed silently as we listened to the song that branded itself onto my skin like the golden lightning streaking across it, the song of our two souls intertwined.

FIFTY-TWO

SADIE

I SPRAWLED ACROSS THE GLINTING SILVER FOUNTAIN IN THE town square, trailing my fingers under the spitting streams. The whole space had been transformed, candle-topped chandeliers hanging from the street corners, vambraces lit in warm fires, and tables mounded full of decadent food in celebration, not just of Calla and Grae, but of the end of Nero's tyranny, of a new dawn in Aotreas.

Finally we were able to celebrate.

Music filled the streets as people danced and drank and filled their once empty bellies.

I lifted my chalice, catching Maez's eye as I tapped the rim. "Top her up for me, will you?"

Maez rolled her eyes at me. "I am not your personal magical cup bearer, you know."

"For the purposes of tonight you are," I called, flashing her a cheeky smile. "Now come, unentwine yourself from your mate and drink with me."

"'Unentwine' isn't a word."

"You are ruining my well-earned buzz," I said with a scowl. "Come on, I fear it will be our last night together for some time."

"So it's true, then?" Calla asked, rising from where they sat beside me. The Golden Court Queen looked along the fountain edge at each of us in turn.

"Calla—" I began.

"No." Calla held up a hand, cutting me off, and I smiled at the assertiveness. I liked how confident they had become, once so unsure of every step forward; there was none of that in the Queen anymore.

"Of course, I selfishly hoped we'd all return to Olmdere together," they said. "I wished I could bottle us all up together, the Golden Court, in my own little daydream forever. But I know now that there is no perfect forever, only perfect moments. Like right now." They raised a glass to each of us in turn. "I could no sooner stake you all down than I could a river. Nor would I deny you the places that truly feel like home."

"You will always be my Queen," I said.

"And mine," Maez said, rising to stand. She gave Calla a clap on the shoulder before walking over and wedging herself between Navin and me. "Where will you go, Sads?" she asked, and my heart pinched at my nickname once again on her lips. "Travel the realm with your musician?"

Navin threaded his fingers through mine. "We will be staying here in Damrienn," he said. "We'll lend a hand to the reconstruction of the city, and then who knows?"

I smiled at him, grateful. I knew he was trying to take the blame for the decision. It felt good to finally declare it aloud: I wanted to stay in Damrienn. To stay in my *home*.

"Thank the Gods," Ora said. Everyone cut looks to them and they chuckled, their golden earrings tinkling like wind chimes. "I'm sorry." They shrugged. "But there are only so many sea shanties I can sing loud enough to cover the sounds of your vigorous lovemaking."

I snorted sparkling wine out my nose. Maez smacked me on the back as I coughed and pinched my fizzling nostrils. "You heard us?"

"You don't need to have Wolf ears to hear the two of you," Svenja said, lifting her eyebrows at me. She leaned her shoulder into Ora. "I think your travels will be much quieter now, palizya."

"It will give us some room to find other wandering souls, others lost who might need a helping hand." They looked from me to Grae to Calla. "Or perhaps some secret Wolves who simply need a ride."

We all smiled at them, remembering our journeys in Galen den' Mora. How different our fortunes might have been if we'd never crossed paths with Ora.

A softer song drifted up from across the clamor and I spied Mina and Kian gathered tightly on a bench. She played her violin while he sang along, a sad, resonant song—one I'd heard before. My heart twinged at the funeral song and a jealousy bloomed in me once more that Mina had ways to mourn those she lost that I did not. Maybe I'd need to ask Navin to teach me how. Maez leaned her shoulder into mine, just the subtlest press, but I knew she followed my line of sight.

Verena speared through the group, her Ice Wolves in tow as she bowed her head at Calla. "We are leaving now," she announced, tipping her chin in the direction of the Stormcrest Ranges. "The pack wants to run in the full moon, and we have a court that needs to heal. Now our work begins in earnest, Your Majesty."

Calla laughed and shook Verena's hand. "I suppose it does, Your Majesty."

"I look forward to a unified future for our packs, something far better than our predecessors could have ever dreamed up," Verena said. "Be well, friend."

"And you," Calla replied, the two Queens tilting their chins up to the moonlight in unison—a prayer and a farewell.

Maez slung her arm around my shoulder. "Come on," she said. She looked over her shoulder and said to Navin, "I will return your fiancée momentarily."

I let her drag me off the fountain bench and lead me through the boisterous crowd. "Where are we going?"

We walked through the narrow townhouses and to the ruins of the palace, where the streets were still quiet and the festivities were only a distant hum. She raised her glass to the moon as Haestas swept across it, the dragon silhouetted by the silver glow. I raised my glass, too, unsure of why we did so. Maez stared at the sky for many more seconds before she spoke.

"For Hector," she said.

"Curse you," I muttered, roughly swiping at my eyes again. "I am not one to cry so fucking frequently."

"Just for tonight you are," she said.

I held her gaze. She knew I needed this, needed to mourn him, that I couldn't forever ice over my heart with hatred. I had no songs to sing, no words to speak, but at some point I'd have to let him go.

"I don't want to," I whispered, battling to keep my emotions in check. "I want to hate him or at the very least feel nothing. Why did he do it? I'll never have that answer. I don't want the chance we could've ever reconciled to be gone. I don't want to say goodbye."

"I know."

Maez held that silent space for me for a long time, our breaths curling into the cold air as more stars winked to life. She knew I wouldn't let my guard down easily, knew I needed this quiet moment. Maez had known Hector and me her whole life. If anyone could help me untangle this twisted knot of raw feelings it would be her, my best friend.

"It's just us here," Maez said, standing shoulder to shoulder with me as we stared at the moon. "I've got you."

"Fuck it," I said, letting the hot tears spill down my cheeks. The dam broke, the guards fell, and I sobbed. I let the tears wreck me until the moon was only a glowing blur in the black of night. And when I finally found my voice again, I said, "Goodbye, brother."

Maez and I raised our chins to the moon and howled.

FIFTY-THREE

BRIAR

"You realize at some point we will need to put some clothes on," I said, kissing Maez's warm salty skin. "And probably drink some water."

My cheek rose and fell with Maez's laughter as I nuzzled my face into the planes of her stomach. "That is a challenge I'm prepared to win."

I started to rise and her hand playfully tugged me back. "You never fight fair." She sighed, letting out a little grumble as she ran a hand down her face. "Calla's going to be there, and I want to see them. It's my auntly duty to dote upon them right now." I grabbed Maez by the shoulders and shook her, a smile cracking my face. "We have to be the favorite aunts."

She guffawed. "We will be."

"Not if we never show up," I pointed out.

Maez grumbled something unintelligible but finally let me rise. I wandered over to the window, staring out at the open air and the sand far below. Jasmine wafted on the breeze along with the zesty scent of our citrus trees.

Our home at the edge of the world. One we thought we might never live to see.

"We still have time," Maez said, propping herself up on her elbow.

I only glanced at her peripherally. I knew if I turned to her full on, I'd be drawn back into our bed like a moth to the flame.

"We need to be in Damrienn in one hour," I countered, grabbing a sponge from a bowl of lavender-scented water and wiping it across the back of my neck.

"Plenty of time," she teased. "Need I remind you, love? We have magic."

"And as the official flame wielders of Aotreas, I think it's important that we attend the coronation," I countered, crossing my arms. "Fully dressed. Maybe not smelling *so* much like each other."

Maez chuckled. "I suppose you're right," she said. "Sadie seems to really like this Silver Court Queen."

A village elder by the name of Riva Yexshire had been elected to the Silver Throne, moving the capital from Highwick to the high mountains of the Stormcrest Ranges. I wondered what Nero would've thought of his successor—not only a woman, but a human to boot. But the worries of dead kings were of no concern to me anymore.

I lifted my hand and pulled it down, raining sparkling red motes of magic upon me. When I blinked again, I wore a scarlet satin dress, my hair braided off my face, my skin smelling of soap instead of sex. I plunked the sponge back in the bowl and, without looking, waved a hand behind me at Maez.

"I am *not* wearing this," she said, looking down at the sculpted golden chest plate, gem-studded armbands, and emerald dress with two slits that raised *all* the way to the top of her thighs.

"No," I said. "That's what you'll be wearing when we return here tonight."

She rolled onto all fours and prowled across the mattress. "Oh really?" She grinned. "You like this, hmm?"

I shrugged. "Perhaps. Maybe with a few more splatters of dirt and blood." Her eyes trailed down my figure, snagging on my curves in my form-fitting dress. "What are you thinking right now?"

"How much I would like to tear that dress off your body with my teeth."

I clenched my thighs together. "You are making it very hard for me to be the sensible one right now."

"We are good at many things, mate," she said. "Being sensible isn't one of them." She reached for my wrist and tugged me back toward the mattress. "Half an hour. Then we can go."

"We really should—"

Maez lifted onto her knees and kissed me, her tongue sweeping into my mouth. "Come on, Briar; show me your thorns."

FIFTY-FOUR

ORA

TWINS. OF COURSE IT WAS TWINS.

The same green eyes and dark hair. The same golden heart, I already knew it. I could already hear the first notes of their songs: one loud and confident, the other quieter but just as clear. I'd sing them these lullabies on my next turn through Olmdere.

Their entry into the world so much more peaceful than the generation before. A good omen. The continuation of the golden reverie.

I knew their parents would make sure they always had space in their hearts for all the things their children might become. They already had elders in every corner of Aotreas who loved them fiercely. It was the kind of love that made kingdoms crumble, and monsters cower, and new magic bloom.

Many songs would be sung, but none more sacred than the ones yet to be written.

I turned back to Galen den' Mora, a quiet tune on my lips. Time to find more stories yet untold. I'd visit again soon, but first I had new places to discover, new towns to explore, new lost souls that needed finding just waiting to be unearthed.

The wheels of Galen den' Mora would never stop turning. For nothing ever truly began and ended; it simply flowed.

DRAMATIS PERSONAE

PEOPLE

CALLA MARRIEL: Gold Wolf, twin to Briar, child of the late King and Queen of Olmdere

BRIAR MARRIEL: Gold Wolf, twin to Calla, Crown Princess, child of the late King and Queen of Olmdere

GRAE CLAUDIUS: Silver Wolf, Crown Prince of Damrienn

NERO CLAUDIUS: Silver Wolf, King of Damrienn

MAEZ CLAUDIUS: Silver Wolf, cousin to Grae and niece to the King, one of Grae's royal guard

SADIE RAUXTIDE: Silver Wolf, sister to Hector, one of Grae's royal guard

HECTOR RAUXTIDE: Silver Wolf, brother to Sadie, one of Grae's royal guard

ORA: human, leader of Galen den' Mora musical troupe

NAVIN: human, part of Galen den' Mora

KIAN: human, former Rook, Navin's brother

MINA: human, twin to Malou, part of Galen den' Mora

MALOU: human, twin to Mina, part of Galen den' Mora, deceased in battle of Olmdere

SAWYN: sorceress who killed the King and Queen of Olmdere and now controls the kingdom

ROOKS: soldiers of Sawyn's army

EVRES: Silver Wolf, chosen heir to King Nero

INGRID ENGDAHL: Queen of the Ice Wolves

KLAUS: Queen Ingrid's cousin

LUO YASSINE: King of the Onyx Wolves, older brother to Tadei

TADEI YASSINE: Prince of the Onyx Wolves, younger brother to Luo

RASIL: Head Guardian of the Songkeepers

AUBRON AND PILUS: Hector and Sadie's uncles

COURTS

OLMDERE (CAPITAL: OLMDERE CITY): home to humans and the Gold Wolf pack

DAMRIENN (CAPITAL: HIGHWICK): home to humans and the Silver Wolf pack

TAIGOS (CAPITAL: TAIGOSKA): home to humans and the Ice Wolf pack

VALTA (CAPITAL: RIKESH): home to humans and the Onyx Wolf pack

AUTHOR'S NOTE

DEAR READER,

What a journey it has been together!

I've loved sharing the world of Aotreas with you. Calla, Sadie, and Briar have each taken up a piece of my heart and it has moved me greatly to hear how many of you have felt seen in their stories.

I hope you had a chance to get lost in the pages of this book, get swept away to a far-off land, and fall in love right alongside these characters. Now, more than ever, is a great time to support queer and diverse storytelling and I hope this series has encouraged you to seek out more.

Thank you for coming on this adventure with me and I look forward to sharing more adventures in other worlds with you soon!

A.K. xx

ACKNOWLEDGMENTS

THANK YOU TO ALL OF MY READERS WHO HAVE LOVED THIS series and have shared about these books far and wide. Your support, as always, means the world to me. I can't wait to share more bookish adventures with you!

Thank you to my editor, David Pomerico. You've helped me to become a better writer and I've loved working on this series with you. Thank you for championing diverse fantasy and storytellers. Thank you to my patrons for cheering me on throughout the writing and publication of this series. I love connecting on Patreon with you! A very special thank-you to: Luce, Aleah, Bethany, Aussie, Morgan, Samantha, Kat, Stacy, Lauren, Patricia, Naiomi, Latham, Kelly, Jaime, Marissa, Ciara, Linda, Katie, and Chantal!

Thank you to my agent, Jessica Watterson, and the whole team at SDLA for all of your support.

Thank you to Chloe Gough at Harper Voyager UK, and to the entire Harper Voyager team, who have worked on this series. I appreciate all of your hard work in making these stories happen and sharing them with the world.

ABOUT THE AUTHOR

A.K. MULFORD is a bestselling fantasy author and former wildlife biologist who swapped rehabilitating monkeys for writing novels. She/they are inspired to create diverse stories that transport readers to new realms, making them fall in love with fantasy for the first time, or all over again. She now lives in Australia with her husband and two young human primates, creating lovable fantasy characters and making ridiculous TikToks.